1

Leander McKinney was a likeable fellow. It was Leander who'd found the Chickasaw rocks on the ridge, Leander who'd shown Alemeth how to make music with two thumbs and a blade of grass, and Leander's rope that swung across the swimming hole on Bynum's Creek. Because of Leander, summer meant scrounging for mudbugs at the sandy springs, luring catfish with crickets, catching fireflies after dark.

But there was one problem. Leander had been acting biggity lately – enough to make Alemeth wonder if he remembered the size of his britches. He'd given instructions on how to fix a night crawler as if he were older than he was, and better. He'd described how to spot poison ivy as if no one else knew anything about the three-leaf devil. And now, here he was, whistling turkey, which he did a lot when his attitude was near to unbearable. Truth be told, Leander couldn't carry a tune in a bucket, but there was no telling him that. The simple fact was that Leander McKinney needed comeuppance.

So when Leander said, "Mawnin, Alemeth Bahrs," it seemed natural to make clear he was not the helpless youngster Leander made him out to be.

"Mawnin Leander. I'm gonna kill the painter."

"*You* gonna kill the painter? How you gonna do that, Mr. Alemeth Bahrs?"

"How do you think? With a gun. Pa's gun."

"Now, if that ain't –"

"He lets me use it."

There was no need to mention that Pa had been trying to teach him to shoot, or that he'd never found it easy to kill an animal. Besides, Pa and he *were* going to hunt down the panther. Pa had said so. And Pa had said they were both going to shoot the gun. So he wasn't *lying*.

"When?"

"Tomorrow."

"Your Pa ain't going with you?"

"Nope."

His show of confidence put a lid on things, for a moment. But in short order, Leander spoke again:

"Mind if I come along?"

The question had no good answer. "You don't have no chores or nothing?"

"Nope. No chores. I can come along. What time you goin'?"

Leander's question was an arrow headed his way. His answer – "before dawn" – was a feeble attempt to put Leander off the scent.

"Great, then, Alemeth. Before dawn. I'll be outside waitin.'"

After that, there was no way out.

Pa kept his muskets up against the wall, just inside the front door. His ammunition was on the shelf above the muskets. It would be easy to take one of the guns, and some balls and powder, without being heard. But could he get out of bed without Pa hearing? What if, as he tip-toed past, Pa asked where he was going? He couldn't be sure. Anything could happen.

The first, faint lightening of the dark. *Dawn is near. Pa'll be up soon.* He slid the blanket off. Pa snored. *Good. He's asleep.*

Out of bed, Alemeth grabbed his britches and socks, and waited. At the next snarl, he lifted the latch, slipped through the door, and nursed the latch closed, all before Pa's nostrils stopped trembling. In the main room, he pulled up his britches, put on his socks, and moved the stool to reach the ammo shelf. The stool made a faint thud as its legs came down, but Pa snored on. And outside the front door, Alemeth pulled his boots up to his shins.

A last glance back: the door closed.

Everything right so far.

Outside the cabin, Leander was waiting, just as he'd promised, sitting on the edge of the well, scratching Wolfie's haunches. The dog was backing into Leander's hands, turning and slobbering into them.

"Good mawnin,' Alemeth."

"Good mawnin,' Leander."

"Can I see the gun?"

"Not with that dog spit in your hands."

Leander wiped his hand on his pant leg.

"Alright, I'll show you how it works."

Pa had always said that to find a panther, you want to look up, as panthers like to hunt from the limbs of trees. Apart from that, there was no telling where the killer could be; it could be anywhere; 'just always look up.'

"We'll take the highest ground, Leander. That's where the painter'll be. That means the old Chickasaw camp."

"Dangit, Alemeth, that don't make sense. The highest ground around here is that hill your cabin sets on. If the only thing the painter wants is high ground, he oughta be sittin' on top of your roof right now."

That was the problem with Leander. In a world of possibilities, he always thought he knew the answer.

"Second thing, at first light, the painter'll be needin' water. Cats come down at dawn to drink. *Everybody* knows that."

ALEMETH

jwcarvin

Copyright 2017
by Joseph W. Carvin

Illustrations and maps by jwcarvin

Printed in the United States of America

ISBN 978-0-9768183-6-6

For Corinne

If we could first know where we are, and wither we are drifting, we could better judge what to do and how to do it.

— Abraham Lincoln

Maddening. "Alright. If you're so smart, what do *you* say we do?"

"We should follow the creek – up toward the swimmin' hole. That's where the painter'll be."

Wolfie pawed in the dirt and sniffed the air like she was preparing to move, then looked back at Leander. She was as loyal a dog as you could ask for, and as good a quail hound as any in Panola County, but she wasn't about to leave the hand that scratched her. Meanwhile, she'd already sniffed out that something was about to happen. So when Leander finally stopped scratching her, her head was up, looking for signs of what he wanted her to do. But Pa had said that a panther could take down a dog, so for Wolfie's own sake, he shut her inside the fence – and while caught up in caring for Wolfie, he didn't see that Leander had already started off on the path to the swimming hole.

He had little choice but to follow.

It was a good walk, and not too steep. A mile up the creek, at the oaks called 'the herons' wings,' Leander turned on the path.

"Hey, Alemeth, let me have another look at the gun."

Leander had a way of telling him what to do. *He'd* been the one who'd insisted they leave the barn door open, the day the horses got out, but he'd never gotten into trouble because of it: *Alemeth* had. That was another thing about Leander: he had a knack for escaping blame, no matter how reckless he was. And that was saying something, because Leander could be as reckless as a winter wind. Could he be trusted with the gun? Maybe not.

But a voice said, *At the end of the day, Leander is harmless enough.*

"Alright," said Alemeth. "Here."

It had *seemed* like everything was going great. But as soon as Leander had the musket, he turned and walked away, firearm in hand.

"Wait a minute!"

Leander was ignoring him, as if the weapon made him bigger than he was.

"Give that back!"

"You had it a while. Now it's my turn. I'm in front. I ought to have the gun."

"But it's my gun."

"No it ain't. It's your Pa's. Said so yourself."

"Alright, you carry it for a while. Then it's my turn again."

There was nothing that bothered him more than somebody no better than him, no older than him, telling him what to do.

The sun began to rise, but 'a while' never came. Not long after taking the weapon, Leander put his finger to his lips and looked up. Alemeth obeyed and followed his gaze. Hanging from a branch above them was the goat. The victim that had finally put the panther at the top of Pa's priorities.

The cat wouldn't have strayed too far; it was probably still close by.

Alemeth had dreamed of taking it down, of standing over its lifeless carcass, victorious. And he'd dreamed about panicking, about lacking the nerve to kill, about not having time to reload as it charged. He'd been curious how a real confrontation might actually play out. This time, the real cat was close. It should have held his attention. But there was a problem even worse than the nearby catamount: What would he tell Pa about taking the gun? What would he tell Pa about going off, to hunt the panther alone?

If he made the kill, any scolding he got would be nothing compared to how good it would be: everyone gathering, congratulating him, telling him (and each other) how excellent a hunter he'd become. There'd be plenty of glory in that. But what if he couldn't make the kill? What if he came home a failure? Pa would ask where he'd been. What would he say? What would he say about taking the gun?

Forcing himself to think of the cat's killing ways, he scanned the limbs above the creek, branch to branch, tree to tree: no sign of the panther.

Leander, however, was already moving on. Resentfully, Alemeth followed. Near the swimming hole, with the creek just below, Leander put his finger to his lips again, to tell him to be quiet.

Does he think he's so much older? So smart? It would sure be sweet to bring him down a notch or two...

*   *   *

Twenty yards ahead was clear, deep water. The swimming hole had a sandy bottom. The panther, nearly on its belly, its front claws touching the water's edge, was lapping up a morning drink, minding its own business, as quiet as a kitten. Again, Leander motioned to be quiet, then stepped forward, closer to the cat. For a moment, the cat paid no mind, and Alemeth almost relaxed. But then, Leander's foot came down on a stick. *Snap!* The cat locked its gaze on him. Leander jumped back – his foot catching a tree root – and he fell down the bank toward the creek, musket in hand. *(Dang it!)* Leander was off balance, scrambling, and the panther was crouching, as if to spring at him.

What could Alemeth do? Leander was pointing the gun toward the sky. The panther's teeth glistened in the early light. Was this to be Leander's last moment before claws pierced his sides? Before deadly feline teeth exposed the bones of his neck? Would the cat be the last thing Leander McKinney would ever see?

Then Alemeth remembered something else Pa had said.

A panther won't mess with a whole pack of dogs.

He jumped into the air, high and screaming, charging down the bank, waving his arms as he hit the water. "Whoopee Yee! Whoopee Yee!" The cat's charged eyes zeroed in on him, its irises like sabre blades. He turned to Leander, "Get up!" Get up! Attack! Whoopee Yee!" Hobbling upright, Leander swung the musket over his head with both hands. Alemeth splashed walls of water the panther's way.

For a moment, only the cat's eyes existed, peering at him, cold and primeval. But when the cat leapt, it was not at him.

It bounded out of sight.

Alemeth's fearless show of force had worked.

Alemeth clambered out of the water, britches dripping, heart pounding.

"We scared her off!" Leander shouted, wide-eyed and proud.

On the walk back home, the thrill of confrontation gone, pleased with himself, Alemeth's heart rate slowed. But Leander was carrying on about how they'd scared the panther off. The truth was, Leander had nearly cost them both their lives. By taking the gun and being useless with it, he'd proven he wasn't half as smart as he thought. If only the world could know what had really happened: Leander's incompetence; his own quick thinking. It wasn't easy being quiet in the face of that. It wasn't easy having to bite his tongue when Leander was so full of himself.

But even Leander was not the biggest problem. The closer to his own doorstep he drew, the colder and harder was the reality that awaited him there. He was late for breakfast. He had nothing to show for his adventure. He had no explanation for his wet clothes, for why he'd gone out before dawn, or (most important of all) for why he had taken the gun without Pa's okay – at least nothing that would save his rear end.

He could always say, 'I was brave,' or 'I thought quickly,' or 'I remembered your lesson about painters and dogs.' He could even say, 'I saved Leander McKinney's life.' But Pa would be fit to be tied about his disobedience. And when Pa got that way, he was dangerous. With Pa so mad, talk of saving Leander's butt would sound silly.

Besides, Leander was his only witness to what had happened, and Leander would never admit that anyone had saved him from anything.

2

The boy's bed was empty. The crumpled sheets and unkempt blanket – without the familiar hand and leg hanging over its edge – made Amzi wonder.

It's not like him to be the first one up. If he went out to make water, he'd be back by now. He pulled his night shirt off. *But where else might he have got to?* He draped the night shirt over the back of a chair. *He could have gone swimming, or fishing, but if he was getting up early to do something like that, why not say so at dinner last night?* He put his shirt and trousers on. His socks were in the seat of the chair. His boots were by the door. He put them on and laced up the ankles.

Mary Jane and Little Semmy Lou were not yet up, Leety not yet getting breakfast ready. The cabin was quiet, nothing stirring. But –

One of the muskets by the front door gone.

Alemeth was not in the yard. A call got no answer. Outside the outhouse door, another call, and still, no answer. Behind the outhouse door, no sign of him at all. Plainly, Alemeth had taken the gun. He knew not to take it alone, but obviously, curiosity had gotten the better of him again. He'd crept out early to avoid being seen. He knew he was doing wrong.

Yesterday, after the goat was taken, Amzi had said they'd have to get the panther before it killed any more livestock. But he'd said '*they.*' *Not* Alemeth alone. Not at nine years old.

The boy had spunk, at least, to go after the panther himself. No more need to worry that he lacked the nerve to try his hand at hunting. He could handle a musket alright, at least with straw targets. He wouldn't likely shoot himself. On the other hand, if the McKinney boy was with him, there was no telling what might happen.

And the cat worried him. Alemeth didn't understand the danger. He'd shot at smaller creatures, but squirrels don't turn on their predators when they get cornered; a rabbit can't kill with a shake of its fangs through the back of the neck. Alemeth had no idea of what he was up against. The boy was too young to be taking on a deadly predator. He'd made the rules for good reason, and he'd made them very clear. Alemeth had disobeyed them, and something *had* to be done about that.

*   *   *

When Alemeth finally returned, apologizing for being late, he looked down, making no eye contact.

"Alemeth?"

"Yes, sir?"

"Look at me. Where's my musket? What did you do? Leave it on the porch?"

Alemeth's face got bright red. Leety carried Semmy Lou outside.

"Yes, sir."

Amzi grunted.

"So you think you're a panther hunter now, do you?"

"Yes, sir. We almost – "

"'Almost'? Son, you don't know if you could kill a panther. But I promise you, the panther could kill you. Ever stop and think what might have happened, had you found it?"

Alemeth didn't answer.

"Well, son?"

"'Course I've thought about it. I—"

"We wouldn't want to lose you, son. Just be thankful you *didn't* find it."

"Yes, sir. Pa?"

"You shouldn't've taken my gun without asking me. You know you're not supposed to use it unless I'm around."

"Yes, sir."

"Looks to me like you don't have enough to do, getting' up before dawn for such foolishness."

"Yes, sir. But –"

"There's a bunch of rocks up on the east ridge. You know the ones from the old Chickasaw camp. They need to be brought down to the creek. "

"Yes sir."

"See it gets done. And I'll see to the panther myself. I don't want you having anything to do with that animal."

"Yes, sir."

"And one last thing."

"Yes sir?"

"There'll be no using my guns for a month, for any reason, even with me."

Alemeth nodded.

"Now, give Aunt Leety your dishes and get to those rocks."

As Leety took the plate and mug Alemeth handed her, she gave the boy a disapproving frown of her own. Amzi liked that about Leety. She was almost like a mother to the children. She understood the importance of following the rules. After Alemeth left the cabin, Mary Jane giggled, like she thought it was funny her brother had gotten in trouble. She was a darling girl, but she'd always resented Alemeth's being older. Even when she stopped giggling, her smile remained, looking more than ever like her mother's.

Semirah's death had hit them all hard. Little Semmy Lou had been small enough to absorb the shock, or at least not to understand it, and with Leety's help, Mary Jane had managed to cope. But Alemeth had known his mother the longest. He'd been hurt the most, whether he realized it or not – ever since, he'd been doing things just to prove he could, claiming there was nothing he needed to talk about. But the loss of his mother had made him act strangely at times, misbehaving just to get attention. And if the rocks were needed for the bridge across the creek, Alemeth didn't need to know that. If he thought moving them was just punishment, no matter: it would be good for his self-discipline. It wouldn't do for him to grow up like some blue-blood, thinking all the hard work was for negroes. A boy needs to be strong. Pulling a hoe, splitting wood, suffering through sore shoulders, were powerful remedies for a sulking heart.

*   *   *

The house on Bynum's Creek lay almost at the county line, about half way between Panola and Oxford. Panola was his kind of town, simple and unpretentious. But today, Amzi was taking Cracker east, to Clear Creek, just outside Oxford, which was Semirah's kind of town. The invitation he'd received, written in fine lettering on rag paper, was for a "Social" at the home of Colonel James Brown, among the biggest landowners in Lafayette County. Semirah used to say the Colonel and his wife were 'people of distinction,' and that he could learn something from them. As he approached the two story mansion, he wondered if he was making a mistake.

The mansion was set on high ground cleared to keep it safe from fire, and fronted by four Corinthian columns. A gate in the center of a white fence opened to an entrance drive. Several negroes stood waiting in front of the house. Amzi spit out his plug and reined Cracker to a stop in front of them.

"Good evenin.' Let me take that please, Suh. Who kin I says callin'?"
He dismounted. "Amzi Byers."
"Right this way, Mist' Bahrs."
Up steps, a front porch and a maw of oversized doors. Through them, an ante-room of crinoline dresses, petticoats, and laced bodices, enough to drown a man. An ample-figured woman approached, a corset pushing up her bosom, pinching her waist. Her dress was a deep blue-green that reached her ankles, a yellow lily lay in auburn hair, fastened with a silver pin; about her was a hint of lavender perfume. He recognized the Colonel's wife from going to church with Semirah.

"Welcome to our home, Mister Byers. It's a pleasure to see you again."

Though she was a Connecticut Yankee, her manner could have passed for Memphis, Charleston or New Orleans.

"The pleasure is mine," he said.

A stairway cascaded from a balcony. There was complex, multi-surfaced crown molding.

"Your house looks well put together."

"Why, thank you, Mister Byers. As the poet said, 'There's no place more delightful than one's own fireside.'"

In gray suits and brown dresses, guests circled like eddies in a river. But from among them, he heard a rising pitch: *Aawwwk*! And then another *Aawwwk*! There before his eyes were two creatures more colorful than the Colonel's wife: blue wings, a scarlet tail – bright lime underbellies – beaks the color of oranges – perched on a polished mahogany stand across the room.

"Ah," said Mrs. Brown. "Clio and Calliope. My parrots. Aren't they beautiful?"

"They sure are, ma'am."

"Birds like that are everywhere in the Indies. Have you ever been?"

"No, ma'am. I'm afraid not. I sailed from Charleston to Savannah once. As a boy."

(He'd gotten sick over the side of the boat.)

"If you like birds, you must make it to the Indies one day. Totally exotic birds, the most striking you'd ever care to see. Daddy sent these two home when I was little. A rather splendid gift for a young girl, don't you agree?"

"Certainly."

"So. Do you know the Hunters? The Bradfords?"

Mrs. Brown seamlessly introduced him to the Hunter-Bradford conversation, then disappeared just as smoothly.

"Gentlemen," said Mr. Hunter, "What do you think? Will cotton ever bring ten cents a pound again?"

"Those days may be gone forever."

"I'm an optimist. I'm planting as much as I can. Of course, we all know the problem there."

Amzi knew all too well the challenges of cotton – crusty soil, pests, disease, late frosts, damp storage, jammed balers. Too little rain, too much rain. But he couldn't think long about cotton because the parrots were looking at him: their eyes concentric circles, round glossy black pupils in the center of full moons, the moons themselves centered against red face feathers. And no sooner had he realized that *he* – Amzi Byers – had been singled out for the bird's special attention, than the Hunters and the Bradfords excused themselves, leaving him alone with the birds.

People were in closed circles now. Hard to enter a conversation.

"I'm Calliope," said one of the birds. "Pleased to meet you."

He'd never heard a bird talk, much less introduce itself.

"I'm Calliope," the parrot repeated.

It seems to expect a reply. Do I have to oblige?

The bird lifted one leg slowly, then, putting that one down, lifted the other, sidling down the perch, its stare fastened upon him.

He looked around, but no one else was paying any attention to the bird, and the bird seemed unconcerned about anyone else. It was clearly looking *at him.*

He looked again for something else to relate to. At last, a bell's ringing called attention to the staircase, where the Colonel – a large man to begin with – stood on one of the lower steps, waiting for silence. As large as he was, the tiny bell only made him seem larger, and he had a demanding way of ringing the bell. As he made eye contact with more and more guests, one after another, conversations wound down. And when the last of them had stopped, the bell stopped too.

The Colonel glanced at a silver pocket watch, returned it to his waistcoat, thanked everyone for coming, and said he felt honored that Senator Alexander Pegues had agreed to give them a report regarding the status of the University.

Senator Pegues took the floor. He spoke of "years of struggle." Of the selection of Oxford as the site of the new University. Of having classes begin within three years. Of tuition, and of the number of students expected. He outlined plans for the construction of buildings. He deftly handled Mr. Smither's question about the shortage in the seminary fund. He addressed the mystery of whether the Legislature had intended to fund a religious seminary or a secular university, and he did so with tact and good humor.

"The Master's gone to sea!"

One of the parrots was behind Amzi's shoulder, and once again, had him flummoxed.

He couldn't address the bird – pretending at intelligent conversation with a mere animal was out of the question without Mary Jane there to laugh at him – so he decided to move. Making his way through the crowd, through bootlicks and puffery, he looked for an approachable face, his gaze alighting at last upon Mary Ann Brown talking to Dr. Waddell.

"Having the University in Oxford will improve the town's moral character, don't you think?"

"Without question. I suppose the folks in College Hill aren't too happy."

"Indeed. I wonder what will come of their college now?"

Amzi took his measure of the crowd: cultured people, people who thought too highly of themselves, people dressed in fine visiting clothes, kow-towing to prove their enthusiasm for the University.

Amzi was skeptical of "cultural improvements." As far as he could see, Mississippi was fine as it was. When Papaw had sent him to school in South Carolina, it had not been a happy experience. He had as little use for intellectuals as he had for preachers. A university in Oxford could only bring upturned noses – and more socials.

But then again the sound of the tinkling bell.

"Gentlemen," said the Colonel. "Will you join me outside for cigars? Mary Ann doesn't let me smoke in the house."

3

Leander McKinney's father said that Chickasaw savages had brought the rocks all the way from Pontotoc to make an altar to the devil. Pa said to pay Moses McKinney no mind, there was no altar to the devil; the Chickasaw had probably just wanted a fire pit; stones were just stones: there was no reason not to touch them – and, by the way, he wanted the biggest Alemeth could gather. So, wondering all the while whether the devil was hiding somewhere among them, Alemeth swallowed hard and put his hands on the largest he could see. But it was as heavy as a tree stump, and polished smooth, with no place to grip. It took a whole minute to wrestle it over to the wagon.

Dang. How many more?

Straining, he heaved it into the wagon. He could handle nothing heavier. Turning back to the pile, he stooped to lift another, a little smaller.

Pa had said the land could be his someday, but it depended on whether he proved himself. He wanted nothing more than to prove himself, but this business with the panther had messed things up. Pa didn't know he'd saved Leander McKinney's neck; Pa thought he'd done something stupid. Meanwhile, might the panther strike again? Take another goat, or even Wolfie or Cracker? Pa'd said they had to be rid of it. Alemeth didn't much like killing things, but to kill the panther could put him back in Pa's good graces. Killing dangerous animals was what men did; he wondered if he had it in him.

When he threw the next rock into the wagon, he half expected it to break the first. After taking a deep breath and stretching his back, he reached for another, this one smaller still. He could take the gun again, take one more stab at killing the cat...

But it made no sense to disobey Pa now. Not after the trouble he was already in. He heaved the next rock into the back of the wagon. Pa had said to leave the panther alone. There was no way. He shouldn't go after the cat.

After one more stone, he stopped for a moment, wondering if the goat's carcass was still on the limb. It had to be, if it hadn't been eaten already. Pa hadn't said a word about not going after the goat. He wouldn't need a gun, if the panther was away, and a goat could make a meal for the whole family.

The creek trail, the tree, the carcass on the limb, all called out to him. The last thing he needed was for Pa to find out he'd skipped out on a chore, but Pa was gone, all the way to Clear Creek. He could hike up toward the swimming hole for a quick look – just to see what was up – and Pa would never know.

He was mulling it over when Leander McKinney reappeared.

"Hey, Alemeth Bahrs. Your Leety told me I'd find you up here. You want to go hunt some rabbits? We could take your Pa's gun again."

"I got work to do. Pa told me to get these rocks."

"You know you're messin' with the devil's rocks."

There it was again: Leander saying things as if he knew they were true.

"Pa says that ain't so."

"I told my Daddy what we did this mornin'. How we scared off the painter. He said we done good."

"He said we done good?"

"Sure did. Said we done real good."

"Really?"

"That's right. He said, 'You boys done good, not to get yourselves killed.' Said, 'If I'd been you, I'd a shot the cat and fed it to the wolves.'"

Feeling ill, Alemeth sat on the pile of rocks. As Leander looked down at him, shaking his head, the idea of going after the goat closed in. Just to find out if it was still there. Just to see what was what – if it would be *possible* to get it down, to bring it home, to show Pa what he could do.

"That goat's probably still up in that tree," he eventually said.

"Yeah? So?"

"I'm fixin' to go get it. Want to come?"

"Heck yea. I'll wait here. You go back and get your Pa's gun."

"Naw. It's too far. Besides, we won't need it."

"Alemeth Bahrs, don't you know anything? The painter will be there. You think she's just gonna *give* us the goat? We can sneak up on her, shoot her right there on the limb – *if* you bring the gun."

"Naw. No need."

"You're not allowed to take your Pa's gun, are you?"

"Heck no, that ain't it. Pa's a better shot than me. If the painter's still there, we'll let Pa know. He should be the one to take the shot."

"You're just scared."

"No I ain't. *You're* the one that's scared. You comin' or not?"

As he took a step toward the creek trail, he looked at Leander over his shoulder. Leander was hesitating. So he turned his back and started up the narrow path, wondering what Leander would say.

It worked.

Leander fell in behind him.

"Dangit, Alemeth Bahrs, hold on! 'Course I'm comin.'"

4

Following the Colonel's lead, men were converging on a door behind the stairs. As Amzi considered making excuses for an early departure, Mary Ann Brown approached again.

"Mr. Byers, it's a shame we haven't had time to talk more. We miss you at church. But I'm so glad to see your interest in the University. It will be a splendid thing, when it opens."

"I imagine it will, ma'am."

"You have a son, do you not, Mr. Byers?"

"I do, ma'am. John Alemeth is nine."

"Isn't it wonderful? He'll be able to attend a university in his very own town."

"Yes..." His words had to be chosen carefully – "if that's what he wants to do."

"I hope you won't think me forward for saying this, but – it's been a year now since your wife passed away?"

"About that. It was in June — "

"Do you think you might ever marry again? — to the right woman, of course?"

If her question was unexpected, at least her smile was warm. "Oh, I don't know, Mrs. Brown. Not too many women could put up with an old coot like me."

"Well, I'm sure you could make some young lady a fine husband."

"Even a worm looks good to a bird, Mrs. Brown. But a young lady's got plenty more than me to pick from."

"I do believe you sell yourself short."

Flattery made him uncomfortable. The men by the staircase would make easier company, and it was them, after all, he'd come to be with.

"Will you excuse me, ma'am?"

"Of course, Mr. Byers."

Outdoors, in a terraced garden, orchids sprawled from clay pots hung from the limbs of magnolia trees. The Colonel was handing out cigars. When his eyes engaged Amzi's, he tilted his head sideways, as if trying to remember.

"It's been a good while," Amzi offered. "I'm afraid I haven't been to church much lately. I'm Amzi Byers."

"Yes, yes. Don't worry about church. It was good of you to come today."

The Colonel offered him a cigar. The rolled brown leaves were moist to the touch and sweet to the nose.

"Thank you," he said at last.

The Colonel introduced Senator Pegues and Mr. Smither.

"Mr. Byers, you know the Senator, I'm sure."

Of course.

"Mr. Smither's a merchant in Oxford. Mr. Byers is a planter down in Panola County, on Bynum's Creek."

"How do you do, Senator?"

"Very well, Mr. Byers. Thank you. What are you planting?"

"Cotton, of course. Is there anything else?"

"It doesn't seem so. Not these days."

Amzi had never seen the likes of what the Colonel did next. It was a quick movement,— so quick, in fact, he wasn't sure if he'd seen it correctly. But the movement had produced a tiny, finger-sized flame. The Colonel had struck something against the brick wall of his house, and it had caught fire. Now, he used the flame to light his own cigar, and then the one he'd given to Pegues.

"Colonel, that – what sort of – what is that?"

"A lucifer, Mr. Byers. You haven't seen one?"

"No..."

"Well, they're ingenious little things. Here, look."

The Colonel handed him a small wooden stick: something white on one end.

"Much quicker than a tinder box. It's just a pine stick, dipped in lead and white phosphorus."

Amzi struck the lucifer against the Colonel's house, and a flame appeared.

"Well, I'll be!"

He lit his own cigar and drew a puff into his mouth, where a dark Caribbean aroma infused itself into the taste of Mississippi tobacco.

"I'll give you a box to take home with you. Don't let me forget."

"I'm much obliged, Colonel."

What a fascinating item! How useful! And a box would sure delight the children. Semirah had been right. He *could* learn something from Colonel Brown.

Senator Pegues finished a long drag. "Very nice tobacco, Colonel. Did you say where it's from?"

"West Indies. Jamaica."

"I thought so."

"I'm glad you like it. I'll get you a box of them. Do you like the cigar, Mr. Byers?"

"I do—"

"Wonderful. I'll get you a box as well."

In groups of fours and fives, men talked of land prices, steel plowshares, the price of cotton, the Colonel's stage coach lines, steamboats on the Mississippi, new locomotive engines, the best gauge for railroad track, and the coming of the telegraph. At every turn, Amzi heard predictions of things to come, perspectives on how to gain advantages and prosper. Late in the afternoon, the Colonel pulled out his silver pocket watch again and opened it with a flip of his thumb. After glancing at it, he looked at the parrots, and as if on cue, Clio screeched: "*Aawwwk*. I'm sorry. It must be late."

Amzi chuckled at the parrots' almost human observations and the absurd thought that the parrots might understand what they'd said. But a few seconds later, Mr. Hunter said to Colonel Brown, "Your parrot is right. It's getting late. We must be going home for supper." Within moments, others were saying it too. Amused that the words of a witless parrot had triggered the movement of intelligent men, Amzi joined the herd as it entered the house to bid goodbyes, making his way to Mrs. Brown to do likewise.

"Thank you, Mrs. Brown. You have a wonderful house. I've had a fine time."

"But of course, Mr. Byers. You're welcome any time. We're sorry we haven't seen you in church lately."

Had coming to the social been a mistake after all? "It's such a long way..."

"I understand. It was delightful talking to you earlier. I *so* wanted to have a chance to chat some more. Perhaps you'll join us for tea some time?"

"I'd be honored, Ma'am, I'm sure." But it would never happen.

"Till next time," said Clio.

Amzi dismissed the meaningless bird.

Mr. Smither came in with Colonel Brown.

"Those are some exotic parrots you have, Mrs. Brown. They look like African chieftains in tribal robes."

"They certainly are colorful. How they make me think of the Indies!"

"The Master's gone to sea," said Calliope.

"Mr. Byers," said the Colonel, "if you'll wait just one moment, I'll get you those cigars I promised, and some of those lucifers."

5

When the boys reached the tree, the goat was still on the limb, just a day old and not much eaten.

"You should have brought the gun," said Leander. "Just in case."

"Why? You scared?"

"Course not."

"Neither am I," he said, starting toward the tree. But the lowest branch was too high to reach, so Leander told Alemeth to make a foothold with his hands, then used it to climb onto Alemeth's shoulders, lifting himself into the branches. He pulled Alemeth up after him.

The goat was slung across a limb, its head cradled in branches on one side, its rump hanging over the other, limbs lifeless, eyes dull, pieces missing from its belly, the back of its neck torn open, bones like rocks dug up by the tilling of soil. Should the two of them carry it down? Was it better to let its own weight take it down? Did it make more sense to drop it? From which side of the branch?

But his thoughts were rudely interrupted. On the ground, fifteen feet from the base of the tree, the panther crouched, poised for a jump toward him. To repeat his earlier success, Alemeth screamed as loud as he could and tried to shake the branches, but the big branches didn't move, and this time, the cat didn't scare. Its legs flexed taut like a bow. Alemeth imagined the release, the cat springing like an arrow loosed, its maw open wide, its teeth set to pierce. Lest he never see the age of ten, he jumped from the branch as far from the cat as he could, landing in a patch of tall grass. Behind him, though the leaves still trembled, the goat remained on the limb, and Leander (dislodged by Alemeth's departure) fell hard.

Screaming as if to let the whole world know that it was not to be trifled with, the cat leapt into the tree. Leander, on the ground, yelled as if hurt. The cat screamed over their heads. Leander ran, and Alemeth ran after, looking back to be sure it was just a two-person run.

Taking stock a moment later, he reflected: he hadn't taken the gun; he hadn't tried to hunt the panther. True enough, he wouldn't be able to show off the goat; there'd be no trophy to brag about; but it was Leander who'd be bringing home a swollen ankle and bruises. And there was still time to make progress with the rocks. This time, he'd be able to answer all Pa's questions.

So after Leander went home to nurse his wounds, Alemeth spent the rest of the day filling the wagon, thanking his lucky stars that everything had turned out all right.

6

Back from Clear Creek, Amzi found Mary Jane and Semmy Lou playing house on the porch. Mary Jane looked up.

"How was the social?"

"Oh, it was a lot of talk about business. Adult talk. It wouldn't interest you."

"Papa, I want to know what's going on in the world. *Something* interesting must have happened."

"Well, actually: it did. I was just teasing. If you want to know about it, come over here and sit down."

Mary Jane rushed over and sat in her straight-backed chair; Semmy Lou followed, climbing a rung to the top of a stool.

"Senator Pegues was there. And Ike Davis – you know Mr. Davis. Mr. and Mrs. Smither, Mr. and Mrs. Hunter."

Mary Jane raised an eyebrow, her interest in question again, as he'd expected. The trap was set.

"On the other hand, there was a couple there you might have found interesting."

Mary Jane perked up. "What sort of couple?"

"They were covered in bright feathers."

"*Feathers?*"

"That's right, covered in feathers. And not like those on a nut hatch."

"What do you mean?"

"They were orange, red, and the brightest green you've ever seen. Like emeralds."

"Oh, Pa..."

"They were strutting around like Tennessee Walkers. And you wouldn't believe what they said!"

"*Pa-ah*! You're making the whole thing up. I'm not a baby any more, you know."

"I am not making it up."

"People dressed in feathers?"

"I said nothing about people. Have you never heard of parrots?"

"Parrots?"

"Yes. Talking parrots."

"I – They really *talked*?"

"That's right."

"Like us?"

"Well. Not quite like us. But almost."

"Promise you're not making it up!"

"I promise."

Enter Alemeth, climbing the steps to the porch.

"I'm back." He looked beat. He was rubbing his left shoulder.

"You get all those rocks?"

"Yes, sir. Wagon's full. Down by the creek, like you said."

"Good," said Amzi. "Now, both of you, watch this!"

He removed a match from a box and struck it against a stone. Just like the Colonel's, his match burst into flame. The children's mouths opened wide.

"Wow," said Alemeth. "What was that?"

"It's called a lucifer. It's got chemicals on the tip. Colonel Brown gave me a box of them."

"Can I see one?"

"No. You're still being punished."

"Pa," said Mary Jane. "Can we see the parrots? Can you take us to see them?"

"What parrots?"

"I was just telling your sister, son: the parrots belong to Mrs. Brown, the Colonel's wife. They really do talk, just like all of us, almost. But we can't just drop in, not without an invitation. You know that."

"Let's get an invitation, then," said Alemeth.

Amzi exaggerated a frown, but it was to no avail. The children's eyes made clear that their interest in the parrots would not be quelled.

"I tell you what. Tomorrow, if you want, we could all go to church together."

Alemeth made a face.

"If you tell Mrs. Brown you've heard about her parrots, maybe she'll invite you to meet them."

Mary Jane's eyes brightened.

"I could wear my dress!"

Mary Jane was nothing like her brother. She loved going to church. But even Alemeth's sour reaction softened as Amzi answered all his questions about the lucifers.

7

That evening, Alemeth watched Leety wring the necks of two chickens. The first flapped its wings and ran in a circle before falling to the ground, legs kicking reflexively. The killing of chickens still made him a little queasy; he wondered what it would feel like, to have his neck broken that way. He could kill a pest like a squirrel, and maybe even a panther, but a harmless chicken? Leety had performed the execution without hesitation, then quickly caught a second. When she wrung its neck, the chicken flew out of her hand, its detached head remaining between her fingers, clear-eyed. She threw it into the pig pen with no apparent thought. One of the pigs put a toe on it and started ripping the skin from the head with its teeth. Alemeth cringed.

After dinner, Pa threw some table scraps to Wolfie, trying to teach her to play dead.

"Pa," asked Alemeth, "do chickens feel pain, the way people do?"

"Good Lord, Alemeth. What would make you wonder such a thing? No. Only people feel pain, really. Killing a chicken is no different than training a dog." He held Wolfie down to the ground. "Animals were put on earth for us. A chicken's best use is to be killed and eaten. That's all you need to know."

Alemeth was on the porch, mulling over what Pa had said, when Leander's daddy rode up.

"Your Pa here?"

"Yes, sir. He's inside."

Mister McKinney did not look happy. Whatever was troubling him surely had something to do with the goat in the tree.

"Pa, we got company."

The front door opened and Pa came out.

"Good evening."

McKinney gave no hello, but started right in.

"Leander come home this afternoon with a broken arm. Come to find out, your son was with him. Seems they was out lookin' for a mountain lion. I thought maybe you'd want to know about that."

Pa's eyes were on him like stink on a polecat. He turned, as if to find a way out, but there were only empty fields, dark woods, and everything that had happened at the swimming hole.

Nothing to do but tell Pa about all of it.

The tree. The goat. The panther.

That night, Alemeth got a real shellacking, but he didn't blame Pa. It was Leander who'd opened his big mouth.

8

Single fatherhood is no easy occupation. With land to be worked and livestock fed, the widowed father must not only be planter, shepherd and judge, but in whatever time is left for the children, he must be teacher, comforter and disciplinarian – and all the while, must suffer alone whatever emptiness is in his heart. In addition to his cotton and his children, Amzi had fifty mules, more or less. Fifteen horses, a hundred hogs, four hundred sheep, twenty oxen, seventy-five cows, two hundred chickens, and fifty negroes to provide for. He had to grow enough corn, oats, hay, and potatoes to keep them all fed. And while Semirah's loss still saddened him, he could ill afford to stew in memories of her. An entire plantation depended on him.

Besides, he'd only known Semirah a quarter of his life. The children had never lived a day without their mother. So at Mary Jane's urging, he'd let them visit her earthly remains every Sunday, though College Hill Presbyterian was some two and a half hours from Bynum's Creek. Mary Jane's sad but loving gaze on Semirah's headstone had made the trip worthwhile. His daughters would grow up to become like their mother, if he could help it. He would keep away anything that could hurt them – including his own hand. A moment of anger could never be undone, Like breaking a petal off a flower, a pretty thing that could never be re-attached. So Amzi was careful with his daughters, lest his interference keep them from becoming the girls Semirah had wanted them to be.

Alemeth was a different story. He was never meant to be another Semirah. Amzi's duty toward his only son was to make a man out of him – and that meant making him strong enough to bear the sort of burdens that were a father's to bear. Alemeth would have his own plantation, his own family, his own negroes someday, all depending on him. He would need the strength to build a barn, break a horse, set a broken leg, or lose a wife. He would have to bear every adversity life could pile on him. And at nine years old, he was a long way from being that man. He'd put up such a stink about the long ride to College Hill on Sundays that Mary Jane had suggested they forego the trips. (She better understood sacrifice than her older brother, and because of her concern for his feelings, they hadn't been to the church or the graveyard in months.)

Alemeth was a dreamer; always had his head in the clouds. There was much he had yet to learn about the way things really were. He'd have to toughen up if he was ever to be the man Amzi wanted him to be. So when he balked at going back to church again, Amzi had told him to take it like a man and do what he was told.

*　　　　　*　　　　　*

Colonel Brown had no sons, only daughters. And as curious as Alemeth was about the parrots, it was Mary Jane who asked Mrs. Brown about her parrots as soon as the service was over. Three of the Colonel's daughters were more than twice her age, and the fourth was just a toddler, but she was so friendly to all of them that the invitation was soon forthcoming. That afternoon, the whole family were guests at Clear Creek.

Six white chairs faced each other in a circle, surrounded by a flower garden. Clio and Calliope shared a perch on a long wooden arm that projected across the top of a gatepost.

Calliope: *Aawwwk!*

Clio: "Welcome. So pleased to meet you." (Amzi was relieved. This time the bird was looking directly at Mary Jane.)

"And *I'm* so pleased to meet *you!*" she said.

Aawwwk.

While the children paid attention to the parrots, Mrs. Brown asked Amzi about his background. As he told her of his childhood on the rice plantation, Mrs. Brown's knowledge of the palmetto state became apparent.

"Charleston has so much to offer. Don't you think so, Mr. Byers?"

He hesitated. As far as he was concerned, there wasn't much good to be found in any big cities, Charleston included. "I —"

Then the black man appeared again.

"Tea now, Miz' Brown?"

"That would be good, Harl. We'll have it here, on the terrace."

Harl nodded and turned to leave.

Aawwwk.

The rising pitch of the parrot's screech vied for attention.

"The Master's gone to sea."

"They seem so intelligent," said Mary Jane.

"It's an illusion," said Frances Brown. "They're not really talking. They have no idea what they're saying. They're only repeating speech they've heard."

"'The Master's gone to sea?'" repeated Alemeth. "What on earth does *that* mean?"

"John Strong was a sea captain. He got the parrots when Mama was just a child. She's simply repeating something she used to hear Harl say when visitors came to call."

"They've been alive since your Mama was – "

"They're nearly thirty years old," said Mrs. Brown

"I'm four," announced Julia.

"I'm seven," said Mary Jane.

"Here," said Julia, taking Semmy Lou by the hand once everyone had been heard from. "Come with me."

The younger girls left in one direction, the older girls in another, following familiar patterns. Colonel Brown talked to those remaining – Mrs. Brown, Amzi and Alemeth – about the stage business, using a pocket watch to make a point, giving several examples of why, in the stage business, even more than in the rest of life, it's important to keep to a schedule. Alemeth fidgeted, more interested in the parrots than the adult conversation. Amzi tried to learn what he could.

Later, over goodbyes, Mary Jane asked if they could come back again the next week. Mrs. Brown chuckled, but when she saw Amzi frown at Mary Jane, she put her hand on his arm.

"It would be wonderful to see you again," she said. "Your children are delightful. They should get out more often."

It was a long ride from Bynum's Creek to College Hill. But Mrs. Brown's words had delighted Mary Jane, and now their pleas were united. Surrender seemed the only course.

"Alright, then. Church again next week."

Alemeth winced.

"Pa –"

"Not now, Alemeth."

"We'll be looking forward to next week, then, Mr. Byers. You'll be able to meet my sister, Eliza."

What?

He should have known better. Mrs. Brown's *sister*? Taking the children to church was one thing. But he didn't need another widow in search of a husband. He'd thought he could learn something from Colonel Brown, but maybe getting involved with strangers again had been a mistake. He shook his head, seeing no way to extract himself from what he'd agreed to do. And as he climbed into the wagon, he couldn't wait to put a plug of tobacco in his mouth. The sweet, familiar pleasure gave comfort whenever things didn't go well.

9

At the first splash of the paddlewheel, the movement of the deck underfoot had interrupted Eliza's heartbeat; she had held tight to the rail, fearing that with a sudden change of direction, she could topple from the steamboat. She'd imagined plunging into the water below, the river swallowing her up, clenched teeth and all. She was hardly the seasoned sailor her father had been. But as she imagined what dangers lurked below, it occurred to her that God himself had made the river for some purpose – whereupon, praying for strength and peace, she felt the comfort of the river's power. Her grip on the rail relaxed. For God spoke to her personally, and now He reminded her that the river had swept through the country every day, every hour, every minute since Creation, and it would keep flowing until Judgment Day. Paddle wheels might break, engines might explode, but the river was everlasting. Besides, the deck steward had advised that, in the unlikely event she fell in, she should not try to swim back toward the boat, but let the river's flow carry her to shore. Divine and earthly authorities agreed: the river was more powerful than she; she simply had to trust it. So as the shoreline passed by, the river pulling rafts, driftwood, and *The Alex Scott* along with it, Eliza put her trust in God's mercy.

Eventually the river led to New Orleans, and *everyone* knew what that meant: Drunken brothels. Worldly temptations. New Orleans was as wretched and depraved as Sodom or Gomorrah, and in similar need of salvation. Along the way there were countless other souls with similar needs. With Faith in God's mercy, even New Orleans could be saved from decadence. The river's power was His power. It would always be with her, if she let it into her heart.

And therein lay the purpose of life: to obtain for herself and others the mercy and comfort only He could offer, simply by submitting to His will. Eventually, she relaxed enough to take a seat on the hurricane deck, where she took stock of all that had led to this juncture of her life.

Her first memories were of Uncle William Strong's house, where she'd been taken before she could remember. There she'd learned the benefit of faith and prayer. Dear Uncle William. Dear Aunt Harriet. With eleven children of their own, they barely had enough room for themselves, much less taking in an orphan, but what was there to complain about? By their charity and their example, she had come to know God, and God had proven as reliable as any parent could have been.

In the shawl in her lap, her autograph book carried parting messages from Sarah and Saphronia, Nancy and Oliver. How insignificant those relationships now seemed, when compared to the comforts of faith! The most meaningful signature in her autograph book was Henry Hitchcock's. While Aunt Harriet had taught her the value of faith, Henry Hitchcock had taught her the importance of acting on it And he had signed her book, "H. L. Hitchcock. *Your friend and pastor.*" His joyful vision of America as the "new Promised Land" became her vision, too. Together, they were part of the new Eden, under the new Covenant with the faithful, soldiers of the Lord, God's promise to Abraham soon to be fulfilled.

*   *   *

Everything changed in Memphis. The frontier was a Sinai desert, a Gethsemane, a trial God had created for His soldiers. The hotel bed had been lumpy, its odor unpleasant. Now, the stagecoach was cramped; it could not have been meant for nine. Had she been in the middle row, her knees would have dovetailed with those of the malodorous drifter in the front seat. Next to him, a sack-coated man fidgeted and tapped on a chest he carried in his lap. In the far corner, behind the other man's chest, slouched a man with his hat brim down, as if trying to sleep. Three young men on the middle bench, their backs toward her, formed a welcome barrier between her and the drifter up front, but the barrier caused its own discomforts: the talk of one of them, in a buffalo robe, was crude; he chewed tobacco, and he was so close to her that, with each jostle, she lurched toward him, her nose nearly touching his buffalo hide.

Her own space, on the rear bench, was no wider than her hips. Dust came in through the window, past the handkerchief hung there. To her left, an older couple, a Mr. and Mrs. Cleary, shared a blanket. Since Mrs. Cleary rested against her husband, Eliza had room to shift a little, so her muscles didn't cramp. Nine souls packed into a six by six coach that rocked insistently. With no one to brace against, she fought the urge to feel sorry for herself.

An envelope was folded as a bookmark into Mark, and the book opened, as if of its own accord.

> *Verily, I say unto you, there is no man that hath left house, or brethren, or sisters, or father, or mother or wife, or children, or lands, for my sake, and the gospel's, but he shall receive an hundredfold now in this time, houses, and brethren, and sisters.*

Julia had suggested the verse to her. It was just what she needed now.

Dear, *dear* Julia. She had been living with Uncle Henry Strong in the finger lakes until she married Dr. Webster. When Uncle William took his family there, Eliza and Julia had come to know each other at last. Julia had become her best friend. Eliza had moved with the Websters to Columbus, and later to Carondelet. Her five years with Julia had been the happiest of her life. Now, she was leaving her best friend behind. No more afternoon strolls along the river bank. No more conversations about their work in the church. No more evenings on the porch, among the fireflies, with Julia's children. What lay ahead for the youngest of the Strong women was a new life. A life with Mary Ann – her senior not by seven years, like Julia, but by fourteen. A sister, yes, but completely unknown to her, as remote and unfamiliar as a faraway star.

Years earlier, Eliza had read one of Papa's old letters to Mama. "I wished you to write very often," John Strong had written, "and particularly about Mary Ann's eyes." Eliza had asked Julia what Papa meant about Mary Ann's eyes. Julia had explained that Mary Ann once had a problem with a wandering eye, her left sometimes focusing on something other than her right. The eyes had looked 'crossed' at times. For all the years since, Eliza had pictured her oldest sister looking like Julia, but with crossed eyes. Julia said she believed the problem had been long corrected, but there was no portrait of Mary Ann hanging on a wall, no etching by which Eliza could know what Mary Ann looked like. So when Eliza imagined Mary Ann, the image always included eyes that wouldn't stay put.

The image was responsible, no doubt, for the emotion Eliza had long felt toward Mary Ann. It couldn't have been love, as she didn't know her oldest sibling. It was something more like pity. A compassionate sorrow for whatever woes had caused the wandering eye, and for whatever additional woes it had brought. Problems at school? Ugly nicknames? Teasing? She could only imagine. But on the example of Christ, she would do what she could to show her sister compassion.

*   *   *

A gooey white slime splattered on the rim of the open window.

"You might want to close that window," said Mr. Cleary.

"Can you believe how many birds there are?"

"There's a reason they call this Pigeon Roost Road. Andrew Jackson built it to remove the Chickasaw. He managed to get the Indians to leave, but not the blasted birds!"

Through Watson's Crossing, through Byhalia, the pigeons reminded her that among God's creatures, people were vastly outnumbered by animals. In a country of catamounts, rattlesnakes and heathens, good, god-fearing souls were clearly in the minority. Every bump, rock, rut and jar was a trial of faith.

After the first way station, the men on the middle bench opened a flask of whiskey. Soon they began boasting to the others, and the men in front boasted back. When the odor from their mouths reached the back seat, the man on the middle seat rose and leaned across the man beside him, spitting through the window, while the gaze of the drifter up front fastened on her. She lowered her eyes, but that left her unaware of what the drifter was doing. Her gloved hand trembled. When she looked up, his gaze was still straight on her, his tongue wandering from its den like a cat's. Again she lowered her eyes. Again she looked up.

His eyes were still on her. She summoned the iciest stare she could. It seemed to put him off. But she had no guarantee that it would work very long. Perhaps she could just ignore him...

A bump in the road sent hard wood into the back of her neck. If she leaned forward, to rest on her duffle bag, her forehead would brush the back of the man in the buffalo robe. She'd be closer to the man who'd spit out the window. She'd be closer to all their foul breath and unwelcome attentions. So she sat erect, her eyes closed, trying to shut out everything around her.

At the next stop, the man closest to the door had trouble opening it. (He'd clearly had too much whiskey.) Two of the men from the middle seat got out first, then the man with the chest. The man in the buffalo robe waited for the Clearys to step out. Then, at last, Eliza followed, taking her first step into the land that was to be her home. If ever she'd need the strength that Faith could provide, it would be settling into this heathen territory.

As it happens, Chulahoma station was but a single cabin that sat among rolling hills of grass. She wondered what was to become of her in this unfamiliar place, civilization nowhere in sight. Even in the Finger Lakes, with no roads or buildings in view, a person was never far from farm or mill. Here, there was no sign of humanity beyond the station.

In front of the coach, the driver was checking a new team of horses.

"Can you tell me, sir – are we in Mississippi yet?"

"We've been in Mississippi about an hour now, Miss."

Beneath the open sky, the billowing clouds, the sunlight, everything seemed small.

"This surely is God's country," she said out loud.

"'Sgod's country 'ndeed," blurted the drifter, cocking his head, exposing his tongue, coming closer. "Purdy country for a purdy girl..."

She stiffened. The man in the buffalo robe shot a quick glance at the drifter, then called out, "Are you alright, ma'am?" as he approached her to help.

Eliza thanked God that someone had noticed.

10

Amzi had known for a while what had to be done. If you're going to keep livestock, you have to keep it from wandering off. The fence had served that purpose well. But by fencing in his goats, hogs, and chickens, he'd made his stock easy prey for predators. Now, there was only one way to protect them, one way to be a good steward.

Alemeth had said the goat was hung up in a tree, right along the path, no more than a hundred yards short of the spring. So it didn't take long for Amzi to find the right tree. The big cat was on the limb, on all fours, looking over the goat's remains.

His Kentucky long rifle had a range of a hundred yards or more, but a miss would give the cat time to strike, or get away, while he reloaded. So what he needed most was a steady hand. He drew a bead. The cat turned and looked in his direction.

No time to consider the possibilities. Squeeze.

Arms and legs folding, the cat fell from the tree and hit the ground.

There. It wasn't moving. That was that.

Amzi bled out the cat and detached the goat's shoulders and legs. (Leety could feed them to the hogs.) As he made his way home, his meat on a makeshift sled, he enjoyed the contentment of knowing that his livestock were free of imminent danger. It had been a job well done. His fields were coming up healthy and green. The joint grass had been pulled; the soil had been worked. The cotton blossoms had started to turn white. There was nothing now but to let the sun do its work. As long as the weather didn't turn foul, the crop would be healthy and good.

That evening, there was plenty of pink in the sky. After dark, there was no halo around the moon. Years of experience brought comfort in the knowledge that tomorrow's weather would be good.

11

The stagecoach stopped in front of the courthouse. The nervous man and the drifter headed toward the Butler Hotel. People and wagons approached, but there were no familiar faces, no friendly eyes. There was an empty bench on the store's porch. Eliza took a step in that direction.

Then a woman called down from the back of a wagon.

"Eliza Strong?"

"Mary Ann?"

The woman stepped down, her hands on Eliza's arms, her cheek bringing a pleasant scent of lavender to Eliza's. Then she stepped back, holding Eliza at arm's length, leaving plenty of time for the sisters to examine each other's faces.

"How marvelous! Reunited at last. I haven't seen you since – how long, sister? I do believe you were still in diapers –"

Mary Ann's eyes were large, brown, and becoming: no sign of a wandering eye.

"Well, we certainly have a lot to catch up on. So, Julia – she is doing well?"

"Yes."

"And Doctor Webster?"

"Yes. How is Colonel Brown?"

"Oh, the Colonel is always busy with one thing or another. He's out now looking at some property he wants to buy – Oh, give that to Harl, dear! – so we'll have some time to ourselves. Isn't that delightful? Oh, Sister! You are a sight for sore eyes! Well we mustn't stand here all day. Harl, you be careful with that luggage, hear?"

"Yas', ma'am."

"How is everything in Carondelet?"

"How is Doctor Webster's medical practice?"

"How are Julia and the children?"

"How were your students?

All the way to Clear Creek, Mary Ann kept up her questions.

*　　　　　*　　　　　*

Harl stopped the buggy in front of a columned, Greek Revival home, as grand with its two rows of windows as anything Eliza had seen in Saint Louis or Carondelet. When she reached for a piece of luggage, Mary Ann stopped her, then glanced at Harl; Harl called to some boys standing nearby, and two of them ran over to hoist it down.

"They'll get it all, Eliza."

Mary Ann led the way up the steps. When Harl opened the door, Eliza spotted the parrots on their mahogany perch.

How time had dulled her memory! The deep royal blue feathers, the flaming scarlet tail, the bright green undersides and white eyes!

Aawwwk. Good morning. Aawwwk.

They were strutting with excitement

Aawwwk. How do you do?

Aawwwk.

"I am very well... thank you... Now, tell me –"

I'm Clio.

"It's so wonderful to see you again, after all these years..."

Aawwwk. Glad to meet you.

What other-worldly creatures!

I'm Calliope.

And their speech! What it must have been like to grow up with such fantastic creatures! "Mary Ann, I'd forgotten how striking they were!"

"Indeed, sister, they certainly are that. But you've been on the stage now – *how* many hours? You must be terribly tired. You'll want a chance to freshen up. Come with me."

Mary Ann led the way up palatial stairs. Crown molding. Oak paneled walls. A globe. A bronze bust. On one wall, a painting of Cupid and Psyche. In the room Mary Ann said would be hers, a dressing table topped with white linen and polished silver trays.

Lord Jesus, into what splendor had she ascended? Was this what it *could* have meant all these years, to be a daughter of John Strong?

*   *   *

Later, in the parlor, Mary Ann insisted she tell her everything about the past twenty years. Eliza took her through the story of her life, describing Somers, and Redding, and Uncle William's call to the Finger Lakes. How, by the time she was fourteen, she'd been taken from her friends five times. How Julia had become her only lasting friend. How, in Columbus, Lyman Beecher and Henry Hitchcock had instilled in her the importance of missions to the west.

"Julia has told me about your admiration for Reverend Hitchcock. He was a young man?"

"Twenty-seven."

"I see. Good looking, I suppose?"

"Mary Ann!"

"I understood you thought rather well of him."

"We *all* thought well of him."

"I see. Tell me, sister. How did you find Saint Louis?"

"Oh, such a town! It began as a Romanist mission, you know. It was obvious everywhere you went. Saint Charles. Fleurissant. Portage des Sioux. The Sisters of Charity. With so many papists, the need was apparent. I'd intended to locate a position as a teacher – I made inquiries at various schools – but I received no offers. I'm afraid the best I could do was occasional employment; some tutoring in private homes. But I do think I accomplished something with my Irish Marys."

"Your Irish Marys?"

"Yes, Henry Blow's servants – *all three* of them named Mary!"

"Well, sister, you won't have a problem finding a position here. Oxford is to be Mississippi's center of education. We already have the North Mississippi College, and the boys' and girls' academies. Even the new state university is to be ours. And the Colonel is not without influence, you know."

"I'm so excited! But tell me, Mary Ann. I can't delay asking any longer. What was it like, living with Papa?"

"Oh, I got an excellent education from it. We saw and did everything."

"Everything?"

"He took me to concerts in Charleston, to balls in Savannah. Papa's friends included the best people in the South, you know."

"Were they good Christians? I mean, truly, not just Christians in name?"

"Oh, sister. Whatever do you mean? I suppose they were a mix..."

While Emily brought tea, Eliza searched Mary Ann's eyes again, looking for hints of abnormality.

12

The following Sunday, Amzi tried to prepare for a difficult time.

"Remember, Mary Jane, Mrs. Brown is bringing her sister. You remember your manners, okay?"

"Yes, Papa."

"Alemeth, you too."

"Yes, Pa."

But when introductions were made in the church yard, Amzi was pleasantly surprised. Miss Strong looked ten years younger than Mrs. Brown. Same nose and jaw, but cheeks fuller, skin softer. Seated directly behind her during the service, he couldn't avoid looking. Her frock was plain and gray, but through it he could imagine the structure of her bones: her frame was more slender than her sister's, but supple. And when the congregation rose for the hymn, her singing voice was cool and clear.

> *Oh, for a thousand tongues to sing*
> *My great Redeemer's praise*
> *The glories of my God and King*
> *The triumphs of his grace!*

It was not a Charleston drawl, not black-eyed peas or jambalaya. More like apple cider. After the service, Amzi found himself face to face with the young lady.

"Mr. Byers, my sister has said good things about you."

"She's spoken well of you too, Miss Strong."

"Oh? You're a gentleman to say so."

There was a freckle half way down her neck.

"Your children are lovely, Mr. Byers. How old are they?"

"Alemeth is nine. Mary Jane is seven. I also have a little one at home."

"We've been telling Mr. Byers about you, dear. How you've prepared yourself to be a teacher."

"Well, until now, I'm sorry to say, I've only taught a few Irish girls. But I hope to find a position in Oxford, Lord willing."

"You needn't simply hope," said the Colonel. Then, to Amzi, "Eliza will likely be teaching at the College Hill Girls' Academy."

"Colonel, please," said Miss Strong. "We don't know that for certain."

"Sister, I'm sure if you decide that's what you want to do, they'll have a position for you. The Colonel is not without influence, you know. We'll soon be a University town, and everyone will want an education."

"I believe in education," said Miss Strong. "But I have a question. So many colleges these days – well – will the University have the right emphasis?"

Amzi liked the young woman's skepticism, and wondered if she shared his distrust of education.

"The more reason to be involved," said the Colonel. "To ensure the emphasis is where it ought to be."

"I understand your concerns, sister. If we leave the whole business to the men, we'll have nothing but chemistry and mathematics. James is right. If we want the University to pay attention to the arts and to literature, women would do well to stay involved."

Miss Strong looked as if she might be biting her tongue. Instead of another pompous academic, thought Amzi, Mrs. Brown's sister might be a kindred spirit.

*   *   *

That evening, after the Colonel had withdrawn to his study and the Byers family were all gone, Eliza was alone with her sister.

"Mary Ann. About the University. I feel I need to explain my concern about the proper emphasis. I – "

"Yes, dear. If the men have their way –"

"No. I mean, I agree with you about the importance of literature. But my greater concern is about faith. What will be *Christianity's* place in the curriculum?"

"Eliza, that's exactly the sort of thing the Colonel was talking about. If we're involved, we can be sure it will be the institution we want it to be. And you'd be surprised how important having the Colonel on our side can be. You should raise the matter of religious studies with the Colonel. But speaking of education, what about the education of Mr. Byers' children? A pity they'll grow up with no formal education at all."

Indeed, thought Eliza.

"His son will never be able to attend the University if he has no schooling beforehand."

True.

"You know, sister, even if you don't get a position at the female academy, you can always take in students of your own, as you did in Carondelet."

13

Eliza's first weeks at Clear Creek were filled with luncheons and teas, but her inquiries about teaching positions bore no fruit. Meanwhile, expressing concern about the distance Mr. Byers and his children had to travel to church, Mrs. Brown invited them to Clear Creek every Sunday – "for the children's sake." The Byerses became familiar visitors.

One Sunday at church an announcement was made: there was to be a meeting of the faithful from all over northern Mississippi. It would last several days. People would camp at the site. Christians of all churches were welcome.

Eliza's heart stirred at the thought of so much praise and worship. "Oh, Mary Ann, I so hope we can attend."

"Well, I thought you might be interested. But of course I could not."

"Why not?"

"In my condition?"

"Why not? You –"

"Sister, I can't leave Oxford. Doctor Isom advises plenty of rest. Nothing strenuous."

Having a child on the way had never kept Aunt Harriet at home, nor Julia. Eliza worried that the luxuries with which her oldest sister had been blessed might have made her weak, or spoiled.

"It could be a time of great revelation," she tried. "Something the children will long remember."

"Oh, sister. For your sake, I might risk it. But the Colonel cannot come. He has to go to Jackson. I'm sorry, but I won't be able to go."

"Mary Ann, you can bring Emily. You can bring Harl, or Sam. Between all of us, we can keep you comfortable. We'll all pitch in to take care of you. We'll make you feel like a queen. Please. For the children?"

"Sister, you're as tough as week-old bread. Alright. I'll come. But on one condition: we must be properly escorted."

"Why, of course…"

"It wouldn't do to go camping without a man in our group. Since James will be in Jackson, we'll need to find someone else. Shall I inquire of Mr. Byers?"

14

If there were ever to be a sermon Alemeth could tolerate, it would be one on a hilltop somewhere, under a starry sky, surrounded by fireflies and crickets. (Pa felt the same way, and had said so.) But on the wagon ride to revival camp, the girls talked about teas and table settings, chattering enough to drown a flock of jays, while Amzi's eyes and ears stuck to everything Miss Strong said. It was clear he wasn't going to be any company for Alemeth. Revival camp had already taken a turn toward disaster, and Alemeth would have rather been alone, beneath the surface of the swimming hole, than suffering through the jabber on a wagon headed toward hell in the name of salvation.

The swimming hole had long been his favorite escape. Breaking through the surface, into the clear, still pool, entering that silent world, free of the chatter of girls, the grunting of frogs, the arrogance of Leander McKinney. It was a clear world, free of the smell of wet dogs, stinking skunks, and rotten milk. A world in which there was no dust or dirt, in which chiggers, lima beans and liver had never been known, in which all things moved with grace, where he could float weightlessly, up and down. Where a simple spiral flutter of his palms could send him into acrobatic displays impossible on dry land. Most of all, it was a world in which he could look into the eyes of fish and wonder what they were thinking, while their ease in the water dispelled all sign of grief, loss, or hurt. Sometimes he thought he could stay beneath the surface forever, transforming himself into a wide-mouthed bass, and that there could be no better life. But then, when a pain in his lungs forced him up for air, reality inevitably returned.

The jostling of the wagon and the sounds of those around him were all too real. Among a hundred other campsites, the Browns and the Byerses unpacked, Mrs. Brown giving instructions to everybody, seeing that everything was exactly as it ought to be. She called for Harl to bring her her chest of personal things, told Emily she had some clothes that needed washing, and told Eliza to summon Dr. Isom if anything went wrong with the baby. As Eliza tried to help Mrs. Brown, Amzi tried to help Eliza. Alemeth started to wander away, but Amzi called to him. First, help Sam put up the tent. Then help Sam build a stack of kindling and logs. And when that's done, take this bucket. I saw a well as we pulled in. We'll need plenty of water.

Alemeth did as he was told. First he helped Sam. Then, bucket in hand, he ascended a hillside full of people crawling with salvation and damnation, singing, waving, and lifting up arms. As far as the eye could see, the land had become one big church, crowded wall to wall. He was in no mood for a sermon, but Eliza – and Amzi – had made clear he was there until it was over. He'd have to make the best of it, though he still had no idea how.

*   *   *

The program began at seven. The benches were full; those late to arrive stood in the back. The first speaker preached that sin was everywhere, to be stamped out by the soldiers of the Lord. The next said most people were going to hell. The third preached that by translating the Bible into Latin, the pope had stolen the very word of God. The final preacher of the night was the Reverend Leroy Gaston, his voice alternately soft and strong.

"And I ask the Lord Jesus to come down among us now, and I ask him to reveal himself to each of us. I trust in him. That if I will only do that one small thing, that little act of accepting him into my heart, with total trust, he will bless me with eternal life. I ask that he let us share in the brilliant light of salvation – *His* light – the light of life everlasting, at the right hand of God.

"And though I know that his Will be done, I know also that his will is for me to read his Holy Word. And I ask you, brothers and sisters, as we read the good book, what does Scripture tells us about a man's obligation toward God? Nothing, I say to you tonight – and it is not me speaking, but the Word of God – He asks of us nothing more or less than the complete obedience by which Abraham would have killed his only son. This is why Saint Paul describes himself as a "*doulos*" – a *slave* of Jesus Christ. If a man only give up his heart to God, in complete submission to the will of the Divine, then God will bless him, with many sons and daughters. That was the promise God first made to Adam – to give him dominion over all the other animals – nay, over all the rest of Creation – and the promise was repeated to Abraham, to give him a land of milk and honey on this earth, and far more wonderful things in the next, if he only have faith. Abraham obeyed, and so should we."

Despite his lack of interest, Alemeth listened to every word. Only when the Reverend had ended did he find himself recalling what Leander had said: "My Pa says Leroy Gaston's the best preacher since Lorenzo Dow. The same what preached to thousands."

But while he couldn't deny the Reverend's preaching skills, he couldn't see the wisdom in his message. Total submission? To something he could neither see nor hear, himself? Surely, it made no sense to be a slave, to God or to anyone else.

*   *   *

After the preaching, back at the campsite, Alemeth listened closely when Miss Strong asked Amzi, "Mr. Byers, what do you think about education's place in the church?"

What Pa thought about the church – and education's place in it – had always made sense. Religion is fine for folks that profit by it, but a man can get by just fine without it, if it suits him better. And besides, God is as likely to be found outdoors at night than stuck in a church, listening to a sermon. So here was a perfect chance for Pa to let the preachers have it. To tell Miss Strong what he really thought.

But when Pa answered, it came out sweeter than fruit jam.

"It depends, I suppose, on what you mean by education, Miss Strong. I'm all for a man's getting educated. The question is, educated about what?"

"What would you educate folks about, Mr. Byers? Something other than the Bible?"

Pa cleared his throat. "I believe in doing what the Lord would have us do, Miss Strong. I believe that's the first Commandment."

"Undeniably. But what do you believe the Lord would have *you* do, Mr. Byers?"

"I believe I have an obligation to be a good steward. Take care of what He's left to my care. In my case, that's my family. It's Bynum's Creek."

Miss Strong nodded.

"Fancy ideas don't impress me," Pa went on. "The way I see it, a man that keeps his head in the clouds can trip over his own boots. But as long as a man keeps that in mind, and keeps his mind on his land, the Bible can only do him good, Miss Strong."

What? Had Miss Strong worked some sort of spell on him? Where were Pa's criticisms of pompous preachers? His distrust of organized religion?

Then Mrs. Brown: "Permit me to be bold, Mr. Byers. I've been thinking about your children. There must be some way to give them an education. An education you'd approve of, of course."

Dang. Leave it to a woman to stick her nose where it don't belong.

"That'd be nice. But Oxford is so far to go. It's all we can do to go into town on a Sunday now and then."

"What about Mount Sylvan? At least for Alemeth. It's closer than Oxford."

Dang. Things could sure go downhill fast. He had no interest in going to school.

"It's still a long way from Bynum's Creek."

Good again, Pa.

"Well, if you can't bring the children to school, you could always bring school to the children."

"What are you suggesting?"

"Well, for example, Eliza could come out to the country to teach your children, Mr. Byers."

Dang! No –

Pa held up a hand, to ward him off, still looking at Miss Strong.

"On Sundays, after church, you could bring them to Clear Creek. Have lessons at our house. And two days a week, Eliza could take our buckboard out to Bynum's Creek."

Pa wouldn't take his eyes off Miss Strong, and Miss Strong was smiling – just as sweet and awful as could be.

*   *   *

The first chance Alemeth had to get away came when Leander McKinney arrived with two younger boys he introduced as the Reverend's sons, William and Charles Gaston. With Mrs. Brown's encouragement, it was easy to wander off with them. But what to do? Alemeth hadn't had time to think it through, and that left the decision to Leander, it having slipped Alemeth's mind for a moment what a bad idea it was to leave things up to Leander.

"Alemeth here's got some lucifers," said Leander to the Gaston boys.

"What? *Lucifers*?"

"Just watch," said Leander. "We'll show you. Alemeth?"

Alemeth hadn't intended to show them off. He hadn't intended to do *anything*. But now that Leander had the boys' interest up, he was stuck. So from his pocket, he produced a lucifer, held it up, and told how it worked. Still, Leander McKinney couldn't keep his mouth shut.

"Show 'em, Alemeth. Show 'em how it works."

"Naw…"

"Give it here. I'll show 'em."

"Yeah," said William.

"Show us," said Charles.

"Alright, then. Just one. But we need to get out of the wind."

Mrs. Brown had brought a covered wagon big enough for all of them. They sat in the dark, facing each other, crammed into bedding, extra blankets, and a kitchen's worth of pots and pans. Alemeth struck the lucifer. The others' jaws dropped; they peered at the flame until it dwindled, the pine turning to ash.

"Here, let me light one," said Leander.

"Let me," said William.

In an effort to keep things from getting out of hand, Alemeth agreed to light a second lucifer. Leander jumped out of the wagon and was back in a heartbeat with some dry leaves and a caterpillar. William found a tin plate and put the caterpillar into it. Leander arranged the leaves under it.

"Light it!"

"Yeah, light it!"

He had to admit it would be fascinating to see what would happen. Striking the lucifer, he waited until the flame was strong, then lit Leander's leaves.

There was nothing to gain by wondering what might have been. As it was, when the caterpillar tried to crawl off and Leander moved the plate to stop it, it brushed a burning leaf aside; the flame caught a tassel on the wagon floor and scaled a table cloth. Charles Gaston screamed. Leander swung at the flames. Suddenly everything was on fire, the wagon ablaze, the fire out of control. With the heat pummeling his back, he could already feel Pa's anger. It made him small, childish, and wrong. How had he ever let Leander talk him into it?

Pa, Sam, Harl and Leety attacked the flames. Alemeth tried to help, but Pa told him to stay back – "With the rest of the children."

How had he been so stupid?

Pa's face was red and glowing, light and shadow flashing back and forth. As angry exertion blackened his eyes and the firelight reflected in his cheeks, Pa looked more devil than man. He handed Sam a shovel, telling him and Harl to throw dirt at the wagon. He pulled down the tent and threw it over the flames, telling the negroes to throw more dirt on top.

Just moments had set Alemeth back years in his effort to prove himself to Pa, to be treated like a man someday. It was as if he'd had a taste of Hell, and in his case, Hell meant being sentenced to childhood forever.

When the fire was finally out, Pa kept his distance, not saying a word. But he was listening to Miss Strong. As she talked, Pa was shaking his head. She was looking mostly at Pa, but sometimes, over her shoulder, at *him*. Finally, Pa walked off. It was Miss Strong who approached him.

"Alemeth," she said "You're a very smart young man. But remember. God gave you your brain. He expects you to use it wisely. Okay?"

"Yes, Miss Strong."

"Remember what the Irish say: 'Curiosity killed the cat.' Lighting that fire wasn't wise, was it?"

"No. It wasn't."

And that was it.

Pa never said a word about what had happened.

15

"Oh, come on, Alemeth. It won't be so bad. I promise you."

"But Pa –"

"Go on, son. Show Miss Strong some respect."

Respect was something owed to older people, and Miss Strong was young enough to be his sister. But Pa meant what he said, and Pa could see right through his heart if he wasn't doing what Pa wanted. He'd have to go to Miss Strong's 'school' with a good attitude, or Pa would smell a skunk. So he went out to the porch, where Miss Strong and Mary Jane were reading the Bible together. The idea of school was bad enough, but having to go through it with just Miss Strong and Mary Jane made it especially hard. What would she try to teach him? There were things he wanted to know about, but he doubted Miss Strong could teach him about striped bass or bull frogs' habits. And whatever she had in mind, he could probably learn it just as well from Pa, or Grote, or Aunt Leety.

It didn't take long to find out.

"So, Alemeth, tell me. What do you know of your Bible?"

"Same as most folks, I reckon. I know about Adam and Eve, and Moses, and Jesus."

Mary Jane rolled her eyes, like she thought his answer stupid.

"Alright," said Miss Strong. "Let me see… Alemeth is a Biblical name. Do you know what it means?"

He knew what his name meant – it meant *him.*

"It's in Chronicles, Alemeth. Have you read Chronicles?"

He'd never even heard of Chronicles.

"No, ma'am."

"Here's what I'd like you to do, Alemeth." She handed him a Bible. "Read Chronicles. When you've finished, let me know. And tell me what you learn about Alemeth."

Reading the Bible was worse than listening to a two hour sermon on a hot day. And there was even less reason to think it would be interesting now, with Miss Strong telling him what to read. But then another thought occurred to him: the Bible had never been about 'Alemeth' before. If there was a story about Alemeth in there, it might be worth reading. His curiosity about the Biblical Alemeth grew. And he needed Pa to be happy with him again. So he started to read Chronicles.

In the first chapter, he found Adam, and Noah, and others less well known, like Seth, Enosh, and Kenan; Shem, Ham and Japeth; Gomer, Magog, Madai, Javan, Tubal, Meshech and Tiras, and then their sons. Alemeth stopped paying attention to other names, looking only for his own. He scanned the lines for 'A,' and when that became tedious, he began to scan whole columns for the letter – yet no sign of *Alemeth*.

There was no sense reading lists of the dead. Had he somehow missed it? He started in on Chapter Two, where Reuben, Simeon, Levi, Judah, Issachar, and Zebulun nearly put him to sleep. Faceless names, all, without lives or meaning. In Chapter Three were David and Absalom, but also Shephatiah, Ithream, Eglah, Shimea and Shobab. Four. Five. Six. Nothing.

In Chapter Seven, finally, he came upon the namesake he'd been looking for. There, among the sons of Bechar was *Alemeth,* at long last. But not a word about who the man was.

Miss Strong was listening to Mary Jane read Galatians.

"I've done it," he told her. "I've found Alemeth."

She looked up.

"Very good. Tell me, then. What does your name mean?"

"Nothing."

"Nothing? The Bible gives you no clue?"

"Nothing."

"Read it to me."

His finger was on the page.

"'And the sons of Becher, Zemirah, and Joash, and Eliezer, and Elioenai, and Omri, and Jeremoth, and Abijah, and Anathoth, and Alemeth. All these were the sons of Becher.' See? It's just a name, ma'am. The last of the sons of Becher."

"Keep going. Read some more."

"And they were reckoned by genealogy. After their generations, heads of their fathers' houses, mighty men of valor, twenty thousand and two hundred.'"

A man of valor! No discovery could have pleased Alemeth more than to learn that he was a man of valor.

"*Alemeth* means *valor*," he announced with pride at his success.

"I see. And what about all those other names – Omri and Teremoth, Abjah and Amathoth? Do they mean 'valor' too?"

They were *all* men of valor, said the Bible. The names themselves couldn't all *mean* 'valor.'

"I don't know."

Mary Jane giggled, but Miss Strong ignored her.

"Did you read the entire chapter?"

"No, ma'am."

"I asked you to read the whole chapter. Please read the rest of it."

Dang! Persistent, this Miss Strong!

When the name appeared again in Chapter Eight, Alemeth was begat by Jehoadah. But still, nothing at all was said about this Alemeth, either. He scoured verses for signs of what the name might mean. Valor? Strength? Wisdom? Anything? But there was nothing.

Then, after forty more verses in Chapter Nine, the name again: But this time, Alemeth was the son of Jarah, and still, no story. No clue about the meaning of the name. And was he one person, or three? And was his father Becher? Jehoadah? Jarah? He wondered.

"I can't find anything. I read the whole book. I found him three times, all with different fathers, but other than that, Chronicles says nothing about him."

She closed her Bible and put it in her lap.

"Remember, Alemeth, the good book is the word of God. There has to be a reason for every scripture – even those lists of names."

"I'm sorry, ma'am, but I don't see the point."

"Perhaps, God wanted the lists to remind us that a person isn't so important as an individual; that a person's importance comes from relation to his family."

Miss Strong was an outsider, a stranger. According to Mary Jane, she was an orphan. If there was anything she had no business teaching him about, it was family.

"Are not all the lists the sons of Noah? And of Abraham? And of the house of David?"

"I don't know."

"Perhaps the Scriptures mean that Alemeth is less significant as an individual than he is as a member of a family. I'm talking about the Lord's chosen people, Alemeth. If this plantation is to be yours someday, you need to understand Chapter 17, verse 21."

She was worse than Leander McKinney when it came to making a suggestion sound like a command, but Pa had told him to do what she said, and if it didn't involve cutting off a finger, he would. And so he read:

And what one nation in the earth is like thy people Israel, whom God went to redeem to be his own people, to make thee a name of greatness and terribleness, by driving out nations from before thy people, whom thou hast redeemed out of Egypt?

"Alright," he said when he was finished. "I read it."

"Who did God choose as His people?"

Mary Jane opened her mouth as if to blurt out the answer.

"You don't say a word, Mary Jane. Alemeth?"

"Israel?"

"Yes, Alemeth. Good. But what one nation in the earth is like Israel? Isn't that the question being asked in this verse?"

"I don't know."

Mary Jane giggled.

"Shush, now! Alemeth, if the Jews crucified our Lord, and if Jesus made a new covenant, who then, are God's chosen people now?"

"Christians?" he guessed again.

"Exactly. His new chosen people are those who *believe* in Him. We are a tribe, in a way. A family. The name Alemeth may only *seem* to have no meaning at all. Perhaps all the meaning it needs is that Alemeth is one of a family: the family of God's chosen people."

And so the lessons began. At Bynum's Creek twice each week, and at Clear Creek on Sundays, Eliza Strong taught school, delighting Mary Jane and driving Alemeth crazy. When she'd finished teaching about Abraham's faithfulness to God over Isaac, and Noah's faithfulness when the rest of the world was killed, she followed with Adam and Eve, and then with Cain and Abel: in other words, it was all about dead people. When he complained that he had no interest in the dead, that all he cared about was the future, Eliza added grammar, diction, and penmanship. She said he'd didn't appreciate how lucky he was, that Bynum's Creek Plantation was like a new Eden and he had a chance to know and love God if only he'd open his heart. As far as Alemeth was concerned, Miss Strong's school had nothing to do with what a boy really needed to know. It was about words and symbols, and the hidden meanings of things that seemed to mean one thing, but Eliza insisted meant another. She wasn't his mother. What gave *her* the right to tell him what he ought to know?

As best as Alemeth could tell, Mary Jane enjoyed every minute. It was all he could do to show her respect. Pa dropped in from time to time to see how things were going. Alemeth tried scrunching up his face to let Pa know he hated sitting in class all day, but Pa always answered with a look of his own, and Alemeth always turned his attention to the lesson in the end, since that was what Pa wanted. He tried resigning himself to accepting the sentence for what it was – being forced to satisfying the whims of another person – but a day with Miss Strong was worse than a day of fishing without a nibble. She made *him* feel like bait that was being nibbled. Three days a week of it was about all he could handle. On the four days he had without her, he did his best to keep his life the way it had always been, but most weeks, four days didn't seem hardly enough.

One day soon after school began, the Reverend Leroy B. Gaston became pastor at College Hill Presbyterian. Leander McKinney had been right: Leroy Gaston was indeed a wonderful preacher – or at least everyone said so. Granted that his booming voice managed to pull you right out of your wooded daydreams and into church, at least for a moment or two. But still, no preacher was going to make any lasting impression on him.

Then something happened that made the preacher seem like a miracle worker. As it happens, Alemeth was right there to witness it. As Reverend Gaston exchanged pleasantries with the departing congregation, he said to Miss Strong, "I understand you are teaching on the Sabbath."

"That's correct, Reverend Gaston."

"You are not concerned about – the Commandment?"

"The Commandment only forbids work, Reverend. Not teaching."

"But your teaching *is* work, dear."

Alemeth wasn't sure what they were talking about, and probably wouldn't have noticed, except that he was next in line, and the confrontation took place just inches from him. Miss Strong's voice had taken a decided edge.

"Reverend Gaston, I come from a very Christian family. Perhaps you know of my Uncle – the Reverend William Lightbourne Strong? I was raised in his house. He always condoned teaching scripture on the Sabbath. And the Reverend Hitchcock, my pastor in Columbus, held the same view. Sunday has been a day of scripture study all my life. Surely, Scripture does not make it a sin to teach scripture on the Sabbath."

There was something of a bottle neck forming in the line behind them.

"My dear, I do not mean to presume, but I feel sure Mr. Byers is paying for your labors?"

"Yes. Of course."

"When a preacher living by the kindness of the congregation preaches the Gospel on the Sabbath, there's no sin in that, of course. First Corinthians, chapter nine. But my dear, you have no commission from the church to preach. You are teaching, and you are teaching *for wages*, at that. How is that anything but work?"

By now, several people were listening to the conversation, and Alemeth could see that Miss Strong was aware of them.

"Reverend Gaston, I – "

"And even if not work for you, my dear, it is for the children. Do they say their ABC's? Do drills? Perform exercises, as you assign them?"

"Why, yes…"

"Learning is work, my dear. The children must be taught to abide by the commandment. Your teaching on Sundays sets a very poor example for them."

"But, Reverend, my purpose is to prepare my students for an understanding of – "

"The Commandment says nothing of purpose, Miss Strong. Exodus thirty-one. Teaching and learning involve work. Therefore teaching on Sunday is a sin. Once we begin coming up with our own exceptions to the word of God, there can be no end to the error of our ways."

Miss Strong's face was red. Her head teetered on the edge of her neck, mouth open a little. And when she finally tried to speak again, the Reverend cut her short once more.

"You have six other days of the week you can teach, Miss Strong. The Sabbath is a day of rest. Scripture could not be more clear."

It was the first time Alemeth had seen Miss Strong at a loss for words, and he envied Reverend Gaston for it. The pleasure he felt at the sight was all the sweeter because Miss Strong was being fed a dose of her own medicine. Even if Reverend Gaston wasn't a miracle worker, he had something even the McKinneys had missed.

In any case, neither on that day, nor on any of the Sundays that followed, were there any lessons taught by Miss Strong. Classes were cut to two days a week at Bynum's Creek, and Alemeth could not have been more delighted – unless, of course, the Reverend had said that school was wrong altogether.

16

Mary Jane and Semmy Lou took to Eliza from the start. And after weeks with her, even Alemeth, despite all his resistance, started speaking less like Leander McKinney. There was no denying the good Eliza's school did for all his children. So Amzi asked her to come to Bynum's Creek three days a week, instead of two. Alemeth complained, of course, but Amzi was certain it was for the boy's own good.

Then, something else happened, more serious still: Amzi asked Eliza one afternoon if he might be allowed to call on her at Clear Creek. She agreed, and within a month or so, they were engaged in full scale courtship. The difference between Amzi's age and Eliza's was no greater than the difference between the Colonel's and Mary Ann's, and Amzi drew upon his years in the mercantile business to reckon accounts: ten cents a pound was what he'd have to get for his cotton before he could afford to remarry. A year later, the price of middling cotton rose to ten cents a pound.

When he asked her, she asked if he understood her calling to do the work of the Lord. And when he said he did, she accepted.

When the planning began for Amzi and Eliza to join in holy matrimony, no one needed to remind Amzi that planning a wedding had nothing to do with the groom. It would be all about Eliza.

*   *   *

Young ladies in Uncle William's congregation had married in their Sunday woolens. So had the women in Henry Hitchcock's church. Gray, brown, or dull green at best, it was always dark; Eliza had never considered a lighter color. In fact, she'd never even thought about a wedding dress, until she saw the one Julia had been married in, and began to wonder whether she, too, might say her vows in it. (It had been a beautiful shade of dark gray.)

Then Mary Ann showed her a portrait of Queen Victoria in her white wedding gown.

"What do you think, sister?"

"Oh my goodness: the money it must take to buy a dress like that!"

"Eliza, dear, they're not that expensive. What do you think of the dress? Would you wear it?"

"It's too showy, I'm sure. And all *white*?"

"But sister, dear. Since the Queen did it, it has become the thing to do."

"It's so pretty – I couldn't bear to get it soiled."

"No matter. A wedding dress ought to be worn only once."

"But, Mary Ann – it's a question of taste. Don't you think it, well –

promiscuous?"

"Hardly, dear sister. White is the color of angels. And purity."

"Well. Alright then. Perhaps I could – I mean, as long as it were simple."

Mary Ann's thoughts about the sleeves made sense enough. The gloves and the veil were fine, though she hadn't worn a veil since Uncle Henry died. The problem was not the gloves or the veil, but the neckline. It could not be lower than the collar bone.

"Sister, are you certain –"

"Yes," insisted Eliza.

"I might concede on the neck line," said Mary Ann, "*if* I could be the one to have the dress made."

"You? Have the dress made? By whom?"

"You would leave that to me."

"You'd keep it simple?"

"Fashionably, yes."

"The neck line will be higher than the collar bone?"

"No lower."

"Well, then, well enough."

The wedding would be at the Brown's house, at Clear Creek; the Colonel would give her away; Reverend Gaston would perform the ceremony.

"It will be a large wedding," said Mary Ann.

"How much will it cost?"

"The cost need not concern you. The Colonel and I will take care of it."

"But – Mary Ann – I don't want to seem ungrateful, but really – I don't know who I'd invite."

"Really, sister?"

"Really."

"I'll draw up a list, then."

Mary Ann's list would include 'people of importance.'

No matter.

As long as the Lord was present, everything would be fine.

17

When the Websters arrived for the wedding from Carondelet, Alemeth's girl problem only got worse. In addition to Mary Jane, Semmy Lou, and the Colonel's daughters (of whom there were now five), there were three Webster girls. Julia, Mary Ann, and Harriet Webster *ooh*ed and *ahh*ed over Mrs. Brown's things – the embroidered linen, the gold leaf china, the sterling. Alemeth didn't want to sit on brocaded cushions, between girls in toile or lace. Perfume smothered him – "That stuff stinks to high heaven!" he'd said the first time he'd smelled it on Mary Jane – and the stiff white Sunday shirt, the collar, the old suit of Pa's, a hand-me-down much too large for him – none of it was comfortable. Worst thing was, it all had to stay clean. Having to stay completely clear of all dirt left Alemeth very little to do.

Only wire-hooped, stiff-corseted women could make a man dress so stiff. Why men tolerated it made no sense. Dressing up, combing hair, minding manners. Just because girls did was no reason he should have to. It was unnatural. In fact, everything about Clear Creek was unnatural. Most Sundays, when it was just the Byerses and Browns, if he'd try to wander off, Pa would stop him, make him sit with everyone else, to be "civil." But on this day – the day Pa and Eliza were to get married – with house guests all over and everyone readying for the ceremony – there was no one paying attention to him. He could do cartwheels on the terrace or yelp like a scalded dog, and no one was likely to notice. And as it happened, Fortune was smiling from above. On a drawing room sideboard was a porcelain bowl, and it was full of the new friction matches.

Outside, Alemeth found a spider web spun out between two peach trees. In its center was a little white-bellied fellow, his construction done, waiting for prey. Alemeth wasn't going to burn the spider, but the matches had to be used for *something*. The way the spider's web shimmered, all but weightless between shadow and light, its strands thinner than the hairs on his arms, cried out to him with a question: how would it burn? Would it go up in a quick flash? Would it burn slowly, strand by strand, each one a separate fuse, the whole thing collapsing as it came apart in stages? He didn't know, and he couldn't reason through to an answer. And when things got like that, you could count on one hand the number of times Alemeth was able to let the question drop without an answer. For if there was one thing Alemeth couldn't stand, it was not knowing what would happen.

Pa had always called him curious, and Miss Strong had hard started saying that, according to Henry Blow's three Irish Marys, curiosity "killed the cat." When he'd finally asked what cat, Miss Strong had just laughed and wouldn't tell him. The more she refused to explain, the more frustrated he got. But when Pa came in and saw his frustration, he hadn't made Miss Strong tell, he'd said it was 'just an expression.' Alemeth had never stopped wondering about that cat, and today, with Pa and Miss Strong about to be married, he couldn't stop wondering how that spider web would burn.

He pulled a lucifer from his pocket. There'd be nothing wrong with destroying it; he wouldn't burn the spider. And the spider could rebuild the web in no time. So he struck the match against the bark of a tree.

The match broke. Then, as he looked for a better surface, a voice called from the house.

"Come in, everyone! Come in! The ceremony's about to begin!"

Inside, people were whispering to each other, turning around in their seats, looking over their shoulders. His instructions were to sit on the bench next to Mary Jane and Semmy Lou. ("Up front," Mrs. Brown had said. "Where everyone can see you.")

Eyes were gazing. The seat was hard. Pa stood next to the stairs with his brothers, Reverend Gaston on the first step. After Mrs. Brown came the Colonel, and on his arm, Miss Strong, dressed all in white, her face beneath a short veil. When everything was quiet, Reverend Gaston started in about marriage. About God giving Adam dominion over Eve, and all creatures, and the whole earth. About each thing bearing the seed for generations, according to its kind. About God telling Adam and Eve to multiply. About marriage, and the difference between freedom and union. All Alemeth could think about was how a spider web would burn.

"What therefore God hath joined together, let not man put asunder."

When Amzi lifted Miss Strong's veil, Mary Jane sighed as if she wanted the whole world to hear her. There was applause. Everybody made a point of calling Miss Strong 'Mrs. Byers.'

Alemeth couldn't get outside fast enough.

On the terrace, the air was cool and the spring sky sunny, but the ground was wet, as if there'd been a brief shower. If he went back to the spider web, the heels of his trousers would pick up dirt. Harl and Emily held silver trays with *petits-fours*. From their cage, Clio and Calliope had an older lady under their spell. Alemeth took a *petit-four* that looked sweet and moist, but it turned out to be savory and dry. A glance at his pant leg revealed a small grass stain already there, so he decided to try the spider web again, anyway. Then the door from the house opened. Amzi's two brothers, Alemeth and Johnson, came onto the porch: Uncle Alemeth a tall, gawky man with large eyebrows and deep set eyes, a little like Pa's; Uncle Johnson pale and freckled, with a shock of carrot red hair. He wondered how the three could be brothers.

"You know what Papaw used to say about that."

"Yeah, I remember. If you put a Gordon and a skunk in a sack together –"

" – the skunk'll pass out from the smell of whiskey!"

Uncle Johnson laughed. Uncle Alemeth shook his head.

"Hello, John Alemeth. Johnson, why don't you sit out here and talk to our nephew. I've got some business I want to discuss with Amzi and Colonel Brown."

Uncle Johnson smiled and sat down next to Alemeth. When Uncle Alemeth went back inside, Johnson pulled a cigar from his pocket.

"How are you, John?"

"I'm okay, I guess. Folks just call me Alemeth, though. How are you?"

"I feel like a long-tailed cat in a room full of rocking chairs. You smoke?"

"Naw. I –"

"That's alright. I don't much care for it myself. I'd rather chew anyway. Do you chew?"

"Naw…"

He'd seen Pa chew plenty, and he'd asked if he could try a plug, just once, just to see what it was like, and Pa almost gave him some, but after Eliza got wind of it, the answer had been no.

"Well, suit yourself. How about a little whiskey, then?"

"Sure. Some whiskey'd be good."

He'd always wondered what whiskey was like.

"I can see you're a man after my own heart."

"Pa says I'm liable to do just about anything."

Uncle Johnson chuckled and poured a small glass about a third full, and Alemeth downed it in one swallow.

Dang!

Uncle Johnson laughed. "Whoa, Alemeth. Take a minute. You're allowed to sip it, you know. Here, try again. But sip it this time."

Uncle Johnson poured the glass half full again. Alemeth lifted it, but stopped short of putting it to his lips.

"You gonna drink that whiskey?"

He shook his head.

"Sorry. You don't really like it, do you?"

"It smells like a kerosene lamp."

"Don't worry. I understand. Here, give it here."

Uncle Johnson took the glass.

"Don't worry, Alemeth. You did good. Real good."

After finishing the glass, Uncle Johnson went off to find Uncle Alemeth. When he did, Alemeth set out for the spider web. When he found it still there, he struck a lucifer on one of the bricks bordering Mrs. Brown's garden. This time, it lit. He moved the flame toward the web, imagining all sorts of crackling color and sound, a dazzling show of finery gone haywire. But before the flame even reached it, the web just vanished, instantaneously, from the heat. The spider was nowhere to be seen; he'd escaped to parts unknown. There'd been no fire at all, nothing that was ugly, or plain, or even boring – just nothing. He'd simply made the web disappear. He reflected on what he'd discovered, as if to be sure he had seen it right, then tucked the information away, one more thing about how the world worked. Meanwhile, with nothing about the burning of a spider web to delight or amuse him, he decided to save the rest of the lucifers for a time he could keep a fire going. Turning back toward the house, he noticed large spots of mud splattered on the back of his trouser leg.

For the next couple of hours, while grown-ups mingled and laughed, Alemeth sat, wondering who might see the mud on his pant leg, wondering what they would say, what they'd make him do; but no one noticed. He walked out to the outhouse, and sat again, and thought how awful was a house full of girls, how awful it was to have to stay clean, how awful things would be with Miss Strong in the house, and who would be first to call attention to the mud on his trousers when they got home. He looked for Uncle Johnson again, but Uncle Johnson was talking to Pa and Miss Strong.

When time came to go back to Bynum's Creek, Amzi left in a buckboard with Miss Strong. Uncle Johnson drove the rest of the family home in a separate wagon, telling stories about his brother that Alemeth had never heard. The only good thing about the day was that no one said a word to him about the mud.

The next day, Leander McKinney and Alemeth were playing horseshoes when their conversation took a familiar turn.

"I wished I'd been at your Pa's weddin'," said Leander, tossing a shoe at the stake. "I'd go anywhere to hear Reverend Gaston preach. He gives a right powerful sermon. Gets people actin' full of the spirit."

"Not this time, Leander. That man was slow as Christmas without fruit pie."

"No way. Not Reverend Gaston."

"My Uncle Johnson could give a better wedding sermon than Reverend Leroy."

"Alemeth Bahrs, you wouldn't know a good sermon if it hit you square in the head. And you shouldn't call him Reverend Leroy. It ain't respectful. My Pa says Reverend Gaston's the best preacher since Lorenzo Dow."

"Don't talk like you know everything, Leander McKinney. You weren't there. Maybe Reverend Leroy can preach alright on Sundays, but this wasn't no Sunday sermon. This was a weddin'. Weddin' sermons ain't like Sunday sermons."

"Oh yeah? What was it like?"

"Like I said. It was awful. It put me half to sleep."

Leander said nothing for once, and that was good. But it wasn't good enough, so Alemeth said one more thing:

"And I drank whiskey. Two glasses full."

Pa had warned him that little white lies could lead to big ones, but the words were already out, and besides, this was Leander McKinney he was talking to.

"Heck you did."

"I swear to God I did."

He hadn't planned to swear to God. That made it worse than a white lie. He knew what God thought of disobedience. So he hurried back to the truth.

"My Uncle Johnson gave it to me."

Again, Leander had no answer for that, and it seemed, for a moment, that he'd had the last word. But not to be bested, Leander changed the subject.

"Hey Alemeth Bahrs. Now your teacher's your mama!"

"No she's not, Leander. My mama's dead."

"And she's a Yankee!" Leander said gleefully. "How's it feel, havin' a Yankee for a mama? C'mon, Alemeth Bahrs, tell me. How's it *feel*?"

18

The Lord expects a woman to live for His glory in everything she does. Suffering is her lot, and she is to endure it as He endured his. Uncle William had explained the role of women in a sermon: how God gave Eve to Adam. How Saul gave his daughter to David as a reward for valor on the battlefield. How Laban gave both his daughters to Jacob in return for years of labor. A daughter is always subject to her father's command; a wife must submit to her husband. The man is not of the woman, but the woman of the man, and a woman's service to her husband should reflect her service to the Lord.

Would Mr. Byers be good to her?

After the wedding, on the buckboard to Bynum's Creek, Eliza had prayed that he'd be tender, and she had prayed for the strength to obey him, whatever he turned out to be. *Commit thy way unto the Lord; trust also in Him; and He shall bring it to pass.*

Since then, her prayers had been answered. On her wedding night, her dread had turned to happiness. Mr. Byers had proved to be caring and tender. And in the days that followed, she had felt the glory of promise fulfilled. Mr. Byers listened to what she had to say. He didn't curse or drink to excess. He proved himself a good father to the children. He asked her to call him by his first name. Twenty years her senior, he had his warts and blisters, and his tobacco chewing was the dirtiest thing she'd ever seen, but what concern are warts and blisters, when compared to the goodness of the heart? If his own prayers focused on the weather rather than salvation, so be it; at least he was a man of prayer.

May brought rain, then warming sun, then more rain, days perfect for the crops, he said. It seemed to Eliza as if the Lord stood on high, moving the sun and the clouds in answer to Amzi's prayers and those she had added to his. The cotton grew tall. After weeks of hesitation, when she finally summoned the courage to say something about his habit of getting in bed with the day's dust and grit on his legs, he asked why she'd taken so long to mention it, and began taking a barrel shower before supper, with soap. He agreed not to spit tobacco in front of her. He was a good man. While not always clean, he was making an effort. He was strong; he was reliable; she found much to take comfort in. And for that, she thanked the Lord.

To do her part, Eliza did everything she could to treat the children as if they were her own. Mary Jane was a good student; little Semirah Louisa as obedient as a stepmother could ask. Alemeth was the only one who resisted her, and there were times even he seemed to come around. He'd asked her, once, what the Bible said about the relationship between people and animals.

When she told him that God had given man dominion over all the animals of the earth, and all the fishes of the sea, he seemed satisfied; and another time, he asked her if the Bible said anything about punishment for telling a lie. Maybe, she thought, just maybe, these small expressions of interest meant he was finally coming around.

*   *   *

One morning, Eliza woke to daylight in the window, to birdsongs in the air, to a bed that was empty beside her. Her first thought was of the trousers she was mending for Alemeth, that she'd left on the table a few feet away, to finish first thing in the morning. But when the urge to pass water prompted her to rise, her head spun with the churning of seas. She grabbed a pail. Wrenching, she came face to face with what had been inside her, and tasted it in her mouth. Pulling the pail closer to her mouth focused the smell around her nose, and she disgorged again from deep inside her.

There was more upheaval, but nothing came out. Eventually, the nausea subsided and she managed to rise, to dress, to go about the business of the day. But at times she felt faint, and when Johnson saw her, he said she looked lower than a snail at the bottom of a dry well. Leety said she might be going to have a baby. And in the hours and days that followed, everyone came to understand that Leety was right.

As days turned into weeks, what had been fertile ripened and grew. Green bolls appeared in the cotton fields like thousands of tiny cabbages, and as if of one mind, the people of Bynum's Creek hoped for the appearance of what people called "white gold." As summer turned toward autumn, and as Eliza grew large with her gift from the Lord, the bolls in the fields grew hard, turning first to gold and then to brown, and when it seemed they could not get any larger, they burst open by the millions. Cracking. Dividing. Becoming the prizes for which all their labor had been spent. Acres on both sides of Bynum's Creek turned whiter than fleece, as if, in the still waning summer, an early snow had started to fall.

19

Alemeth looked forward to the day he would know as much about the world as Amzi did. Lessons about rutting pigs, brooding chickens and how to mill trees for good lumber were a never-ending feast for the appetite. And if some things – like the cold slaughter of a defenseless animal – didn't come easily, it didn't detract from his faith in his father, or his desire to learn whatever he could about the world from him. So he listened faithfully to Amzi's lessons about the land, and about a man's responsibility toward it. As they rode the plantation together, Amzi talked of the sun, and of the soil: how the crop needed rain when it was green, dropping its roots, and preparing to bloom; how it needed sun when the bolls were forming and turning brown. How now (with the bolls open) the cotton didn't want rain at all – for rain would ruin a crop that was ready to pick. But as Amzi also pointed out, you didn't want to pick it early, either. As long as the cotton was dry, it would keep on growing; every day of sunshine would add to the harvest.

Amzi had answers to all Alemeth's questions. How you could tell it was time to start picking. Which rows to pick now and which to wait a little longer before picking. That a red sky at night meant rain the next day; time to pick all the cotton you could.

"Every boll has its perfect day: the day before it rains."

But one day, the lesson was about something else.

"There's something else we need to talk about, Alemeth. You have a new Ma now. It's time to start calling her 'Ma,' like your sisters do."

Alemeth winced. Miss Strong wasn't old enough to be his mother. With Semirah still so strong in his heart, he couldn't think of Miss Strong that way.

"Pa, I've tried, but I can't. Miss Strong is not my real Ma."

"I know you loved your real Ma, Alemeth. I'm glad you still feel so much for her. But it would mean a lot to Eliza, if you could call her 'Ma.' She thinks you don't like her."

"Pa, it's not that. I don't know if I can."

"Well, you can't go on calling her Miss Strong. That isn't her name anymore. It sounds ridiculous. You need to try harder."

He might as well start calling Ann Brown 'Ma,' he thought. Then, he had an idea.

"Could I just call her 'Eliza'?"

Amzi sighed; started to talk; then stopped again.

"I guess so, Alemeth. She's got to understand how much you loved your mother. I'll talk to her about it. But no more 'Miss Strong,' okay?"

"Okay, Pa. I'll try to remember. 'Eliza' it is."

20

One day in late October, Leander McKinney knocked on the door.

"Hey, Alemeth – you heard Doctor Egger's in town?"

"Who?"

"Doctor Egger. My cousin says he talks to spirits."

"Spirits?"

"Yeah. You ain't never heard of that?"

"Sure I have."

"Oh yeah? Tell me about it, then."

"Well – it's like prayin'."

"Heck, Alemeth Bahrs. You don't know nothin'. It ain't prayin'. You can talk to people who've died, and they talk back to you. Really. They tell you things. My Daddy says he's done it himself. Twice."

The very idea of hearing a ghost talk sent chills up Alemeth's spine; he was fascinated. Alemeth readily agreed to go see Dr. Egger. But he also insisted on secrecy, because, he said, "some folks don't approve." They needed a plan. They needed to wait for the right time.

A few days later, when Eliza asked Alemeth to get her a piece of lace from Neilson's, to make a piece for the baby she was expecting, it was the chance Alemeth had been waiting for. He let Leander know their chance had come. In Oxford, instead of going straight to Neilson's, they stopped in at Butler's hotel to look for Dr. Egger.

"Good morning, boys," said Mrs. Butler. "What can I do for you?"

"Good morning, ma'am. Is Doctor Egger staying here?"

"You mean, Doctor Edgar? No. He's not staying with us. He sleeps in his wagon, in a lot off North Street."

"Oh. Thank you, ma'am."

"You're Alemeth Byers, aren't you? And you, a McKinney?"

"Yes, ma'am."

"Yes, ma'am."

"Do your parents know you're looking for Doctor Edgar?"

"Yes, ma'am. They know all about it."

It was a lie, of course. (Not *his* lie, this time.) Leander was always speaking for both of them, and sometimes, you just had to go along with Leander's white lies, no matter how crazy the scheme. So when Mrs. Butler looked his way, Alemeth just nodded his head.

Dr. Edgar's big covered wagon sat around the corner from Dr. Isom's. A sign printed across its middle read, "DR. O.W. EDGAR," and in larger letters,

below, was the claim Leander had talked about: "GUIDE TO THE SPIRITS."
A tent was set up next to it, and a man sat on a chair in front of the tent. On a
sign in the ground were the words, "Your Surer Path to Knowledge."

"Good morning, gentlemen."

Leander was gleaming. "Good morning."

"Good morning."

"Are you gentlemen interested in the Spirits?"

"Yes, sir," said Alemeth and Leander at the same time.

"Well, that shows your intelligence. I've always valued the company of
intelligent people. So please, consider me a friend. What can I do for you?"

"Is it true what they say," asked Leander, "that you can talk to dead
people?"

"Quite true, my friend, though I prefer to think of them as spirits. And
with my help, you can too. Are there any particular spirits you have in mind?"

Leander and Alemeth looked at Dr. Edgar wide-eyed. Alemeth hadn't
thought about *who*. Surely not his mother. Who else did he kmow?

"And, while you think about who you'd like to talk to, do you gentlemen
have ten cents? I usually charge twenty-five, but for you boys, I'll gladly make
an exception."

Leander, as usual, had no money. On most days, there'd be none in
Alemeth's own pocket either, but Eliza had given him money for the lace. He
counted it, to be sure. If he gave ten cents to Dr. Edgar, he might not have
enough for the lace.

"No. I guess – "

"Sure you do," said Leander. "That's forty cents you got there." Leander
whirled around to face Dr. Edgar. "My grandpappy. That's who we want to
talk to. We'll talk to my grandpappy." Whirling back, he stuck out his hand for
the money. "Unless you got someone else in mind?"

Alemeth hadn't planned to pay, but his curiosity about talking to a ghost –
any ghost – proved frighteningly irresistible. He handed over ten cents of
what Eliza had given him, and they followed Dr. Edgar into the tent.

"My friends," the doctor said, "my most excellent and intelligent friends –
according to Varley's Treatise on Zodiacal Physiognomy, the alignment of the
planets in relation to the stars at the time of a man's birth determines the rest
of his life. When were you born?"

Alemeth answered: "I was born on the first of January."

"Oh, really? You're a Capricorn, then. Ruled by Saturn. Persistent, like a
goat. Hardworking. You make good decisions, when you think things through.
You want to be independent, but you find yourself wanting the approval of
others. And you?"

"I want to talk to my grandpappy."

"Alright, alright. Give me just a minute."

Dr. Edgar pulled down flaps at each end of the tent, making everything dark. Then, in the center of a small table, he lit a candle that lit up his face and cast a shadow behind him. He bid the boys to sit beside him; when they did, the three silhouettes on the tent's side looked like shades of the dead.

"Put your hands on the table," said the doctor. "Palms down, like this. A spirit will come to the smoke of a fire," he explained, and then — addressing spirits unseen — "We are looking for Leander's granddaddy. What did you say his name was, son?"

"Zephaniah. Zephaniah McKinney."

Alemeth couldn't wait to see what would happen next.

"We are looking for Zephaniah McKinney. Are you there, Zephaniah? Leander wants to speak to you."

Nothing.

"Boys, it's very important. Don't think of anything else but Leander's granddaddy."

Alemeth had never seen Leander's granddaddy; how was he supposed to think of him?

"Ask for him, Leander. Maybe he'll respond to your voice."

"Grandpappy, this is Leander talkin'. Your grandson. Are you there?"

After a moment, there was a quiet rapping from their midst.

"Ssshh!" said Dr. Edgar. "I think we may have him. Ask him again."

"Grandpappy, this is Leander. Are you there?"

There was silence for just a moment, then two quick raps, a pause, and then two more.

"I hear him," said the doctor. "It's – yes, it's him. He says his name is Zephaniah McKinney."

"I don't –"

"Ssshh! He says he is very glad to see you, Leander."

"Well, dang, I cain't see him!"

"Of course you can't, Leander. He's only a spirit."

"But I cain't hear him, neither."

"Listen, closely," said the doctor. "It takes practice. Sometimes, it takes a medium to hear the voices."

Alemeth listened as closely as he knew how, but all he could hear was the thumping in his own chest, then more rapping.

"He wants to know how your Ma and Pa are doing."

Leander looked like he'd swallowed a watermelon.

"Ma and Pa are fine," he said.

"Do you have any questions for your granddaddy?"

"I sure do. Tell me, grandpappy, — are you up in Heaven? Or —"

More rapping. Leander stopped, but it didn't matter.

"He is," said Dr. Edgar. "He says he is."

"What're things like there?"

"'It's wonderful,' he says. 'Absolutely wonderful. The weather's always sunny. The birds sow seed. Crops never need working. People have nothing to do but fish all day."

"How's the fishin'?"

The doctor listened, and Alemeth did too. Nothing beat fishing,

"He catches fish every time his line goes in the water."

Leander and Alemeth both gasped.

"The fish clean and fry themselves."

"Dang, dang, dang!" proclaimed Leander, eyes bulging as if they'd seen Heaven itself.

After the séance, Leander raved about his granddaddy's report. "Sure beats angels sitting around and singing hymns, don't it, Alemeth?"

"Sure does."

"Sure was dandy talking to him."

"Sure was." But Alemeth was already thinking about the money.

"Alemeth Byers, you reckon we can come back some time? Your Ma got anything else she needs in town?"

"She ain't my Ma."

At Neilson's, Alemeth was five cents short on the lace. Dr. Edgar's ten cents had made a difference.

"No problem," said Mr. Neilson. "You're Amzi Byers' boy, aren't you?"

"Yes..."

"I'll put it on account."

Relief calmed Alemeth's anxious heart. He'd be able to get the lace for Eliza after all. But on the way home, he stewed over his new problem. He was going to have to give Eliza the lace, but what about the money? If he gave her only a few cents, as if he'd gotten change, he'd be stealing. If he told her he'd spent it all, he'd be lying again. And it wouldn't be a little white one. He couldn't think of anything he could do where things would turn out right. So, when the time came, he gave Eliza only the lace – suggesting, perhaps (but without having to say so) that it had cost the whole forty cents. In order that he wouldn't have to lie, all the coins stayed in his pocket.

For a couple of weeks, no one said anything, and Alemeth thought maybe he'd done the right thing (or at least the smart thing). But his worries returned when, in Oxford to get new stirrup leathers for Cracker, Pa said, "As long as we're in town, let's go over to Neilson's."

"What do we need at Neilson's?"

"Nothing. But I thought I'd pay up the account."

The mere mention of the account made Alemeth's heart jump a beat, and he lagged behind. He didn't want to see what would happen next. But he could have predicted it: the greetings, the general inquiries about health, the getting down to business, the furrowed brow on Pa's face when Mr. Neilson's account book didn't match his own. Or maybe, somehow, it would be better.

When Pa ran a forefinger down the page of Mr. Neilson's ledger, it showed 35 cents on account for the lace.

"There's the mistake. Alemeth paid for that lace. In cash."

"No he didn't. He was short."

Both men looked at him. He swallowed.

"He was short," Mr. Neilson repeated. "So I told him I'd put it on account. Isn't that right, Alemeth?"

There was nothing he could do. He'd been caught red-handed.

"Yes, sir, Pa. He's right. He put it on account."

"Then what happened to the money Ma gave you?"

"I still have it. Back home."

Pa scowled, apologized to Mr. Neilson, and paid up the account. On the ride home, Pa kept saying, "I don't know why you didn't say something." Still, Alemeth said nothing. There was no sense volunteering. Nothing he could say would help. No matter how he counted it, he had only thirty cents to return, not the forty he'd been given. Maybe, when he turned the coins over to Pa, Pa wouldn't count it. Or maybe they'd forget how much they gave him in the first place, and that would be the end of it.

Help me, Lord.

But as it turns out, Pa did count it. And Eliza knew she had given him forty cents. There was nothing to say but what had really happened.

For a moment, it seemed it might be his lucky day, because Pa seemed to focus on Leander.

"What comes over you when you get together with that McKinney boy? Every time you two get together, you get into some sort of trouble. You need to find yourself someone else to hang around with."

But then, reality.

"Go get my switch, John Alemeth. I'm going to beat you into next week."

Alemeth got a licking he wouldn't soon forget. But finding someone else to hang with? Besides Leander McKinney? There was no one close to their age for miles, unless you counted girls.

21

The existence of spirits is well attested by Scripture, as Eliza knew well, but as she saw it, Dr. Edgar's summoning of Zephaniah McKinney was an abomination. True, Alemeth had stolen the money, more or less, and had all but lied about it. He probably deserved the licking he'd got, and was obviously in need of a thorough Christian education. But he was just a boy; he could be forgiven such things. Dr. Edgar was a grown man.

Amzi said Edgar was a fraud, a swindler, with no regard for the truth, like all mentalists and spiritualists. All that was true, she knew, but the real danger was worse than fraud. To raise a man from the dead is something only God could do. And even if Dr. Edgar – or whatever his real name was – didn't intend to raise the dead, what he was doing was *very* dangerous. Satan looks for openings into our lives. To sit in a dark room summoning spirits is to welcome him into your heart. If your object is to cheat young boys of their errand money, who can deny that Satan has a foothold?

First, she told Alemeth he'd better start making smarter choices, or he might never get to attend the University. When that seemed to have no impact, she got Amzi to agree there'd be no more trips to town until further notice, to keep Alemeth out of harm's way.

Alemeth said it wasn't fair. That he'd already been punished by Amzi and didn't need 'someone else' trying to tell him what he needed. That she wasn't his real Ma, and had no right. She let him know that what she wanted was for his own good. That if he resented her for it, she'd simply have to bear that burden. That it was a small price to pay for protecting him.

But then, when Amzi said maybe the boy was right, she got to wondering, and after a quick prayer, she said, "Amzi, I think I ought to adopt the children. Legally. Before God."

It wasn't so strange a request. Uncle William and Aunt Harriet had legally adopted her. Uncle Henry had celebrated his adoptions with a family meeting at the altar. But Amzi didn't see it that way.

"I see no point in it," he said.

"Alemeth doesn't accept me, as things are. You can't expect me to protect him from evil influence if he doesn't respect me as his mother."

She tried several more arguments, but none of it got her anywhere. For a reasons she couldn't understand, Amzi would hear nothing of formal adoption. Her suggestion, meanwhile – made, to her regret, in front of the children – had made Alemeth look even more defiant and resentful.

It was a look she'd see often in the months to come.

22

The way Eliza kept on about the Word of God and the need for 'a good Christian education' was getting on Alemeth's nerves. "Chronicles is a message from the Lord," she would say. "If you want to understand yourself, Alemeth, you must pray for an understanding of Chronicles." And it wasn't just Chronicles; it was all of Scripture, every chapter and verse. "The Holy Ghost is always with you," she would say. "And He's always sending you a message, Alemeth. If you'll just open your ears, you'll hear the message as clear as I do. You simply have to ask Him to give it to you."

He tried, but he didn't hear a thing.

"Have you read your Scripture yet today? You'll never get into the University unless you study."

His interest in the University was less than his interest in brocaded seat cushions. Pa understood about Universities. It was one thing to learn about things that really mattered, things that existed, that he could touch and feel; it was another to learn about people who lived thousands of years ago. It was the one part of Eliza's browbeating that made him chuckle. She had no idea how little the idea of a University – or Scripture – or anything about the past, meant to him. She had no idea, in short, who he really was.

Then, as Alemeth's twelfth birthday approached, Eliza said it would be the perfect time for him to "stand up," to make his profession of faith. She invited Reverend Gaston to have a talk with him.

The Reverend Leroy B. Gaston's gravity had to be acknowledged. (He'd once knocked a tray of *petits-fours* out of Harl's hands with the flesh that overflowed his suspenders.) After Reverend Gaston and Miss Eliza spoke privately for a minute, Eliza asked Alemeth what he believed. Of course he believed in God, and Jesus, and all that. But the Reverend Gaston wanted more detail. Was Alemeth *saved*? Did he believe he was among the *elect*? What did he think of the Westminster Confession?

When he said he wasn't sure, Reverend Gaston said Faith doesn't mean freedom from all doubt – only recognition that doubt is the work of the devil. The Faith God expects of us, he said, is to believe in the divinity of the Lord *despite* one's doubts. "When the mind begins to question the Word of God, you know the Devil is at work. If possible, doubt should not be entertained in the first place, but if it does arise, it must be dismissed and kept far away."

Eliza asked the ultimate question.

"Alemeth, are you ready to declare yourself bound to the service of Jesus Christ, your Lord and Savior?"

She showed no sign of giving up. And there couldn't be any good to come from entertaining the devil. And so, on Saturday, the first of January, 1848 – Alemeth's twelfth birthday – he stood up for the Lord.

"Do you declare, John Alemeth Byers, before your family, and before your friends and neighbors, that you are ready to submit, with all your heart and all your soul, to the will of God, as your Lord?"

"I do."

At Reverend Gaston's invitation, people stepped forward and laid hands on him, praying out loud for his soul. One woman's hand on his neck made him wonder if Zachariah McKinney felt as cold; another's shook as if palsied. When it was all done, he needed fresh air. Escaping from the house, he made his way to the tool shed, where he found Uncle Johnson taking a drink.

"Don't say anything about this to your stepma. Alright?"

"Of course. I won't say nothin'."

It felt good to hear Johnson call Eliza his 'stepma.' "Uncle Johnson?"

'What?'

"How come Pa acts so different around Miss – around Eliza?"

"Men fall in love, Alemeth."

"I can't ever talk to him anymore. He only listens to her. She's got him bewitched or something."

"Oh, Alemeth. She's not a bad lady. You ought to give her a chance."

"I've tried, Uncle Johnson. I've tried to hear what she hears, but I don't. And she won't lay off it. Always talking to angels and stuff. It's, well, it's like there's somethin' wrong with me if I don't hear angels talkin' too."

"Eliza takes her Scripture serious, Alemeth. And maybe that's a good thing. She knows more about the good book than I'll ever know."

"But she keeps at it. I'll bet she's talked about Chronicles a dozen times."

"Chronicles?"

"Yeah. It's just a bunch of names. But she keeps telling me to study it, to pray about it, to find out what the Holy Ghost is trying to tell me about what my name means."

"Well, I guess I see that a little different than your stepma does."

"You do?"

"It wasn't the Holy Ghost that named you, Alemeth. It was your Ma. I was there, at your baptism. Your uncle Alemeth was your sponsor. Your Ma named you John Alemeth, after him."

"Why?"

"Because he stuck up for what he believed in. Back in Union County, your Uncle Alemeth was famous for how he stood up to Papaw."

Well. If that didn't beat just about anything. Miss Strong didn't know everything, and Alemeth resolved not to forget it.

23

For Eliza, teaching, prayer and the study of Scripture served practical purposes as well as spiritual ones. Without them, she'd have only had to decide what dress to make, what shawl to knit, what socks to mend. Leety did the laundry, kept the garden, made the meals; with occasional help from Annie, she made all the negroes' clothes. Grote and Kep did the yard work. Simply put, there was not much else for the mistress of Amzi's three-room cabin to do. The nearest neighbor was over a mile away, Clear Creek nearly ten. Neither Nancy McKinney, Anna James, nor Mary Crawford visited often.

Nor did Amzi occupy much of her time. Early every morning, he went out to see what the night had done to the plantation. Sometimes he'd come back for dinner in the early afternoon, but he was always gone again soon thereafter. He rarely returned before dark. Sometimes, she thought the crop and the soil were his mistresses.

So there was little to do during daylight hours but knit, teach, and study Scripture, and she did her best to see that they filled her day. But as weeks passed, she thought as well about the life inside her. The child's elbows and legs were pressing, little feet pushing against her spine. Eventually, despite ministrations from Leety and Mary Jane, she longed for the day the baby would come. She faced the last few weeks propped up on pillows, wondering if *that* day would finally be *the* day, wondering what it would be like to have a child of her own.

*   *   *

When the day finally came, childbirth rocked her frame. In the throes of labor, hips splitting, back aching, insides nauseous, her flesh stretched beyond all reason, she wondered if such suffering was really needed for a life of service to the Lord. But when the pain was over, she knew He had lifted her up by seeming to beat her down. Through the mystery of His ways, He had strengthened her will draw on His strength, not her own. To be always obedient to His will.

Besides: the child was warm; fragile; crying out to be cared for. Love for the child took a place it in Eliza's heart it would never give up.

She named her daughter Medora Roxanna, after the character in Lord Byron's poem, and after her mother. Byron's Medora and her own mother had both been faithful to wandering husbands. *Medora the adorable. Dora, little Dora.* A faithful little angel.

Cooing in her ear, she welcomed the infant to the army of the Lord.

24

Alemeth's curiosity about the new baby ranged from the curious worm coming out of her navel, to the shock of dark hair, to the wonderment and confusion evident in her eyes. Would she be thin and small like Eliza? Have the same small knot at the front of her throat? But his curiosity lasted little more than a few days. He soon concluded that having Dora in the house was both good and bad.

On the good side, the baby occupied a lot of Eliza's time. The hours she spent nursing, washing and dressing the girl – cooing to her, reading to her, singing to her – were all hours Eliza was not focusing on him. For the first couple of weeks after Dora was born, there were no lessons. And even when school started again, lessons lasted only two hours, not four. Best of all, for months after Dora's birth, there were no Sunday trips to College Hill or Clear Creek. More time to spend outdoors, swimming or fishing. More time hanging out with Leander McKinney. More time to spend with Pa.

But on the bad side, Amzi now had one more person to pay attention to. Sometimes *he* cooed to the baby just like Eliza. He even sang to her, though he couldn't sing any better than Leander McKinney. And every time Amzi seemed ready to leave the baby to itself, Eliza would ask him to bring Dora something, or do something for her, or she'd say, "Oh, Amzi, look what Dora's doing now!" One way or another, she was always bringing his attention back to Dora.

Encouraged by nudges from Eliza, Amzi paid more attention to the baby than he paid to Alemeth, Mary Jane, or even Semmy Lou. One day, he told Semmy Lou he couldn't call her "Little" Semmy Lou any more. Being four, she was 'all grown up' compared to Dora. "In fact," he said, "it's time you started acting more grown up. There's only room for one baby in the house."

The words sent Semmy Lou into tears. Amzi told her to stop crying, she was too big to be crying like a baby, but that only seemed to hurt her more. It was obvious why the words had stung. Sometimes, Amzi just didn't seem to understand; he didn't see his own favoritism, though his preference for Eliza's child was as clear as the midday sun to Alemeth and Semmy Lou.

Leander McKinney had two younger brothers. Pa had several. A brother could be a life-long friend, someone to go swimming or fishing with, someone who'd always be right there, available for a romp or friendly tussle. Everyone knows how close brothers can be. Alemeth would have loved to have somebody that close – somebody like Leander would be, if Leander weren't trying to tell him what to do all the time. But another sister?

Somebody more like himself would have been just about perfect.

Cotton Plantation
FOR SALE.

I OFFER for sale, Section 13 and 14, in Township 9 Range 7 West, 1280 acres, situated 5 miles South East of the town of Panola; over 500 acres cleared and in a fine state of cultivation, divided by cross fences into from 60 to 90 acre fields. Some two to three hundred acrewoods enclosed for lots, with good water-- all under a good fence, and more than 20 gates well arranged, good gin house and cotton press; a comfortable double log house, a story and a half high, good negro quarters with good plank floors, good sta bles, cribs &c.

This place has proved to be one of the healthiest and most productive plantations in the country.   I will sell it for $7,000. half cash, balance in 12 months.   Some 10 to 20 first rate mules from 2 to 4 years old, would be taken in part payment at a fair cash price, or Negroes would be taken in part or whole, at such prices as may be agreed on.

The overseer on the premises will show the place to such as wish to examine it.

JAMES BROWN.
Clear Creek, Lafayette County, Miss.

25

In Colonel James Brown's plantation house at Clear Creek, two oil portraits hung in the entrance hall. On one wall was the portrait of the Colonel's grandfather, James Brown, who'd fought a war to get land in Indian country (though the hatchet of a 'savage' denied him the fruits of his labors). On the other hung a portrait of Joseph Brown, the Colonel's father, who'd done very well for himself as a soldier, first, as adjutant for Andrew Jackson, and later, as Minister of the Lord. The Colonel was proud to display the portraits, but no prouder, one might suppose, than he was of himself, and of his own successful decisions.

He'd once read an article in the Chickasaw Union that summed up his attitude about the Chickasaw perfectly. After asserting that the agent charged with the removal of the Chickasaw has made a "clean job" of it, so that the presence of an Indian in the village had become "almost a curiosity," the article had referred to "the demoralizing, brutalizing effects of contact between the white man and the savage" and concluded: "Every well-wisher of his species, every friend of the redman, must rejoice at the breaking up of an intercourse which, as it existed here, was fraught with the most pernicious consequences to both the white man and the Indian – two races, which all time and experience prove cannot exist prosperously together."

One of the first white settlers to arrive in Chickasaw territory, the Colonel had made a good deal of money operating a stage line from Memphis to Jackson. Then, with help from the Indian Removal Act, he'd started buying up Chickasaw land. First, two sections – 1280 acres – from Tobotubby, at the ferry where Tobytubby's creek flowed into the Tallahatchie; then three sections from Ish Tah Chock Athla and Ah Fah Mah Tubby, along the Yoknapatawpha; then, from Mish Um Tah Umby, the land on Clear Creek, another tributary of the Tallahatchie. Further investments followed. It paid to have connections in the Department of Indian Affairs, and the Colonel was a master at making connections. As his stage business brought more settlers to the area, there'd been more buyers for everything, and more profit for those who'd bought land when prices were low. By the late 1840's, Colonel Brown was one of the wealthiest men in northern Mississippi.

His desire to sell a 1280 acre working plantation in Panola County was not a sign of financial trouble, nor of any plan to leave the area. The plantation was only one of many properties, and the sale was simply to make a profit on his investment, generating cash (or other negotiable property, like negroes) for other ventures. His desire to sell coincided with his new focus on the University, of which he had become a Board member. The Trustees had needed an Executive Committee to oversee daily operations and a local member of that Committee to oversee construction of the campus. Colonel Brown had been their man.

The Colonel's offer to accept negroes in payment for his plantation may say something about the value he saw in Africans. Perhaps he told himself it was hard to believe his neighbors were so oblivious to the fact that a skilled negro could do more than just pick cotton – that he could clear land, build structures, or simply be rented out as day labor. Those who came later would only be able to guess his private thoughts on such things. But the Colonel's investment in negroes was almost as great as his investment in Chickasaw land, and it seems safe to say that it wasn't only another source of profit, but another cause for pride.

Another article, this one in *The Oxford Organizer*, offers further insight into the Colonel's character. On the 30th of April, 1849, the paper informs us, the Colonel was elected chair of a meeting of the local Democratic Party. As chair, it would have been his responsibility to keep the proceedings running smoothly. Smoothly, in fact, is how the meeting appears to have run. The Honorable Jacob Thompson, Congressman – whose Congressional duties included serving as chair of the Committee on Indian Affairs – explained the high patriotic object of the meeting. Mr. Dill moved that Colonel Brown appoint a committee of ten to report upon the objects of the meeting. And when Brown appointed said committee, he made sure to include Dill among the committeemen. Thompson moved that a number of those present, including Brown, be appointed delegates to the District Convention, and that Dill be made a delegate to the State Convention. Both motions passed.

The meeting, it seems, was a model of smooth politics. Thompson, Dill and Brown kept their fingers in every aspect of the affair, and ended with approval of a motion that the minutes of the meeting be printed in Dill's newspaper, *The Organizer* — which they soon were.

By August, Colonel Brown was not only a delegate to the state convention, but a candidate for the state house as well. One can suppose it was the sort of life that befitted a man of the Colonel's stature. In fact, as best those who came later could tell, everything about the Colonel's life operated like the silver pocket watch he carried, never missing a beat, everything always in its place, working together to give him everything he wanted. There was but one exception to the fine-tuned ordering of affairs that would permeate the record of the Colonel's life: neither his late wife nor his current one had been able to give him a son. His wife's sister's stepson, Alemeth Byers, was the closest thing to a son he'd ever have.

*   *   *

Amzi Byers, the Colonel's brother-in-law and Alemeth's father, was a very different sort of man. The record of his life would leave no evidence of a taste for politics, or of any public involvement at all. He was private man, a quiet man, a man who believed in hard work, and in doing hard things with his own hands. And in the spring of 1849, though his plantation was growing, the crop in two of his fields was turning yellow. The unfurled seedlings had come up green and healthy, at first. There'd been no sign of cut worms or seed rot. The plants had deep tap roots, and lots of branches. But then, as they'd reached their botanical adolescence, they'd started turning yellow.

His family depended on that crop, on that land. It wasn't worth a hoot if it didn't produce. So when Colonel Brown invited him to attend a Tuesday lecture on the chemistry of growing cotton, it seemed he had nothing to lose.

The speaker was Dr. John Millington, M.D., the University's professor of Geology and Chemistry. Well past his seventieth birthday, an Englishman, and a complete stranger to Mississippi, it seemed doubtful Millington knew anything about growing cotton in the American west. When he began apologizing for his ignorance of the white fiber, Amzi sighed, steeling himself for boredom, wasted time, and a sore backside. With the voice of an old man, Millington talked about Emanuel Fellenberg, the Earl of Leicester, and Sir Humphrey Davy. Clay. Lime. Flinty sand magnesia. Amzi had a hard time staying awake.

"Chemistry shows us that all earths in their pure state are white as chalk, but nearly all the earth of our plantations is more or less colored; consequently it is not pure but has been colored by something extraneous to itself."

Ike Davis nudged him, trying to keep him from nodding off.

"We find, likewise, that this colored earth is clothed with vegetation, while the white and pure earth is incapable of sustaining it."

He tried to focus on Millington.

"There can be no doubt, therefore, but that a great portion of the nutritious quality of the soil must reside in the material with which it is colored. The next question that arises is as to the nature and quality of that coloring matter."

What he needed was information that could help him get his cotton looking green again. Might Millington share anything he could use for that, or was he just another educated windbag?

"The weight of the globe never increases or decreases. No matter what happens to the fifty elements that make up the earth – no matter what sort of change they undergo – the same elements exist, in the same quantities, as before. They simply move around. The elements are merely *lent* to things for a time, to serve the period of their natural existence. And this being accomplished, the materials are not wasted and thrown away, but are carefully restored to their parent earth, to be used again and again in a chain of endless existences."

The lecture itself seemed headed toward an endless existence.

But then the doctor leaned forward, speaking in a near whisper, as if to reveal the answer to a great mystery.

"The great secret that has been laid open to us by studying Agricultural Chemistry is this."

Millington glanced around as if to make sure that no one could hear him but those fortunate enough to find themselves close.

"The soil must contain the elements that are to enter into the composition of the plant to be grown upon it."

The idea caught Amzi hard. If the soil had everything the crop needed, the crop could hardly go wrong.

"To be sure that this is the case, we must analyze the plant by chemical means. We must ascertain its elements. And then the soil must be analyzed to ascertain that it contains at least all the elements necessary to the plant."

It made undeniable sense. If the elements remain, then the stock of the plant, and all its fruits, came up through the roots, and the roots must be drawing up those same elements from the water and the soil. If chemical analysis could reveal exactly what the crop needed, a man could determine – and provide – the perfect soil.

Amzi sat up on the bench, contemplating the banks of Bynum's Creek, eager for a closer look at the earth.

26

Alemeth could hardly believe his own ears: Mrs. Gaston was telling a shocked group of church-goers about a bull found on the Lyceum roof. The church yard was filled with chatter.

"I declare, it's enough to make a soul wonder, what *is* that University teaching?"

"What do you mean?"

"You haven't heard? They found *a bull* on the roof of the Lyceum. snorting and knocking about. I thought surely your sister would have told you."

"No, I – How on earth did it get up there?"

"That's the question everyone's asking. Why, here comes your sister now. Mary Ann, what can you tell us about the bull? What do the faculty think?"

"Isn't it outrageous? What will the trouble makers think up next?"

"Do they know who did it?"

Alemeth wanted the answer to that question as much as anyone did, if for different reasons. He thought whoever had put a bull on the roof deserved some kind of award.

"There is no suspect; not yet. But James went up on the roof this morning, with Professor Bledsoe. They found the strangest thing: a pile of ashes. And in it, a charred bone. They're thinking it may have been some sort of sacrifice."

"They were going to sacrifice a bull?"

"Who knows?"

"Well, if that isn't the end of things!"

"A sacrifice. To what, I wonder?"

Alemeth recalled what Leander had said about the Chickasaw altar to the devil.

"What *is* getting into these young people's minds?"

"Perhaps it was a morality play."

"More likely a sacrifice to the devil, if you want my opinion."

There it was. Maybe it *wasn't* a student prank. Maybe it *was* the Chickasaw.

"I must say, in *my* opinion, it doesn't matter what heresy was involved. Can you imagine *any* young people involved in such nonsense, if properly versed in Scripture? Whoever the pranksters may be, the real responsibility is clear. It's the lack of Christian doctrine that's to blame. What's the world coming to, when a University can't teach Christianity, but *can* teach Hades and Zeus?"

"Indeed."

Alemeth was in no mood to hear more about Scripture, but he was still listening when something Mrs. Buford said caught his ear.

"Speaking of radical ideas, have you heard about Doctor Millington's lecture to the Agricultural Council? I've heard it was *most* interesting."

"I've heard the same," said Mrs. Pegues.

Alemeth had heard plenty about Dr. Millington's lecture from Pa. Like Pa, he'd wondered whether Millington could help the Plantation. They were having to wait another year to find that out. But what interest the ladies from church could have in understanding the soil, and what Dr. Millington's soil had to do with the bull on the roof, he hadn't the slightest idea. Then Eliza joined the conversation.

"I understand from Mr. Byers," she said, "that what Doctor Millington said about chemistry could be a great help to farmers. With soil samples, and fertilizers, and things like that."

"That's *hardly* what *I* heard he talked about. Don't you know what everyone's been saying?"

"Perhaps not. Are you going to tell me?"

"Well, how shall I say it? We all know the doctor seems a kind old man. But advanced age cannot excuse, well – I don't know what other word there is for it: blasphemy."

What?

"What?"

"As I hear it, he claimed that turnips have habits, and tastes – likes, and dislikes – just like people. And that the breathing of a human being is no different than the burning of a candle!"

"Well, perhaps there are similarities…"

"No, Mrs. Byers, I have it on good authority. The professor used the word 'identity'. He said there's an *identity* between animal and vegetable life. He said that a human being consists of nothing more than that which he has eaten, from the grasses, and the livestock. Nothing more!"

"Such reasoning degrades the race. We were not made mere poultry! Isn't it obvious?"

"It's ungodly; that's what I say it is."

"Well," said Eliza. "His remarks were printed in *The Organizer*. We can read them for ourselves. I feel sure that he didn't – "

"As I hear it, Mrs. Byers, the worst came *after* his reported remarks. He said that yeast 'reproduces' itself just like people do! Can you imagine – that the Creator made us no different than fermenting sugar?!"

Pa had said nothing about turnips having tastes, or people being like fermented sugar.

"I heard he said both plants and animals – including human beings – are nothing more than *machines*. That all living things are made of the same materials, and these are the same materials as non-living things, like rocks and sand!"

"Scripture says the same thing," said Eliza. "From dust to dust,"

"Calling human beings machines? Even God's chosen people? I don't see that anywhere in my Bible. I ask you, ladies. Pagan sacrifices on the roof? Human beings no different from rocks? Lacking a soul? What is happening to our University?"

*　　　　　*　　　　　*

Alemeth was thoroughly confused. Had Dr. Millington really said that people were machines? O that they lacked souls? And if he'd started talking about people's souls, why hadn't Pa laid into him for sounding like a preacher? Alemeth wished he'd been there, to hear it all for himself, and draw his own conclusions. What Dr. Millington really said could make a big difference for crops to come. For the Plantation. For all of them.

In contrast, the ladies' inability to resolve exactly what Dr. Millington had said did not stop them from agreeing on the exact cause of the real problem: that the University was turning its back on God. The decision not to include *The Evidences of Christianity* showed just how godless the University had become, and the appearance of the bull on the roof showed the predictable consequences. Dr. Millington's speech to the Agricultural Association gave proof that, in the guise of higher learning, the secular powers were taking God out of *everything*.

On the ride back to Bynum's Creek that night, Eliza said to Amzi, "You know, I'm not so sure Alemeth ought to be attending this University. I think a seminary might be a much better choice."

And in the back of the wagon, pained as he'd been that she wanted to adopt him, offended by the lengths to which she'd gone to dictate the course of his life, Alemeth was filled with hope based on what Eliza had said. Pa didn't like preachers or seminaries, either one. And the nearest seminary was in Huntsville. If Eliza was losing interest in the University, college might be off the table altogether – and wouldn't *that* be a dandy stroke of luck?

27

In June, the weather warmed; showers brought the right amount of water, and Eliza's 'school' let out for the summer. By July, the crop was flowering pink and red. And then, as if beckoned elsewhere, the showers grew short, letting the sun do the work. Pa said things could not have been much better, and as far as Alemeth was concerned, there was reason to agree.

It was hard to see the point in learning about diction, literature or dead people. Whether out in the fields with Pa, or fishing with Leander McKinney, his future would depend on the land. What Eliza wanted to teach was useless to the land *or* to his future. So he began to consider arguments he might make to Pa about why he shouldn't have to go to class with his sisters.

He'd be more useful outside, on the plantation.

Pa himself said it was important to focus on the land.

If Eliza didn't have to spend time with him, she could pay more attention to Mary Jane, Semmy Lou, and little Dora.

Each time he imagined another reason, he imagined Pa thinking it over.

Then, at the next Sunday dinner, Eliza read a note she'd received from her sister. It was news about the University. At their last meeting, the Trustees had voted to replace President Holmes with the Reverend Augustus Longstreet, a man of the cloth. And in an even clearer signal of a return to righteousness, the Board had reconsidered the curriculum, voting this time to *include* The Evidences of Christianity. Eliza read the note with excitement.

"Amzi, dear. It seems some good may come of the University after all."

"Maybe."

What did Pa see in her?

"Shouldn't we see that Alemeth is at least prepared to attend, when he's old enough? In case he decides he wants to? He'll need to prepare himself for the entrance examination, or he'll have no choice in the matter. I can't teach Caesar or Virgil to him; I'm not qualified. He ought to attend one of the academies, to prepare himself. Don't you think?"

Pa looked up from his plate and nodded. "You're probably right," he said without even looking Alemeth's way. And then, as if from the depths of a trance, he repeated himself the way a man does when he's talking in his sleep. "You're probably right."

Alemeth's great expectations for a life without book learning had lasted less than a month. Now, once again, Eliza's obsession with religion threatened to ruin everything good in his life.

28

That summer, the cotton was hit hard by the wilt disease. Planters grumbled about attacks by vermin they couldn't see. In their frustration, they started talking about going to California. Some spoke of prospecting for gold. Others of swinging the vote for slavery in the west. But while there was plenty of talk, most folks didn't leave Mississippi. Most just stayed and grumbled.

That fall, when the cotton was hit again by an early frost, planters cursed the weather. There were fewer wagons outside the baling barn; fewer bales to sell in Memphis; less cash coming in from the crop to buy seed, and tools, and dry goods for clothes. High tariffs imposed by Washington made manufactured goods ever more expensive. Sour news and grim predictions joined to make things even worse than they really were. Seeing no way to make ends meet unless farming was made more profitable, men spoke of seceding from the northern union. Talk of secession was heard at every meeting, meal and social.

But Colonel Brown returned from the state secession convention to report the sense of that convention: secession by Mississippi alone would be premature; no one southern state should act alone. There was to be a meeting of representatives of all slave states in Nashville. The question of secession would be discussed in unison, by a representative group of like-minded planters across the whole South.

Then, at the end of October, Eliza gave birth to another baby. For a short while, the birth of Henry Walton Byers filled Alemeth with high spirits. The idea of having a brother had brought visions of someone to swim in deep water with, someone to fish and explore with. But now that the baby had been born, Alemeth realized what a difference fourteen years could make. He did the math: by the time the boy was seven years old, he'd be twenty-one – almost old enough to be the boy's father.

If Walton had been born to his real Ma, they'd have had a lot in common. But Walton was Eliza's boy, and she *coo*ed over him like she'd *coo*ed over Dora. The younger girls of Bynum's Creek and Clear Creek appropriated Walton to themselves, treating him like one of their dolls, fussing over him like mothers and aunts.

In short, as far as Alemeth was concerned, having a little brother proved too little, too late. He retreated to the safety of his swimming hole, where he peered into the eyes of fish as if to seek an answer there. Maybe – in some way he couldn't imagine – the Christmas holiday would bring something good anyway, despite what was wrong all around him. After all, Christmas was Christmas – a time for miracles if ever there was one.

Back when Samirah was alive, Christmas Eve had been the best of times. Aunt Leety had made fruit cake; Pa had told stories; Ma had passed out presents. For the last few years, Christmas Eve had been different: filled with Scripture – Mary and Elizabeth, King Herod killing babies, no room at the inn – and with Henry Hitchcock, Lyman Beecher, and all the work still to be done to 'save the West.' Lately, Christmas Eve had not been the best of times. Still, Alemeth let himself hope that, this year, it might somehow be better.

Then, early in December, hope took a hard blow. Mrs. Brown's daughter, Fredonia, would be getting married on Christmas Eve. Everyone would go. For the first time, the Byerses would not even be staying home as a family.

"Christmas Eve isn't a very good time to get married," he said to Eliza.

"I agree with you, Alemeth. But Mary Ann has already sent invitations. There's nothing to be done about it now."

"I just don't see why I should have to spend Christmas Eve with Miss Fredonia."

"You know what, Alemeth? I think you're right. The birth of Jesus should be the center of attention on Christmas eve. But I'm afraid you have to go. If you stay home, you'll be alone. Pa and your sisters, and even your Uncle Johnson – we're *all* going."

"I won't be alone. The negroes will be here. Can't I spend Christmas eve with them?"

"No. I'm afraid that's not an option."

"I'm going to talk to Pa…"

"I've already spoken to your Pa. And I can tell you, he agrees with me. So you're coming with the rest of us. We're all going. Together. As a family."

Mrs. Brown, of course, was the one who'd chosen Christmas Eve. It was as if she wanted to steal attention from Bynum's Creek, away from the family, to make everyone pay attention to her daughter. What an awful hive of bees that family made! Strongs, all right. All of them. All the stuck-ups would be there. The educated people. Senators, judges, preachers, professors. 'People who matter.' He was going to have to get all dressed up, like on Sundays. Wear a tie. And he'd definitely have to stay clean the whole time.

He couldn't stop wondering how bad it would be.

*   *   *

On Christmas Eve, as they approached the front doors of the Colonel's home, Amzi took hold of Alemeth's elbow, stopping him.

"You'd best mind your manners tonight, Alemeth."

"Yes, Pa."

"In a few days, you'll be fourteen years old. Time you started acting like a man. No stunts like you did at the camp meeting that time. And no putting your nose where it doesn't belong. You understand?"

Alemeth's desire to become a man had only gotten stronger with time. "Yes, Pa," he said.

"Stay away from the matches. And no liquor. Make me proud."

"Yes, sir."

*   *   *

The Reverend Burney made quick work of the formalities, pronouncing Miss Fredonia and Colonel Walter husband and wife without fanfare. But the preaching that followed rose from humble beginnings to high oratory, from simple advice to the bride and groom about the benefits of prayer to bold pronouncements about who was going to hell to join Satan and fallen angels. That such spirits existed, Alemeth had no doubt. And he'd have been willing to spend an hour in hell, just to see what it was like. But he couldn't understand the difference between Beelzebub, Abaddon and Leviathan walking around in the fires of hell, and Zephaniah McKinney walking around in heaven, the experience of which Eliza had gotten so upset about. For that matter, he couldn't see the difference between Beelzebub and the invisible creatures Dr. Millington said were crawling around in the soil. At least he'd *heard* Zephaniah McKinney. He'd never seen *or* heard devils or germs, either one. Yet people talked about them with great confidence, as if they could be seen, and heard, and touched. Was it possible to know for sure they were really there?

As the Reverend showed signs of finishing his sermon, Alemeth started to slide quietly off the bench, intending to escape. When Amzi noticed him, Alemeth recognized the disapproving glance. (Alemeth knew that glance all too well.) So on his way out, he made conversation with others in the receiving line. When Dr. Conkey, the dentist, said something about the best way to clean his teeth, he listened. When Mr. Smither droned on about the role of 'classical studies' in the University curriculum, he listened. He offered Colonel Walter and the new Mrs. Walter his 'sincerest congratulations,' and when Miss Fredonia started to talk about the distinguished history of the Walter family, he listened – though the bride's face was covered with the most horrific white powder. Standing alone among families, trapped between linens and crystal, straight as he could in his Sunday clothes, Alemeth introduced himself to others, and listened.

Then, with the ring of a bell, Mrs. Brown announced it was time to be seated for dinner. Tables in long rows were covered with white linen, crystal and place cards. His seat was between Mary Jane and Ann Brown. As Harl and other negroes brought dinner in, barefoot children entered holding palm fronds; mounted the tables; and seated on the tables with their shins in front of their faces, began to wave their fans back and forth.

"What are they doin' *that* for?" he asked Mary Jane (to his left).

"Why, John Alemeth Byers," interjected Ann Brown (from his right). "Boys never cease to amaze me."

"Excuse me?"

"You've never had your flies shooed away before?"

Even without the palm frond in his face, it would not have been easy, one fork for this, another for that, food brought over his shoulder from behind him by a black man in a white shirt and black jacket. So when dinner was over, the guests out back with the parrots, Alemeth didn't hesitate to make his escape.

Rounding the corner of the house, passing an open window, he breathed a sigh of relief. But when he heard giggling inside the house, he had to know what was causing it. He stood on his toes to look through the window. He saw a crowded room; more petticoats and underclothes than he'd ever seen. He quickly looked away from the girls' private chamber, but though he continued in his path around the house, the petticoats wouldn't leave him alone.

*   *   *

Later, on the porch, recalling the sight yet again, he felt a hand on his shoulder. It was Mrs. Brown.

"Alemeth, look there. Do you know who that is?" She was gesturing to a tall, sharp-angled man in the center of a crowd.

"No, Ma'am."

"That's Reverend Longstreet. If you're going to attend the University, you ought to meet him. It's not too early to make an impression, you know."

Longstreet was sallow-cheeked, stern-lipped, a black bow tight around his neck, wire frames straddling the tip of his nose. Alemeth wondered if he'd ever so much as laid a hand on the handle of a hoe.

"I think I've had too much lemonade," said Alemeth. "I need to find the privy."

And so he made his escape. But before he knew it, the Colonel put a hand on his shoulder, and his hand was a good bit larger than Mrs. Brown's.

"So, Alemeth. I understand you'd like to meet Judge Longstreet. Come with me." He guided Alemeth along with him. "I'd be happy to introduce you."

Longstreet had large teeth set in a jaw that looked like the beak of a bird.

"Judge Longstreet," said the Colonel, "Allow me to introduce Master

John Alemeth Byers. His father's one of our major planters, and a good Democrat, I must say. Young Mr. Byers here is interested in attending the University someday. He wanted to meet you."

"Glad to meet you, sir."

"Glad to make your acquaintance, young man. Tell me, then: what school are you attending?"

"I'm taking some study with Miss — with Mrs. Byers."

"My sister-in-law," said the Colonel. "He'll soon be attending Mount Sylvan."

What? Did the Colonel know something he didn't?

"Mount Sylvan. That's Reverend Burney's School, is it not?"

"Yes it is."

"I should see that you do, my boy. At least if you're serious about your education. Reverend Burney will prepare you well."

"Yes, sir."

The new President looked down a long, thin nose.

"It's a shame more young men don't see the importance of a good education."

"Yes, sir."

Longstreet gave him another look up and down. How long would he be on display?

"You know, my boy, appearance is also important: a gentleman must make a good impression on people."

"Yes, sir."

"A Christian gentleman does well to set an example as to good manners and proper dress."

"Yes, sir."

"So tell me, young man: — is that your only pair of trousers?"

President Longstreet was staring at his right pant leg. Alemeth looked down too.

Dang it. He'd felt something tugging when he'd pulled himself up to the window. Splinter, nail – whatever the cause, a dirt-rimmed, two-finger hole now gave a view of his knee.

"You should wear something nice," said Reverend Longstreet. "You don't want to look like a savage."

"Yes, sir."

It wasn't all bad, Alemeth thought. At least the man hadn't asked how it happened. Nor did Colonel Brown give any sign of inquiring; he only looked at his pocket watch, as if he were late for an appointment. But a moment later, after Alemeth and the Colonel had left Longstreet to the attentions of others, Mrs. Brown pointed it out to her sister. Before he could escape to the garden, Eliza was asking him about it.

"Alemeth, how *on earth* did you get that hole in your pants?"

"It got caught on something. A nail, maybe."

"How did that happen?"

"It's hard to explain."

"It can't be that hard. Where was the nail?"

"In the house. Stickin' out of the house. A nail, or a splinter or something. I must have been leaning up against it."

Mrs. Brown, too, had been listening. "Well, we'll have to get Harl to get that fixed. Where is this nail?"

"At the window, down that way." He pointed as vaguely as he could.

"Alright. Well. I understand the hole. Still, how did it get so dirty?"

That was the hard question, as if some invisible power was pointing the way toward the truth.

"I slipped."

He'd hit mud right where the hole was.

"How did that happen, Mr. Alemeth Byers?"

He'd been pulling himself up, to see into the window.

Suddenly, Ann Brown had her mouth open and her hands up, one of them cupped over her mouth.

"My word, Mama, don't you see? He was standing outside the powder room, while we were changing! Why, Alemeth Byers! Were you spyin' on us?"

"Is that true, Alemeth?"

He looked at his feet. If only for a moment, he *had* been curious.

"You should be ashamed of yourself!"

Mary Jane put her hand to her mouth and started to laugh. Once she'd started, Ann Brown joined in. He'd have liked to walk away; nothing was worse than being laughed at by girls; but he couldn't leave Mrs. Brown and Eliza without being excused. So he suffered until Mary Jane had finished.

The worst part came later, when Eliza told Pa about it.

Looking at him like he thought he'd never do anything right, Pa said to Eliza, "I don't know what's wrong with that boy."

"But I – I – only looked for a second. I – "

"Don't try to defend your behavior, Alemeth. Can't you just admit that what you did was wrong?"

Altogether, it was the worst Christmas Eve ever.

The Oxford Organizer
Oxford Mississippi
25 May, 1850

WHAT IS DIRT?

Old Doctor Cooper, of South Carolina, used to say to his students, "Don't be afraid of a little dirt, young gentlemen. What is dirt? Why, nothing at all offensive, when chemically viewed. Rub a little alkali on that dirty grease spot on your coat, and it undergoes a chemical change and becomes soap. Now rub it with a little water and it disappears; it is neither grease, soap, water, nor dirt.

"'That is not a very odorous pile of dirt,' you observe there. Well, scatter a little gypsum over it, and it is no longer dirty. Everything you call dirt is worth your notice as students of chemistry. Analyze it! Analyze it! It will separate into very clean elements.

"Dirt makes corn, corn makes bread and meat, and that makes a very sweet young lady that I saw one of you kissing last night. So, after all, you were kissing dirt, -- particularly if she whitens her skin with chalk or fuller's earth. There is no telling, young gentlemen, what is dirt. Though, I must say, that rubbing such stuff upon the beautiful skin of a young lady is a dirty practice. 'Pearl powder,' I think, is made of bismuth – nothing but dirt."

29

It was a slow, wet winter, and Bible lessons mixed with penmanship and grammar as cold rain mixed with a light snow. But that spring, things began to look up when Amzi took Alemeth and three glass jars of soil to see Dr. Millington. Their aim was to get any wisdom Millington might have for how to improve the crop. When Millington was finished examining the soil, he announced that in his judgment, the loess was in need of fertilization, as they'd imagined, but Amzi's reliance on sheep manure was misplaced. According to Millington, it was an excess of sheep manure that was responsible for the yellow color and ill health of the crop. Dr. Millington suggested adding limestone in one field, old, sun-baked chicken droppings in another, and potash everywhere.

The field hands turned Dr. Millington's medicine into the soil. After they planted the cotton seed, Alemeth couldn't wait to see whether the changes would make a difference – and they did. When the plants finally came up, there was no sign of yellowing. And in late June, in the stand where the limestone had been added, the plants opened at least two weeks earlier than in prior years. The crop was green and vigorous. It would bring twice the revenue of past years, as long as calamity didn't strike first.

Everyone started arguing about the soil. Plant next year in the south eighty again? Plant cabbages beside the cotton? Legumes? Go ahead with a grass burn? Let the livestock roam? No matter what the question, the talk was about Dr. John Millington, M.D. And though some said the year's success was due to Divine Providence, Alemeth always wondered, whatever the question, what the doctor would do, in light of the makeup of the soil.

"It's all about dirt," Amzi said, and Alemeth agreed.

*   *   *

Another turn for the better came in July, after Medora's and Henry Walton's baptisms at College Hill Presbyterian. Midway into a bumpy, three-and-a-half hour, backside-breaking ride home, one of Eliza's hands sprung to her ribcage. Aunt Leety asked if she was alright, and Amzi pulled up the reins.

"Dear, are you alright? You look…"

"I think another child might be on the way."

While Aunt Leety handled Medora's questions about a new sister, Amzi kept quiet for a while, considering ramifications, then made an announcement.

"We'll have to cut out this Sunday trip to College Hill."

Alemeth's ears shot up.

"Amzi, we've always done it."

"Eliza, you're not as young as you once were."

"Where would we attend worship?"

"You know Bob Nickle? Nate Gray?"

"They go to the Cumberland church in Otuckaloffa. It's hardly closer than College Hill. And they can't even get there when the river's high. Amzi, I'm not going to church in Otuckaloffa."

"There might be others looking for a change. Maybe some Methodists and Baptists would share a building. If we all got together, we could start a new church, this side of the river. Three congregations together. Not a college church, or a town church, for Presbyterians. A union church, for farmers and their families. People close to the earth. It could be right here, on Bynum's Creek."

"It's a thought," said Eliza. "Did I tell you what Angus Johnson said?"

"Angus Johnson?"

"Reverend Angus Johnson. Reverend Gaston said that only an ordained minister could teach on the Sabbath, and Reverend Johnson disagreed. He said *anyone* could teach scripture on the Sabbath, if the Spirit moved them."

"And?"

"If Reverend Johnson would oversee us at the new union church, perhaps I could teach Sunday school there."

And so, before Alemeth's very eyes, a wonderful idea was born. Within weeks, Dr. Angus Johnson had agreed to service the Presbyterians, and by the end of September, the Baptists, Methodists, and Cumberland Presbyterians who lived north of the river were raising the roof on a new log church on Bynum's Creek. Someone suggested calling the new church *Sand Springs*, because of the springs that fed the creek. Eliza said the name reminded her of Moses in the desert, getting water from the rock. Alemeth couldn't wait. No more rides to College Hill. No more afternoon teas with girls at the Browns'. With six hours freed to spend at home every Sabbath, he'd be fishing, swimming, and doing as he pleased. Once the new church let out, Sundays would be the next best thing to paradise.

Then, a few nights later, he heard Eliza and Amzi talking about whether the negroes would be attending the union church. When Eliza said it was their Christian duty to teach the negroes the word of God, Amzi said it'd be fine with him, but he'd have to talk to the other elders about it. And when Eliza asked what the objection could possibly be, Amzi pointed out that the new log church was not as large as College Hill Presbyterian or the other churches in Oxford. Unlike them, Sand Springs would have no balcony. If the negroes were to attend services, whites and blacks would have to sit together.

IN A FIX – we met with a friend in Pickens District a few days since, returning from a hunting excursion, who related to us the following curious incident which he had witnessed that day: He saw a Hawk of the common blue wing species, on the ground, fluttering, seemingly in great distress, and on approaching, he was surprised to find a long, black snake coiled around it – both alive and evidently trying to part company. The hawk had its talons fixed in the snake, whilst the snake had its folds coiled, not very lovingly, around the neck and wing of the hawk. Whether the hawk had caught the snake, or his snakeship the hawk, our informant was unable to say, but one thing was evident: one or the other had waked up the wrong passenger.

30

Alemeth could have sat next to Grote, or Kep, or Ike. He'd have thought nothing about it. But try as he might, he couldn't imagine Mrs. Brown sitting next to Harl or her Emily; he couldn't image Mrs. Pegues sitting next to Grote, or even Aunt Leety. Dressed to the nines, showing off their finery to their neighbors, they just wouldn't do it. After all, wasn't that why the negroes sat in the balcony? Would it be any different at Sand Springs?

As it turns out, the negroes didn't sit in the union church at all. The Baptists and Methodists wanted the building on Sunday afternoons for schools of their own, and it was hard to work out a schedule satisfactory to all. In the end, due to what people called their 'general ignorance of the good book,' it was decided the negroes would not attend the regular worship service at all – at least not until they gained some understanding of the Faith. Sundays at the union church would begin with the Methodist worship service, followed by the Sand Springs service, followed by Mrs. Byers's Sunday school for whites; then there'd be a couple of hours set aside for the Presbyterians' dinner, while the Baptists held their service; Mrs. Byers's colored school would be after dinner. Once that was decided, it didn't take long to determine that since negro Sunday school would be held after dark, and since Eliza was the teacher, and since most of the negroes belonged to Amzi anyway, negro school might as well be held at the Byers plantation. And as Eliza pointed out, according to Lyman Beecher, negroes did better in their own schools anyway.

None of which was of interest to Alemeth until that evening, when Amzi had a surprise for him.

"Alemeth, you should go with your Ma. When she goes out back, with the negroes. No sense her bein' alone with them. You know how things are these days."

"To *colored* Sunday school?"

"Yes."

"Are you saying I have to go to Sunday School *twice*?"

Amzi glanced at Eliza before he answered.

"If you're going to go with your Ma, to the negro school, that's enough."

Alemeth thought it over. Out of church by mid-day; time to himself, to do whatever he wanted, while the girls were in Sunday school; it actually might be worth it. This time, he was happy to do what Pa said.

*   *   *

Eliza spent most of the week planning her lessons, asking Amzi, Mary Jane, and even Alemeth what they thought of different scriptures for different purposes. She put pieces of paper in her Bible to mark parts she wanted to share, numbering them, changing the numbers, experimenting with sequences, enough to drive Alemeth crazy if he hadn't been able to spend time outdoors. It was a difficult week. But when Sunday came, after Reverend Johnson preached at the union church, while Eliza taught white Sunday school, Alemeth got to go fishing with Leander McKinney and he caught five good bream, with crickets, while Leander only got one. At the church dinner afterward, Alemeth met Noff and Ben Spears, who'd been at white Sunday school, and told them all about it. After dinner, catching a glimpse of Charlie Orr kissing Melissa Hudgepeth, he tried to imagine what it would be like to do such a thing himself – a troubling thought that he quickly put out of his mind. Then, after the others went home, he went down to the negro camp with Eliza, for negro Sunday school, wondering what he'd got himself into.

*　　　*　　　*

There were ashes and embers dying in the pit, charred bones left over from dinner, stumps cut for sitting around the fire.

"Alemeth, would you be so kind as to bring those stumps over here, in front of me? They'll make fine seats."

There were only enough stumps for those who'd sit up front. Grote and Aunt Leety, Aunt Mary and Aunt Harriet looked like they wanted to sit as close as possible. Alemeth had been thinking about staying toward the back, but others kept looking his way, like they weren't going to sit until he did.

Then, in front of everyone present, Eliza spoke clearly to him.

"Alemeth, come up front and sit next to me."

He hesitated. Eliza asked Grote and the three negro women to sit as well – but still, they wouldn't sit till he did. So he had to sit up front, with Eliza. She motioned for him to sit at her knees, with his back to the stump where she sat. He did. Grote and the women sat on stumps close by. As other people came in, they moved up close, too. But Kep, Ike, and Moses McKinney's negro, Sally, came in last, and they held back, behind the others. They said they could hear fine from where they were. When Eliza let them stay put, Alemeth wished he could be so lucky.

He could hear the Bible open behind his head, Eliza's fingers flipping to one of her marked pages.

"The Bible is the word of God," she began. "This very book I hold in my hands. And the first Commandment in God's book is right here." (She held it up for everyone to see, pointing at the verse with her finger.) "I'll read it to you. I am the Lord thy God, which have brought thee out of the land of Egypt, out of the house of bondage. Thou shalt have no other gods before me."

She paused. The women were looking at her; behind them, the men were restless. Kep whispered something to Ike.

"Thou shall not make unto thee any graven image, or any likeness of any thing that is in heaven above, or that is in the earth beneath, or that is in the water under the earth: thou shall not bow down thyself to them, nor serve them: for I the Lord thy God am a jealous God."

There was silence up front, and in the back as well.

"As you see, He forbids us from serving any god but Him. How does He tell us we can serve Him? Does anyone know?"

Still silence.

"First and foremost, it is that we believe in Him. Now, Mary. Harriet. Everyone. Believing in God means having faith in him."

Mary and Harriet leaned forward at the mention of their names. In the back, Kep had stopped whispering, but was still looking at Ike.

Alemeth could hear Eliza behind him, flipping through her Bible. A new set of pages fell into place with a thump.

"In Galatians three twenty-three, the Apostle Paul tells us, 'Ye are all the children of God by faith in Christ Jesus. For as many of you as have been baptized unto Christ have put on Christ. There is neither Jew nor Greek, there is neither bond nor free...'"

Kep looked at Ike as if saying *I told you so.*

"...there is neither male nor female: for ye are all one in Christ Jesus.'"

Eliza spoke to the women up front as if from her heart, to each of them.

"And if ye be Christ's, then ye are Abraham's seed, and heirs according to the promise.' Does anyone know what that promise is?"

Everyone looked at Eliza, unsure if they should answer.

"The promise of Abraham?" she asked again, looking to the back of the room. "No one has heard of the promise of Abraham?"

Still, no response.

"Leety, please tell everybody about the promise of Abraham."

"The promise of Abraham is, we'll be rewarded, if we have faith in God and obey him."

"Good, Leety. That's right. Very good."

Eliza explained the ramifications of the promise. A Christian's duty, she said, was to study the word of God. For that, a Christian needed to read scripture. And so, when there were no questions, she announced it was time for a reading lesson. She took out a hickory stick and used it to draw an 'A' in the dirt. Then she gave the stick to Harriet and asked her to make the same letter, next to hers.

Harriet accepted the stick carefully, as if it were a snake she wasn't sure was dead. Then she pressed it into the dirt, making her own 'A' beneath Eliza's.

After showing Harriet a few more letters, Eliza handed Alemeth a stick and asked him to help. Kep came over and took a stick, followed by Ike and the rest of them. Alemeth did as Eliza had done, showing them how to make letters. Within half an hour, everyone had a stick, and everyone was drawing letters in the ground. Eliza identified each of the sounds and Alemeth repeated them. (He was glad, at least, to be standing up and doing something.)

Kep seemed much taken by the whole lesson. He studied the shapes and drew them again and again, saying the sounds as he did so. Before the entire alphabet had been covered, he asked Alemeth to show him how to spell his name, and when he'd finished scratching it out, he smiled.

When time for schooling was up, Eliza said she'd see everybody again Sunday next.

"You all did very well today," she added. "Before long, you'll be reading the Bible yourselves."

31

There was a lot of talk about slavery that summer, and with it, talk about secession. At the beginning of November, Uncle Johnson came in to supper one evening with a copy of *The Organizer*.

"Look here," he said. "*The Organizer* has printed Colonel Brown's letter."

"What letter?" asked Amzi.

"His letter to Ben Dill about the slavery question."

"Oh, really? What does the Colonel have to say on it? He doesn't seem like the sort to quote the Bible."

"No, not at all. He sticks to the political. If the Colonel's anything, he's realistic."

"Has he come out in favor of secession?"

"The Colonel's a practical politician," said Uncle Johnson. "If you ask me, he's keeping his options open before the convention. But I think he's made his sentiments plain enough. Here, I'll read the last line of his letter." He lifted the paper close to his face. "He says, 'As to the best way to secure our rights, I confess I am unprepared to advise; but we have the example of our forefathers before us."

"The example of our forefathers?" asked Alemeth.

"Yes, to be sure," said Uncle Johnson. "They had to fight a war to win our independence from England. The Colonel's saying we might have to do as much to win our independence from the north."

Uncle Johnson handed the paper to Amzi.

"Sounds like you've got the Colonel figured out," said Amzi, taking the paper and starting to read.

War?

Alemeth wondered what a war would be like. Would he be a part of it? Would he *want* to be a part of it? Was he man enough to handle a real war? To kill another man, if need be? He didn't even like killing chickens.

He asked Amzi if he could read the Colonel's letter himself. Amzi not only let him have the newspaper, but said he could take it with him to the fishing hole, to show Leander McKinney.

The Colonel wasn't really related to him – not by blood anyway – but the next day at the fishing hole, when he handed Leander the newspaper, he said, "Look here, Leander McKinney. My uncle's got himself a letter printed in *The Organizer*."

The Oxford Organizer
Oxford Mississippi
November 2, 1850

LETTER OF COL. JAS. BROWN.

To the Editor of the Organizer.

SIR:--In your number of 26th inst., you have been pleased to call on me as one of the Representatives of Lafayette County, to make public my views on the all absorbing questions of the day. To this call I most cheerfully respond, and through your paper make known to my constituents the position I occupy on the question of northern aggression on the South, and submission or resistance on our parts.

That the tendency of the acts and doings of the last Congress has been to deprive the southern population from participation in the settlement with their slaves of the newly acquired territory from Mexico, none I presume will deny. The acquisition of this immense and valuable gold region was made by the common blood and treasure of the whole Union; but the abolition majority, having no identity of interest with the South, have seized upon the whole joint stock and appropriated it to themselves.

In ten years, by a very moderate and reasonable calculation, we shall not have more than eleven slave States and thirty-three non-slaveholding States. Three fourths of the States can alter, amend or change the Constitution. Who can doubt that the free States will exercise that power at the first moment they obtain it? They will then be able to prohibit the slave trade between the States; to annul the slave basis of representation in Congress, and to abolish slavery in the States. This is no idle dream. It is a plain practical view based upon facts which everyone can see, who will examine the subject.

What then shall be our position? Shall we submit to the monstrous wrongs of the past, and shall we make no effort to arrest the terrible evils impending over the future? It is a question of right and wrong. The South had a right under the constitution of the Union to an equal participation in the newly acquired territory; but the North has wronged the South out of the whole of it.

In casting my vote on the measure or measures that may be proposed, I shall be governed by what I believe to be to the interest of the South. I am not disposed to ask anything not warranted by the Constitution, nor to abandon any right we have under the Constitution. As to the best way to secure our rights, I confess I am unprepared to advise; but we have the example of our forefathers before us.

Yours, &c.;

JAMES BROWN.

32

By the end of the year, the politicians in Washington had worked out a compromise on slavery, and by the following spring, the most passionate talk had cooled. People were back to planting again, hoping for a good crop. But then one summer evening, as the night sky filled with stars and the family took in air on the porch, listening to the calls of whip-poor-wills, the birds' singing was joined by the sound of horses, and there were lights approaching the house.

It was Bill Starr, with Jim Murdock, Zeke Avery and Al Cansler. With the light of torches behind him, Starr's face was impossible to read.

"Howdy, Amzi. Howdy, Mrs. Bahrs."

"Evenin', Sheriff. What brings you boys out this time of night?"

"Nothin' in particular. We're just ridin'."

"Everything alright?"

"Everything alright. What about here? Everything quiet?"

"No trouble here. I suppose I wouldn't complain of a little more sun."

"Yeah. We could use more sun."

Then Starr's voice became serious.

"Uh… Excuse my rudeness, ma'am, but – could we speak to your husband alone?"

Amzi looked at Eliza. She gathered the younger children and took them inside. Alemeth couldn't stand to miss whatever was about to happen, so he held his ground. Amzi made no objection. Starr waited for the door to close.

"Listen, Amzi. This is nothing official. Just friend to friend. Your Missus, she's teaching Sunday School, ain't she? To the coloreds?"

"Yes. She is. Is there a problem?"

"Let's just say it might be best if she stopped."

For a moment, Alemeth imagined getting out of Sunday school altogether.

"Well now, you don't know my Eliza. She has her heart set on her teaching them. I see no harm in it."

"You might be right. But it'd still be best if she quit. On account of what people might say."

Murdock, Avery and Cansler were staring at Amzi.

"Think of your neighbors. Not everybody's as confident in their negroes as you. People are naturally concerned. You know. With Mrs. Byers being from up north and all."

"Bill, I –"

"Neighbors got to be able to trust one another. You understand."

*   *   *

After the men rode off, Eliza returned to the porch.

"What are those men up to?" she asked.

"Just ridin' the beat."

"What did they want with you?"

"Eliza, darlin', I've got to ask you something."

"What's that? You look serious. What's the matter?"

"I'm sorry, but come over here."

"Alright. What?"

"I think you better stop your lessons to the negroes. People don't think we should be teachin' the colored to read."

"What?" She backed away.

"Why Amzi. You can't mean – "

"I do."

"Amzi, we've talked about that, remember? It's a Christian's obligation to rescue all those lost to the Truth – especially savage races. I have a Christian duty –"

"I don't know about that."

She took another step backward. "Pardon me?"

"How sure are you of your Christian duty?"

"We brought them here as slaves, to make good Christians of them. The church would never have approved of it, were that not so. We have an obligation."

"'According to his kind,' Eliza. Don't forget that. That's in the good book too. Maybe education's not for everyone."

"I can't believe you're saying that. What about those that have the capacity for it? Aren't we God's own disciples, Amzi? Go ye therefore, and teach all nations? Matthew twenty-eight nine?"

"Eliza, I didn't say anything about not teaching them Christian ways. I'm just saying, you can't be teaching them to read."

"How can that be? A Christian has a duty to study Scripture."

"Eliza, dear, are they *capable* of studying Scripture? On their own?"

"Amzi, some of them take right to it. They practically teach *themselves* to read. You should come down and watch them some time. Or ask Kep to show you how much he's learned."

"Well, I'm sorry, Eliza, but it'll have to stop. You can't be teaching negroes to read."

"Sir: With this letter comes a Negro (Tom) which I beg the favour of you to sell, in any of the Islands you may go to, for whatever he will fetch... That this Fellow is both a rogue and a Runaway...I shall not pretend to deny. But . . . he is exceedingly healthy, strong and good at the Hoe... which gives me reason to hope he may, with your good management sell well (if kept clean and trim'd up a little when offered for sale... [I] must beg the favor of you (lest he should attempt his escape) to keep him hand-cuffed till you get to Sea."

-- George Washington, letter to Joseph Thompson, 2 July 1766

Besides those of color, figure, and hair, there are other physical distinctions proving a difference of race. They have less hair on the face and body. They secrete less by the kidneys and more by the glands of the skin, which gives them a very strong and disagreeable odor...

They are at least as brave, and more adventuresome. But this may perhaps proceed from a want of forethought, which prevents their seeing a danger till it be present...

They are more ardent after their female: but love seems with them to be more an eager desire than a tender delicate mixture of sentiment and sensation...

Comparing them by their faculties of memory, reason, and imagination, it appears to me, that in memory they are equal to the whites; in reason much inferior, as I think one could scarcely be found capable of tracing and comprehending the investigations of Euclid.

— Thomas Jefferson, Notes on the State of Virginia, 1785

"Amzi Byers, I can't believe you're saying that."

He just looked at her.

"What's the point of having our own land and our church here on Bynum's Creek if we can't do what we want to do? Amzi, I told you it was important to me. You led me to believe it was important to you too."

"That may be so, Eliza. But it seems to me I also recall the good book sayin' a wife's duty is to obey her husband."

"Amzi, I'd never disobey you, but you know my calling. And you promised. Jesus ministered to lepers and harlots. Surely the negroes – "

"Eliza!"

"If I can't teach letters to the others, at least let me teach Kep."

"Why should that boy be any different? The Agricultural Association – "

"Amzi, Kep is so intelligent. The other planters will understand your wanting to make him more useful. What makes a man more useful, if not education?

"Eliza –"

"It'll be an experiment."

Amzi stared intently, not an eyelash or a nose hair moving.

"An experiment, like Professor Millington talks about. I'll teach the others without reading scripture – for now. I'll teach Kep to read Scripture himself. And we'll see how it goes."

Still, Amzi's face was stone.

"Reverend Hitchcock was always very clear about the importance of Scripture. Every man has to be able to read Scripture for himself, else he becomes dependent on someone else's interpretation, and that only leads to Papism. If teaching Kep to read bears good fruit, I can teach others. If it bears ill – if teaching turns Kep into any sort of problem at all — "

Amzi held up his finger to Eliza.

"Then you'll stop," he said at last.

"Then I'll stop."

"Agreed."

"Thank you, Amzi. You'll see. I'm certain of it."

33

Alemeth knew he was curious; everybody told him so. In fact, Pa said he was *too* curious. He'd once asked why a fishing line looked like it bent when it left the water. (He knew it didn't *really* bend; but a person's arm seemed to bend the same way. Why?) But when he asked, Pa had gotten mad. "I have no idea," he'd said; "why are you always asking about things you don't need to understand?" Eliza had agreed. She had told him more than once that curiosity killed the cat, and when he'd asked what cat, she'd said it was just an expression and told him not to be silly.

Was "just an expression" the same as a little white lie? He'd wondered about that, too. He longed to understand how a hawk could fly, how a frog made the sounds it made. He wanted to understand what made the cotton grow, and what made a fish take bait. He wanted to learn more about how the world worked – about the things he didn't yet know, the strange new things that kept coming up in the everyday life around him. He'd never felt much interest in what was already familiar; never cared, for example, about his own bed, or his own britches. He had no interest in dead people, grammar, or the other things that filled the pages of books. There was no point in curiosity about things if you already knew as much about them as you'd ever need to know. And that, he supposed, was why he'd never been curious about the negroes. He loved Aunt Leety like he'd loved his real mother, but while he knew that the palms of a Grote's hands weren't as dark as the rest of him, he'd never wondered why. What difference could such a thing make to anything he did? Pa was right about that. Some things just were what they were.

So every Sunday, when Eliza taught the negroes about the promise made to Abraham, about the sacrifice of Isaac, about the coming of Jesus, doing it all from memory so no one could claim she was teaching the negroes to read, Alemeth thought nothing of it. That was just the way she was. And when Eliza took Kep into the house, and they read Scripture together from the big Geneva on the bookstand, he thought nothing of that, either.

"You really think he can learn to read?" Leander asked Alemeth one day.

Kep was one of the smarter Negroes. "I reckon he can."

"Well. Time'll tell. My Daddy says God can work all sorts of crazy ways. But you know what my Aunt Lucy says? She says keeping slaves is a sin."

"Really? What about your Sally?"

"She's my Daddy's. But my Aunt Lucy says it ain't Christian to keep a slave. Told my daddy he ought to give Sally her freedom. You never heard such a fight."

"I'll bet."

"My Daddy says the Bible's the word of God, and in the Bible, there are lots of slaves. Says God never says it's wrong to keep a slave. In fact, in places, God tells people to take slaves."

Alemeth had never thought about it before.

"And ten commandments don't say nothin' about slaves. Nope. And slaves were everywhere around Jesus. Jesus never said a word against folks that owned 'em. Saint Paul told slaves to be good to their masters. Daddy says he told one slave to *go back* to his master."

"So then how can it be a sin?"

"Dang it, Alemeth, I ain't saying it's a sin. That's what my Aunt Lucy been sayin."

"Well, ain't no one knows the Bible any better than Eliza, and she hasn't said anything like that."

"What does your Pa say?"

Alemeth had no idea what Amzi thought the Good Book said about slavery. So that night, he asked him.

Amzi chewed on his tobacco plug for a few seconds, then leaned over the porch rail and spat.

"You're askin' me what the Good Book says about slavery? For cryin' out loud, Alemeth. You and your questions. Why don't you ask your Ma?"

"Ma's dead, Pa."

"You know what I mean."

"Okay. I know. But I want to know what you think."

"All I know is this, son. God told Adam all the creatures were his; He gave Adam dominion over all of them, and that means taking good care of them. Now, I can see that a dog is smarter than a horse or a pig. And they're all smarter than fish. It seems to me, what's true for animals is true for people, too. When a civilized man takes care of a savage, he's doing what God charged him to do. It's part of a man's responsibility. If one man is meant to be a field hand – if he isn't fit to take care of himself any other way – then it would be wrong to let him go off and get into something else. Just like it would be wrong to let a dog eat a rabid squirrel."

"Thanks, Pa. I understand."

That winter at the gin house, watching the negroes clean motes from the cotton, Alemeth could only think how lucky they all were, to have good land, crops enough to provide food to eat, and clothes to wear. It was a noble thing to be a planter, with so many people depending on you. A noble thing to look after everyone else, the way Pa did.

34

The Sunday after Alemeth turned sixteen, a place was set for him at the adult table. Mary Jane had said getting to sit at the table was going to change his life for the better; she couldn't wait for the day *she'd* get to. Alemeth felt suddenly taller. Imagined Amzi and Colonel Brown making lifting glasses to his health, welcoming him to the table as they would a grown man.

But it was not to be. Alemeth sat between Eliza and Ann Brown. Four years older, Ann showed him the proper way to hold his spoon. When he spoke to a negro child who'd mounted the table with a palm frond, Ann scolded him. "Alemeth Byers, if you're going to sit at the adult table, you're going to have to learn how to behave. And the first thing you ought to know is that you're not supposed to talk to *him*; you're supposed to talk to *me*. And another thing: see my daddy, at the head of the table? When he turns his attention to the right, you should turn and talk to your right. When he turns to his left, you should too. It's so no one is left with no one to talk to."

Turning this way and that between two women, ignored by the older men and at a loss for anything to say, he found dinner all but intolerable. So when Alemeth was included when the men retired to the back terrace for cigars – Amzi, Harvey Walter and Buck Avent, Frances Brown's new husband – he held out hope that something might yet come of being sixteen.

The Colonel showed his pocket watch to the others. Made in Connecticut by someone named Pitkin, its mix of interconnected metal parts was more involved than the scriptures of the Bible, more complicated than the guests at Frances's wedding, but far more interesting. Alemeth wondered how such tiny levers and gears could be made to work together. But he kept his questions to himself, trying instead to listen and learn from the talk of the older men. The upcoming election. A railroad tax in Lafayette County. Bonds, subscriptions, capital investments and returns. There was nothing of interest for him, or for Amzi either, as best as he could tell. It seemed that smoking with these city men could turn out to be as bad as eating with girls.

"You know," said the Colonel, "if we pass the tax, it should benefit us all."

"No question. It's the one thing the Whigs are right about."

"Some folks don't believe the government should get into business. The railroad business, or any other."

"That's short-sighted. The railroad will pay for itself in no time."

"People have to understand the railroad's importance to the University. The best students will never come to Oxford unless we get the railroad."

"It'll come through Holly Springs," said Mr. Walter.

"To be sure. What do you think, Amzi? What are folks in Panola saying?"

"Most folks in Panola don't much care about the railroad. Folks feel it's more a matter for the people of Lafayette."

"I see. And do you share their views?"

"I suppose I do."

Harvey Walter turned to the Colonel. "I'll bet we could net fifty per cent, at least. Maybe double our money."

The conversation returned to banking. The Colonel and his sons-in-law talked about money, numbers, rates and percentages. How state government depended on the slave tax for its revenues, and men like the Colonel, and Amzi and Harvey, paid more in slave tax than just about anyone. For Alemeth, it was like being in school. And there stood Pa, in school right beside him, looking as out of place as Alemeth was. There seemed nothing good about being sixteen, or sitting at the adult table.

Then the Colonel asked if the men would like to take a look at the new saddle horse he'd picked up in Memphis. Alemeth's interest soared. He could appreciate the features of a fin saddle horse, and the Colonel's was likely as fine as they came.

Inside stables, among bins and troughs, draught horses and shadows, the Colonel opened a stall to a powerfully handsome creature with chestnut haunches whose sheen, when the horse was led into the light, reflected the moon. A stallion, with a creamy mane and a soft white blaze that complemented its impressive form.

"He must be sixteen hands," said Buck.

"Look at the arch in that neck," said Mr. Walter.

"That's a fine animal, Colonel."

"Thank you, Amzi. Got him from a gentlemen in Memphis. Gets his horses in Kentucky."

"Is he fast?"

"A mile in two minutes. And he hardly breaks a sweat."

"You don't say. Alemeth, look at the size of those thighs. Ever think of racing him, Colonel?"

"I might, in the fall. I'm also thinking of breeding him, if I can get the right mare."

"I know where I can find you some fine Virginia mares," said Buck. "I'd consider it a privilege to choose a few for you."

The men eyed the horse from every angle. They discussed breeding, and the right time to let him out for stud. And as they did, Alemeth watched with admiration. There was not a trace of fat to be seen beneath the skin. Every inch muscle. Even his tawny tail swept away flies with authority. And spending time in the company of Pa and Colonel Brown, of Buck Avent and Harvey Walter, admiring the horse together, made the men seem a little more familiar. Maybe, *something* good would come from sitting at the adult table.

But time with the stallion was not to last forever. After closing the stable gates, the Colonel addressed Amzi.

"You know, Amzi, the railroad isn't just about the University."

"What do you mean?"

"You know what steam did to the paddle wheel. It's going to do the same thing on land."

"I suppose you're right."

"Transportation," said the Colonel. "Efficient transportation. Getting a man from one place to another faster. It's always been the key. Where would we be without our rivers? And look at how the stage has opened the way for civilization! When I started in this business, it could take a man weeks to go a hundred miles. The stage made that possible in a day and a night. But a coach can carry just a few passengers and bags. Look at the cargo a steam boat carries – hundreds of bales on a single boat. If we can transport cotton over open country, in large quantities and at great speeds, just think of the advantages. One steam engine can pull a train at three times the speed of a stage. Five times the speed of a steamboat upstream. No more cost of wagon trains to Memphis. No more two and a half for the factor there."

"No more barges downriver to New Orleans," added Mr. Walter. "We can bypass the sea. Load railcars here in Oxford and haul them overland to Memphis, Charleston or Philadelphia at a fraction of the cost."

"Amzi, they're paying twenty cents a pound for cotton in Philadelphia."

Amzi set his elbow in the palm of his other hand, like he was thinking over what the men had said.

"Sounds fantastic, Colonel," he said at last. "Getting twenty cents would be real nice, Harvey. But if we lay railroad lines, what's that going to do to the land?"

"Growth, Amzi. Opportunity."

"Is that always a good thing?"

"Think of the revenue traffic can bring. If Oxford is a major stop on the line, there will be people staying over. Food. Lodging. Supplies. You know there's money to be made in the mercantile trade."

Alemeth cared little for the profits of mercantile trade. While the men talked investments, shares, and revenues, he wondered what a locomotive engine looked like up close.

35

The next day, at the bottom of the swimming hole, Alemeth and Leander came face to face with more catfish than Alemeth had ever seen. He was unable to count them, unable to mimic them, unable to swim with their light, finned ease, unable – as hard as he tried –to breathe as they did. But staying under so long, trying to imagine himself a fish, his lungs began to burn. When he finally gave up and broke out of the deep, the air that filled his lungs felt so clean he felt rescued, as if from a grave – accepted into a life that was freer than the slow, stupid doldrums of the fishes' world. He and Leander quickly returned with their fishing poles, catching a slew of catfish, pulling them into the air as if they were freeing the fish from the same confining world they'd been freed from. They went up to the house with the fish on a string, to tell Kep what he'd missed.

But neither Eliza nor Kep were there. The big Geneva was not in its usual place on the bookstand, but lying out on the table, in the light by the window, where Leander took an interest in it.

"Hey, Alemeth. Come here. Look at this."

Leander was pointing at one of the pages and grinning – one of those grins so broad Alemeth started grinning too, without knowing why.

Alemeth hadn't even started to read when Amzi walked in.

"What's so funny, boys?"

Amzi strode forward, repeating his question.

"Come on now, Alemeth. What's so funny?"

"Nothing, sir."

"Leander?"

Amzi looked down at the Bible. What began as a glance turned into a stare. The boys had to wait before he looked up.

"What are you boys doing, reading this?"

They looked at each other.

"We weren't!" said Leander. "We just got here."

"Don't give me that: I saw you reading it. I saw you smiling. Alemeth?"

"I wasn't reading nothin' Pa. We found it here –"

"You're telling me it was open to this page when you came in?"

"Yes, sir," said Leander.

"The wind flipped the pages to this nonsense?"

"No, Pa. We came in to look for Kep. Miss Eliza and Kep must have left it this way, after their lesson."

"You boys get going. Get on out of here. And put that stool back in the kitchen where it belongs."

There was no doubt what Amzi was thinking: that, yet again, Alemeth had put his nose where it didn't belong. In fact, he'd done nothing wrong, but yet again, he was getting blamed for something Leander had done. He took the stool and put it back by the table in the kitchen. Outside the house, he asked Leander what had got him grinning so.

"What Charlie Morgan said is true," said Leander, grinning still more. "But you'll just have to read it yourself."

Not knowing what Leander knew proved more than Alemeth could bear. So that night, by candlelight, he went back and read from the still open page. It was easy to figure out which verses had put Leander in such a tither.

> *Thy two breasts are as two young roes that are twins, feeding among the lilies...*
> *Thou art all fair, my love, and there is no spot in thee...*
> *My sister, my spouse, how fair is thy love?*
> *How much better is thy love than wine?*

*   *   *

He couldn't understand, at first, what Eliza and Kep had been doing, reading about love and wine. But just two days later, he saw Aunt Harriet showing her little Gilbert the woodcuts in the Bible, in the same bright spot next to the window. It could have been her who'd left the Bible open to the page about love, or Gilbert, or anyone. It didn't have to be Kep and Eliza. The problem was, Pa thought *he* had been reading it. Should he explain that he hadn't even seen it? That it had all been Leander? Since Pa seemed upset with everybody, he decided it was best to leave to say nothing for a while. About a week later, he again considered defending himself. But this time, he reasoned, bringing it up would only put the problem – and his guilt in the matter – front and center again. So he kept quiet, again.

His newest predicament remained in place. A part of the permanent record in Pa's mind. He had disappointed Pa yet again. Blamed, yet again, for something Leander McKinney had done.

But all was not bad. Pa had gotten quiet around Miss Strong, too. Hardly looked her in the face. When he spoke to her, the words came one at a time. You could tell that something was going on between them. Like, Pa was angry at Eliza, thinking she'd been reading about love with Kep.

Just maybe, he was finally coming out from under her spell.

36

The coming of the railroad put people scrambling: some clambered to get out of the way, others were like cats at meal time, trying to get as close as they could to where it would go. Amzi Byers held fast to his land, with an eye on his neighbors' parcels, hoping that the railroad would not be laid across his land or theirs. Others – like the McKinneys – moved into town, with their eyes on the mercantile trade. To hear Leander talk, he and Alemeth might not ever see each other again. "After all, I'll have no reason to come to Bynum's Creek anymore."

It didn't seem possible they'd never see each other again, never swim together again, never go fishing again. So when Leander asked if Alemeth wanted to go with him and a new friend from town to 'the trial of Jesus,' Alemeth hesitated only a moment before saying yes, of course, he'd be glad to go. He couldn't have explained why, but the idea that Leander had a new friend who lived in town left Alemeth feeling jealous.

The trial was better than Alemeth had expected. Sheriff Butler played Pontius Pilot, Dr. Gabbert Judas, and Dudley Isom Jesus. The 'Romans' cracked real whips, so the whipping sounded great. And while they couldn't tell how it had been managed, the spear in Jesus's side seemed to draw real blood. Leander jumped to his feet when he saw it. When Dr. Isom spoke the final words, "Forgive them, Father, they know not what they do," Leander declared the show better than any sermon he'd ever heard.

Afterwards, Alemeth, Leander and his new friend, Nat, were passing through the square toward the Butler stables, for Alemeth to pick up his buckboard, when a stallion trotted up. Before Alemeth could see that the rider was Colonel Brown, he recognized the horse's magnificent chest and shoulders. Then the big man's face came into the light, staring directly Alemeth's way.

"Good evening, boys."

"Good evening, sir."

Without breaking stride or saying another word, the Colonel passed up the street as if he hadn't recognized them.

"Wow," said Leander. "Did you see that horse? I wonder who that was…"

"It was Colonel Brown."

"No kiddin'! That was some horse."

"He can run a two minute mile without breaking a sweat."

"The hell he can! Says who?"

"Says the Colonel."

"Aw. That don't make it so."

As Alemeth considered a suitable retort, the Colonel reached the stables and handed the horse's reins to the liveryman. Leander held his own hands out in front of Alemeth and Nat, bringing them to a halt fifty yards short of the stables.

"Stop," he said with emphasis. "Don't say anything."

They stood in the shadow of an elm tree, waiting as the Colonel finished his business with the liveryman and walked down the street to President Longstreet's house.

"Wouldn't it be something to have a horse like that?" asked Leander. "What do you say, Alemeth Bahrs? Wouldn't it be something?"

"What do you mean?"

"I mean, we *could* have a horse like that. In fact, we could have *that* horse."

Leander grinned.

After putting the horse in the stable, the liveryman looked up and down, then crossed the street and entered the hotel.

The boys looked at each other.

"It'd sure be something, to have a horse like that," said Leander.

"What are you sayin'?"

"Just that it would sure be something if we could have it." Leander smiled again.

"You're *not* sayin' we could *steal* it..."

The accusation left Leander grinning even more broadly. Nat looked back and forth, between Leander and Alemeth.

"Just think what the guys would say," said Leander to Nat.

"They *hang* folks for stealing horses," said Alemeth.

"You chicken?"

"I ain't no chicken, but I ain't a fool either, Leander McKinney. Where you gonna put it, where someone won't know it was us that stole it?"

Leander had the devil in his eye; he wasn't backing off; and as Alemeth well knew, he was always figuring a way to get what he wanted.

"We wouldn't have to keep it," said Leander. "We could just let it go."

"Taking it a while is as bad as taking it for good. It still ain't right. Besides, we could *still* get caught in the act. It'd still be stealing a horse."

"Horse thieving?" said Nat. "They'd probably just whip some nigger for it."

"Okay, then, we don't let the horse go. We don't steal him at all." With wide open eyes, Leander pulled a large knife from his belt. "We just cut off his tail."

"We can't do that," said Alemeth.

"And why not, Mr. Bahrs?"

"That's Colonel Brown's horse."

"Yeah? So?"

Leander McKinney and Nat went into the empty stables. After a moment in the street alone, unsettled by the thought of cutting off the horse's tail, Alemeth followed, checking over his shoulder to be sure the liveryman was still at the hotel. There were no other customers. All three boys stood in the darkness, Leander's hand on the stallion's neck and face, stroking, keeping the horse calm. Then Leander motioned to Alemeth. "Take hold of his tail."

"You're crazy."

He could cut a fish open while its gills were still moving. He could even kill a rabbit or a squirrel to eat the meat. But cut off a horse's tail? For what reason?

"Take hold of his tail, doggone it. If you won't, Nat will."

"Leander, this is like – Leander, it ain't right. You're tetched."

"You feeling sorry for this horse, that's ten times bigger and braver than you? What kind of sissy are you?"

"I ain't no sissy."

"You been spending too much time with girls. It's not like it'll hurt the horse."

"You just going to cut the hairs, right? Not his flesh?"

"Now Alemeth Byers, why would I be so stupid as to cut his flesh?"

"Ok, alright. But – "

"Nat, come over here and keep this horse settled."

Nat put a hand on the horse's neck while Alemeth took hold of the tail.

"Closer to his rump," said Leander. "Get him at the dock."

Alemeth's hands inched closer. The stallion seemed ready to rear up.

"Leave me as much tail as you can," said Leander. "I want the whole thing."

He held the dock close to the rump with his left hand and towards its end with his right. Holding the tail a few inches away, Leander brought the knife down less than an inch from Alemeth's clenched hand, making a long, strong stroke. The stallion flexed his haunches and snorted. A clutch of tawny bristles fell to the ground.

"Hold tight, now. One more time."

Leander brought the knife down again. This time, more than half the bristles fell; a nervous whinny; the horse's hind quarters backed sideways, nearly bowling Alemeth over. Leander said "Just one more time. Come on, now," and cut the last of it.

The stallion reared up, whinnying, his fore legs high in the air. Alemeth ducked into cover. Leander took a handful of bristles from the dirt and stuffed them inside his shirt.

"What are you doing that for?" asked Nat.

"Now we can prove it was us."

"What?!" Why would Leander want to keep evidence linking them to the crime?

Up the street, a noise from outside. They searched the darkness and, seeing nothing, burst from the stables. The front door had opened at Judge Longstreet's house. A shaft of light from the doorway illuminated the yard. Hearing men's voices, Leander grabbed Alemeth by the shirt sleeve and pulled him behind a holly bush next to Nat.

The Colonel and Judge Longstreet came out of the President's house, peering into the darkness above the boys' heads.

"I didn't like the sound of that whinnying," said the Colonel.

The older men entered the stables. As they talked, the boys waited and watched from the bushes, unable to make out their words. After a while, the older men went to the hotel looking for the liveryman, and the boys dashed across the street toward safety. When the Colonel dragged the liveryman out of the hotel and back to the stables, he was protesting loudly: no, he had *no idea* what had happened to the horse; no, he *hadn't* seen anyone coming or going; no, he hadn't heard a thing; he'd only been gone a few minutes; he'd had only one drink; and as God was his witness, he'd kept his eye on the stables the whole time.

Once the Colonel and Longstreet were gone, when Alemeth went in again to retrieve his buckboard, the liveryman was muttering and cursing, as if ready to strangle the next person who looked at him crooked. The man asked Alemeth if *he'd* seen or heard anything.

"No," said Alemeth. "I ain't seen or heard a thing. I've been down at the church."

37

It hadn't been a lie; he *had* been down at the church, earlier. And if it was a lie, it was just a white lie. An expression. But in his gut, he knew he'd held the dock. He'd known better. He'd gone along with Leander McKinney for no reason – for his own weakness, and for nothing else. The knowledge plagued him for days. Everybody was talking about who'd done it. So when Amzi asked him if he knew anything about it, his heart raced; his flesh turned sweaty and cold. Amzi stared at him, demanding that he tell him anything he knew. At last, he said he knew nothing. Amzi let out a *hrrumphh!* and walked off.

Alemeth thought he'd heard the end of it, but the next week, at Clear Creek, Colonel Brown took up where Amzi had left off.

"You were in town that night, right? I saw you with that McKinney boy, didn't I?" Alemeth barely nodded. "Do you know who did it?" Alemeth froze. He didn't want to lie to the Colonel. "I won't ask you who, Alemeth. I appreciate loyalty. Just tell me if you know who did it – yes, or no – and I won't ask you anything more."

Wow. That was better. "Yes, sir. I guess – I guess I know."

There were no more questions. Colonel Brown just thanked him and left the room. Alemeth decided Colonel Brown was his best friend. But a few days later, when Pa announced that he would start at Mount Sylvan in the fall, the punishment seemed far worse than the licking he'd feared.

"But Pa. It's harvest time. I need to be here at Bynum's Creek, with you."

"Alemeth, Ma and I have talked it over. You're going, and that's that."

Ma? Was there no end to Eliza's influence? Whatever else may have come from sitting at the adult table, it had not included getting to make his own decisions. He wouldn't legally be a man until he was twenty-one. In the meantime, he couldn't bear the thought of Eliza having such say over his life. When he became a man, he'd never let a woman tell him what to do. In the meantime, he would have to go to school, but there was no reason to do more than what Pa told him. No reason to start treating Eliza as if she was his mother. As if she had any right telling him what to do. He'd be twenty-one in just a few more years.

So when Eliza said that he couldn't start school looking like a country cretin – that she would have to fit him for new clothes – he fumed anew, then looked to Amzi in hopes Amzi would see it his way. Of course, Amzi thought Eliza made sense. And in the end, Alemeth had to strip down to his underwear while Eliza ran up his legs and over his shoulders and neck with a measuring tape.

38

On the second Monday in September, gussied up, hair slicked back, John Alemeth Byers took the buckboard to a clearing at the edge of the woods, half way to Oxford, near Clear Creek. He was alone. He could have turned aside, taken the buckboard anywhere else. But he knew he'd never get away with it. So, even on his own, he drove on, impelled by the power Eliza had over him, even from far away.

A tall man stood outside the school house in a black waistcoat, a high white collar and a black bow tie, bald on top, but with large tufts of hair above his ears and a black goatee under his chin. The three triangles jutting from his face gave the natural roundness of his head angular edges. The man said, "Come in, boys. It's time to become men." Once they were in their assigned seats, he called the class to order.

"You new boys need to learn our ways here at Mount Sylvan. One of our traditions is to begin each day with announcements. Today, I have three announcements to make. First, the Reverend Stanford Burney will no longer be teaching at Mount Sylvan. He has opened a College for Women and will be devoting his attention to it. I am Frederick Coffin Vrooman. I have my Doctor of Divinity from Lane. I will be teaching instead of Reverend Burney."

Vrooman surveyed the class, checking faces, making eye contact.

"My second announcement is that while I am an ordained minister of the Presbyterian Church, I am tolerant of other denominations. As I have assured your families, I'll make no attacks on anyone's Christian beliefs. But I *will* ask hard questions."

That was not reassuring.

"The third announcement is one I make at the suggestion of Doctor Burney. I want to let you know from the outset that, like him, I put much stock in the power of the human brain."

His head and movements made him look like a wind-up clock with handles and levers. As he strode around the room, rigid and erect, he began asking questions about squares: three times three being nine, nine being the square of three, and — "By the way, is anyone prepared to tell me the square of nine?" From squares and triangles, to the genius of Pythagoras. "The square of the hypotenuse is equal to the sum of the squares of the other two sides. Who can give me an example?"

A breeze brought the cool fragrance of the woods and, after wrapping it around Mount Sylvan drew it in through the open windows, reminding him that it wasn't far to Clear Creek, to Sand Springs, and to home. He wondered what he'd do when he got home. First, he thought, he would

"Pay attention, please, Master Byers, or you will not like the consequences, I can assure you."

He tried to pay attention. He tried hard to listen. But he had no use for a hypotenuse. And Latin was worse that Geometry. *Amo amas amat. Ego, te, alter. Gallia est omnis divisa in partes tres.* Greek was even worse. Reverend Vrooman began with a discourse on Homer: how, from Socrates on, the Greeks had venerated him, Socrates passing on his respect to his pupil, the young Plato, and Plato to his pupil, the young Aristotle, and Aristotle to his pupil, the young Alexander who, as Alexander the Great, carried a copy of Homer to war with him and held competitions for excellence in Homeric rhapsody.

From Homer, Vrooman went on to the Greek letters hung around the room on large cards, pointing them out with a hickory stick as he named them. There were majuscule letters, like 'A,' and miniscule, like 'α.' 'B' and 'β'were recognizable, but 'Γ' and 'γ' were not.

There was black dirt wedged under Alemeth's finger nails. His hands had always been in the soil, so dirt didn't bother him unless it was in his eyes, or his mouth. But Reverend Longstreet had stressed the importance of appearance, and Alemeth wondered if Vrooman would do the same.

"Master Byers?"

Vrooman was talking to him.

"Are you going to need some sort of help with your attention?"

Vrooman tapped the inside of his left palm with his stick.

"No. Sir."

"Very well, then. Listen up."

With Vrooman's back turned, he cleaned some dirt from one of his nails with the edge of a pen knife. But then, with excavations just begun, Reverend Vrooman turned down the row toward him again. As his fingers slid beneath the open halves of a book, Vrooman zeroed in.

"Master Byers, what are you doing with your hands?"

"Nothing."

"Master Byers, please be so kind as to remove your hands from under your book."

As Vrooman approached, he slid his hands from under the book. The knife was still out of sight beneath it.

The Reverend raised his eyebrows.

"And?"

"And what, Sir?"

"What is it about your hands that makes you want to hide them?"

Yet again, caught in deception.

"They're dirty, sir."

"Well, it's good news, I suppose, that you're thinking about *something*. What do you think of the fact that your hands are dirty?"

None of the things he'd imagined Reverend Vrooman saying about dirty hands was good, and he was prepared for a scolding, whatever it might be – anything was better than what Vrooman would say if he discovered the knife.

He was not, however, prepared for the question Vrooman had asked. He had no idea what *he* thought of the dirt on his hands. All he could think of was Reverend Longstreet, looking at the tear in his pants.

"Reverend Longstreet says – "

"If I want to know what Reverend Longstreet thinks," said Vrooman, "I can ask him. I want to know what *you* think."

Before the day was out, Vrooman called upon Alemeth to explain what he thought, not only about the dirt under his nails, but about the pyramids of Egypt, the discovery of a megalosaurus in England, and the heliocentric theories of Copernicus. Does the sun really rise in the east? Does the earth really orbit around the sun? Or does everything just depend on one's point of view?

Alemeth had never done so much thinking in just one day. By the end of it, his head had begun to ache. He rubbed his temples, wondering how hard Mount Sylvan was going to be.

39

*The creatures persistently refuse to live together as man
and wife, even after I have mated them with all the wisdom I
possess, and built them such desirable homes.*

— *Augustus Longstreet*

Eliza had no idea what had come over Amzi. Instead of getting better, his mood had gotten worse. He seemed angry at her for something. When cotton dropped to eight cents a pound, he seemed a beaten man. So when, in response to her prayers for understanding, the Lord suggested she speak directly to him, she tried. But he just glared at her. Said he didn't want to talk about it. And the winter brought no relief.

Alemeth was no better. What did you learn today? Anything interesting happen at school? 'Everything's fine' was all he ever said.

"I don't know what's wrong with you, Alemeth, but I'm not going to let go. If I've done nothing to offend you, then I'll keep asking until I get a civil answer. What did you learn in school today?"

He glared. "We're studying Latin. Today I learned the meaning of the word *famulus*."

"Alright. Good. That's very interesting. Let me take a guess. Does it mean 'family'?"

"No. That's what I found interesting. The word 'family' comes from it, but the Latin word means a *slave*." He threw the word "slave" at her like a stone. "Can I go now?"

And so it was. Both Amzi and Alemeth worried her. What could she do for either one? Whatever she tried just made things worse.

Kep, on the other hand, had been a joy and a delight. He was very bright for a colored boy. After a year, he was reading nearly as well as Mary Jane. And most wonderful of all, he was interested in Scripture.

One Saturday morning, the boy approached her on the porch.

"Good morning, Miz Byers."

She was always glad to see him, but this time, she could sense that something was up.

"Miz Byers?"

"What is it, Kep?"

"I'd like to be baptized."

"Really?" Joy filled her heart. "That's wonderful! May I ask you why?"

"Alemeth says I can't be a Christian unless I get baptized."

"Oh, really? Well, I'm not sure about that. But I'm delighted! This is wonderful news!"

There was nothing more glorious than a person becoming a Christian. On the other hand, Lorenzo Dow had proven the ease of confusing an idle wish with a genuine religious experience.

"Kep, are you *sure* you're willing to submit to the will of God, as your Lord and Savior?"

"Yes, ma'am. I am."

"It's very difficult, you know – to always do what *He* wants you to do."

"I know — "

"I'm glad you understand."

"— I'm ready to do anything he asks. I can feel the spirit in my heart. Right here. I want to be baptized, Miz Byers. I really do. I'm ready."

How wonderful! If ever there was proof of the benefit of education, this was it. Her hours with Kep could no longer be questioned. Kep, a Christian who could read Scripture! When Amzi told the Agricultural Council, she'd be able to teach others – she was sure of it.

On the drive to Clear Creek, she anticipated the look on Amzi's face.

"I have good news."

"What is it, Eliza?"

"Kep came to see me this morning. He says he's become a Christian. He wants to be baptized."

Amzi just looked at her.

"Amzi, didn't you hear me?"

"Yes, I heard you."

"You won't believe how well he's learned to read. Scripture has done *so* much for him! Tonight, I'd like him to read for you."

"The boy has learned to read?"

"Yes, Amzi. I – "

"Is that *all* you've taught him?"

"No, no, I've taught him Scripture as well. I've taught him what it means to be a Christian. He's intelligent. He hangs on every word I say. He's a better student than – well – than some white children. You can ask him about Scripture, all you want."

He looked at her before responding. "You expect me to be pleased?"

"Why, Amzi, I thought you'd be thrilled. Kep really feels the power of the spirit. He's an amazing boy. He…"

But the more she talked about Kep, the angrier Amzi got, and the more he dug in his heels.

40

"You never know what an African is thinking," said the Colonel. "Has Eliza shared her notions about savages with the boy?"

"I should hope not."

"Eliza ought to know better. It's not just what that Nat Turner did. Her own family history shows what happens when you educate a negro."

"What do you mean?"

"There was a negro, a slave named Henry, in Haiti. They sent him to Spain and gave him a real highbrow education. You know what he did with it?"

"What was that?"

"He stole every plantation in Haiti. Including the Strongs'. The slaves ran Eliza's grandfather off the island. Took all his land."

"I don't think Eliza knows that."

"I'll have Mary Ann talk to her. She knows what they did to Adonijah Strong."

It couldn't hurt for Mary Ann to talk to her, but Amzi doubted it would be enough. Kep had been rutting about in her thoughts, and she couldn't see the danger that created. She was always talking about how intelligent he was. She'd spent more time with him than with her own stepdaughters. She was past the point of seeing him for what he was. The boy'd always had a big head. He couldn't change who he was, any more than Eliza could. Now, with Eliza, he was doing – what? Had he come on to her? What had he already done, with Eliza praising him all the time? All that stuff about reading, and being a Christian – God only knew where it would lead. Even if the boy hadn't acted on his urges yet, he *had* to be thinking about it. Sure as sunrise. It was in his nature.

Besides, even if the boy was as innocent as Eliza seemed to think, he still had a young boy's body. Watching his muscles grow, for heaven's sake. Close to her age. The boy could hardly help his own nature. What in God's name was she thinking, teaching him to read about 'breasts like roes'? Her innocence made her easy pickings.

In the end, whether Kep would or wouldn't forget his place with Eliza didn't really matter. His brother John Alemeth had explained it well. Kep was an investment. Once he got dangerous ideas, that investment was in jeopardy. That he could be a Christian the same as any white man was clearly a dangerous idea. It was simply bad business to keep him.

41

"Amzi, I can't believe you feel that way."

"The boy will not be baptized."

"Amzi, what harm could possibly come from a baptism?"

"That boy's no Christian, Eliza. You don't know what's on his mind. He just thinks that being a Christian will get him his freedom."

"Amzi, I believe the boy's faith is sincere. He spends time with the Bible even when I'm not around. He shows every sign of understanding. He has nothing but the best of intentions."

"Why do you defend him? You've said yourself, Faith means nothing if a man doesn't understand it. It's not just about scripture, Eliza. You really think this boy understands the Christian way of life?"

"Amzi, are you questioning what I've taught him?"

"I'm saying you haven't convinced me that boy has any idea what it means to be a Christian. He could be deceiving you, to get what he wants from you. And you're so – "

"What will it take, then? What will I need to show you?"

Amzi took a long, deep breath, and exhaled slowly, never once taking his eye off Eliza. "Eliza, I've decided to sell Kep."

"Pa, you can't!"

"Amzi, you're not serious."

"Alemeth, you don't tell me what I can and cannot do."

"I'm sorry, Pa. But –"

"Amzi, he's been doing so well."

"You know what's happened to cotton prices. We're spending more than we're taking in. I still owe my brother, and now, there's the cost of Mount Sylvan. We can use the cash."

"Pa, Semmy Lou says Kep's got a thing for Miss Sadie. If you hang on to Kep, I'll bet he and Miss Sadie will have lots of babies."

"Son, I made up my mind. I don't want to hear any more about it. And don't either of you breathe a word of this to Kep, or to any of the other negroes. They don't need to know, until after it's done."

Alemeth and Eliza were both open-mouthed.

"Pa – "

"That's the end of the discussion."

Amzi walked out, closing the door behind him.

42

Alemeth worried he'd never be able to hide what was up. Kep was too smart. Kep would figure him out. Amzi would give him a shellacking. So for the next few weeks, it was all he could do to stay away from Kep.

He stayed away from Eliza, too, though for different reasons. She seemed ashamed of something, or embarrassed. She so prided herself on doing the right thing, if she was embarrassed, she'd have tried to make it right. Whatever the trouble, it had to be still going on. Maybe it was tension between her and Amzi. Maybe things were starting to wear between them. In any case, as the two bad moods grated at each other like Reverend Vrooman's glaciers went at rocks, the tension wore them down. Life at Bynum's Creek moved perceptibly away from what it once had been.

There weren't many things that could have made things worse, but then one day, Jim Murdock came to the house. He'd heard that Amzi wanted to sell Kep, and was interested in buying him.

Amzi invited Murdock to have a seat on the porch. From his loft in a nearby tree, Alemeth could hear bits and pieces of the conversation.

"I'd rather hang a dozen dead possums in my yard than trust a *nigger*."

Murdock slung it like mud from his tongue, not *negro*, or even *niggra*, but as if the second syllable was hardly there. A moment later, he said it again, the same way. With Murdock his master, Kep's life would not be good.

"I never knew a field nigger worth more than two horses when one of 'em's lame."

Murdock left. Alemeth got Amzi's attention.

"Pa. I know you gotta sell Kep. But do you have to sell him to *that* man?"

"If he'll pay me $800 I do."

"Pa – "

"Enough, son. If you have to know, there's more to it than that."

Alemeth couldn't imagine what Amzi meant by "more to it," unless it was Eliza teaching Kep about breasts like roes.

"What could – "

"Enough, I said. You don't need to know the particulars."

43

The next afternoon, Uncle Johnson came in the door with a letter from town addressed to Mrs. Eliza Byers from her sister, Mrs. Julia Webster. Julia's daughter was getting married. She was hoping both her sisters would be able to come, and to bring their families to Missouri for the wedding.

When Amzi tried to talk Eliza out of it, due to her condition, Eliza told him not to be concerned. "A girl only gets married once," she said. "Julia is my closest older sister, and her daughter Julia is practically a younger sister to me. Besides, I won't be alone: you must come as well. Mary Ann is going. We'll *all* go."

Alemeth groaned. Something about weddings disagreed with him. He was determined to avoid this one, whatever it took.

"You'll enjoy Carondelet," she said to him. "You remember my sister Julia, and Doctor Webster."

Just barely.

"And you remember their daughters."

Maybe. There'd been a lot of them.

"You surely remember Mary Ann. She's the one who's just your age. I thought you two got along nicely."

He remembered Mary Ann Webster. She'd driven him crazy. She'd even asked if she could come along fishing once. But so what? Eliza and Mrs. Brown were enough. He didn't need another *Strong* trying to arrange his life.

"Alemeth, I promise you, you'll love it. Mary Ann – my sister, that is – will have us stay at the Gayoso, I'm sure."

No wonder John Bates Strong had gone to sea.

Eliza: "What about Walton?"

Amzi: "You and Leety don't need a little one to take care of. We should leave him here, with Harriet."

How unfair.

Eliza: "Alemeth, surely you'll enjoy the steamboat ride."

Well. *That* might be true. But at what price, a steam boat ride?

Amzi: "I think you'd like the river, son. It's bigger than any you've ever seen. And stronger."

Uncle Johnson: "Alemeth, I'd love to see those double wheelers myself. Steam engines. Boilers. Power enough to haul all those people, and all that cotton. I'd think you'd have a good time, checking out that machinery."

If only Pa would say he didn't have to go.

Amzi: "Alemeth, I'm sure we'll have a good time."

"*You're* going to go?"

"Yes. I guess I am. Someone's got to keep an eye on your – on Eliza."

"Well, then. I guess I should go too."

And so Alemeth accepted the inevitable. He would go to Missouri with the rest of them.

Then, two mornings before departure, the day Mr. Murdock was supposed to come take him, Kep disappeared.

*   *   *

First, it was simply that Grote hadn't seen him. Then, that Alemeth hadn't. Then Eliza, and Uncle Johnson. The more people who hadn't seen him, the more places could be ruled out. Soon, Amzi was asking where else he could be, and the more it looked as if Kep had just run off.

"Something alerted him," Amzi said to Eliza. "What did you say to him?"

"I'd prefer not to assume the worst, Amzi. He has to be somewhere nearby. Hurt, perhaps, but not far. He *couldn't* have run away."

"But you told him nothing about selling him?"

"I can't say it's been easy, Amzi, but no. Of course I haven't."

"What about you, son?"

"I haven't seen him since – "

"Since when?"

"Since you said you were going to sell him."

"For that long? "

"I've been avoiding him. I didn't think I could – "

"Well, then, there it is. You've done it again. You made him wonder if something wasn't right. You tipped him off."

The accusation stung, but there was no time for feeling wounded. They spent the morning looking everywhere around Bynum's Creek, Alemeth trying to imagine where he'd go if he were Kep. But further searches produced no leads. None of the other negroes had seen him. Bill Starr came out, along with Al Cansler and Jim Murdock, to widen the search. Dogs strained against leashes, yelped and sniffed, pulling the hunters along all morning and most of the afternoon, but there was no sign of Kep.

Amzi speculated out loud, saying Kep might be here or Kep might be there, the whole time looking at Eliza to see if anything caused a reaction. Before long, Alemeth, too, was looking for a sign in her eyes, wondering whether she wasn't letting on to something.

Mary Jane pointed out what Semmy Lou had said, that Kep 'had a thing' for Sadie. After Amzi took Sadie to the smokehouse to ask her what she knew, he came back saying he hadn't been able to get anything out of her. Eliza showed no sign she was keeping a secret. Nor could anyone be found who had anything to say about Kep and Sadie. Kep had no family in another state, no known relations in nearby counties. He'd been born at the Byers place in Coosa County. He'd never lived anywhere but there and Bynum's Creek. He had no place to go, unless he was headed north.

The search lasted into the evening, but nothing of interest was found. When, late, the dogs were called off, Amzi announced that, with Kep still missing, he wouldn't be going to the wedding after all.

Would anything ever go right? Why the situation didn't let *him* off the hook, he couldn't understand. The wedding itself was nothing to him. The bride and her family weren't really his kin. He'd be out of place among the women. He'd miss out on the search for Kep.

"Julia Webster's daughter is no relation to me. She's Eliza's kin. Colonel Brown isn't going, and now you're not, Pa. If the girls want to go, that's fine, but why should *I* have to? They're not my family."

"Alemeth, I don't see why you have a problem with this. You went to Miss Frances's wedding. You went to Miss Fredonia's."

"I didn't have to be gone for two weeks while you're looking for Kep."

"Ma will need someone to look after her. You should feel *honored*, Alemeth. You'll be the only man. All those women will be in your hands."

What? Eliza always wanted her own way. As for Mrs. Brown, even the Colonel did what she said. All five girls, two negroes, and even the child Eliza was carrying, they'd all be in *the sisters'* hands. No doubt about it, Pa was wrong. But when Pa had his mind made up, there was no use protesting.

"Alemeth, I want you to keep your eye on Eliza. Make sure she's alright. Make sure she listens to what Leety tells her, about the baby."

*   *   *

And so Alemeth's exile began.

As expected, the journey to Memphis was insufferable. Alemeth rode like a prince in the first of two coaches: a flagship of sorts, for Mrs. Brown and the seat of command. Mrs. Brown talked of sundry things – the *Gayoso* – "the grandest of hotels" – the city of Memphis – "Andy Jackson's city" – how the Browns had been neighbors of Jackson in Tennessee – how the Colonel's father had been his aide de camp in the Red Stick campaign – how the Colonel had served under him at New Orleans. Old cities, old wars, people long gone – Alemeth suffered through Mrs. Brown's stories of the past.

At the *Gayoso,* the women followed Mrs. Brown up the steps, a gaggle waddling in to explore the grand hotel. What could he do, but follow? The hotel had a hundred and fifty rooms. Passing through its columned façade, ascending its ballroom stairs, entering the room where he'd spend the night, seeing for himself what so enthralled the girls – indoor plumbing, a marble tub, silver faucets, a flush toilet, everything delicate, expensive and clean – he wondered what it would be like, to live in such a palace.

Then he snapped out of it. What did he care about flush toilets and marble tubs? How much better to be at home, looking for Kep, with Pa.

With the sisters' permission, he left the Gayoso to inquire about the steamboat for Memphis. Crossing onto the promenade, he descended the terraced slope to the river. Ten times wider than the Tallahatchie, it was bringing uncountable tons of water from a land he'd only heard about, a land of mountains, bears, and Dakota Sioux villages, a land he vowed to explored some day.. As close as he could to the water's edge, he looked downriver, imagining where it all ended, past New Orleans. Judging by the current, the Gulf had to be very deep to hold so much water.

Then he looked northward again. The river's massive current was carrying rafts, logs, branches and every sort of flotsam south. The 'mother of rivers,' they called it. The name might have made sense if the river had spawned a brood of smaller rivers. But the mother was herself an accumulation, built up from rivulets of melting northern snow, ice and rain running down mountainsides to lower ground, combining into runs and traces. It was all those hundreds of runs and traces which came together to form her. The 'mother of rivers' was a combination of waters, their coming together what made her what she was. How much rain and melting snow it took to support so many thousands of gallons moving past the promenade every hour, he couldn't fathom, but it made no sense to call the product of so many sources a 'mother,' not to Alemeth, at least.

SOUTHWESTERN
TELEGRAPH COMPANY

At the telegraph office, a whiskered clerk in a stiff white shirt listened to an odd contraption: two cylinders on a metal armature, with parts and appendages click clacking on the desk in front of him, the sound amplified by a tin can. The clock in the corner of the office chimed once, marking the quarter hour.

"Excuse me, sir. Is there any news about *The Calypso*?"

The clerk didn't answer till the click clacking had stopped.

"We've heard just now," he said, looking up through spectacles. "She passed Pikesville just minutes ago. Should be here tonight. Ready to leave at dawn. You looking for a ticket?"

"No, we've got our tickets already."

The machine sounded off again. Once more, the clerk listened carefully, writing a message. When he'd finished, he stuck the message on a nail and turned back to Alemeth.

"Never seen a telegraph before?"

"Sure, I — "

"We get messages from New Orleans to Saint Louis and from everywhere in between. Get 'em as soon as they're sent. In fact, I can tell you the minute a boat leaves the wharf in New Orleans."

Minutes earlier, the river had been gargantuan, the Dakotas to the north and New Orleans to the South each a journey of many days. In just a second, they'd been connected by messages on a wire. In a sense, he could be in both places at once.

"You don't say."

A boy came in and took the message from the nail. Alemeth followed him out the door. Curious as ever, he longed to follow. But he'd be in trouble if he were late for supper, so dutifully, he headed back to the Gayoso.

He spent the evening in a parlor beneath Greek columns, balconies, and cornices. When it came time to retire, he took a full bath, the mere turn of a knob bringing hot water from nowhere in sight to a faucet at his feet. Lying on a fancy bed, looking up at a ceiling fan, he resented having been delivered into the hands of Eliza and Mrs. Brown, and looked forward to the rest of the trip with anxiety. The bed was comfortable – he had to admit that – but when he finally fell asleep, he dreamed of sitting in a coach with women whose bustiers and hoop skirts trapped him, blocking the way to the door, and he woke to find himself tangled in his sheets. He lay awake for most of the night, wondering where Pa would finally find Kep.

The next morning he hurried down to the wharf before dawn. The Colonel's new steamboat had arrived: a wooden-hulled side-wheeler with chimneys like white obelisks. Draymen were unloading wagons, bearing provisions on board. The boat's name was hard to see in the darkness, but as the sunlight broke through the buildings, it illuminated the paddle house, unveiling the name in magnificent blue:

CALYPSO

Beneath the name hung a sign in smaller red letters:

DEPARTING PROMPTLY AT 8 A.M.

He couldn't wait to board, to find out what the boat was like. But at the ramp, he was stopped by a steward. Mrs. Brown had kept all the tickets with her. He didn't want to go back to the Gayoso, so he went downriver a way, and as the sun rose behind him, observed the water passing, none of it the same as the water he'd seen a few minutes before, but all of it still headed toward New Orleans. But now, the whole massive mother struck him as connected, from the Dakotas to the Gulf, by wire. It was an impossibility, yet he'd seen it himself. It was real.

Back at the Gayoso, Mrs. Brown was at the head of her brood, in control, giving instructions to Emily. Alemeth asked for his ticket, but Mrs. Brown said no, she would hold them: the group should stay together. So Alemeth – far from having everyone in *his* hands – waited for the women. When the bell of *The Calypso* signaled time to depart, Eliza fretted that the group might miss the boat on account of her condition. Mrs. Brown told her to take her time: the Captain wouldn't leave without them. And sure enough, though they didn't reach the boat until ten minutes past eight, the boat waited for them.

When they were all on board, poles came out. Lines came loose. People talked about the distance to Cairo and the probable time to Saint Louis, which depended on the wind, the current, refueling times, sand bars and snags. Mrs. Brown informed the others that if all went well, they'd be in St. Louis in two days.

One by one, the four boilers were fired. The engines built up steam. The paddlewheels churned. In a white, watery foam, black smoke billowing from its chimneys, the *Calypso* moved away from the dock. As the river broke against the bow, Alemeth felt the power beneath him. He'd been on the Tallahatchie; he'd swum in the Yocknapatawpha. But they were shallow, rocky rivers; you couldn't put a big boat on them. The Mississippi was no mountain stream. The *Calypso* was no raft underfoot. Standing on the Texas deck as the boat plied its way up between Arkansas and Tennessee was like going up the Nile on one of the Pharaoh's boats, or on the back of one of Reverend Vrooman's prehistoric creatures.

*   *   *

On the second day, past Cairo, without the Ohio to strengthen it, the river narrowed slightly. The vague Illinois shoreline turned into trees and branches. Occasional fishermen, canoes, tents, cabins and sometimes even little villages passed by. Hours of watching the shoreline made clear their northbound progress, and Alemeth's eyes faced forward, but his thoughts were with the flat boats, rafts and launches and the river that lumbered south, behind them, back toward Arkansas, Mississippi, and the search for Kep.

Maybe Kep hadn't run off at all. Maybe there'd been some sort of accident, like Eliza said. Kep might have been hurt. And even if not – even if some crazy idea had put it into his head to run off – he could have had a change of heart, and come home on his own. He didn't want to think of the alternatives.

After mid-day dinner, on the catwalk of the hurricane deck, Mrs. Brown said to Eliza, "Sister, you've lived in Saint Louis. What can you tell the girls about the city? I've heard the whole sky lights up at night. Is that not true?"

"Yes – "

"Tell us about it."

Eliza turned to the girls.

"Well, as you know, St. Louis is where the Mississippi is joined by the Missouri. That's why St. Louis is called the door to the west. It's the gateway to the future of America. It was founded by papists, named for King Louis IX of France, the Grand Inquisitor of the Catholics. (The pope declared him a saint, of all things!) But even as we speak, God is delivering Saint Louis. That's why Lyman Beecher sent us there. To play a role in that deliverance. To help realize his plan for the new Promised Land. Next month, when we read *A Plea for the West*, you'll better understand the significance of Saint Louis in the life of a Christian. "

Alemeth tried to imagine living in a Catholic country. But he couldn't focus on St. Louis. Even as the steamboat pulled him northward, with the sisters, to a wedding he dreaded, the river pulled him back to Bynum's Creek, and Pa, and whatever Pa had found out about Kep.

*   *   *

They disembarked at the wharf amid a hubbub of porters, chandlers, passengers and well-wishers. They took a carriage past the Cathedral of Saint Louis, where two nuns in habits were wearing hats that made them look like swans. In Carondelet, they passed timber-framed German homes on stone foundations, and painted window sills full of flowers. On Kraus Street, they pulled up at last to the Webster's door, where they were met by Aunt Julia Webster and her family. There were greetings all around.

Six years had made a big difference among Eliza's nieces. Julia, the bride-to-be, directed her attention to her elders, her etiquette no longer that of a child. Harriet, now eleven, was skinny. And two more girls had been born since the Websters' last visit to Clear Creek. But it was the second oldest Webster girl, Mary Ann, the one his age, who had changed the most. She'd ignored him six years before, except for that one request to go fishing. Now, she wouldn't let him go, as if she'd made it her personal mission to put him in touch with everything going on.

She told him how the bride had met the groom. (William's older brother, Henry Blow, was a friend of her father.) She told him who would perform the ceremony. (The pastor at Westminster Presbyterian, the Reverend Samuel McPheeters.) She told him who had been invited. (All the leading citizens of Carondelet, including some Germans.) She called him "cousin," then a minute later told him that, on second thought, they were not really cousins; that although 'Aunt Eliza' was her mother's sister, he was not really any relation to Eliza. (Still, she would call him cousin, if he didn't mind.) He said he didn't care. She asked about Bynum's Creek, and Oxford, and Mount Sylvan. She asked about the union church, and about Uncle Johnson. She even asked about Leander McKinney.

"You sure are curious."

"I have to be curious; I'm going to be a writer."

"Really?"

"I think it's amazing what a writer can do, to weave an enchanting story. It's a wonderful gift that I hope someday to develop myself. Have you read Elizabeth Browning?"

"No, I – "

"Mary Shelley? Ann Radcliff? Shakespeare?"

"Well, no…"

"Dear Alemeth, whatever are we going to do with you? You *do* read, don't you?"

"Yeah, of course I do."

"Well, you must read more. You'll never be happy if you spend your whole life on the plantation."

"It's not simple, being a planter. This year, the soil was different everywhere. Do you know that soil *changes*? And we had to make all sorts of changes ourselves. And – "

"How many slaves does your Pa own?"

He wondered. How many children did Annie have now, and Harriet?

"About fifty, I guess. Maybe a few more."

"Do you know them all?"

"I know most of them pretty good. Why?"

"Are they happy?"

"Well, they're like other people, I reckon – happy some of the time, not so happy others."

"Have you had any runaways?"

Dang – her nose was like a hunting dog's. "No. I mean, not until…"

"Until what?"

"Right before we left to come here, there was one that disappeared. That's why Pa didn't come with us. He's home, looking for the boy now."

"Why was he unhappy?"

"He wasn't unhappy."

"Alemeth, he wouldn't run away unless he was unhappy." Her cheeks fell into a sad smile. "I can't imagine having so many slaves. Where do they sleep?"

"Out back. Behind the house."

"In what sort of shelter?"

"They have cabins, Mary Ann. You'd think you'd never seen a slave. You've got slaves in Missouri."

"Well, that's just the thing. I mean, yes, there *are* slaves here. But they're mostly household servants: coach drivers, cooks and nannies. There are no plantations, no field hands, no overseers. I hear things are different on the plantation."

"How do you mean?"

"Well. With that many negroes, together, in the hot sun... Does your father have an overseer?"

"Naw. Not a white one, anyway. Grote looks after the others."

"Does your father whip them?"

"What? Mary Ann Webster –"

"Does he?"

"Well, maybe. I don't think so."

"Why not?"

"He's never had to."

"They're lucky, then. I hear plantation slaves get whipped all the time."

"It's only some of them, Mary Ann. Those that have to be. It's no different than white folks."

"Really?"

She paused. He said nothing.

"Do you think slaves should have rights?"

"I don't know. What kind of rights?"

"*Legal* rights. Like, the right to marry whoever they want; the right to own land, or buy their own freedom."

Kep could be hiding beneath the floorboards of a house somewhere. That's what *he* wanted to know. *Rights?*

"I don't know. Why do you ask?"

"William's father used to own a negro who practically raised the boys. A few years back, they sold him. Now, he and his brothers have a lawsuit. They're trying to get him free."

"They're abolitionists?"

"No, Alemeth. Not hardly. William keeps a servant himself. She's his cook and housekeeper. Reads. Goes to church. Julia's mad about her. But they're talking about the legal rights of negroes. About the right ways a slave can win his freedom. Some are raising Cain about it all. I don't suppose you've seen this?"

She lifted a book from her handbag.

UNCLE TOM'S
CABIN
OR
LIFE AMONG THE LOWLY

"I've seen it," he lied.

"What do you think of it?"

"Oh, I don't care for that sort of thing."

"You don't want to read about slavery?"

"I – … right."

"You don't sound very sure. What sort of books *do* you read?"

What books did he even know? *The Bible*, of course, but he wasn't about to mention *it*.

"I like *The Odyssey*." (There was a copy of it at Mount Sylvan. Reverend Vrooman had read a little from it.)

"What's your favorite part?" (She was a bloodhound!)

"I guess I like… the Cyclops."

"You know, Alemeth, if you like to read, you ought to consider going into the newspaper business. There's amazing stuff in the newspapers." She held up a copy of the Missouri Republican. "They take articles brought to them. If they're good enough. I've submitted some things…"

"I've thought about going into the newspaper business."

"Why, Alemeth, I think that's marvelous!"

*   *   *

Over the next few days, Mary Ann Webster paid a great deal of attention to wedding plans, making sure that Julia's dress fit perfectly, that her hair was fixed just right, that she had everything she needed. But unless Alemeth was badly mistaken, she also maintained a distinct interest in *him*. He grew more sure of it with every glance, and after several days, accepted it as fact. The following Tuesday, during the ceremony in Dr. Webster's garden, with the Blows on one side and the Strongs and Websters on the other, she stood with her sister and the other attendants, and sometimes, instead of looking at Reverend McPheeters, or at the bride, she looked his way instead.

That night, in one of his dreams, she handed him a newspaper and asked if he wanted to read a story she'd written. He told her he wanted to read it. But as he held the paper up, the print became blurry, and he couldn't read a word.

He awoke thinking only about her. She was like no one he'd ever met. And her smile was – well – the sort of smile you can't stop thinking about.

The following day, their paths didn't cross until the family was packed and preparing to leave. Mary Ann drew him aside and said they ought to have something to remember each other by.

"Alright."

"What shall I give you?"

"I don't know. That book, maybe? The one about the cabin?"

"I'm sorry, Alemeth. That book belongs to Mother. I couldn't do that... But since you like books, might I make a present to you of this bookmark? I've always held it dear."

She held it up for him to see. The letters "M.A.W." were printed elegantly on it.

"That would be nice."

She brushed the bookmark to her lips and dropped it into his palm, her little finger touching his for an instant.

"Though we'll be apart, we'll be together, in a way."

He fumbled for the brass button on his jacket, hanging on by a thread.

"Here. You can remember me by this."

Their goodbye was all too clumsy. But on the southbound steamer, he discovered a note she'd written on the back of the bookmark.

> *To Alemeth,*
> *Best wishes and good luck in the*
> *newspaper business. I'll be thinking of you.*
> *— Mary Ann*

                    *   *   *

The river swirled, water birds called from the grasses, and a great blue heron, wings flapping like carpets, landed on the moonlit river. Behind him was Mary Ann Webster. Ahead, back to Memphis, Mississippi, and Kep.

It wasn't right, Kep's running off without saying anything to him. A friend shouldn't treat a friend that way. Much as he pitied the boy – much as he understood why he couldn't stomach working for a hateful man like Jim Murdock – Kep had betrayed him, running off and getting himself into trouble, one way or another. How he'd fare, a runaway, deep in Mississippi, Alemeth shuddered to think. But maybe he'd thought better of running away. Maybe he'd come home. Maybe his running away had caused Murdock to change his mind. Maybe Pa had even had a change of heart. A lot could have happened in just a couple of weeks. His thoughts shot back and forth, from Mary Ann to Kep and back again, competing for his attention.

*　　　　*　　　　*

In Memphis, with two hours before the stage was to leave, Alemeth wandered through Court Square, looking for the cotton market Mrs. Brown had told him about. But the cotton market was empty and lifeless. Flyers tacked to posts and walls spoke of small lots for sale, but there were no traders or agents among the stalls, just wisps of cotton snagged by nails and empty pallets, refusing to submit to the wind. He wondered when he'd next see Mary Ann Webster. He wondered if he'd *ever* see Kep. Then, on his way back toward the Gayoso and the river, he came upon a pair of large warehouse doors, and a sign overhead:

BOLTON BROS.
COTTON-ACCLIMATED SLAVES.
WADE & ISSAC BOLTON, PROPRIETORS

One of the doors was half open. Hearing voices, he went in. The place was like a revival hall. But rather than a preacher, a man was on a platform calling out numbers. Sweltering heat. The odor of human sweat hung like fog. Alemeth got closer. The man on the platform was not alone. Standing behind him were a dozen negroes, and in front of him, two more hung onto each other.

"Look at this youth. Look at the muscles there."

From the crowd that had gathered, a well-dressed man ascended the steps of the platform to have a better look.

"And this pretty thing will be pregnant for many years to come."

A rough-hewn man ascended too, to do his own inspection.

"Don't bother looking for lash marks," said the auctioneer. "These here are top field hands. Don't they make an excellent couple? Only twenty-two hundred dollars! Who will give me twenty-two hundred?"

There was a flurry of human voices, but no takers.

"Not today, eh? You're missing a fine opportunity there. These two Africans are made for each other. Sure to give you a fine return. Oh, come on now! Don't make me break up a pair! Do I hear two thousand?"

Still, no takers. By now, he'd made his way close to the block.

"Well, then, if you insist. You can have just this fine buck for twelve hundred. Eight years picking, and not a scar on him."

"A thousand," said a voice from the opposite side.

"I've got a thousand. Do I hear eleven hundred?"

Alemeth looked into the eyes of the negroes. They were silent, like the children on the table tops at Clear Creek. For some strange reason, the young woman's eyes as she looked at the man reminded him of Colonel Brown's horse, about to lose its tail. But the man was peering at *him*, his stare stinging like an accusation. As if Alemeth was the one splitting the pair apart. As if Alemeth had cut off the horse's tail, flesh and all. As if *he had anything to do* with what was happening on the platform.

'Eleven hundred!"

"Twelve!"

On the stage home, in a coach this time with both Mrs. Brown and Eliza, Alemeth described the sale at Bolton's – how arms had been pulled apart, man from woman, mother from child. It was hard not to see Kep and Sadie in that warehouse, begging not to be separated. Hard not to see Jim Murdock going up the steps to make an inspection, taking one but not the other, showing no concern at for consequences, ignoring the duty a civilized man owes to those who depend on him.

"It's a shame you couldn't see the cotton market," said Mrs. Brown. "To see the cotton market, you need to be on Front Street when the harvest comes in. That's when the new Memphis really comes alive."

She was speaking to him; he wasn't allowed to ignore her.

"The *new* Memphis?"

"Yes, Alemeth. The *new* Memphis. *Our* Memphis was modeled on the Memphis of ancient Egypt. From the bluffs, overlooking the greatest river in America, the site reminded the founders of ancient Memphis, overlooking the greatest Old World river, the Nile. They imagined America someday becoming as great as ancient Egypt."

"With pyramids and sphinxes?"

"I don't know about that. But Memphis was a great marketplace for cotton, and for slaves. The trade had made it wealthy. Andy Jackson envisioned the same for his new Memphis. I'd say he got it rather well, wouldn't you? The same great city upriver? The biggest cotton and slave markets in the Americas?"

"Well," interjected Eliza, as if correcting her. "Don't forget the biggest difference between the old Memphis and the new."

"What's that, sister?"

"The old Memphis was a pagan city. Ours is a Christian one."

*   *   *

When the stage was met in Oxford by Amzi and Harl, Alemeth bounded out of the coach, finally free of his the sisters who'd abducted him. He made no effort to hide what was on his mind.

"Howdy, Pa. Have you – "

"Kep's back at home, son. We found the devil not a quarter mile from home. We think he was coming back for Sadie."

"Oh, thank Heaven!" said Eliza from behind him. "Coming back home. Was he alright?"

Amzi's eyes narrowed. For a moment he looked angry at Eliza; then his gaze settled on her enlarged belly, and his face softened. "So, Eliza, did you get plenty of rest?"

"Of course, Amzi."

Alemeth wanted to ask about Kep. Apparently, he hadn't been handed over to Jim Murdock – at least not yet. But Amzi was talking to Eliza and the girls, who were telling him about the wonders of Carondelet, the Gayoso and *The Calypso*. All at once. Kep would have to wait.

At home, out back, in Harriet's cabin, Kep was not to be found. Harriet's frown and shrug toward the smokehouse was all Alemeth needed to see.

The door to the smokehouse was barred shut; a padlock secured the hasp. A brief, muted moan confirmed Kep's presence, holed up inside, but for reasons Alemeth couldn't understand, he didn't answer questions. Alemeth scolded him for running off without talking to him. (If only he had, he could have explained why it wasn't a good idea to run – they'd have found a way to keep him from Murdock.) Still, Kep didn't reply.

"It isn't right, you know. Running off without saying anything to me. A friend shouldn't treat a friend that way."

Nothing.

"Have it your way, then."

It wasn't until the next morning that Uncle Johnson told Alemeth about the whipping Kep had got. And it wasn't until Eliza had pleaded with Amzi for hours that Kep was released from the smokehouse, and Alemeth saw the raw tracks across Kep's back. The deep cuts caused Alemeth to shudder, and remembering the sting of hickory on his own buttocks, he wondered if Kep's lashing had been more than necessary. But by that time, Alemeth was convinced that *some* discipline had been necessary. Kep had been in the wrong to run away. He'd been in the wrong to say nothing to Alemeth beforehand. Kep had brought it on himself. He deserved punishment, of some sort or another.

44

During the trip to Carondelet, Eliza's condition had been evident enough, but she'd never complained. None of the women had suggested there was cause for alarm. So Alemeth had given it little thought. He'd done everything he could think to do, and that wasn't much, but it was, apparently, enough. Eliza was fine.

But Eliza took Kep's punishment badly. Seeing the sores on his back, she had started to cry. Then, behind closed doors, Amzi had yelled at her. And now, Amzi was railing at *him*: he hadn't kept his eye out, *he'd* let her do too much. (As if Eliza had ever done anything he thought she should do!)

Aunt Leety and Harriet were in her room, the door closed, and Alemeth was feeling sorry for himself, mystified by Amzi's rage, when Aunt Leety came out of Eliza's room for towels. Through the open door, Alemeth could see her in the bed, disheveled, and a baby in a porcelain tub.

The baby had come! (Ugly as sin!) Leety went back in, and after wiping the baby down, wrapped her in a blanket. Was she thinking to keep the girl warm? Then it occurred to him. There was a certain look, like the cloudy eyes of a killed rabbit or deer, no movement of the chest, no heartbeat, hearing or thought. The baby wasn't breathing. It bore the stone cold look of death. Maybe Leety had wrapped the baby so that Eliza wouldn't have to look at it.

That day, and for the next several, the women closed around Eliza like prairie wagons. They talked to her of the infant's heavenly soul, and of the earthly trials she'd never have to face. They offered condolences. They asked what they could do for her. But nothing could hide their grief. Attempts at conversation brought tears. Even the trivial was shrouded in a somber air. Alemeth lay awake at night, thinking of the baby.

If the corpse could keep him awake, what did it do to Eliza? She had carried the child; she had held her in her arms; she had felt the baby's flesh. What a terrible thing it must be, to feel a new life inside you, to feel it grow, to imagine all the things it may someday be, only to think of it as a lifeless corpse. Or – worse – that the child was alive just hours ago, until your own body gave up the fight and put a stop to it

He tried, as best he could, to see things as Eliza saw them. He tried to imagine her suffering, and how, unlike Kep, the infant had done nothing to deserve its punishment. And at supper one evening that week, he told Eliza what he'd been feeling.

"I want you to know, I've been thinking about what you're going through." She managed a sad but appreciative smile.

"I just wanted to say how sorry I am for you – Ma."

45

Alemeth's new-found sympathy for Eliza drew him closer to her, and he tried as never before to see things her way. He noticed a warmth in her eyes as she looked at him, and she smiled when she saw him. He started calling her 'Ma.' For the first time, Amzi's occasional kindness to her also warmed his heart, and brought him closer to Amzi as well. The possibility of loving them both drew Alemeth to work harder than ever, hoping to convince Amzi he was growing up; that he understood the necessity of Kep's punishment, just as he understood the necessity of hunting for food; that he'd be able to run the plantation someday; and that, for none of that would he need school.

But no matter what he said to Amzi about school, Amzi wouldn't answer until he'd talked to 'Ma' – and Eliza wouldn't budge. Mount Sylvan was good for him, she said. He should 'show appreciation' for the education his father was giving him. And so Alemeth came to realize that being kind to Eliza, calling her 'Ma,' didn't change her opinions about education, or the mothering way she talked to him. She only pressed her own wants harder. Trying to see things her way did nothing to get *her* to see things *his*. So his new-found sympathy had a very short life. And when the harvest was done, he found himself back in school, where his curiosity had all the life of a stillborn child.

The first day of the new year, Reverend Vrooman greeted the boys with a lecture about the importance of keeping an open mind. He had a copy of the very book Mary Ann Webster had shown him, and asked if anyone had read it. He elicited arguments for and against slavery, asking the class to analyze the problem, first from a Biblical perspective, and then from an economic one – all, he said, in order to get at the truth.

The truth, as Alemeth saw it, was that he might not make it at Mount Sylvan another year. At the market, in Memphis, he'd wondered if slavery could be wrong, but Reverend Vrooman was harder than Miss Strong. His lessons, like his maps, were full of lines and numbers that made no sense. And the worst of it was, after forcing the class to express reasons and conclusions, he refused to say who was right and who wrong. The isosceles triangle. *Gallia est omnia divisa.* Odysseus and the Laestrygonians. Was it possible to concentrate with a blue jay on the window sill? Reverend Vrooman made his way around the room. Alemeth's desk could have been bolted to the schoolhouse floor, his ankles bound to the base of it, for all he could escape from it. Hard as he tried to focus on the difference between the active indicative and the passive subjunctive, Vrooman loomed ever closer.

The year ahead could be unbearable. The only thing he knew for sure was that he'd have never been stuck at that desk, were it not for Eliza Strong.

46

In the midst of torment under the ponderous weight of Frederick Coffin Vrooman, there was one small bit of good news. One of the new boys at Mt. Sylvan – shorter than most of the others, but dressed very smartly – didn't seem cowed by the Reverend as much as the others did. When school let out at the end of the third day, he introduced himself to Alemeth.

"I'm Gordon. What's your name?"

"Alemeth Byers. How come I haven't seen you before?"

"My family's from Ripley."

"You coming to school all the way from Ripley?"

"I'm staying with Reverend Vrooman."

"Oh…"

"What do you think of him?"

"I swear I've seen steam come out of his nose."

"I know what you mean. He can sure work up pressure. But wasn't it interesting, the way he used his body when talking about the subjunctive mood?"

"What?"

"His gestures. Like he was pretending to wear a yoke around his neck. You didn't notice?"

Gordon not only knew Greek and Latin; he was actually interested in them. As Alemeth soon learned, it was part of his love for the dead, his love for words, his love for invention and discovery. He wanted to be a writer, like Mary Ann Webster. Like Mary Ann, he was curious, self-confident, and prone to speak his mind.

When Reverend Vrooman released class at the end of the first week, Gordon led Alemeth to a hickory tree in the woods nearby the schoolhouse, and in the hollow of the tree, from beneath an old bird's nest, he took a box of half-smoked cigars. Lighting a stogie with a lucifer, he passed it to Alemeth.

"Be sure you don't draw smoke into your lungs."

Alemeth was dying to test the cigar, but knew better than to say so.

"I know, I know."

He knew not to draw it into his lungs, but it tasted bitter and stale, and after a third puff, he was dizzy.

"This is good." He was just being nice. "Thanks."

Gordon put his hand back into the hollow of the tree, this time removing a deck of playing cards bound together with a cord.

"Play cards?"

"Sure. I've played cards."

"I mean, do you *want* to?"

He had handled cards once, but he didn't know any games.

"Nah…"

"Oh come on. Let's play poker." Gordon was untying the cord. "What'll we play for?"

Alemeth was still reeling from the cigar.

"I've got no money."

"Whoever loses will do the other's homework. For a week. Why don't you get us some acorns?"

Alemeth wondered if the dizziness would ever end or if, filled with smoke, he might rise into the air as if from a campfire. He stumbled about, searching for acorns, and soon after he found some, Gordon was penetrating the haze somehow, teaching him to play cards.

The next Monday, Alemeth did Gordon's homework, but he confused the imperative with the subjunctive, and on Tuesday, Gordon told him he didn't have to do it anymore. Gordon, it turns out, was an affable fellow. Brotherly, in fact. In the weeks that followed, the boys became fast friends. Gordon was always finding a way to sneak a cigar; always surrounded by the smell of smoke, if not the sight of it; always looking to play cards. Though Alemeth finally found a way to pass on the cigars, Gordon never tired of them.

Between cards and cigars, Gordon let out opinions, stories, and speculations, casting his line as if into a fishing hole in search of a bite. His friendship – and especially his curiosity about the past – made it easier for Alemeth to handle just about everything at Mount Sylvan – especially the endless display of knowledge that spewed from the volcanic mind of Reverend Frederick Coffin Vrooman. One day, Vrooman was talking about Homer being more than one person. The next, about Erasmus and someone named Tischendorf, who believed there could be more than one Bible. (That night, Eliza assured him there was only one Word of God.) To Alemeth, all such talk about people who were dead and things that had been written long ago, were things he would never need to know. Thank goodness he had found Gordon, someone who could help him deal with it, someone who could bring the dead to life while playing cards and smoking his cigars.

It was Gordon, for example, who explained to Alemeth, later, what Reverend Vrooman had meant when he said that Homer's true greatness came from showing how a well told story can lead a listener to see the world through several sets of eyes. It was a concept that, without Gordon, Alemeth would have never been able to understand.

47

The separatist spirit had driven Eliza's grandfather to join the rebellion against the King. It had emboldened Amzi's grandfather to join in the Snow campaign. It had inspired the Colonel's grandfather to risk his life at Guilford Courthouse. Even before they'd focused on the need to separate from the King, that same spirit had led them to separate from the King's Church, just as the King had separated his from the Pope's. It look a lot of courage to throw off an unjust yoke, and Eliza had long admired those willing to do so.

But not long after they severed their ties to the King's church, the reformers had separated from each other. Adonijah Strong's line had become Congregationalists; William Byers's Baptists; James Brown's Presbyterians. More recently, the Cumberlands had separated from other Presbyterians. The Church was a prolific mother, spawning new churches that went their separate ways as if, unbound to anything in the material world, the spirits of men led naturally in different directions.

At first, the experiment with the union church had seemed an excellent idea. Eliza liked not having to go all the way to College Hill, and there was meaning to her life when she taught Sunday school. But sharing a church with Methodists and Baptists created problems of its own. The former lacked doctrine, as if it didn't matter what a person believed. The latter had no regard for education. And the Baptists themselves were split – some being Landmarkers, who complained about having to share a church with Methodists and Presbyterians.

"It's just a building," Amzi had said. "There's no harm sharing a building. Think of it this way, Eliza. Sharing a building is the price for being able to teach Sunday School. That's not too high a price to pay, is it?"

But the problems kept getting larger.

The first problems were minor, like who would have use of the building for a meeting, or who would refit the hinges on the door. Then, one of the Baptist children told Semmy Lou she'd been an 'ignorant infant' at the time of her christening, adding that because Semmy Lou had been ignorant, she hadn't ever *really* been baptized. It took Eliza most of the morning to assure Semmy Lou she was not ignorant, and was fully a part of the visible church.

While there were other problems at the union church, none proved as significant as the problem that started when Kep – apparently afflicted with a separatist spirit of his own – said he'd had enough of Sunday school and Bible lessons, and that he didn't care to read with Eliza any more. Amzi said it proved him right: there was nothing good to come of teaching negroes to read. Then, a few weeks later, Kep disappeared a second time.

This time, the hunters and the dogs couldn't find him. A week passed. Then, on an errand into town, Eliza saw one of the Methodists, Hugh Pike, outside the post office talking to Sadie. He was looking over his shoulder as if trying to draw Sadie aside, as if not wanting to be overheard. Sadie's demeanor was equally strange: hanging, first, on every word Pike said; then, the smile on her face departing, wiping her face with her sleeve and hurrying away, as if Pike had given her some piece of bad news. What news could Hugh Pike *possibly* have for one of the Byers' servants?

When Eliza told Amzi what she'd seen, he got with Sadie right away. When he returned from confronting her, he summarized what she'd said. "She denied speaking with Pike at all, at first. But then, when I pressed her, she admitted they'd talked. Claimed Pike had only complimented her dress. Said she didn't think she'd cried; then said she'd cried because Pike had embarrassed her. There were several contradictions. She was obviously lying."

The first chance Eliza got, she talked to Sadie herself.

"Please come here, Sadie. Listen to me. You know the questions Mr. Byers was asking you are serious. And you know that God wants you to tell the truth."

"Yes, ma'am. I do. I don't want to cause nobody no trouble."

"Then tell me, Sadie. What was Mr. Pike talking to you about?"

Sadie looked desperate to be believed. "Like I told Mister Byers, Ma'am. Mr. Pike, he just told me he liked my dress."

"The colorful one with all the pinks and blues?"

"Yes, ma'am. The one Leety made me. Miz Byers, I swear, that's all it was."

"He said nothing about Kep?"

"Why – no, Miz Byers."

Eliza believed her, but in the meantime, Amzi rode over to Hugh Pike's place, and when he returned, he brought a very different opinion.

"Pike denied saying anything to Sadie about Kep."

"Did you ask him what they were talking about?"

"Yes. He said he just passed her outside the post office. They hardly had a word or two; he didn't recall exactly what. He's lying, too."

"Amzi, you can't be sure of that."

"He knows somethin' about Kep; I'm sure of it. And now, so does Sadie."

"Sadie may be telling the truth. It wouldn't be good to try to force anything from her."

"Tell Semmy Lou I need to see her. Now."

Semmy Lou answered all Amzi's questions. She had seen Kep and Sadie holding hands. They'd gone off alone together. Yes, she'd seen that herself. But no, she'd never seen them try to hide a conversation. Nothing that looked like they were plotting anything together.

For the rest of the week, Amzi stewed over what Sadie, Pike, and Semmy Lou had said, doing nothing, mulling over options and possibilities. The following Sunday, at church, several Methodists stood around Hugh Pike, keeping their distance from the Presbyterians. The Presbyterians likewise kept their distance. But the two groups couldn't avoid all contact with each other, and before they parted company, words were exchanged. Antagonistic words and accusations. Not the sort of thing you expect to hear at church.

That afternoon, at Clear Creek, Amzi told the Colonel and Mrs. Brown what he knew. That Pike and Sadie were lying. That Hugh Pike knew something about Kep, and that was what had made Sadie cry. That something had to be done.

The Colonel offered to speak to Hugh Pike personally, and for three days, Amzi considered what he'd do when the Colonel got to the bottom of things. But at the end of the third day, the Colonel came out to Bynum's Creek to report his judgment: that Pike was telling the truth.

"If you ask me, he doesn't know anything at all about your negro."

It was not what Amzi expected. He knew that Sadie and Pike had been talking about Kep. He confronted Pike again the following Sunday at church. The gossip afterwards, from Long Creek to Oxford, was that Amzi had accused Pike of knowing where Kep had gone; that Pike had denied it, saying that if anyone was an abolitionist, it was Mrs. Byers; and that the two men had nearly come to blows. Friends naturally supported whichever man they knew, and from friends came opposing descriptions of what had occurred. Relations between the Methodists and Presbyterians had never been worse.

The whole time, Eliza made it known that she believed Sadie. That whether Hugh Pike knew anything about Kep or not, he hadn't been talking to Sadie about the boy at church.

"You don't know the negroes like I do," said Amzi.

"Well, I know Kep, and I think I know something about Sadie."

Amzi's brow furrowed, unable to understand what Eliza thought she knew.

The Colonel, meanwhile, had not achieved success without a good sense of politics. One of his fundamental beliefs was that a man cannot be successful if there's disunion among those who support him. Amzi was the Colonel's brother-in-law; Pike was the Colonel's wholesale agent; both were Democrats; both had been supporters. So to no one's surprise, the Colonel kept the feud from boiling over any further. With the wisdom of Solomon, he donated some land for the construction of a new church in Lafayette County, just a mile east of Bynum's Creek. With the Colonel's help, the Presbyterians would be able to worship by themselves.

Everyone agreed about the Colonel's solution to the problem, applauding him for his wisdom and generosity. It would be good for the Presbyterians and Methodists to have their separate churches. 'Good fences make good neighbors' was heard both east and west of the county line.

*   *   *

Land had to be cleared, of course, roots dug up, a foundation laid where moisture wouldn't ruin the plank floor. The walls were fifteen feet tall. The front had two massive entrance doors, one for the right aisle, one for the left. There were three tall windows on the north wall and three more on the south, where the light would enter the church as high as the walls would allow.

Alemeth was standing in the center, in front of where the pulpit was to go, when the last wall was hoisted up around him. Suddenly, the breeze he'd been feeling was gone. Even with six windows and no roof, the church was quiet and dark, the air inside still. Alemeth felt very much alone, and he wondered what the new church would be like, with a building all to themselves.

48

With the new Sand Springs church less than a mile away, there was little reason to leave Bynum's Creek. Reverend Angus Johnson came to the church on Sundays to deliver the sermon. There were no visits to College Hill, and few as far as Oxford. Clear Creek was as far as there was need to go. Amzi thanked the Colonel for the church every time he saw him. In his gratitude he offered to be of service anytime he could.

Before long, the Colonel offered Amzi a loan to start work on a new plantation house at Bynum's Creek. Telling everyone what a generous offer she thought the Colonel had made, Mrs. Brown took the lead in suggesting designs for the house. Next door to the existing cabin, it was going to have three chimneys, a parlor, a dining room, a library, two rooms in the back for Leety and Grote, and six bedrooms upstairs, everything the family could want, large enough for all the children they ever might have, stores enough to let the household be self-sufficient, come what may.

Two years passed. Kep and the problem with Hugh Pike became collective memories, ghosts whose absence was felt only on Sunday afternoons when Eliza taught with no Bible in sight, lest anyone accuse her of teaching the negroes to read. And with little reason to leave Bynum's Creek, the family circle became the people of Sand Springs. Apart from the Byerses, the congregation was related by blood, as well as by faith – kin who'd followed Reverend Johnson from Mecklenburg. There was the matriarch, Narcissa Gray; Narcissa's sons, Charles and Nate Gray; her daughters, Mary Ann Orr and Drucilla Weir; her niece, Jane Spears. With their spouses and numerous children, the families of Grays, Orrs, Weirs and Spears were a close knit congregation with a single history, and (as far as any of them knew) a single set of beliefs. Sundays were easy and peaceful again, compared to the days of the union church. Amzi was delighted at the new arrangement, as it allowed him to focus on making the most of his plantation. Eliza, too, was happier.

But if Sand Springs was an enclave of peace, it lay in the center of a world that lay beyond visible horizon, a world connected by steamboats, railroad tracks and telegraph wires. Overland trade and travel had always been slow. But having connected the cities to the great rivers – Philadelphia to the Ohio; Charleston to the Savannah; Jackson to the Mississippi – the railroads were now connecting the Atlantic to the Mississippi; the Gulf of Mexico to the Ohio. The M. & T. was building south, from Memphis through Panola County toward Grenada. The M. C. R. R. would soon connect Oxford to the Memphis and Charleston at Grand Junction, and to the capital. The country was being overlaid by railroad tracks, and along every railroad right of way were telegraph lines to facilitate the movement of the cars and bring the rest of the world closer. Nothing was slow any longer, except a person's own two feet.

Men like James Brown said connections added value for the community. Having a railroad depot in Oxford would facilitate the export of cotton. It would enable the import of manufactured goods from all over the world. Having the depot at the University's doorstep would make it easy for students, and their families, and lecturers, and supplies, to come and go. And so, with Colonel Brown's support, the Trustees approved a right of way at the edge of the campus, on which to build a railroad depot.

The Colonel was also acutely aware of his responsibility to seek what he could for himself and his household. By the spring of 1856, he had bought several lots for himself, next to the depot site. If the railroad and telegraph were going to connect Oxford to the rest of the civilized world, the Colonel intended to be at the heart of that connection.

*   *   *

Years had passed since Alemeth had first affirmed the beliefs that joined him to the rest of his family. On Sunday mornings at Sand Springs, he now listened to the sermons of Reverend Johnson with Charlie Orr and Ben Spears; on Sunday afternoons, he helped with lessons at the negro Sunday School; the rest of the week, he listened to Amzi, Uncle Johnson, and Grote, and during the summer months, he did what he could to learn the secrets of the land, the livestock, and the cotton crop.

But unlike the rest of the family, Alemeth had one foot outside the plantation, and outside the congregation at Sand Springs. Five days a week for two winters, he left the enclave at Bynum's Creek to attend Mount Sylvan. And much as he'd have liked to be elsewhere, much as he longed to be fishing, or following the blue jay in the windowsill, he did his best to keep up with his studies. Thanks to Reverend Vrooman's efforts, Alemeth eventually grasped the basics of Archimedes' lever and Newton's apple. He'd always had an interest in how things work, and in time, math and mechanics began to come easier. As for old artists and philosophers – the letters of Cicero, the *Anabasis* of Xenophon, or the tragedies of Shakespeare – Gordon made sure Alemeth understood enough to get by. And while Charlie Orr and Ben Spears were nice enough fellows, Gordon became Alemeth's closest friend.

As graduation neared, the Gordon and the other seniors at Mount Sylvan spoke of the future, of attending college. Alemeth wasn't sure he could keep his nose in a book for four more years. Eliza wanted him to attend the seminary in Huntsville. Amzi wanted him to stay at Bynum's Creek. Colonel

Brown – careful not to interfere with either Amzi's or Eliza's desires – told Alemeth that if he wasn't ready to attend the University he might consider a career in the railroads; the Colonel could get him a position with the M. C. R. R.

Alemeth dodged being pinned down, unsure who he agreed with, unsure what he himself wanted to do.

As it happens, it was another visit from Mary Ann Webster that sprung the catch of Alemeth's indecision. She came to visit Clear Creek that spring from Carondelet, and on the occasion of her visit, the Browns invited the Byerses for Sunday dinner. Alemeth was happy that Eliza would cancel Negro Sunday school for the occasion. More than that, he was anxious to see if Mary Ann was still the girl she'd been three years before – the same who'd given him her bookmark, to remember her by.

When dinner came, he got something of his answer right away. Mary Ann, now an attractive young lady, was as talkative as ever. Among the usual reports about people's health, marriages, births and deaths, she brought news of the hubbub in St. Louis over the Blow brothers' lawsuit.

"Oh, dear me, it's been the talk of the town. Passers-by in the streets, total strangers, applauding Julia or insulting her, depending on their views about slavery. It's simply terrible. It's not as if Julia or William have anything to do with his brothers' views. The way feelings on the subject are so strong, it's a wonder no one's been killed."

"I agree," said Mrs. Brown.

"It makes you wonder where the country's headed. Insurrection in Kansas. Women's Rights conventions in New York. The Whigs endorsing the Know Nothings. There's always something in the news. How about you, Alemeth. Have you pursued your interest in the newspaper business?"

The newspaper business? He'd forgotten the little white lie he'd once told her, that he was interested in the newspaper business. But Mary Ann Webster seemed to forget nothing. He'd given no thought to the newspaper business in years. He hardly knew what to say. In the gap left by his silence, others didn't hesitate to speak.

"Oh?" asked Mrs. Brown. "I didn't know you were interested in the newspaper business, Alemeth."

"Neither did I," said Amzi.

"Newspapers," said the Colonel, nodding. "Very important to the community. Indeed, important to the nation. If you like, I can have a talk with Judge Ballard, over at *The Star*. He's a good friend of mine."

"Oh, Alemeth! What a wonderful opportunity!"

Mary Ann was smiling, imploring him to be all that he could be. And in a rush of unfamiliar sensations, he wanted to be whatever she wanted him to be.

"Would you like that?" asked the Colonel.

He looked at Amzi, but Amzi was just looking at *him*.

"Yes, or no?"

"Yes," he said at last. "It would be good of you to talk to him, Colonel Brown. Thank you."

The Colonel put a big arm around his shoulder.

"I'm happy for you, son."

It was awkward, being in the Colonel's arm, in front of Pa and Mary Ann.

"You don't mind if I call you 'son,' do you? I always regretted not having one of my own. You don't mind, do you, Amzi?"

It would prove to be a turning point in Alemeth's life. Coming under the Colonel's wing would lead to other things. But at the time, Alemeth was focused less on the future than the present, less on the newspaper business than on Mary Ann Webster. He had said what he'd said because of her, and he wanted to reap the rewards of his decision. He'd have liked to take a walk with her. But keeping his big arm firmly around Alemeth's shoulder, the Colonel walked onto the porch. He had Harl bring out cigars. The women stayed inside, in the parlor. Having watched Gordon as much as he had, Alemeth managed to smoke a cigar without choking on it. But it was the end of the evening before he was able to escape from the men, and find his way back to her. And by that time, there was no time for more than a brief, hurried good night.

The next day, after school, he dropped by Clear Creek, hoping there'd be another exchange of gifts, or at least some sort of special moment before Mary Ann left for St. Louis. But Emily said Harl had already taken her and Mrs. Brown to Oxford, for the stage. And no, she had left nothing for him, not even a message.

Back at Bynum's Creek, he looked again at the book mark she'd once given him and wondered what it meant that, this time, she'd left with no special good bye.

Then, a few days later, Colonel Brown said he'd arranged a meeting with Judge Ballard. He would meet Alemeth at Mount Sylvan after school. They'd ride down to Panola together, and see about getting Alemeth started in the newspaper business.

49

The *Panola Star* was a joint venture of two lawyers, Barton Ballard, the magistrate judge, and his law partner, Martin Ward; the presses were in the back room of their law offices. Ballard and Ward agreed to give Alemeth a trial apprenticeship, limited to Saturdays, until school was out. On his first day at work, Alemeth learned that a pressman, Jim Horton, actually printed and distributed the paper. While Alemeth helped distribute it, Horton described how the paper was produced. When they were finished, back at the office, Horton showed him the cast iron Columbian press and explained how it worked. And that was it. Horton said he was ready to call it a week.

Delivering newspapers wasn't likely to impress Mary Ann Webster, so Alemeth asked if he could come in earlier the next week, to help Horton run the press. The following Friday night, after supper, he took the buckboard back to Panola and helped Horton run the Columbian. It was heavy work, but it felt good. Mesmerizing. Hundreds of sheets of newsprint, one sheet identical to the next, running off the press. He slept on a law office couch. The next morning, after delivering another issue, Alemeth drove home tired and sore, but a little pleased with himself.

As soon as Eliza saw him, she scolded him.

"Alemeth! Would you look at yourself? You won't be able to afford work at *The Star* if you ruin your trousers every week."

Alemeth looked down to see black ink all over his hands and black lines on the thighs of his pants. Amzi just looked at him, shaking his head. No questions about the press, or the paper, or even how he'd gotten ink all over himself. Just a scolding. Just a shaking of the head.

So much for curiosity. His own excitement was something he'd have to keep to himself.

The following Friday night, he helped Horton again, and Saturday morning, helped him distribute again, and when they were back at the office, Horton asked Alemeth if he could stay a while longer. He readily agreed.

"Come here," said Horton. "You need to know about setting type."

From a slot in a maple letter case, Horton removed a tiny cast metal block, holding it up for Alemeth to see. On the face of the block was a single letter: I.

"This is called a sort," he said. "See those pieces over there?" Horton pointed to the galley. "The pieces we ran last night need to be broken down. The sorts need to be put back in the letter cases."

Alemeth spent the rest of the day moving sorts from the galley to their proper compartments in the letter cases. Though the arrangement of the letters made no sense at first, in just a few hours, he had the boxes memorized – capital letters at the right of the case, small at the left; large boxes for frequently used letters like *e*'s and *i*'s, small boxes for the uncommon *x*'s and *q*'s. Before long his motions were rhythmic and smooth, like letting out a line behind a moving skiff. The following week, he broke down the galleys again. Speed and accuracy improved. Before long, Alemeth's return of the sorts to their cases was almost as fast as Horton's.

For several weeks that spring, Alemeth spent his days looking forward to Friday nights with Jim Horton. The materials provided by Mr. Ward covered a burglary at Benjamin Brown's grocery store and a speech by Henry Ward Beecher. *The Star* announced its support of Millard Fillmore and the American Party (the Know-Nothings). At the end of April, it reported the damage from a storm that had passed over. *The Star*, Alemeth discovered, was actually interesting. He developed the habit of reading the articles. He asked questions of Horton and Ward. Back at Bynum's Creek, when Eliza or Uncle Johnson wondered what was going on in the world, Alemeth often knew. His job at *The Star* became a source of pleasure and pride.

*   *   *

At the end of May, Mr. Ward asked Alemeth to read a piece he'd written about some shootings in Kansas. Five people had been killed. The abolitionists had cut pro-slavery men to pieces with swords in the middle of the night. Mary Ann Webster's prediction that people might start getting killed over slavery was coming true. Mr. Ward asked Alemeth what he thought.

"Terrible," he said to Mr. Ward. "What happened, I mean."

"Terrible, indeed," said Mr. Ward, taking the manuscript back. Ward then wrote out a headline in capital letters at the top of the page:

WAR IN KANSAS

"What do you think of the headline?"

He mulled it over.

"You call it a war. Does killing five people make something a war?"

Mr. Ward smiled as if a prediction had just come true.

"John, my boy, it's not just five people. There've been more than a dozen people killed in the last two years. But let me tell you something important about the newspaper business. Even if it was only two people, I'd call it a war. Good journalism depends on there being a story. And story with no point of view is a sorry story indeed. There's no point printing a paper no one's going to read. Consider that your first lesson, if you really want to be a newspaperman."

That night, Alemeth thought more about what Ward had said. He'd always liked a good story. Maybe, that was why he liked *The Star*. It seemed, in any case, that the right decision about his own future was apparent. Graduation from Mount Sylvan would mean the end of school and time to work more at *The Star*. *A newspaper man*. Taking out pen and paper, he began a letter to Mary Ann Webster.

He'd gotten a job in the newspaper business, he wrote. He was helping Mr. Ward keep the people of Panola informed about the world. The killings in Kansas were evidence of how deep feelings ran, across the country. She'd been right to predict that things were headed in that direction. He saw the world much as she did. He hoped that all was going well for her personally, and he'd be pleased if she saw fit to favor him with a reply.

He looked for her reply every day. But none was forthcoming. Every day he wondered why she hadn't written, and what could explain her lack of interest.

Graduation from Mount Sylvan came and went. With no word from Mary Ann, and with Gordon making plans to attend the University, Alemeth was lost. Amzi took it for granted that, when graduation came, he would return to work on the plantation. Now, the sorts, broken down from the galleys, became senseless things, with no more meaning than if they'd been spilled on the floor. The newspaper business was little better than life at Bynum's Creek.

The following week, Jim Horton was rifling through a letter case, one of Mr. Ward's manuscripts in hand, when he muttered something about runaway slaves. Alemeth thought he heard the word "shooting." Kep was the only runaway Alemeth had ever known. Could anyone have wanted to shoot Kep?

Horton motioned for him to approach.

"Come here, Alemeth. Watch me." Horton took a sort from the upper case with his right hand. "This," he said, looking pointedly toward his left hand, "is a composing stick. You set the sorts in the composing stick. Here. Look."

Horton demonstrated the motion, then held the stick out to Alemeth.

"It's just a metal slide. Here, look: a screw tightens the knee."

Alemeth took the stick in his left hand, rolled it over, feeling its weight, and handed it back to Horton, who glanced at the manuscript, then delved into the letter case, removing sorts with his right fingers and adding them to the stick he held in his left.

"When you set the letters," he said over his shoulder, "you have to set them backwards and upside down. Watch this."

He set several lines. Then, grasping them at the margin, he transferred them to a larger frame, which he held for examination by both of them:

IMPORTANT DECISION

Overseers, and Owners of Slaves would do
well to read and remember the following
important decision.

The High Court of Errors and Appeals of
Mississippi have decided that an act of homicide committed upon a negro slave, merely
because he runs to avoid capture, cannot be
justified by any principle of morality, of law,
or of policy, growing out of the institution of
slavery. The Court held the killer of the slave
liable in such a case to the owner for damages.

"It looks like Greek."

"That's alright," said Horton. "Just watch." He laid the frame in the galley of the proof press, blocked it in, and rolled it with ink. Placing a sheet of paper between two guideposts, he drew the roller across the galley. When he lifted the piece of paper and examined its underside, the finished piece made sense:

IMPORTANT DECISION

Overseers, and Owners of Slaves would do well to read and remember the following important decision.

The High Court of Errors and Appeals of Mississippi have decided that an act of homicide committed upon a negro slave, merely because he runs to avoid capture, cannot be justified by any principle of morality, of law, or of policy, growing out of the institution of slavery. The Court held the killer of the slave liable in such a case to the owner for damages.

So. If one of Amzi's slaves got killed, Amzi would get paid by whoever had killed the slave. It seemed a fair remedy. He gave it no more thought. Rather, he was intrigued by the sorts. He had known them only by size (in points) and where to put them in the letter cases. After seeing the readable print, he looked again at those set in the galley. The words they formed still looked like Greek. How such type could produce intelligible sentences remained an inscrutable mystery.

Then Horton held a mirror to the galley and told him to look at it upside down. He was able to read the piece through the mirror. Even so, he could not read the sorts directly. He imagined himself standing apart from himself, looking back in the direction of his eyes, through the metal from the other side. Still, without the help of the mirror, the meaning of the words defied him.

The next week, Horton asked if he'd like to compose some type of his own. Reluctant at first, he eventually gave it a try. It didn't take much time to 'think backwards,' as Horton called it. Within an hour, Alemeth was wondering how the task could have seemed so hard. Even his speed at returning the sorts to the cases improved, as he saw the sorts as parts of words and unwrapped them from the back end to the beginning, mentally deconstructing.

"You know," said Mr. Ward, "a typesetter has a hand in what people read. Setting the type means bringing information to the people of Mississippi. It's a part of the spread of knowledge."

He paused.

"John, an ambitious young man could do a lot worse than the newspaper business. If you're interested, we could use another hand around here. Would you like to learn to set type?"

Of course, there was only one possible answer for that. It looked easy enough. It wouldn't be hard to get good at it. He could become a real newspaperman, without ever attending the University. Mary Ann would have to notice, then.

His efforts came out far from perfect at first. A *p* and a *q* are hard to tell apart when one of them is upside down. Horton's warnings didn't keep him from confusing his *n*'s and *u*'s, his *b*'s and *d*'s. But over the days that followed, he practiced whenever he could. Before long, he amazed himself at the speed with which he was able to set type.

When Horton said he was ready, Alemeth composed his first piece: a report for the number of June 21st. The Mississippi & Tennessee Railroad announced that it had begun taking passengers and freight from Memphis as far as Hernando, Mississippi. Except for Mr. Ward himself, Alemeth was the first person in the county to read the news. And he had actually set the type by which everyone in the county would learn of it.

It was a far cry from building a pyramid or a Parthenon. But it was enough to be a reminder that he was part of a bigger world. He had a hand in making a written record. A role in the creation of *The Panola Star*.

Later that week, after Mr. Ward made a comment about the power of the modern printing press, Alemeth said to him, "I wonder if someday people will read newspapers like they read the Bible."

Mr. Ward looked puzzled. "What do you mean?"

"I mean, someday, maybe people will look back at newspapers as a sort of scripture. As a source of *truth*."

It was a grandiose thing to say. Had he sounded pompous?

"Scripture is scripture because it's the word of God," said Mr. Ward.

"I know. I'm not saying we're like God. But we *are* making a record of history."

"Scripture isn't scripture just because it's the word of God," said Mr. Ward. "It's also because it's been around since Moses. Practically the beginning. Newspapers will never be that. Think about it, John. We use the cheapest wood-pulp paper around. People crumple it up and use it to kindle their fires. It's gone within days of printing. It's hardly more permanent than conversation."

Alright. So it wasn't scripture. But still, when something is written down and printed, to be read by hundreds or even thousands of people, it could have an impact on the world.

Horton congratulated him.

"You know what you are now, don't you?"

"What. A newspaper man?"

Horton laughed. "My goodness, no. You're a far cry from a newspaper man. But you're a printer's devil, at least."

"A what?"

"A printer's devil. A printer's assistant. Everybody calls it that — everybody but Mr. Ward, that is. He doesn't like the name."

He didn't think Eliza would like it either. But he was beginning to realize: being a printer's devil was about the most exciting thing he'd ever done, and he began to imagine what his future would be like, and whether someday he'd be able to call himself a newspaper man.

50

At Panola's Independence Day celebration, the band played rousing marches that had everyone in the street moving together. Mr. Ward gave a speech about the blessings of liberty and the thanks everyone owed for it. People sang:

Our fathers' God, to Thee,
Author of Liberty,
To thee we sing,
Long may our land be bright
With Freedom's holy light.
Protect us by thy might,
Great God, our King.

Liberty. Freedom. Alemeth tasted something dear. Standing next to Mr. Ward, he felt he *was* somebody. One more good thing *The Star* had brought.

After the speeches, there was a fireworks display that lit up the sky with colored bursts. Between the fireworks, adults introduced themselves as if he were one of them. People treated him like he was something more than a child.

After the display, there was music and dancing at the Planter's Hotel, and after Rebecca Rayburn, in behalf of the organizing committee, thanked all the farmers and their wives for coming out for the sake of a unified community, Gordon Falkner appeared, as if out of nowhere.

"Why, Alemeth Byers, I thought I'd find you here."

"Gordon, my friend – what brings you down to Panola?"

Gordon looked straight at him, then purposefully down at his own waist, uncovering the top of a metal flask.

"Whiskey?"

"Of course."

Gordon took a swallow from the flask and offered it to Alemeth. Remembering Uncle Johnson's whiskey, Alemeth braced for the taste, planning to sip the smallest drop. It was surprisingly smooth.

"You like it?"

"I like it."

"I'll tell you something else you'd like, I'll wager."

"What's that?"

"Have another drink first."

He took a breath from the bottle neck. Not bad, really. He took another swallow, feeling the whiskey clean his mouth.

"So. What else do you think I'd like?"

"To spend the night with one of Sally Wiley's friends."

Alemeth laughed and took another swig, feeling like someone else entirely.

* * *

The next day, in a hazy blur, he remembered only that while dancing with a young lady – her hair long, red and silky – he had fallen down, attracting a great deal of attention. By the time he regained himself, the young lady had disappeared. Gordon had gotten him home, somehow. And from the smoky, dull, deadening ache in his head, he heard Amzi in the next room:

"So, Eliza, *this* is the town life your sister says is so good for the boy? To spend his time getting drunk? Making a spectacle of himself?"

"I agree with you, Amzi. But it won't help anything if we're too hard on him. We ought to be praying the Lord keeps him safe from temptation. From the influence of those who've fallen prey to the devil."

51

Though it took some doing, Alemeth eventually got Amzi to agree he could stay on at *The Star* – as long as he worked four days a week at Bynum's Creek and promised not to get drunk any more. The arrangement had its advantages, but it left him close to Eliza, and her nearness didn't endear her. She had scripture for everything, Godliness and cleanliness always on her mind, and him around ink all day, with the inevitable conflict that guaranteed.

The new plantation house was nearly finished. With everyone else saying how nice it was turning out, she could have been happy with it, but she seemed not to care. She was always thinking of "the battle for men's souls," and these days, spoke often of Lyman Beecher's sermons about the war being fought in the halls of higher education. Now, she said, the war was being fought at the University of Mississippi. Reverend Longstreet had resigned. To replace him, the Trustees had appointed neither Reverend Waddel (a Presbyterian) nor Reverend Carter (a Methodist), but Frederick Barnard, a professor of *astronomy*. Eliza wasted no time expressing her dismay to Mary Ann and Colonel Brown.

"For all one can tell, astronomy is his *only* interest in the heavenly domain."

"At least he's a man of the cloth," Mary Ann said in defense of the Trustees' selection.

"But an *Episcopal priest*," countered Eliza. "Whose ordination came only *after* his arrival in Oxford — as if a new collar could make up for a lifetime of secular pursuits! And if that isn't cause enough for concern, I've heard he has a drinking problem."

*   *   *

In the composing room, Mr. Ward handed Alemeth a letter.

"This piece speaks for itself. Set it as it is. But tell me, John, who do you think this letter's about?"

The letter was addressed to Mr. Ward. But when Alemeth got to the words "Bynum's Creek," he stopped short. Mr. Ward was not smiling.

"I don't know."

"Is that so… Well. I have business to attend to. Have the piece proofed by the time I return."

So Alemeth set the type as Mr. Ward instructed: exactly as he read it. The implications of its reference to Bynum's Creek struck him hard.

MR. WARD : --

I have been informed that there is among us, in our own county, at Bynum's Creek, one of the vilest Abolitionist that ever lived. Why don't the citizens call a meeting, and appoint a committee to invite the gentleman to leave. He is advocating his doctrine, and has been known to credit the meanest negro in the country, in preference to a responsible white man.

A SLAVE-HOLDER
Long Creek, Miss.

An abolitionist at Bynum's Creek? Who? Besides Pa and Uncle Johnson, who was there? Charlie Morgan? Effie Adams? Alva Middleton? None of them were abolitionists. They *couldn't* be.

Meanwhile, the letter wasn't signed. Who could have written it? Long Creek didn't have many more people than Bynum's Creek did. It could only have been written by a few people. But who?

*   *   *

When Mr. Ward got back, Alemeth asked, "Do you really need to print that letter?"

"Yes, of course."

"What if it's not true? It could hurt someone's reputation."

Mr. Ward opened a humidor, retrieving a cigar and a match.

"John, I don't know what the problem is down there at Bynum's Creek." He lit the cigar and took a puff.

"And I hope there isn't any truth to what folks are saying. But let me tell you something about the newspaper business." He held the cigar in front of him. "If a newspaper is to do right by its readers, it has to report the news without regard to who it might hurt. You understand?"

Mr. Ward's eyes told the rest of the story. Until the real culprit was identified, everyone at Bynum's Creek would be suspect.

When Alemeth got home, out of breath, Amzi, Eliza and Uncle Johnson were sitting together on the porch. He had to let them know.

"There's a letter gonna be printed in tomorrow's *Star*. Says there's an abolitionist that lives at Bynum's Creek. 'Vilest Abolitionist ever lived.' Says the man ought to be run out of town, for takin' the word of a negro over a white man."

Amzi just stared at him.

"It was written from Long Creek. Signed *Slave-Holder*."

Amzi and Eliza looked at each other.

"Alemeth, hold on. Are you sure the letter said Bynum's Creek?"

"Yes, sir."

Amzi looked up in the air, shaking his head.

"Amzi," asked Eliza, "who do you suppose it is?"

"If there's an abolitionist around here, it's Hugh Pike. He must be talking about Hugh Pike."

"I think he's talking about me," said Uncle Johnson.

"Oh really? Why's that?"

"I was over at Long Creek just a few days ago, at Murdock's place."

"What business did you have with Murdock?"

Uncle Johnson looked Amzi over.

"Annie came to me a few days back. All in tears. She had bruises on her face. Turns out, she and some of the other negroes were over to Long Creek when Murdock came on to her."

Amzi's ears perked up. Alemeth's too. Everybody looked at everybody else.

"So I went over to Long Creek to talk to Murdock about it."

"What on earth did you say to him?"

"What do you *think* I said to him? I told him we'd all be better off if he left our negroes alone."

"And?"

"He denied doing anything to Annie. Anything at all."

Uncle Johnson's elbows were already on the tabletop. Now he laid his palms on it too, and leaned just a little toward Amzi.

"Now, I know my Annie, Amzi. I'm telling you, she wasn't making this up. She'd have no reason to say anything against Murdock, if it wasn't true."

"I don't see why you couldn't just let it drop, Johnson."

"Amzi, I couldn't do that. Are you sure you know Murdock?"

"Of course I do. He can be difficult at times, but he's not a bad man."

"You know what he said to me? He said, 'All your niggers' must be trouble. 'First one runs away. Next you practically take up house with one. Now she goes around making up lies.'"

Silence. All eyes on Johnson. Johnson looking at Amzi.

"He says we don't know how to treat our negroes. He said we're taking the word of a 'nigger' over the word of a white man."

Eliza's eyes opened wide. She looked at Amzi. "I guess people will be talking about this."

Amzi shook his head. "We don't need this right now, Johnson." He stood up and stepped toward the porch stairs. "I'm going for a walk."

(If there was one thing Amzi never did, it was go for a walk.)

At Sand Springs the next Sunday, everyone was talking about the letter printed in *The Star*. Ben Spears wanted to know if Amzi had written it about Hugh Pike. "Everybody's sayin' so," he said. Alemeth told Ben it was written by somebody from Long Creek. For a few days, if anybody thought the letter was about Uncle Johnson, no one said so. But on Thursday, Mr. Murdock and Mr. Cansler came to the offices of Ballard and Ward, and after they'd left, Mr. Ward came into the printing room and sat on one of the stools.

"John, tell me. Is it true you have an uncle who's a Congressman? From Pennsylvania?"

"No, I –"

On second thought, Mrs. Brown had a cousin who was a Congressman. If Mrs. Brown did, then Eliza did too.

"I think, maybe. Miss – Mrs. Byers's cousin. Why?"

Mr. Ward threw papers that slid across the table.

"It's another letter," said Mr. Ward. "I found it under the door when I came in this morning. It encloses an article from a newspaper in Pennsylvania."

Mr. Ward:

William Strong, the Congressman mentioned, is the cousin of Mrs. Amzi Byers of Bynum's Creek.

— A slave holder.

Long Creek.

The clipping was from the Gazette. It said that Eliza's cousin, the Honorable William Strong, was "one of our more outspoken abolitionist Congressmen."

Alemeth looked up at Mr. Ward.

"John, I know good and well a woman can't control what her cousins will do. On the other hand, I don't know if your mother is like some of those other Yankee schoolteachers. But I can tell you one thing for sure: your family has made some enemies. And without casting judgment on it one way or another, I'd offer a piece of advice: you just might want to start seeing things the way other folks see them."

That night at supper, sharing with the family the new letter and what Mr. Ward had said, there was tension such as he'd never seen. Eliza said, *Yes,* one of Uncle William's sons had gone to Congress. And *Yes,* he had spoken of the evils of slavery. Amzi looked ready to kill.

"First Uncle Johnson, and now you, Eliza. My whole family's falling apart on me."

"Me, Amzi? The article's about my cousin. I hardly knew him."

"The letter's about you, Eliza. See *there*?" He pointed a finger. "'*Mrs. Amzi Byers.*' And you know where it started."

"I do?"

"Your teaching the negroes to read. And filling Kep's head with all sorts of ideas."

"Amzi, I haven't taught any negroes to read. Not since Kep disappeared. You can't fault me for teaching the Bible."

"Eliza. You don't just teach negroes. You ask them to ask more negroes to your meetings. Admit it. The numbers were growing."

"We lost them all, when folks made them stay away."

"That's just the point, Eliza."

It didn't get better from there. Amzi was angry, and in the end, he said "Next time, by God, I'll do what I know to be right, and I won't take my time about it!" Alemeth decided Amzi's anger wasn't all bad – when it wasn't directed at him.

*   *   *

The day after that was a scorcher. There'd been no rain since the middle of June, and the soil had already turned to powder. (According to *The Star's* report, the streets were six inches deep with dust.) In the fields, the hands had to wrap wet scarves across their mouths to keep from inhaling the worst of it. One after another, they had to be sent to their cabins to recover. And in all the dust, and heat, and illness, Amzi moved his family – and all his household possessions – from the old house to the new.

It was another week before the rain finally came, and everybody started to breathe easy again – everybody but Amzi, that is. Amzi had come down with a fever.

"Alemeth," he said, his coughs coming up in thick spurts that he caught in his throat and spat out. "I need you to go down to McGuire's and get me something for my throat. Here's two dollars."

M. J. M c G U I R E

Druggist and Apothecary.

OXFORD, MISS.

INVITES the attention of the public to his stock, embracing every article pertaining to his line, viz:

White Lead and Zinc,

Paints, generally Oils, Varnishes, Putty, and Perfumery, Snuffs, Pens, Sealing wax, Lead and Slate, Shaving Creams, Rosin, Blacking, &c., &c.

B A R K S .

Cinchona, Bayberry, Cinnamon, Ash, Orange, &c.

S E E D S .

Anise, Cardamom, Colchicum, Lobelia, Coriander, Caroway, Canary, Flax, &c

R O O T S .

Columbo, Ginseng, Sarsaparilla, Snake, (various kinds), Golden seal, Blood, Hydrastis, May Apple, &c.

F O L I A G E .

Senna, Buchu, Uva Ursi, Digitalis, &c.

Chemicals, Acids, Ethers.

Acetic, Benzoic, Citric, Muriate, Nitric, Oxalic, Sulphuric, Tannic, Tartaric, Chloroform, &c.

CALOMEL, BLUE MASS, QUININE.

WINES AND SPIRITS

For Medicinal Purposes.

Malaga, Madeira, Port, Sherry, Jamaica and Bay Rum, Holland Gin, Wolfe's Schiedam Schnapps; all kinds of Cordials; Whiskey, Bourbon, and Dexter's.

WINDOW GLASS, *of all sizes.*

The above being only a general list, a great many other articles usually found in a retail

Drug Establishment,

may be found in his stock, all of which will be sold on the very lowest terms for cash.   M. J. McGUIRE.

Aug. 28, 1856.

52

Leety put the ginseng and cinnamon in Amzi's tea, but it didn't help; it just kept him awake. He took the quinine, but that was bitter and made his ears ring. To keep from spreading his noxious vapors in the new house, Amzi stayed outside all day. At night he slept at the old house. At Leety's suggestion he drank lots of water, and when he made his own water, he used the outhouse rather than the new built-in bathroom.

His illness wasn't the only reason Amzi didn't feel comfortable in the new house. There were two porcelain sinks in the kitchen. Windows that slid up and down. Mrs. Brown's architect had put in so much that was modern, it could have been a European palace, as far as Amzi was concerned. It seemed snobbish, all for show. He wanted no part of such pretensions. He stayed outside when he could, and slept in his old cabin, where things were simple and familiar.

But the cough subsided and, persuaded by Eliza, he started, gradually, to live inside. And as he did so, his perspective started to change. To reach his new bedroom, he ascended a stairway. At the top of the stairway was a landing and a balcony. And as he gained experience with the new perspective, he found that by standing on the balcony, he could watch people below without their seeing him. The situation turned out to be very advantageous. From time to time, the mere glimpse of a hat or ruffled head of hair allowed him to choose who to converse with and who to avoid. As the days passed, he began to feel good about his balcony, and the rest of his new keep.

That's why the beat riders bothered him so.

They'd been welcome the first time. Eliza had shown them around the new house like guests at a Sunday social. But when they started coming back every other day or so, asking about the negroes, looking around the house as if there might be something hidden away somewhere, there was nothing social about it.

He didn't need Sheriff Starr coming onto *his* property, checking up on *his* negroes. He could take care of his own plantation. He didn't need anyone meddling in his affairs – least of all someone who thought he had a right to tell him what to do.

53

... [T]he introduction of slavery amongst us was, in the providence of God, who makes the evil passions of men subservient to His own glory, a means of placing that unhappy race within the pale of civilized nations.

— Scott vs. Emerson, 15 Missouri 576 (S. Ct. Mo, 1852)

The tension at Bynum's Creek over slavery was mirrored by tensions elsewhere in Mississippi. Outside the press room one day, Mr. Ward and Mr. Ballard started arguing about the case Mary Ann Webster had described in her letters – the one that had given Julia and William Blow such notoriety in Carondelet. The argument between Ballard and Ward was not whether negroes were the equals of whites. On that point, Ballard and Ward were agreed. (Their common answer was 'obviously not.') Rather, Ballard and Ward were divided on three main questions:

1) whether American law followed the English common law,
2) if it did, whether anything in Blackstone supported slavery, and
3) whether slavery really did exist for the benefit of the African race.

It was all civil at first. They talked to each other the way they talked to each other in the courtroom, making their points in due course and pointing out passages of the court's opinion like preachers pointing to scripture. But as the argument kept on, things began to get heated. Each of the men ended up with a hand on a copy of the court's decision. Like two dogs on the ends of a bone, they started snarling at each other. When Ward accused Ballard of thrusting a finger into Ward's face and Ballard denied it, Ward thrust one back at his partner, and it was only when Ward said, "I suppose we should be gentlemen" that Ballard held back his loaded fist.

The next day, the men avoided each other. Not long after that, Mr. Ballard gave up his financial interest in *The Star.* And as sure as water flows downhill, the next day, Mr. Ward called Alemeth into his office.

"I'm sorry, John. But I'm afraid your services will no longer be required."

Was it the letter about abolitionists at Bynum's Creek? The fact that Alemeth had been brought in by Judge Ballard? Mr. Ward didn't have to give a reason, and refused to do so.

Later, when Alemeth told Amzi and asked if they might talk to Judge Ballard, there was a long pause.

"Alemeth, there's lots of things that can make an idea wrong. Lots of reasons things don't always work out. I never did think much of that foolishness with the lawyers and their newspaper. I've been trying to get you to understand, son: *this* is where you belong; right here, at Bynum's Creek, where you have a Pa that wants to teach you how a man should live."

Alemeth wondered if Pa was right. That he wasn't meant to be a newspaperman. That he should keep his mind on the plantation, and on making it everything it could be.

But as time passed, he found it easier said than done.

If he ever got his hands dirty, Eliza or Mrs. Brown got upset with him. And if he tried to make any decisions on the grounds, like telling negroes what to do, Amzi was as likely as not to tell the negroes to do something else. Wandering the plantation, he looked for a way to be useful. Some days, he tried to get away, just so he wouldn't feel out of place – sneak off – go swimming or fishing – but even that had started to make him feel guilty. He knew he was supposed to be doing something else.

Meanwhile, it wasn't only Ballard and Ward arguing. Amzi and Hugh Pike didn't have a good thing to say about each other. Uncle Johnson and Jim Murdock went at it like fighting cocks, and so did Dr. Isom and Al Cansler. All over Panola and Lafayette counties, ill feelings crossed aisles. And when people found it better to spend time with those who thought as they did, they naturally avoided the ill feelings of those in other churches. And if there weren't always ill feelings, there were often suspicions, and if not suspicions, then doubts about where a person stood – doubts that could give rise to suspicions soon enough. It was pretty much the same everywhere. By the time Ben Spears asked if Alemeth was an abolitionist, it was a question that Alemeth felt he had disprove, the quicker the better.

And when he went swimming, even the fish seemed to look at him differently, as if accusing him, as if wanting to attack him. Pulled out of the water, catfish protested that they belonged beneath the surface. It was wrong to bring them into the air, they screamed. They couldn't possibly survive out of the depths into which God had put them. Alemeth wrestled with the arguments, pro and con. The surface of the water became a wall that divided two worlds from each other.

Then one of Bill Starr's boys called Semmy Lou a 'nigger lover,' to her face, in front of several friends. The next time Starr came out to the house, Amzi confronted him about it.

"Just because Semmy Lou went to one of Eliza's negro classes?"

"No," said Starr. "My boy saw her down at the creek with one of Al Cansler's negro boys."

"How old was the boy?"

"Twelve, but he's a big boy."

Amzi nodded and managed thanks through unclenched teeth.

"Amzi, as for your missus's Sunday School with those niggers. It's legal, as long as she and some other respectable white person is with them."

"What?"

"Any gathering of five negroes is against the law – *unless* it's for Bible study. And that means *only* for Bible study. I hope that's all your missus has been doing down there."

"Bill, I can assure you, all she's doing is teaching Christian values."

"You also need to remember the proviso."

"The proviso?"

"The proviso. Even when Negros meet about the Bible – and I mean *only* about the Bible – there's got to be two reliable white people there. All the time. You or your brother had best be there, or it's against the law. And there are folks who'd argue that your brother can't be considered 'responsible' – not after that business with Murdock."

"I've got my son there with her, all the time."

"A *reliable* white person, Amzi. Your son is – how old?

"Twenty."

"Not even legal age."

"He's responsible."

The sheriff looked at Alemeth and took a long, slow breath.

"Alright, then. But remember, Amzi. I'm sworn to enforce the law. If the boy gets sick, you or your brother had best be there, or there is no school. *Two reliable* white people, Amzi. Remember that. And *nothing* but the Bible."

"I hear you. Thanks for letting me know about Semmy Lou."

That afternoon, Amzi asked Semmy Lou what she'd been doing down at the creek with Al Cansler's boy. Semmy insisted she'd never been down at the creek with any of Al Cansler's boys. Amzi said she'd better not be lying. And he'd better not find out she'd been spending time with *any* colored boys.

That night, Alemeth was already in bed when Amzi appeared in the doorway.

"Alemeth, I need to ask you a question about the negro Sunday School."

"Sure, Pa. What is it?"

""What sort of lessons does Ma give?"

"What do you mean? She talks about the Bible. Abraham, and Jesus."

"She doesn't talk about slavery?"

"No."

"Good. Well. If she says anything about – anything Jim Murdock or Bill Starr could make something of – be sure to tell me. Okay?"

"Right, Pa. Of course I will."

54

Mary Jane got engaged to Willie McKie that autumn. The social at which the announcement was made was the sort of occasion Alemeth had always hated: women with parasols for shade, gentlemen with collars and no hats, servants with tea and cakes. Even Gordon was occupied with Sally Wiley. It had all the makings of a long night at Clear Creek.

The back door was wide open. Above chatting voices, he thought he heard a familiar sound. Even before he reached the porch, he could hear Clio and Calliope.

"*Aawwwk*. The Master's gone to sea."

"*Aawwwk*. He'll be back soon."

"Look who we have here."

A man he didn't recognize was talking to the parrots. He was dressed in a black waistcoat. He had a thin, soft face.

"Can you tell me your name?" he asked, through the bars of the parrots' cage.

"The Master's gone to sea."

"I said, can you tell me your name?"

"He'll be back soon. *Aawwwk*."

"Are you listening? Can you tell me your name?"

"*Aawwwk*. Are you listening?"

The man stepped back, eyebrows raised, adjusting an ear piece of his spectacles. He had a bushy beard, but he was hairless above his lips. The hair on his head was thin and wispy, receding above the temples. But what struck Alemeth most was the earnestness with which he was attempting to communicate with the parrots – not trying to get them to repeat what he was saying, but to answer his questions, to test whether they were really thinking for themselves.

The man noticed Alemeth. He smiled. He held out his hand. "Hello. I'm Frederick Barnard." The man was the new President of the University. How strange! "Glad to meet you." A long pause. "And your name?"

"I'm John Alemeth Byers. I go by Alemeth."

"You said Byers?"

"Yes. Alemeth Byers."

"You're not a student…"

"No. Colonel Brown is an uncle. Sort of."

"Oh. So you are… But no, you're not Colonel Brown's nephew…"

"No. My step-mother is his wife's sister."

"I'm sorry. What did you say?"

"I said my stepmother is THE COLONEL'S WIFE'S SISTER."

"I see, I see. Thank you. I'm partially deaf, you know. But you don't have to shout. It helps if you look at me when you speak. It helps to be able to see your lips."

"Oh."

"I was just having a look at Colonel Brown's parrots."

Barnard rested his chin in the palm of one hand, the elbow in the palm of his other, eyes still fixed on the parrots, thinking. Then he held a forefinger in the air.

"There's one thing I don't like about these birds."

"What's that?"

"No matter how much I try, I can't read their lips."

Could the President of the University really be saying that parrots have lips*???*

Barnard let out an impish chuckle.

"I see I quite got you, young man! Parrots with lips, indeed! But you know, they might as well have, for their ability to emulate speech. Don't you think?"

"I guess…"

"So. You're Mrs. Brown's nephew. I've met Mrs. Brown. Remarkable woman."

"Yeah."

"She can be quite…"

The President seemed to be searching for the right words.

"Persuasive?"

"Yes, exactly! Very well put, my boy! I can see that you're a man who knows how to choose his words!"

He was nothing like Judge Longstreet. Nothing like pompous John Waddell. He was a friendly, unassuming man. He could see Mrs. Brown the way Alemeth saw her. He could see the possibility that a parrot could understand human speech.

Alemeth liked him from the start.

55

NAM MIHI CONTUENTI SEMPER SUASIT RERUM
NATURA NIHIL INCREDIBILE EXISTIMARE DE EA
— Pliny the Elder

With encouragement from the Colonel and Mrs. Brown, and with interest in President Barnard, Alemeth began to attend University events whenever he could. One evening, invited to a social at the Brown's house, Alemeth entered the ante-room to find Dr. Barnard engaged in conversation with Wilson Richardson, professor of ancient languages.

Richardson: "What striking faces!"

Barnard: "Can you see, in the moons of their eyes, the faces of beautiful women?"

"Sirens, you mean?"

"Yes. Precisely."

Professor Richardson peered into Clio's eyes.

"*Aaawwk.*"

"I'm afraid I see no such thing."

"So what is it?" asked Barnard. "What makes them so intriguing?"

"Their colors, I suppose."

"*Aaawwk.*"

"What about their language? Do you suppose they have any idea what any of it means? At some level, I mean. Not as we do, of course."

"Pliny said a parrot not only talks, but knows to salute an emperor."

"Oh really. I dare say, Wilson. Profound."

"They make good pets, he says –"

"*The Master's gone to sea.*"

" – and even better entrees."

"*Aawwwk.*"

"He also said a parrot's head is as hard as its beak, and that in teaching it to talk, you have to beat it with an iron rod."

"*Aaawwk.*"

"Now, I think you've offended her."

"My apologies," said Richardson with exaggerated drama. Then he turned back to Barnard. "Pliny was rather an eccentric, don't you think? I mean, he wrote of things far more bizarre than parrots. Women with two pupils in one eye. Aethiopians twelve feet tall. Races with the heads and tails of dogs."

Dr. Barnard turned to Alemeth. "Being born a freak is actually quite common, you know. Just because you and your neighbors haven't seen some oddity, that doesn't mean it's unknown to nature. We have much yet to learn about the creatures of Java, Borneo, and Sumatra."

"Consider the Circus Maximus," added Richardson. "There were always parrots at the circus. And all sorts of other fantastic creatures. The Romans loved their *mirabilia*."

At that point, Eliza approached the group, not on Amzi's arm, but on that of Captain Edward Boynton. Alemeth had heard about Boynton from Gordon. He was a professor of chemistry, but he liked to be called "Captain" because of his history at West Point.

"And gladiators," interjected Boynton. "Let's not forget the gladiators. The Romans liked nothing better than watching two men fight to the death, or beg for the mercy of Caesar."

"Fascinating," said Eliza. "So, tell me, gentlemen. I've been listening to Captain Boynton's views, and I'd like to hear yours. Was it right that the pagans used slaves as gladiators? That they not only used their slaves for labor, but made them fight, like roosters?"

"Oh dear, Mrs. Byers," said Professor Richardson. "I don't think it was all that bad. The best gladiators were very popular. Famous personalities, with a good life. At least on days they weren't competing."

"*Competing?*" asked Captain Boynton. "That's an interesting choice of words."

"Why so?"

"It makes it sound like the Pan-Athenian Games."

"You think it a poor comparison?"

Disengaging from Eliza, Captain Boynton freed up his hands to move as he spoke. "You're talking about making a man fight to the death – whether he wants to or not."

"Wants to or not, Captain Boynton? The gladiators trained to fight. They competed to be the best. It was a life of glory, fame and honor. They were the Edwin Booths and Anna Mowatts of their day."

"But the gladiators were slaves," said Eliza. "And their fights were to the death."

"They were," said Dr. Richardson. "At least most of them. But it's no demeaning thing, to live in service to a master."

"Oh my God," said Boynton. "I can't believe you're saying that. *Not demeaning*? Where have you been?"

"I think it all depends. Saint Paul –"

"I'd watch my language if I were you, Boynton. *And* my tone. People around here don't take kindly to other people telling them what's right and wrong. If you've got northern sympathies, then perhaps you should take them north when you leave."

"Don't be foolish, Richardson. I'm not going anywhere."

"Don't call me a fool, Boynton."

"I didn't."

"Gentlemen – "

"What? You most certainly did."

"I did not."

"You did, and you're a damned fool if you don't admit it."

"Come now, gentlemen," said Barnard. "Let's not get personal."

Barnard's plea for civility came too late. Richardson and Boynton were already standing toe to toe, and now pressed each other's shoulders with little pushes. There might have been an all-out wrestle had Colonel Brown and Harvey Walter not descended upon the pair, hands out, palms up, saying enough was enough, it was time to stand down before something happened they would all regret.

It was not the sort of conflict Alemeth was used to witnessing at a University event. But he'd been seeing more anger whenever anyone said anything bad about slavery. The common wisdom was in favor of the institution, and more people were getting vocal about it. Anyone seeing a problem with it was treated as a freak, blind to plain common sense. And when such people insisted on making their views known, without regard for the disruption it caused to basic civility, the defenders of common wisdom felt obliged to indict the heretic in the strongest of terms. Isolate the pariah. Keep his damaging views from infecting the rest. To do any less could itself be seen as a sign of doubt on one's part, and there were people saying the matter did not admit of doubt.

It was enough to make Alemeth wonder if people could maintain civility much longer.

President Barnard was different.

"Dear me," he said later. "If people would only behave themselves. To see two grown men go at it the way those two did, well – Pliny had a saying, you know: 'The more I study nature, the more I consider nothing beyond belief.'"

The more Alemeth studied Barnard, the more he liked him. And in early December, when the Colonel invited Alemeth to hear Dr. Barnard's presentation to the Lafayette County Agricultural Association, he decided to attend. By this time, he wanted to hear anything the man had to say.

56

Barnard cleared his throat.

"Thank you. Gentlemen, if you would bear with me for just a moment, I'd like to share a few thoughts I've had on the subject of lenses. He removed his spectacles. "As you know, a lens is any device which uses refraction to cause rays of light to converge or diverge."

He held up the spectacles, wiggling them in the lamplight for all to see.

"Consider the two surfaces on each, the front and the back."

Holding the spectacles in his left hand, he pointed and made gestures in the air with his right, drawing imaginary lines.

"There are two curved surfaces that concern us, the inner and the outer."

He cut two swaths into the air with a flat hand, modeling the curvatures of the lenses.

"Each surface redirects the path of the light."

His right index finger, headed directly at the lens, made a slight correction, then took a different angle out the back.

"It's Snell's law: when a ray of light passes from one medium into another, there is a change in the angle of the ray. A lens can be a very predictable method of redirecting light. Next time you're swimming in clear water put your elbow under water and leave your hand in the air. Look how the surface of the water seems to break your forearm. That's Snell's law, too. Your forearm isn't really broken. It is just the refraction of light."

Amzi had told him not to concern himself with such things. Barnard was telling him it mattered, and giving him the answer.

"Consider how we can make use of such knowledge. By redirecting the path of light, lenses can not only be used for magnification, but for the collection and concentration of light. Colonel Brown, would you be so kind as to draw the shades?"

As the Colonel drew the window shades down, the room became as dark as Dr. Edgar's wagon. Barnard lit a candle and held it just inches from his face. The room was quiet enough to hear a spirit rapping. The light cast shadows across the bridge of Dr. Bernard's nose. His eye sockets darkened. His cheekbones got bright. He looked like a corpse from the grave.

"What happens when I move the candle away from my face?" he asked the captivated crowd, his face falling into darkness.

"As the distance between my face and the light increases, the light must travel farther from the flame to reach it, and its illuminating power weakens. Its rays become diffuse. Individual particles of space are catching less light. (Can you raise the shades again, Colonel Brown?)

"Now, before I move on, I should make another point about light and lenses. Seeing things up close is not just about magnification. It's about the sufficiency of light. With the tiniest things catching so much less light, a microscope designed for things very small must use its lenses and mirrors to bring the maximum light to bear on the point." The room brightened as Colonel Brown raised the shades. "Our ability to see the very smallest things in the world depends upon our success in focusing light on a precise point in space. It is these angles, and the size and polish of the lens and mirrors, that enable all the rays of light to align precisely and illuminate the tiniest smidgeons of space."

Things smaller than dust mites. Things invisible to the naked eye.

"When Janssen invented his microscope, he used an objective lens to gather light, while the eyepiece magnified the image. When he did, a whole new world was revealed. Joseph Lister's lenses were so clear he could see the parts of blood; now, doctors examine blood under microscopes every day."

Once again, Dr. Barnard removed his spectacles and held them up as a prop.

"I can't emphasize enough how strongly I believe in the importance of our lenses! So I'll say it again: I believe in the importance of our lenses! Our understanding of the world depends upon them. The study of light gives us a new understanding of the nature of things. Someday soon, we may have a lens good enough to examine the elements themselves. And lest you suppose, gentlemen, that I have forgotten the peculiar interests of my audience, I should mention the work of Doctors Millington and Hilgard. Imagine, if you will, the advances possible in agriculture if we can direct more light into the soil."

Eyebrows rose on the planters' faces. There was a chorus of *ayes* and *indeeds.*

"This situation *forces* me, I'm afraid, to make a request, directed to your generosity. The attainment of academic recognition depends on having the best lenses in our microscopes. It's really very simple, when you get right down to it. Without the best lenses, we cannot make the most dramatic discoveries. In fact, I have already ordered a number of lenses and related instruments for Doctor Hilgard's use in the chemistry department."

"What of the department of physics and astronomy?"

"Eh? I didn't catch – "

"What of PHYSICS and ASTRONOMY?"

"Ah! Astronomy! I'm glad you asked, Mr. Hunter. For that, too, comes down to lenses. Kepler's lenses made great advances in magnification possible, and science was never the same again. Galileo's led to the discovery of Jupiter's moons. Gentlemen, I'm unashamed to say how strongly I believe that discovery in space, too, out among the stars, depends on the quality of our lenses. Indeed, I'm proud to say, our University will soon be at the forefront of telescopy. For we have recently placed an order for a lens of eighteen and one half inches. It will be our means of passage to the deepest reaches of the night sky."

Heads nodded.

"But there again, gentlemen, to have such world class instruments costs money."

"What good does studying the stars do us?" asked Mr. Smither. "At least we can grow crops in the soil. But the sky?"

"The sky is where we find things much bigger than ourselves, Mr. Smither. Bigger than our planet. But whether the big or the small is where our focus lies, the better the lens, the closer we can come to the true stuff of which the universe is made. We will all be indebted to those whose generosity will keep the University in the best of lenses."

Barnard continued taking questions for another twenty minutes. When there were no more questions, he thanked his listeners and looked at Colonel Brown. Stepping up to the podium, the Colonel expressed confidence that the planters of Lafayette County would support Barnard's efforts to make their institution a first class University. Then he led the audience in applause. And in the days that followed, Alemeth pondered light.

He noticed spectacles large and small, thick and thin. He tried hard, with only the lenses of his eyes, to see the surface of the moon. He looked again at limbs and fishing lines as they passed into water, and at the fading of color at dusk. And he wondered how many creatures might be in the dirt or even the air, if only he could see them.

How might they affect the cotton? How might they affect people? How could he know if they were really there? It seemed everything came down to light.

Then he thought of the differences between people. The distrust between Amzi and Eliza. The arguments between Ballard and Ward, and those between Boynton and Richardson. The disdain of slaveholders for abolitionists, and vice versa. The one thing you could count on, he thought, was that all of them couldn't be right. Yet that didn't keep them from being sure of themselves. If better lenses were a way to see how things really were, then who could be opposed to better lenses?

The next time Alemeth saw Gordon, he told him about the lecture, and Gordon enthusiastically agreed. "It's all about lenses," he said, as if he'd thought about it all before.

57

At Sunday School, Eliza told the negroes that every Christian should think of himself as an instrument of God's will. Afterwards, Alemeth was standing right next to Eliza when Ike came to her with a question.

"What do I got to do to be a instrument of God's will?" Ike asked. "What's God will tell a man to do?"

"That's an excellent question, Ike. And as always, the answer can be found in Scripture. It's in Exodus Nineteen and Twenty. It's in Deuteronomy Five. It's the first commandment: serve the Lord thy God."

"I mean, a black man, ma'am. How we supposed to do everything a master tells us, and still obey God?"

"You can make your service to Mr. Byers your service to God. Has Mr. Byers ever asked you to sin?"

"He's had us work on the Sabbath."

"I see, Ike. I understand." Alemeth thought she looked a little taken aback, but she continued. "Let me see if I can answer your question this way, Ike. Paul tells us in Ephesians 6:5, Servants, be obedient to them that are your masters."

Ike seemed troubled, but Eliza kept going.

"I understand, Ike. You're talking about freedom. It's something everyone wants, of course. I can only say this: Someday, you'll be free. It's all a part of God's plan. You simply must be patient. There are some things better left to God."

"And getting our freedom be one of them things?"

"That's right. Suffering can be God's way of teaching us things. Wisdom lies in accepting whatever Providence brings."

Ike didn't seemed convinced, but he didn't press the point further. And as the last of the negroes went about their business, Alemeth took his leave of Eliza and reflected on what he'd just heard. There was no question, Eliza and Ike had been talking about the end of slavery. And as far as Alemeth was concerned, there was no need to wonder what Jim Murdock or Bill Starr would thinking about discussing the end of slavery with a black man.

So that evening, finding Amzi alone on the porch, Alemeth did what Amzi had asked him to do.

"They talked about getting rid of slavery?"

"Yes, sir. About how it would end."

Amzi coughed up some spittle. "What *exactly* did they say?"

"Well, I don't remember. Not exactly. Eliza said God was going to put an end to slavery. That it was part of his plan."

"God? Anything else?"

"Not really. Well, Ike didn't want to have to wait anymore, to be rid of it."

"Anything else Eliza said? Anything at all?"

"No, I — I remember she said she thought Ike was right."

"Right about what?"

"About the end of slavery, I guess."

Amzi turned, stood up, walked into the parlor, took a long look at Eliza, and without saying a word to her, walked out of the house.

"Alemeth, do you know what's bothering your father?"

"No. Not really."

But he knew what Pa wanted.

"Eliza?"

"What is it, Alemeth?"

"What you were saying to Ike, earlier – about the end of slavery being a part of God's plan – you really meant that?"

"Everything is a part of God's plan, Alemeth. Slavery will end when God provides for it to end. I hope soon. But the time is in his hands, not ours."

'But you think God's going to bring slavery to an end? That he made the world wrong the first time, so now he's got to fix it?"

"My Uncle William gave a sermon on that very thing, Alemeth. Do you believe that an African has a soul?"

"Why, sure. I guess so."

"And that he can have faith?"

"Of course he can."

"Well, 'They which are of faith, the same are the children of Abraham.' Galatians chapter three."

"So?"

"As one of Abraham's children, he must be capable of realizing the promise made to Abraham, about his children. So yes, Alemeth, the day will come when all mankind will be free, serving God and God alone."

"That's the way they teach it up north?"

"Why, yes. Of course. Why do you – oh, Alemeth! I'm delighted at your interest in Scripture!"

58

That Christmas eve, there was a candlelight service at the church, with a guest speaker, a Reverend Stewart from Pontotoc, who people were saying gave a sermon a person simply *had* to hear. So the whole Byers family went to hear him together, Amzi and Eliza in the front of the wagon, the children in back, the night sky full of stars.

"There, look," called out Amzi. "Can you see it? It's the brightest star you can see. It's the North Star."

Alemeth pointed it out to Walton. Walton spotted it, and grinned. Alemeth pointed elsewhere. "Look there, Walton. That's the Big Dipper. Do you see how it looks like a ladle?"

"Yeah."

"And look at that broad band of stars that arches across the sky like a cotton rainbow. That's called the Milky Way."

From up front, Eliza called back: "Imagine, children, if you saw a star three times as bright as the North Star. The star of Bethlehem was that bright, maybe brighter. Do you think, if you saw such a thing, you might follow it, as the three kings did?"

"I don't know."

"Look, Walton," said Alemeth. "There's Orion's Belt. Maybe someday you and I can look at it through a telescope."

"Are those the three kings?"

Eliza answered. "No, Walton. The three kings were on the ground, following the star."

"Look over there," said Alemeth, pointing out Venus. "There's the evening star."

"Walton, would you like to come up front and sit here, between your Mama and Papa?"

A placard on the door of the church announced that Reverend Stewart's sermon would be titled, "Slavery: A Christian's Duty Toward the Institution."

Alemeth hoped it would be short. He wanted to be outside, looking at all the night stars. Soon after they took their seats in the front of the church, Reverend Stewart's sermon began.

59

"To consider what should be done about slavery, it is necessary first to ascertain the nature of the trust committed to us by God. A nation often has a character, a character as well defined as that of the individual, due to the providential training which has formed its education. The particular trust assigned to that nation by God comes with a pledge of divine protection for those who are true to that trust. A people's fidelity to this trust, to their particular covenant with God, determines how they'll be judged on Judgment Day."

Alemeth coughed into his fist, then looked down at the Curtis pocket watch the Colonel had given him. It was nearly seven o'clock.

"If we in the South are such a people, then what, at this juncture, is our providential trust? I answer, that it is to *conserve and perpetuate the institution of domestic slavery.* Let us, my brethren, look our duty in the face. With this institution assigned to our keeping, what reply shall we make to those who say that its days are numbered? I say we should lift ourselves to the highest moral ground, proclaiming to all the world that we hold this trust from God, and we are prepared to stand or fall as God may appoint."

Benches squeaked. Shoes shuffled. Someone coughed. It was hard to pay attention when he could have been looking at the evening star. He wondered how much longer the service would last.

"Need I pause to show how this system of servitude underlies and supports our material interests? That our wealth consists in our lands and in the serfs who till them? That any other than a tropical race must faint and wither beneath a tropical sun?

"And need I pause to show how this system is interwoven with our social fabric? That these slaves form parts of our households, even as our children? Or that the relationship of mutual dependence is recognized and sanctioned in the scriptures of God?"

Slavery was as much a part of God's plan as cotton itself; Alemeth's question was whether God intended, somehow, to end it.

"The so-called free States of this country are working out the social problem under conditions peculiar to themselves. With a teeming population which the soil cannot support – with an eternal friction between the grades of their society – with labor and capital grinding against each other like the upper and nether millstones – with labor cheapened and displaced by new mechanical inventions – amid these intricate perils, we have ever given them our sympathy and our prayers, and have never sought to weaken the foundations of their social order. God grant them complete success in the solution of all their perplexities!"

A voice from one of the front rows said, "Amen." Alemeth wondered if Kep had ever found his way north.

"But we, too, have our responsibilities and trials. And they are all bound up in this one institution, which has been the object of such unrighteous assault through twenty years and longer. If we are true to ourselves we shall stand by it. This duty is bound upon us as the constituted guardians of the slaves themselves. In our mutual relations we survive or perish together. We who live among them know better than others that every attribute of their character fits them for dependence and servitude. By nature the most affectionate and loyal of all races, they are also the most helpless; and no calamity can befall them greater than the loss of our protection."

More *amen*s filled the church. Reverend Stewart waited for silence. Alemeth wondered if Kep was happy, wherever he was.

"If the South should, at this moment, surrender every slave, the wisdom of the entire world, united in solemn council, could not solve the question of their disposal. Their transportation to Africa, even if it were feasible, would be but the most refined cruelty; they must perish with starvation before they could have time to relapse into barbarism. Their residence here, in the presence of the vigorous Saxon race, is the best thing for them.

"I know this argument will be scoffed at abroad as the hypocritical cover thrown over our own cupidity; but every Southern master knows it's true. My servant, whether born in my house or bought with my money, stands to me in the relation of a child. Though owing me service, which, providentially, I am bound to exact, he is, nevertheless, my brother and my friend; and I am to him a guardian and a father. He leans upon me for protection, for counsel, and for blessing; and so long as the relation continues, no power but the power of almighty God shall come between him and me."

"The preservation of slavery is a duty which we owe *to the entire civilized world.* All branches of industry fall back upon the soil, and we in the South know, we must come to the bosom of this great mother earth for nourishment. In the happy partnership which has grown up between the tribes of this confederacy, our Southern industry has been concentrated upon agriculture, while to the North we have cheerfully resigned all the profits arising from manufacture and commerce. These profits they have fairly earned, and we have never begrudged them. We have sent them our sugar, and bought it back when refined; we have sent them our cotton, and bought it back when spun into thread or woven into cloth. Almost every article we use, from the shoe-latchet to the most elaborate and costly article of luxury, they have made and we have bought. And both sections have thriven by the partnership, as no people have thrived since the first shining of the sun."

He looked up at the windows of the church. They were open. The night air was like the stars his last evening with Mary Ann in Carondelet. She'd asked him if he'd read *Uncle Tom's Cabin*, and wanted to know what he thought of it. Now, nearly everyone was talking about it.

"The blooms upon southern fields gathered by black hands have fed the spindles and looms of Manchester and Birmingham not less than Lawrence and Lowell. Strike now a blow at this system of labor, supporting the arch of the world's industry like Samson's pillar, and the world itself totters at the stroke."

Reverend Stewart's idea of God's plan for slavery sounded nothing like Eliza's. Did God plan for slavery to end, or didn't he? Alemeth wondered what Mary Ann Webster's answer would be.

"Scripture contains many proofs of God's will. Just look at Leviticus, Chapter 25. 'Both thy bondmen, and thy bondmaids, which thou shalt have, shall be of the heathen that are round about you; of them shall ye buy bondmen and bondmaids. And ye shall take them as an inheritance for your children after you, to inherit them for a possession; they shall be your bondmen forever.'"

So there it was. Reverend Stewart had finally gotten his attention. It didn't matter what Mary Ann Webster thought, or anyone else. Scripture *did* sanction slavery. He began to listen to what the preacher was saying.

"To the South the high position is assigned of defending, before all nations, the cause of truth, which is, of course, the cause of all religion. In this trust we are resisting the power which wars against constitutions, and laws, and compacts, which wars against Sabbaths and sanctuaries, against the family, the State, and the church. In this trust, we are resisting the power which invades the prerogatives of God.

"If the northern churches are going to proclaim us sinners for our part in Providence, then no principle of scripture or law compels us to sustain our communion with them. Paul advised the Corinthians to turn out the vile one from their midst. He would tell us the same thing. I say to you, my friends in Jesus, it's time we disassociate from the northern Church."

Someone in the back of the church clapped, and everybody started clapping. Caught up in shared enthusiasm, Alemeth started clapping with the others.

"This trust we will discharge in the face of the worst possible peril."

"Amen!"

"And should the madness of the hour appeal to the arbitration of the sword, we will not shrink from defending it."

"Amen!!"

When the service let out, a cold wind had driven out the crisp night air. A misty cloud cover blocked the stars. Reverend Stewart's sermon had made one thing clear: the Bible contained a very explicit endorsement of slavery. A *commandment* to take slaves. And if God himself had told his people to take slaves, and to keep them in bonds forever, how could any Christian claim otherwise? How could thinking people be so ignorant of the Bible? The realization that he now had truth at his fingertips, in the Word of God itself – a truth that spoke directly to what was the most talked about issues of the day – left him feeling confident and powerful, as if armed with a weapon not everyone shared. And he wanted nothing as much as to be with Mary Ann Webster, and to tell her of his new-found discovery – of his confidence in it – of his conviction.

But no sooner had Alemeth conceived of putting this truth on display for the benefit of Mary Ann Webster – of telling her *exactly* what he thought of any book that contradicted the Bible – he overheard Eliza telling Uncle Johnson she thought the sermon was the worst she'd ever heard. That it was "ludicrous" to think Providence called for people to maintain slavery forever.

Standing nearby, witnessing Alemeth's confusion, was Ben Spears. After a moment, Ben took Alemeth aside.

"Did you hear what your Ma said? She hated the sermon. She's talking like an abolitionist. Is she?"

Alemeth looked up at the sky. She'd fought with Pa over Kep. She was against the preservation of slavery.

"I don't know. Maybe she *is* an abolitionist."

The past is disclosed; the future concealed in doubt. And yet human nature is heedless of the past and fearful of the future, regarding not science and experience that past ages have unveiled.

— The Panola Star
December 24, 1856

60

Christmas and the week that followed passed in a cold drizzle that was sometimes snow and sometimes rain, making the wait for New Year's Day seem endless. Alemeth would be turning twenty-one. It would be the day of his legal emancipation; the day he'd finally be answerable only to himself.

When it came at last, the snow was gone. Tree branches waved. Sparrows and finches crisscrossed the sky. At Clear Creek, where Mrs. Brown had invited the University crowd to another social, Gordon was talking to Professor Richardson on the terrace.

"But how," Gordon was asking, "do we understand the truths for which we have no lenses?"

"Like what?" asked Richardson.

"Like what happened at any moment in time, once it has passed?"

"Indeed," said Richardson. "You're talking about history. There *are* lenses by which we can better understand history. Voltaire gave us details, dates, facts, a better understanding of what really happened. How much better a lens Gibbon gives us, for example, than Herodotus."

Alemeth looked around the terrace, considering how best to avoid the conversation. Mrs. Brown's parrots were out of their cage, on their mahogany perch, a crowd gathered around them. Stage actors could not have enthralled an audience better, and after seeing the attention Dr. Barnard had given them, Alemeth decided to engage them too. But before he could move in their direction, he heard the voice of Captain Boynton.

"I couldn't help overhearing," Boynton said. "But I've got a question for you, Professor Richardson. How can you applaud the factual understanding of history, yet teach from Smith's *expurgated* edition of Gibbon?"

Richardson grimaced. "Why, Captain, you wouldn't have me spread Gibbon's libels against the church, would you?"

"I'm not so sure that's the right question to ask, Professor. Isn't history more than just the study of the past? Isn't it also the writing of it?"

"Certainly."

"Well then," Boynton challenged, "isn't Gibbon, himself, and what he said about the Church, a part of history? And doesn't it follow that the expurgation of his work is the corruption of history?"

"That's absurd."

"What's absurd about it?"

"That's absurd," said Clio from the other side of the terrace.

"Well! It seems the parrot agrees with you, at least!"

Alemeth didn't hear what Boynton said next, because coming out of the house beside Ann Brown was Mary Ann Webster. Gordon nodded an immediate *excuse me* to the two professors and headed in the young ladies' direction. Alemeth was right behind him.

"Well, well," said Ann. "Hello Gordon. Happy birthday, Alemeth."

"Thank you, Ann. Hello Mary Ann."

"Good afternoon."

"Gordon," said Ann, "I'd like to introduce you to my cousin, Mary Ann Webster. Mary Ann, this is Gordon Falkner."

Mary Ann curtsied to Gordon, then looked his way.

"I didn't realize it was your birthday today, Alemeth. How interesting, to be born on the first of the year."

"Like I've said before, Alemeth," said Gordon; "you could be like the Roman god Janus, if you'd ever look to the past. Just looking to the future, you have no perspective."

Ann laughed. "I've told him he'll end up cross-eyed."

"What birthday is it?" asked Mary Ann.

She was eight months younger than him. (He knew it well; why didn't she?) "I'm twenty-one today," he replied.

"A new beginning," said Gordon. "He's a man now. Time to get out of his rut." Then Gordon added, with a sly grin, "Or to start rutting."

"Are you enjoying the newspaper business?"

It pained him to admit it, but he had to. "They let me go."

"Oh, dear me. And you had your heart set on being a newspaperman…"

"No, I'm – I'm trying to figure out what my best course is."

"Janus was the God of transitions, Alemeth. Maybe it's time for a change in your life. A clean break."

"Mary Ann, about that book of yours: you know, the Bible supports keeping slaves."

His discovery took all three of them aback. Gordon looked at him in disbelief. "I said you may need a change, Alemeth – but becoming religious? I didn't think you were the type."

Ann Brown laughed again. "Nor did the rest of us!"

There was little he could say. For the rest of the evening, Gordon told stories. And as Ann Brown and Mary Ann Webster hung on Gordon's every word, Alemeth was as dumb as a tree stump. At the end of the evening, Mary Ann produced a *carte de visite*, apologizing that she had only one left. As she held it out between them, Gordon began to reach for it. But Mary Ann said, "Alemeth, it's your birthday. I suppose I should give it to you."

He took the card, and looked at it. And on the ride home that night, he was hardly able to put it away, thinking how pretty she was.

61

That night, back at Bynum's Creek, Eliza called Alemeth onto the porch. Uncle Johnson and Semmy Lou stood off to the side, Amzi in a chair in the middle. Gilbert, Harriet's son, stood, nervous, next to him.

"John Alemeth?"

"Yes sir."

"This being your twenty-first birthday, I've decided to make you a gift. Something to mark your coming of age."

Amzi pointed to Gilbert. Gilbert's arms were moving, but he was looking at his feet. Then Amzi held up a piece of paper.

"Look here. This is a deed of gift. Congratulations."

It was his birthday – his legal *man*hood had arrived – and Amzi was making him a gift. He threw his arms around Amzi's neck.

"Thank you, Pa. Thank you very much."

"Gilbert, it's time you stopped calling Alemeth "Master Alemeth.' From now on, you call him 'Master Byers,' same as me. Understand?"

"Yessuh, Mast' Byers."

That night, Alemeth couldn't sleep.

The whole Plantation would likely be his someday, but he'd never imagined owning just one negro. What would he have the boy *do*? Gilbert had been a house boy his whole life; but *he* didn't keep house, so what use did he have for a houseboy? *He* didn't know what needed mending. *He* didn't need leaves raked, a vegetable garden weeded, or cows milked. *He* didn't need errands run in town. Pa and Eliza saw to such things. The idea of deciding things for Gilbert's day was like wearing a coat that was too large – it just got in his way. Leander might have said that owning a slave was a fantastic opportunity; he could make Gilbert do *anything he wanted*. But what he *really* wanted was for Gilbert to join him down at the fishing hole, and pleasant as that would be, it would hardly meet with Amzi's approval. Having finally gotten a small piece of Pa's favor, he couldn't afford to lose it.

The next morning, in the shed, Alemeth was still pondering his newest dilemma when he came across Gilbert. He asked the boy what he was doing.

"Fetchin' a sharpnin' stone for Mast' Byers" was the reply.

When Gilbert found the sharpening stone, he nearly forgot to look Alemeth's way. "Can I go now? Mast' Byers is waiting for me."

Over the days that followed, Gilbert looked to Amzi for direction as he always had. Amzi gave instructions to Gilbert as he always had. Apart from the deed of gift, it was as if there'd been no gift at all.

62

By the middle of March, middling cotton was selling in New Orleans for over eleven cents a pound. The cotton in the fields at Bynum's Creek was high. But Alemeth was still being treated like a child. It wasn't just Gilbert that Amzi wouldn't let loose; Amzi kept on telling *him* what to do, as if his birthday hadn't meant anything at all.

Eliza told him to have faith, things would be different in time. But how much time? If things had not changed a scratch on the occasion of his twenty-first, then when would they *ever* change? Would things remain as they were until Amzi was too old to walk, or talk?

He didn't know what to do. But he had to do *something*. Being free meant nothing if not getting to make his own decisions about what he was going to do. Otherwise he was no more than a slave. He was named for Uncle Alemeth, who had stood up to Papaw. He was determined to find the key to a *real* emancipation.

So things stood, the day news of the *Dred Scott* decision reached Bynum's Creek. After that, conversation about anything else seemed trivial. Everyone had an opinion to share.

President Barnard counseled harmony. "Whether we agree with it or not, we should be thankful that the Court has at least settled the matter once and for all. I'm looking forward to getting back to work, to rededicating ourselves to the betterment of mankind. It's high time all this acrimony came to an end."

Captain Boynton was in no such mood. His condemnation was sarcastic. "Forget the Missouri Compromise, forget popular sovereignty, even the government can't take a slave from his owner! The decision would be laughable if it weren't so offensive!"

Professor Richardson praised the decision. It was, he said, an affirmation of the righteousness of the southern cause.

Eliza saw the hand of Providence in it.

"It seems to me that the Court has agreed with the Church," she said. "Slavery will not be abolished by the government, but by God's blessing on the slaveholders. It will happen when planters find themselves so prosperous they will free their slaves voluntarily, and slaves so prosperous they'll be able to feed themselves. Surely there's glory in that."

"Glory isn't something I can measure," said Barnard. "Especially not God's glory. I suppose that's why I like science. Science subjects opinions to the rigors of academic proof."

"But Doctor Barnard," Eliza said. "If you limit yourself to things provable, then what room do you leave for Faith?"

"Mrs. Byers. Faith is important, to be sure. But surely you could agree, we should only fall back on it where truth cannot be tested."

"You don't believe that truth can be found in Scripture?"

"Of course I do. But scripture is subject to interpretation."

"So you don't really believe in it, then?"

"If it makes good sense to test everything we can about the world, then why, when we encounter something we *can't* test, is it right to be certain of it?"

"Well, why wouldn't we be certain of it, when it's the Word of God?"

"Because of our limited, defective, fallible point of view."

"It's as I thought, then. You have no real trust in God."

"It isn't God I don't trust, Mrs. Byers. It's thinking I'm capable of knowing His heart."

"Permit me to observe, Doctor Barnard: your church was founded on the idea that the King of England is God's surrogate on earth."

Barnard and Eliza went on for another ten minutes while Alemeth listened. Barnard seemed to know what he stood for. He was confident; his own man. And then it dawned on him: Barnard was the sort of man *he* wanted to be. Not his father's son, living in his father's house, expected to work his father's plantation. With every linter of his being, he yearned for something else. And when he finally had a moment with Barnard alone, he felt the urge to make a connection.

"I think you're right, Doctor Barnard. If a person relies on faith, how does he ever know when he's wrong?"

"We'll never know everything," agreed Barnard. "But we can know a great deal more than our forefathers did, if we devote ourselves to the task."

It made sense. And when Alemeth ran into Gordon Falkner a few minutes later, Gordon shared his own perspective.

"If you want to cultivate your mind, Alemeth, remember that nothing's more exciting than the unfamiliar."

That night, back at Bynum's Creek, Alemeth went to the library. Beneath Pa's account book was a stack of old writing papers and a pen.

He placed a piece of paper on the desk, and began to write.

Dear Sir :

I write to apply for admission to the University.

When he finished writing the letter, he placed it in an envelope, and the next day, he went up to Oxford to deliver it himself.

63

As Alemeth approached the campus, he came upon monuments to what Colonel Brown and his friends had accomplished. A new steward's hall. Another new dormitory. A chapel. The Lyceum. Down the hill, to the right of Alemeth's buckboard, were heavy ties and iron rails, some assembled, others in piles. Everybody wanted the railroad now, the sooner the better. But something was seriously amiss. The M.C.R.R. had finally reached Oxford, but there, on the outskirts of town, at the edge of the campus, the tracks ended. Work had stopped, as if the Irish railroad crews had laid down their tools and gone off on holiday.

At the President's residence, a black servant girl answered the door.

"Yes, sir?"

"My name is Alemeth Byers. I have a letter for the President. May I leave it with you?" He held the letter out to the girl, expecting her to take it.

"Please, come in." She didn't take the letter. "Follow me."

He kept several steps behind her, through an atrium, a dining room, and up to a door. The girl knocked only once, then pulled the door open and looked in.

"There's an Alemeth Byers here to see you, Doctor. He has a letter for you."

The sound of chair legs moving across the floor. Then, in the doorway, Dr. Barnard, his wispy hair tousled. He was smiling.

"Why, Mr. Byers. Please come in. Sit down. Make yourself at home. To what do I owe this pleasure?"

"I –"

"Excuse me, but, can I get you anything?" asked the girl. "Before I go?"

She glanced his way, then at Barnard.

"I'm so sorry, Mr. Byers. Jane is absolutely right. Can she get you anything?"

"No, thank you."

He waited for Dr. Barnard to speak, but the doctor just looked at him and smiled.

"Doctor Barnard, I – I couldn't help noticing the railroad tracks when I came in."

"Yes, indeed. The railroad is coming to Oxford!"

"But it has stopped. Why aren't the crews working?"

"Excellent question. They're waiting for us. They're willing to put the depot here, but they can't have the tracks come up the hill. It takes a great deal more to move a locomotive up a hill than to let it roll on level ground. So they're waiting for us to give them level ground. The Board has the question under consideration."

"It isn't the railroad depot they're building outside?"

"No, no. They're laying the foundation for the Observatory. For the new telescope. You have a good eye, young man. And you're curious. I like that."

"Thank you, Doctor Barnard." He made sure to look at the man – and to enunciate. "By the way, I heard what you said about lenses, to the Agricultural Association. I found it very interesting."

"Yes, I remember you were there. I'm a mite passionate when it comes to my lenses. Anyone will tell you that."

"And I think you're right about science."

Barnard nodded, then removed his glasses, looked at them, and wiped them clean.

"You have a good mind, young man. So what can I do for you?"

"Here. I brought this. It's a request for admission to the University. I graduated from Mount Sylvan a year ago. Then, last year, I worked at *The Panola Star*."

"Excellent, excellent. It's always good to further one's education! What a shame – about Reverend Vrooman."

"What about Reverend Vrooman?"

"You didn't hear? He was – well, he's not at Mount Sylvan any more. Are you sure I can't have Jane get you something to drink?"

"I'm sure."

"I'll need to know what subjects you've studied."

"It's all in my letter."

Bernard began to read the letter, but when Jane stuck her head around the corner with news of another visitor, Alemeth made his goodbyes.

That night at Bynum's Creek, a few steps out into the night, his sights on stars millions of miles away, he peered into the depths of Virgo and Hercules. Then he went inside, sat down at Amzi's desk again, and wrote a letter to Mary Ann Webster.

He couldn't wait to tell her he'd applied.

Carondelet

26th May, 1857

Dear Alemeth,

Congratulations! I am so happy for you!

I knew all along that you would make something of your life. A young man who likes Homer and wants to be a newspaper man should not let his life pass without enjoying an education. You are so lucky to have a quality University so close to home. Words cannot express how much I wish I could be there to see you realize the bounty the University will bring you!

I wish you all the best.

Yours fondly,

Mary Ann Webster

64

A knock at the door.

It was the President's servant, Jane.

"I got a note here from Doctor Barnard for Master J. Alemeth Byers."

Jane was a polite and pleasant girl. She might even have smiled. But Alemeth was more interested in the envelope she was holding in front of her.

"Thank you."

He took the envelope she offered without hesitation.

"Good night."

"Good night."

With the door closed, he tore the envelope open.

Oxford, MS
June 10, 1857

Dear Mr. Byers,

I have very much enjoyed our conversations. You are a bright young man, and I believe you will make a fine addition to the student body someday.

However, a first class University depends on achieving a high level of scholarship. The faculty have recently increased our admissions requirements. New students must now have studied Vergil's Georgics and Ovid's Metamorphoses prior to beginning the course of instruction. I have spoken to Reverend Vrooman and he has confirmed Mount Sylvan did not include those authors.

Accordingly, I must decline to accept you as student in the Class of 1861.

On a personal note, I encourage you to attend the Boys' Academy here in Oxford, or some other school which can provide you the necessary studies. I would be very pleased to consider your application for the Class of 1862.

Your friend and supporter,

Frederick Barnard

65

Everything was quiet in the blind, and he wanted nothing more than to kill a deer or two, but it was hard to keep his mind on the task. Rejection had swept in like a hail storm; his thoughts and feelings about his place in the world lay scattered and broken. Bernard had ripped away all hope and expectation. He wanted to lash back. But much as he tried to blame Barnard, he couldn't undo what had been done. And always, the nagging question was, what would he say to Mary Ann?

Pa said maybe it just wasn't meant to be. Eliza was alright with it too. (She acknowledged for the first time that she'd never been much taken with Barnard, and perhaps Alemeth would be better off at a seminary anyway. In the meantime, in trying to decide what to do with himself, what mattered most was Faith. If he could feel the power of the Spirit in his heart, he could have faith that the voice he heard was God's.)

But what was he going to do? Go all the way up to Oxford every day, to the Boys' Academy? Get Reverend Vrooman to teach him *The Georgics* and *Metamorphoses*? Just to reapply? A year was a long time.

He could stay on at Bynum's Creek. Help Pa take care of the plantation. Help Grote with the cotton. Pa would like that. And he could go out, in the mornings, and take a deer whenever he felt like it.

A flash of hide in the trees. He lifted his musket, but his elbow made a noise and the doe ran off.

Maybe Pa had been right about one thing. Maybe, to be truly good at a thing, you have to devote your *whole* life to it. But what was the thing most worth devoting life to? Improving his aim with a gun? Growing a good crop of cotton? Winning the heart of someone he fancied, and who might just fancy him?

He needed time to figure that out; time to think through what to do.

That afternoon, he wrote a letter to Mary Ann. It was all he could do to admit what had happened. She'd be disappointed, but she'd understand. It wasn't his fault he hadn't read the Georgics. But she wouldn't understand it if he gave the whole thing up; if he didn't attend college at all. She'd be very disappointed in that.

So in the end, he decided not to mention that possibility. He'd see what she had to say first.

In due course, after a difficult wait, he received her reply.

Carondelet

1st Aug, 1857

Dear Alemeth –

Please accept my sincerest condolences regarding the delay in your admission to the University. I feel certain that the setback is a temporary one, and that you will enjoy a change in fortune when you reapply next year.

Carondelet has been a lovely place this summer, and I could tell you all about it, but there is news I cannot bear to keep from you any longer: I am delighted to inform you of my engagement to be married. He is a Kentucky gentleman named James Loughborough, most handsome and well-read. We are to be married here in Carondelet, probably in November. Please let your family know the news! I'll write again once we have a date.

I so hope you can join Mr. Loughborough and me on our special day. I know you would like him, if not as much as I!

Warmest regards,
Mary Ann Webster.

66

Loughborough.

Great galumpus. Burrower. Interloper! James Loughborough. A 'Kentucky gentleman.' 'Well-read.' *A prissy fellow; let him have her.* His whole life didn't depend on *her.*

He'd been a bass trying to swim up the creek, Mary Ann a lure in his way. With her and the University out of the picture, there was nothing to divert his attention. His years at Mount Sylvan had been wasted. There was but one place he had good memories of, and that was Bynum's Creek. It had once been his garden of Eden, where he could fish as much as he pleased and every day brought new adventures.

But things were not the same as they'd once been. The new house was stuffed with end tables, clocks and settees. There were busts and vases from New Orleans, a silver service from Charleston. Crystal from New York. Linen, a grandfather clock, and a new piano from Memphis. There were even French landscape paintings on the walls. What it must have cost was hard to imagine.

Leander and Kep gone. Gordon at college. Mary Jane married to Willie McKie. No one around his age. In the house, little Walton professed his faith out loud, repeating passages from scripture. His mother praised him, when she wasn't fussing over Eddy or Medora. *Especially* Medora. 'My adorable Dora,' she called her. The week before, Dora had made up a poem for her:

> *Mother I hope when you die*
> *You will be an angel in the sky.*

And then there was another:

> *My Mother My Dear Mother*
> *I hear thy gentle voice –*
> *It always makes My little heart*
> *beat gladly and rejoice.*

It wasn't a house to spend time in. Even if being outdoors wasn't the paradise it used to be, he could at least go down to the fishing hole, or take one of the horses out for a ride. And neither the fish nor the horses, nor the chickens or the mules, had ever given him trouble the way people did.

*　　　　　*　　　　　*

Pa, I've changed my mind. I won't be going back to school after all.

It should have been good news. Amzi had never cared for schooling. But Amzi just shook his head again, and his disapproval was all too familiar.

"Why can't you just make a decision and stick to it, son? A man's got to have a spine, you know."

There was little to love in that. "I'm tired," he said. He excused himself and went up to his room.

Would he stay at home until Pa died? And what was he going to do, without Kep, or Leander, or Mary Ann in his life?

*   *   *

A knock at the door.

"Come in."

Semmy Lou. "Hi."

"What can I do for you?"

"You can get out of your doldrums, Alemeth Byers." She had the same bones and long straight hair as her Ma – her namesake – Semirah Louisa. There was nothing of Eliza in her. "It isn't the end of the world you know. Mary Ann Webster isn't the only fish in the sea."

She seemed to care.

"I could ask Julia Brown about getting you some introductions, if you like."

She was offering to help out.

"Thanks, Semmy Lou. Let me think about it."

"Alemeth? Please don't call me Semmy Lou anymore. Can you just call me Lou? I'm nearly fourteen, you know."

"Alright – Lou."

"Thanks. I want to be a good sister to you, John Alemeth Byers. In case you hadn't noticed."

She was a good kid.

67

One Saturday evening, Alemeth met Gordon at the Butler's downtown Hotel. Gordon wanted him to meet someone.

"Hey, Byers. Meet my new friend here."

The stranger held out a hand.

"Alemeth Byers, this is Howard Falconer."

"Falkner?"

"No. Falconer."

"The names sound alike."

"He spells his name F–A–L–C–O–N–E–R. We sit next to each other in assembly."

"We talked about the names the first day we met," said Howard. "People are always confusing us."

"What I find interesting," said Gordon, "is that our names are really the same. Some people spell it F-A-L-C-O-N-E-R, like the English. Some F-A-L-K-N-E-R, which is Dutch. But it's all the same. It comes from the latin word *falx*. A falcon." Alemeth shook Howard Falconer's hand. "So. What's going on?"

"We were just talking about Mrs. Brown's birds," said Gordon.

Howard shook his head, then turned to Alemeth: "What we're really talking about is the muses. Gordon and I are having a debate about them. I was saying Clio is the noblest. Gordon here's a big fan of fiction, so he's been championing Calliope. I think he's daft. There can be nothing more noble than the truth. Don't you agree?"

"But that's just the point," said Gordon. "Do you really suppose you find truth in history?"

"Of course. I'm more interested in what's *real*. History – written with an objective point of view, as Doctor Richardson says – can capture what *really* happened. There's nothing more noble than chronicling the affairs of mankind."

"Howard, the past is like the bottom off the stern of a steamboat as it heads upriver. It's been stirred up; it's murky. People make mistakes. Memories fade. Expecting to capture a 'real' situation from the past is like expecting the river bottom to fall into place exactly like it was, once the steamboat passes. Only an artist can capture truth."

"Really now. And how does he do that?"

"With vision. Once he has a vision of something real, he can create characters that capture its essence."

"But if his vision isn't real, his characters will say more about *him* than about his subject."

"Howard, think about what you're saying. A living, breathing human being can't be reduced to a few words; why should we think a dead one any easier? Your history will be a product of your own fiction, as much as mine. You just won't admit it."

Alemeth said nothing. Howard and Gordon talked as if they were writing books to each other. He'd never amount to anything in that world. For the rest of the night – as Howard went on about the virtues of history and science, Gordon about poetry and art – all Alemeth could think was that his decision not to go back to school had closed their world to him forever.

He'd had a dream once. He'd been trying to cross a river, but the water level had risen. The current had grown so fast he couldn't reach the other shore. Trying to follow Howard and Gordon's conversation was like that – he could struggle all he wanted and never reach the other side. In the dream, he had turned and tried to get back to the shore. But the current kept him from getting back, and when his feet finally managed to find a foothold in the shallows, the sand started slipping between his toes, working its way out from under him.

68

The University was full of strange ideas. Dr. Hilgard taught that rocks move; Dr. Barnard that stars grow like living things. And there was no end to the differences of opinion, sometimes over the most inconsequential things. While Professor Richardson taught that Homer was a single genius, Captain Boynton said his epics were the work of diverse authors. "Hermann proved it," he argued. "The earliest versions of Homer come down to us in different versions." Richardson said Boynton's separatist views of Homer defied logic. "*Separatism*, illogical?" countered Boynton. "By God, Richardson, you believe there are three persons in one God, but there can't be three authors behind the epics of Homer?"

One day, Howard and another student, Sam Humphrey, appealed for help in settling a bet. Resolution required that Alemeth and Gordon meet them among the specimens in the Natural History Department: obsidian and silicon, granite and sandstone, sea shells by the thousands, bivalves, helixes, limestone, calcium, bones and teeth.

"So what's this bet all about, Sam?"

"The progression in the human remains. Come here. I'll show you."

In the adjoining room, they came upon three skulls. Sam held up a lantern, castling light on each cranium.

"See the progression?"

"I see a progression from the other room to this one," said Gordon. "Chalk to bone. It all makes sense."

"No, no" said Sam. "Howard and I are talking about the progression from left to right."

"The one on the left, that's a Neanderthal," said Howard. "The one in the middle, the skull of a modern Chickasaw. The one on the right, a modern European."

"No, no, look at the facial features. The set of the bones."

"Sam, I'm telling you, I know it for a fact. The skulls in the middle and on the right have a smaller nose and jaw – see? They leave more room above the ears, behind the eyebrows for a larger skull. That's what distinguishes modern man from the Neanderthal."

"No," said Sam. "I'm telling you, I saw the same thing in a book: one skull a white man, another a black man, the third an ape. Look, you can see it. The black man's skull is midway between the two others."

"Don't be ridiculous. I've seen the papers. The European skull was sent by a German phrenologist from Philadelphia. (It's female, by the way.) The Chickasaw skull came from a dig in Natchez. Sam, I know what these skulls are. Not one is the skull of an ape or an African."

Alemeth and Gordon decided the question in Howard's favor, but they still couldn't persuade Sam. It was all they could do to convince him that since he'd agreed to accept them as judges, he ought to pay, which he finally did, though he never budged from his conviction.

Nor was Sam the only one with strange ideas. Once Howard had Sam's money, he turned back to Alemeth and Gordon.

"Listen," he said. "Don't laugh too hard at Sam here. While we're all alike in our bone structure, we're hardly the same as the Negro. The best scientists attest to the differences among races. Jean Louis Agassiz, Samuel Morton, Josiah Nott, they all say the races a have different origins, anatomies and talents. Have you read Agassiz?"

"No. Why?"

"He says our thinking is too influenced by the story of creation as it is told in the Book of Genesis. Adam and Eve are myths, he says."

"You don't say."

"In fact, God created whole races of people at one time, just as he created different classes of fish, and birds, and dogs. They have different traits, perfectly suited, by Providence, to the climatic zones in which they live."

"He doesn't go in for Darwin, then?"

"I should say not. How could anyone go in for that nonsense?"

As Howard and Gordon went at it like two dogs over a bone, Alemeth thought maybe it was best he hadn't been admitted to the University; he wanted the Truth, and yearned for the day everybody could see it for what it was. He didn't like there being so many sides to everything.

69

Mississippi's 1858 Slave Code prohibited a master from inflicting cruel and unusual punishment on his slave. It required owners of slaves "to treat them with humanity, to provide for them necessary clothing and provisions, and to abstain from injuries to them extending to endanger life or limb." It was not poorly drafted; rather, its major defect (aside from its limited objective) was that it lacked an effective means of enforcement. Sheriffs and judges owned slaves too. So, as enforced, the law did little to curb what men actually did with their negroes.

If a slave refused to work, as directed by his master, there was a practical problem. What could a master do to achieve compliance with his authority? Once formed, the question hung in the air like a dark western sky, everyone wondering when it would finally rain. And when the sky broke open in a downpour of southern reason, it immersed th residents of northern Mississippi in a remarkable, ground-breaking trial, to which Alemeth had a front row seat.

Alemeth's involvement began when Uncle Johnson received a subpoena, ordering him to testify at the murder trial of George Washington Oliver.

At first, no one understood why Johnson had been called to testify. Oliver, a planter, was on trial for the murder of his slave, John. Johnson knew nothing about the murder. But Alemeth, Johnson, Kep and John had all been fishing together, and Mr. Chalmers, the prosecutor, told Johnson he'd subpoenaed him and the Reverend Frederick Coffin Vrooman as 'character witnesses,' to say what they knew about John.

When things got underway in the courtroom, Mr. Chalmers called Dr. Isom as his first witness. Dr. Isom went over his examination of the body. He said the boy had been killed by a blow to the head, by a blunt instrument. He gave his estimate of how long it had taken the boy to die. (No more than a couple of minutes.) Mr. Chalmers then called Reverend Vrooman's name, but Reverend Vrooman was not in the building, a fact that set the courtroom to widespread whispering. Then it was Uncle Johnson' turn. After he put his hand on a Bible and swore to tell the truth, Mr. Chalmers asked if he knew the dead boy.

The People of the State of Mississippi
vs. George Washington Oliver
Excerpt of Testimony of Henry Johnson Byers

Witness:	Yes, I did.
Chalmers:	What sort of boy would you say he was?
Witness:	A bright boy. Helpful.
Barr:	Objection. Opinion. No predicate.

The Court:	Sustained. Members of the jury, please disregard the answer.
Chalmers:	Did you ever see John do anything that might help us better understand what sort of boy John was?
Witness:	I saw him and Kep talking about the Bible.
Chalmers:	Talking about the Bible! I see. Now, this 'Kep': that's a boy that belonged to you?
Witness:	He belonged to my brother, Amzi Byers. Kep and John spent time together.
Chalmers:	I see. Did John and Kep often talk about the Bible?
Witness:	I only saw them once.
Chalmers:	Alright then, Mr. Byers, what happened on that occasion?
Witness:	Kep said he wanted to be baptized.
Chalmers:	Who wanted to be baptized. Kep, or John?
Barr:	Objection.
The Court:	Sustained.

(Pause during the proceedings while Mr. Chalmers consulted his notes.)

Chalmers:	Mr. Byers, Kep ran away, didn't he?
Witness:	Yes.
Chalmers:	Did you ever hear Kep and John talk about running away?
Witness:	No.
Chalmers:	When Kep ran away, did John go with him?
Witness:	No.
Chalmers:	Even though they were good friends?
Witness:	That's right.
Chalmers:	So, it would be fair to say that, between the two boys, Kep was the more strong-willed? Likely to disobey? John the more submissive?
Barr:	Objection. Calls for an opinion.
The Court:	Sustained.
Chalmers:	Well, alright then, Mr. Byers. The day you heard John and Kep talking about the Bible, what did you hear John say?
Witness:	Well, there were several boys there. John and Kep. Gilbert. Some of the others. I don't recall word for word what John said. But it was clear he was interested in it.
Chalmers:	Interested in what, Mr. Byers?
Witness:	The good book.
Chalmers:	Thank you. Mr. Byers, did you ever see John work?

Witness:	Yes, a number of times.
Chalmers:	How did John work, based on what you saw?
Witness:	Well, I'm not sure. Same as most, I suppose. I saw him get yelled at.
Chalmers:	By whom?
Witness:	By Mr. Oliver. And I saw him get whipped once, too.
Chalmers:	By?
Witness:	Mr. Oliver.
Chalmers:	How did John take the lashes?
Barr:	Objection!
Witness:	He didn't talk back or nothing, if that's what you mean.

Mr. Oliver's overseer, a man named Bramwell, took the stand next. Unlike Johnson, he seemed to know exactly why he'd been called to testify.

The People of the State of Mississippi
vs. George Washington Oliver
Excerpt of Testimony of Abner Bramwell

Witness:	How did I know Mr. Oliver? I'll tell you how I knew. He had an ornery streak a mile long and six feet wide.
Barr:	Objection, your honor.
The Court:	Mr. Barr, you know that you can't object to the witness's answer.
Barr:	It's just an opinion.
The Court:	Members of the jury, please disregard the witness's answer.
Chalmers:	Mr. Bramwell, on what *facts* do you base your *opinion* that the defendant had an 'ornery' streak?
Witness:	On things he done.
Chalmers:	What sort of things?
Witness:	Things like what he done to John.

(Pause as Mr. Chalmers reviewed his notes.)

Chalmers:	Mr. Bramwell, were you a first-hand eye-witness to what happened the night George Oliver's boy John was killed?
Witness:	Yes I was.
Chalmers:	Please then, Mr. Bramwell, would you kindly tell the gentlemen of the jury why the defendant, George Washington Oliver, killed John?
Barr:	Objection –
The Court:	Sustained.

The Witness:	For nothing.
Chalmers:	What do you mean, for nothing?
Barr:	Objection!
Witness:	Because John didn't work as fast as Oliver wanted him to. Oliver told him to work faster, but the boy didn't do it.
The Court:	Objection overruled. Go on.
Chalmers:	You're telling this Court, and the members of the jury, that Mr. Oliver told John to work *faster*?
Witness:	Yes.
Chalmers:	He used that very word, '*faster*'?
Witness:	As I recall, he did.
Chalmers:	What did Mr. Oliver do, when John wouldn't work as 'fast' as Mr. Oliver wanted?
Witness:	He beat him over the head with a corn punch.
Barr:	Objection!
Chalmers:	Thank you, Mr. Bramwell. No more questions.

As Mr. Chalmers sat down, Mr. Barr asked the witness a single question: whether he'd been dismissed by Mr. Oliver from his duties as overseer just a few days after John's death. When Mr. Bramwell acknowledged that he had, Mr. Barr cast a knowing glance at the jury, then told Mr. Bramwell he'd made himself quite clear, and there'd be no more questions.

Mr. Chalmers said the people rested. A minute later, Mr. Barr called the defendant, George Washington Oliver, to the stand.

Oliver didn't deny striking the blow that killed John. In fact, what he had to say was illuminating.

The People of the State of Mississippi
vs. George Washington Oliver
Excerpt of Testimony of the Defendant

Witness:	John was mentally deranged, if you ask me.
Mr. Chalmers:	Why do you say that, Mr. Oliver?
Witness:	He had a long history of bad behavior. Harder to handle than a full grown alligator. You know the type: just doesn't know his place.
Mr. Barr:	I see, Mr. Oliver. So what you did was justifiable.
Mr. Chalmers:	Objection. Calls for a legal conclusion.
The Court:	Overruled.
Mr. Barr:	You can answer the question, Mr. Oliver. Would you say it was justifiable?
Witness:	What's a man to do? Of course it was justifiable. Had I

	beat that boy blue, it wouldn't a done no good. Fact is, I'd had to do it the day before all this happened.
Mr. Barr:	Do what, Mr. Oliver?
Witness:	Why, beat him. Make him mind.
Mr. Barr:	Why did you have to beat him, just the day before?
Witness:	When I told him to get to work, he just looked me in the eye and did nothing. So I'd had to whup him a little. The boy acted savage the rest of the day. His natural wildness come out. Time come, the day it happened, he was supposed to be punching corn into the machine, but he wouldn't. Know what I mean?
Mr. Barr:	I think I do, Mr. Oliver. But just to be sure, why don't you tell us what happened next.
Mr. Oliver:	I had to hit him.
Mr. Barr:	Because he was refusing to work?
Witness:	That's right.
Mr. Barr:	Mr. Oliver, did you tell your boy John to work faster?
Witness:	I never said any such thing. He got it in his head he just wasn't gonna do it. He just didn't feel like it. So I had to make a point, you know?
Mr. Barr:	I understand. What happened next, Mr. Oliver?
Witness:	I took the punch away from the boy and said, 'Now, John, you best not make me use this on you.' I made a movement, like this, you know. To make sure he knew what I was talking about. And he did know, too. Next thing he did was turn his other foot toward me, you know, to come square on to me. Can I?"
The Court:	For just a moment, Mr. Oliver.
Witness:	*(rising, demonstrating)* Like this.
Mr. Barr:	*I see. Thank you.* Go on, Mr. Oliver.
Witness:	*(sitting again)* Well, the last thing I wanted was to let things get out of hand, so I held out the punch toward him, just a bit, in his direction. And I said 'John, now, time has come to stop talking and *do what I say.* You take this punch and get to pushing corn, or I *will* have to use it on you. All I'm saying is, it's time to get back to work. Now.' And I swear – just as sure as I'm sitting here – that boy looked at me the longest time, like he was daring me to beat him, you know. Then he lifted his hands and took the punch from me. But instead of pushing corn with it, like I was asking,

he just laid the punch down by the machine and walked away. Had his back to me. Like he was daring me. I'd already warned him, clear as I could. All the others was watching, too. So there wasn't nothing else I could do. I picked up the punch and struck him a blow. He had turned his back to me. I didn't mean to kill him. But if I hadn't hit him, he'd a just walked off. That was the whole point of what he was doing. Like he'd a rather had a pig's ear than listen to anything more I coulda said.

When Mr. Oliver got through his testimony, Mr. Barr thanked him, turned to the jury, and said the defense rested.

The following day, Uncle Johnson came back from town with the news the jury had found Oliver guilty of manslaughter. As far as Alemeth could see, it was a good thing, but Uncle Johnson didn't seem so sure.

"I hope it's good," he said.

"What do you mean? You weren't rooting for Mr. Chalmers?"

"Alemeth, I'm not worried about Mr. Chalmers. I'm wondering about the consequences. A lot of people are angry."

"Angry?"

"They think the verdict was too harsh. Asking how they'll ever get a servant to work again."

Neither Pa nor Uncle Johnson had ever had trouble getting negroes to work. None of them would ever do anything to make Pa want to hit him with a corn punch – not even Kep, when he ran off. There was something very mean about George Washington Oliver. If a man wanted to get work from another man that bad, there had to be better ways to go about it.

A few days later, a dead body was found in the Tallahatchie. After some initial question, it was finally identified as the body of Reverend Vrooman, who hadn't been seen, it turns out, since prior to the Oliver trial. Once again, Dr. Isom examined the body, this time concluding that the death had been by drowning. Some said it looked like an accident; others, a suicide; others still, that someone else had done him in. Regardless, it was said, his death meant there'd be one less abolitionist around to stir up the negroes.

No one was ever questioned about the death, and if there were any complaints about the lack of an investigation into a possible crime, no one made those complaints public.

70

Some weeks after the Oliver trial, Alemeth found himself back in Oxford, this time at the Colonel's new house on Depot Street, for the wedding of the Colonel's fourth daughter, Julia Brown. After three glasses of lemonade, he'd as soon have gone outside and relieved himself behind a bush, but he also had what Uncle Johnson called a 'posterior need.' Being in the midst of other wedding guests, he thought it best to use the outhouse like a gentleman.

The Colonel's privy was not like others: not just a wooden seat over a hole in the ground, with walls close enough to touch your knees, but two whole rooms, each with space to move around in, each with its own bath tub, porcelain sink, mirror, faucets and brass knobs. He looked around. He wasn't even related to Eliza — not really — but because she was the Colonel's sister-in-law, he was preparing to sit on what had to be the fanciest seat for business this side of the Gayoso Hotel. It was enough to make him feel he was supposed to be somebody.

As he waited, he heard a familiar voice through the wall. It was the Colonel's third daughter, Ann — Mrs. Frances Dowd for the past few years — saying something about the bride's dress. There followed a voice he didn't recognize.

"I like the veil. I think it adds a sense of mystery."

It was not a voice he knew; he fancied it a sort of deep, youthful purr. The softly rumbling sound nearly lifted him from his seat. As he listened to the voices, he wondered who the new girl was.

"The lace looks so pretty," said Ann.

"What is a lady, without mystery?"

The voices went on, Ann's voice and the purr alternating, Alemeth entranced by the contrast, doing his business quietly so he could hear them.. When he had given his last, he turned and, finding a pull chain like the ones at the Gayoso, he pulled it, forgetting the noise the flush would make.

The girls' voices stopped. The sound of rushing, agitated water came to an end. He could hear the pipe dripping, but nothing else. Had they heard more than the sound of the flush? And was that a giggle he heard?

Opening the privy door, he found Ann and the other girl coming out of the adjacent privy. Ann had white powder and paste on her cheeks; the other girl's clear skin needed nothing. Ann was talking, the other girl only smiling at him, the green of her eyes like pieces of jade in a clear creek. Her red hair sparkled. The sun glowed from her arms. She turned toward him, lips open, cheeks revealing her smile.

"Please excuse us," she said.

"Alemeth," said Ann, "I'd like to present to you Miss Sarah Fox. We all call her Sally. Sally and her brother William have come to live with Frances and Buck, next door. Sally, this is Alemeth Byers."

"I'm pleased to meet you, Mr. Byers."

She nodded, with a bend at the ankle and knee.

"If I may ask, Miss Fox, what brings you to live with the Avents?"

"Our mother was Buck's aunt, Mr. Byers. She just passed away. I'm afraid we had no place else to go."

"I'm sorry. It's a terrible thing to lose a mother. So, you're Buck's cousin?"

"Yes." She cocked her head to the side. Another smile crept out. There was an awkward exchange of glances before she finally spoke.

"I remember you, you know. You're the boy that had too much to drink at the Independence Ball three years ago. You fell down trying to dance."

"That was you? You were the one I danced with that night?"

"Oh no. I was barely thirteen. I was only watching."

He was sure it had been her. The girl he'd danced with years ago in Panola had red hair. It had framed her face the same way, too. And though he couldn't put a finger on it, there was more that made this girl familiar. She had to be the same girl.

She was looking up, as if about to speak again, when Frances Avent came out the door and said, loudly, "Sally, dear. Ann. I do believe the music is about to start."

"It was a pleasure to meet you, Mr. Byers."

"And – yes. Me too – "

Both girls went into the house.

A minute later, Mrs. Brown announced that the bride and groom were going to dance. Everyone watched as Andrew Shotwell waltzed with Julia Shotwell. And when Gordon Falkner asked Sally Fox if he could have the honor of the next dance, she glanced in Alemeth's direction. But though he faced her, he said nothing.

"Yes," she said, turning back to Gordon. "The pleasure is mine, I assure you."

It could have been *his* arm she took, but it was Gordon's. He knew it all too well: she'd been lured by someone else's bait.

Then, as couples organized themselves into groups for a quadrille, Alemeth's envy turned to relief. He'd spent little time doing reels and jigs. He knew nothing of quadrilles. How embarrassed he'd have been, arm in arm with Sally, only to stumble, or have to withdraw. Gordon had no such problems. He made every move with confidence. He clearly knew the dance.

When the quadrilles were finally over, when the bride and groom had been seen off in a black, covered coach, some of the young people gathered on the Colonel's terrace. In the ladies' discussion of 'beaux arts' and modern novels, both Howard and Gordon proved to be 'in the know.'

Sally Fox:	Ann Radcliffe, now, there's a wonderful writer. I love the way the most inexplicable phenomena are explained. Everything is so obvious, and natural, once it's understood. Like what happens to Julia Mazzini in *A Sicilian Romance*.
Howard:	I love how she deals with the rule of reason. And I thought her portrayal of the totalitarian father was telling.
Gordon:	I think it's the descriptive language that really sets it apart. The castles, the escapes through underground caves. She manages to make it all seem real.
Sally Fox:	What about her treatment of the rights of women?
Gordon:	Yes, indeed! I liked the scene where the servants see her raise her voice to her father!

What were they talking about? Ann Radcliffe? Julia Mazzini? Dead people? Real people? And who was this niece of Buck Avent's, this girl with the deep, purring voice, this Miss Sally Fox? Orphan or not, she seemed to know what the others were talking about. She clearly knew more than he did about such things. She was a part of Mrs. Brown's world; one of the girls he'd been avoiding. Now she was – what? A mystery, to be sure. A fascination, no doubt. An attraction? Perhaps so – bot not a prize, not with Gordon beside her. Not without hope of discussing literature or dancing the way Gordon did.

To say anything about Ann Radcliffe he'd have to bluff or lie, and if he were caught, he'd look foolish. Trying to change the subject was out of the question. But even silence was not entirely safe. Silence betrayed his ignorance as plainly as speech would have. But it was the best he could do. He barely said another word all evening.

Back at Bynum's Creek, he focused on one thing only. As he shut his eyes, a single set of features floated in his mind, trying to assemble. They had all the vagueness of a memory of a dream. Still, in as much detail as he could, he tried to recreate the way Sally Fox had looked at him.

71

The next day, Alemeth seized a chance to run into Sally by delivering a note to Mrs. Brown. But there was no one in the swing; no sign of anyone at the Avent house. Mrs. Brown was away as well, but he found Captain Boynton in the parlor among bright lights. The lights were aimed at Clio and Calliope; he was apparently taking their photographs. Alemeth approached.

"Good afternoon."

"Good afternoon."

"I'm Alemeth Byers. We –"

"Yes, I remember you."

"Those are some birds."

"They most certainly are. Mrs. Brown has given me permission to photograph them."

"You wanted to take their portraits?"

Boynton stopped what he'd been doing. "My dear boy. Photography is not just about *cartes de visites*. Not just about people wanting little copies of themselves on table tops. Such frivolities will be out of fashion in a year or so. I'm rather more interested in the value of photography to science: the ability to *record* things accurately. The fixing of an image that allows others to see *exactly* what the discoverer has seen." Boynton paused as if waiting for a tug on a line. "Think of how long it took a monk to copy a page of Scripture. Can you imagine how long, and how many successive drafts, it took Audubon to draw one of his birds?"

"A while, I guess."

"Etching and engraving made it possible to reproduce pictures, but it takes forever to do an etching. And how accurately can it reproduce, in any event? I'll tell you, Mr. Byers, all of that is about to change. People are discovering new ways of treating glass plates. Soon, we'll have the opportunity to capture images with an accuracy never seen before. Recordings will no longer be made by chisel or pen, or even by the actions of acids on metal plate, but by light itself, on glass. That's what's exciting about wet plate photography.

"Why do the reds and greens in these parrots look different colors to us, when they're made of the same feathers? Helmholtz is right, if you ask me. Something about the molecular structure of the feathers makes light rays behave differently. As if molecules were chains that acted like prisms." Rays of light intermingling in orange and green. Frequencies bent differently by different molecular surfaces. There could just as well have been feathers in his eyes for all Alemeth could tell. "And with a sensitivity as fine as a ray of light. Transferred to a metal plate, or paper, an image can be shared with other scientists. The true nature of things seen the same way, from Geneva to New York, from Charleston to Paris. And not just by the scientist in the laboratory. By everyone."

Captain Boynton paused to reposition one of the lamps to shine more directly at Clio.

"Those yellows, greens and oranges – how awesome to have a lens that could explain them, — eh, Mr. Byers?"

"*Aaawwk.*"

*   *   *

Boynton had confused him at first, but the more he thought about what Boynton had said, the more sense it made. An image took shape in his mind – and image of his own future – a future in which he was famous for the photographs he took – photographs that revealed the true nature of what things were. He wouldn't need Latin, or Greek. He wouldn't need a University education. He would just need some practical learning about photography, and maybe a feel for light. He wouldn't even have to leave Bynum's Creek.

Pa had bought everything for the girls: the house. The new coach. The piano. Maybe, if Alemeth asked him to, he'd buy a camera. Maybe, with his own camera, he could get a photograph of Sally Fox.

That night at supper, he approached Pa carefully.

"I was wondering, Pa. I was thinking about learning photography." Amzi just stared at him.

"I wouldn't have to leave home. I think it would be a valuable skill to have."

"Son, I understand your feelings. But taking *pictures*? For *calling cards*?"

"It's not just taking pictures of people, Pa. It's about Doctor Barnard's lenses. And Captain Boynton's chemistry. Besides, there's bound to be money in it."

"Money in it? Alemeth, son. Listen here. Do you think a manual trade is a way to make money? Let me tell you something. This is Mississippi, not Paris. Land is your number one investment, and always will be. Those who control the soil control the earth. That's the way it is here in the south."

"Pa, I think — I think there's more than just land in this life."

Amzi lifted his head slowly, turning his neck askew. No one else dared say a word, waiting to hear what he would say next.

"Let me tell you, son. Everything else matters less, and so is worth less."

"But Pa. It doesn't have to be one or the other. It can be both. Colonel Brown says that to take on more than farming is the mark of a gentleman."

"He's entitled to his opinion."

"I just don't see what's so important about the land. At the end of the day, it's just dirt."

"Just dirt? It's not just the land itself, son. It's what the land does for us. It's the value of everything we grow on it. The land is what feeds and clothes the family."

"Including the negroes," added Eliza.

"Even more than that," said Amzi. "To maintain our ownership of the land – to control whatever goes on within our own boundaries – that's what freedom is all about."

"Your father is right, Alemeth. We should honor and protect what the Lord has entrusted to our care."

"Have you thought what this land would be like if we lost our cotton? Where would we get money to buy tools? How could we buy feed for the horses and mules? Buy fabrics? Get doctors and midwives for the negroes? Son, we need our cash crop. We need to look after our cotton. And to do that, we need our attention fixed on the land."

"But Pa. Colonel Brown says a man can look after his cotton at the same time he looks after his other investments."

"Enough about the Colonel. This isn't Clear Creek."

"I think it would be worth it, Pa."

"How much money would a camera cost?"

"I'm not sure. I think I could get a good camera for thirty dollars."

Amzi frowned and shook his head.

"Alemeth, it's time you started taking some responsibility for things. And that means you have to be realistic about value. Your Uncle Alemeth – "

"I want to, Pa. Believe me I do. But I also want a camera."

"You don't need to spend money on a camera. A camera won't feed us. It won't put clothes on our backs. The answer is no, and that's final. Now, go on about your business. Why don't you check and see that Gilbert fed the pigs?"

72

"You know what you need?" asked Gordon. "You've got to learn to take control. The same as winning at poker: you've got to make you vision real. Go after things. Remember Lyell's rocks? If rocks can change, then a man's mind can too. Even your Pa's. You need to think of the right way to approach it. There's a way to get him to change his mind. You just have to figure out what it is."

After years at the fishing hole, Alemeth had learned what persistence could do. So after listening to Gordon's advice, the next day, Alemeth set out to find a way to change Pa's mind. First, he asked if he could borrow Captain Boynton's camera. When Captain Boynton said he couldn't lend out University property, Alemeth decided he could build his own camera. If he could find a lens, he could do the rest.

Maybe Pa was persuadable, for just the cost of a lens.

That night, when he went to talk to Pa again, he heard Eliza's voice. He stopped just inches from the door knob.

"I wish there'd been photographs when Papa was alive. I'd so love to know what he looked like. A camera would be a lovely thing for all of us. Please, Amzi?"

"No, Eliza. And that's final. I'll have no more discussion of it in my house. That boy will *not* waste his life making calling cards. He needs to be here, looking after the plantation. It's a full time job, and I won't be around forever. Somebody needs to take care of the family. Now, there'll be no more talk about it. Good night."

Alemeth backed his fingers away from the doorknob.

*   *   *

The prospect of giving up on the camera was depressing, if not unthinkable. If he couldn't get Pa to change his mind, there had to be some other way. A few days later, in Oxford, Alemeth talked to Jacob Thompson's son, Macon. Macon's father was a powerful man. Macon might know a way to make things happen.

Sure enough, after a few days to consider the problem, Macon came up with a solution.

"If we can get together the necessary supplies, and if we can prepare our own plates, Captain Boynton will let us use his camera."

"How did you manage that?"

"I've got my ways. I'm in his class. Meet me in the chem lab Friday afternoon. And bring some of your best unspun cotton. As clean as it comes."

"What for?"

"These days, they don't use egg whites any more. They use collodion. We can make our own; just bring some cotton."

"How much?"

"Why don't you bring a pound, just in case."

On Friday afternoon, when Alemeth reached campus with his cotton, Macon was in the chem lab alone.

"Where's Captain Boynton?"

"He's away this weekend."

"Shouldn't we wait until he gets back?"

"Alemeth, I got all the details from him. Why should we wait? Do you want to do this or not?"

No one else was around. Macon had made notes listing the steps they'd have to follow.

And so they found the acids, the alcohol, the ether. They found a spirit lamp. They poured the acids into a beaker. They warmed the liquid over the lamp. When it had reached a hundred and fifty degrees, they immersed the cotton in it, and ten minutes later, they washed out the acids in water. Macon said it had to dry thoroughly before they could add the alcohol and ether, so Alemeth set it on the window sill.

As they waited, Alemeth reflected on Pa's love for the land, weighing thoughts as if the two halves of his brain were in conversation from opposite sides of a scale.

How incredible it was, the same soil that made vegetables and beans, the same soil that fed chickens and livestock, also made the cotton that was useful for making so much else, from clothing to paper, and now, it seemed, even photographs! Maybe Pa was right. Maybe everything did depend on the land.

But Colonel Brown could also be right. No matter how important the land was, other things could be important too. If the land and the cotton crop were so important, then wasn't it also important how a person made use of what they yielded? If he could only have a camera, he could capture things as they really were. That would be putting things to good use. (All the more interesting since he'd decided to start with an image of Sally Fox.)

"It'll dry faster over here," said Macon, standing up and walking toward the window.

Then everything turned into nothing.

73

Alemeth? Do you hear me?

Was he dreaming?

The smell of alcohol. Ammonia.

No. A bright light.

Was it the sun?

He was awake.

Alemeth?

Against the light, Eliza's face.

"Alemeth, do you hear me? Are you there?"

His head was heavy. He tried to look up.

"Mary Ann, I think Alemeth's waking up. Alemeth?"

"What happened?"

Consciousness flooded in, his brain awash with voices.

It was Eliza above him, and Mary Ann Brown.

They were asking him how he was. Harl was there, too, handing Mrs. Brown a wet washcloth. A thin rag wrapped tight around a hard walnut was twisting inside his head. He rubbed his temples. The Colonel's house. How'd he get there? After — what?

He put his hand on the back of his neck. What was the last thing he remembered?

Macon had gotten the equipment. They'd dunked the cotton in the acid bath. Then, nothing.

"Where is Macon?"

"At his father's house."

"How is he?"

"Macon was hurt pretty bad."

"What?"

"He's still unconscious."

"Can I see him?"

Mrs. Brown looked at Eliza, then back at him.

"We think it best if you stay in bed a while longer."

"He's breathing alright?"

"Yes. He's breathing."

Friday night, in the bed in Ann's old room, the bicarbs were not enough to still the anvil in his head. He wondered if Pa knew what had happened (Surely he did, but Eliza offered no clue about his reaction.) The anvil rang again. It was all he could do to put up with it.

Things were different the next day. The anvil was much quieter. And Saturday morning, he had a string of visitors.

Howard Falconer was first. He came soon after daybreak, determined to know how the accident had happened.

"Try to remember *exactly* what happened before you passed out."

They'd lit the spirit lamp. Taken the cotton out of the acid bath. Set it on the window sill. Waited for it to dry. Then nothing.

Howard wasn't satisfied.

"What was Macon doing?"

Macon had been tilting a stool back on two legs, his feet up on a lab table, his hands behind his head. He'd been confident. Cavalier.

"Concentrate on that last moment. It's there, in your memory. You only have to find where you put it."

He squeezed out his best recollection.

Macon had been sitting there. Comfortable. He'd gotten up.

"He got up?"

"Yeah. He got up."

Still, what had Macon done?

Try as he might, he could not recall more.

Howard, on the other hand, wouldn't let up. "Concentrate on the last thing you can remember," he kept repeating.

Eventually, thanks to Howard's persistence, something came back. Macon had said something when he got up. Something about how they could be there all night. But even Howard couldn't draw more out of him.

His next visitor was Captain Boynton. Upon hearing of the explosion, Boynton had returned to campus immediately.

"How are you feeling, Mr. Byers?" His voice was disturbed.

"I'm doing fine, I guess. I have a headache."

"Can you tell me what happened?"

Alemeth began to tell him. But not far into it, Boynton cut in.

"I see. I can tell you why there was an explosion. Macon took the cotton back to the work station, to get near the spirit lamp. And one of you had moved the ether rack to the work station too. There were shards of glass embedded around the rack. It's obvious the ether exploded."

"But we didn't light it."

"You'd moved it to a place it shouldn't have been. Then, you probably spilled some on the table."

"No, we —"

"When you soaked your cotton in the acid bath, and it dried, it became gun cotton. Nitrocellulose."

"Gun – "

"It'll light up as quick as a hay barn."

"But we didn't put the cotton in the flame."

"No matter. The spirit lamp puts out heat all around the work station. It was obviously enough to set off the gun cotton. When the cotton exploded, it ignited the ether. And *voila* – shards of glass, like shrapnel."

Macon had been standing right next to the ether rack.

Boynton frowned.

"Son, that equipment was only to be used by the University. I don't allow freshmen in the laboratory when I'm not there, and by the first few weeks of class, they know more than you do about chemical reactions."

Had Macon not had Boynton's permission?

"You know, Mr. Byers, there was a great deal of damage. The equipment in that laboratory is expensive. Someone's going to have to pay to have it all replaced. You might want to talk to your father about that."

"Alright…"

"Good day, Mr. Byers."

Pa came in soon after. He'd obviously heard Captain Boynton's assessment.

"Son, I don't understand your insistence on always doing – on your bad decisions. Where am I going to get the money to pay for your foolishness? I don't have to support you any more, since you turned twenty-one."

"I know, Pa. What about Mr. Thompson?"

"What about him?"

"Well, Macon –"

He stopped.

It had all been Macon's idea. Macon had claimed to know what he was doing. And Macon had moved the cotton out of the window, closer to the heat.

"I was just wondering if Mr. Thompson wouldn't be able to pay for some of it."

"We'll not be bothering Jacob Thompson with this, — not while his son's life is touch and go. You'll pay for this, Alemeth. I just have to figure out how. What could get into your head that would make you do something like this?"

"Pa, I don't – "

Amzi was still frowning.

"— I thought you approved of chemistry."

"Alemeth, what you and I know about chemistry is what a planter *should* know, and no more. What soil is good for cotton, tobacco and greens. You need no more understanding of chemistry than that. You're a planter, Alemeth. Not a Doctor Millington, not a Captain Boynton, but a planter."

"But – "

"A few idle hours isn't enough to understand things men devote whole lives to understanding. We're planters, Alemeth. We make it our business to know the soil. Everything depends on what we grow, and if we're not going to let down those who depend on us, we need to devote our lives to planting."

"But – "

"Your Ma's been trying to convince me your mischievous ways are all the result of Leander McKinney's bad influence, but I'm beginning to wonder." The ache in his head got louder. "It seems we can count on you to find trouble, whatever you get into. I don't know what we're going to do with you, son. I just don't know."

*   *   *

When Dr. Isom told him he was free to leave, he hesitated. He'd never had such an aversion to going home. But being under the same roof as Pa, the same roof as Eliza, it seemed there'd always be disapproval, always disappointment, one way or the other. Maybe Uncle Johnson would put him up for a while. He'd have to ask him, just as soon as he got home.

But before leaving Oxford, Alemeth stopped in at the Thompson house to see how Macon was doing.

Macon was not well. From the looks of him, he'd had enough laudanum to drop an ox. He was bandaged in cotton gauze. But he was conscious.

"Once the bandages are off, my father's going to send me out West," he said.

"Why out west?"

"Doc says dry air will be good for me."

"Yeah. I guess so."

"But you want to know the truth? I think there's another reason."

"What's that?"

"My father thinks you're a bad influence on me."

74

The harvest of 1859 was one of the most profitable on record. Amzi knew he had much to be thankful for. But doggone it, he'd have enjoyed the fruits of the season a great deal more had Alemeth not caused so much trouble. Now, he'd asked Johnson if he could move in with him. The question made no sense on several counts. Once again the boy was avoiding responsibility – not to mention, putting Amzi into the awkward position of having to explain to Johnson everything about the camera and the explosion. The nonsense with the gun cotton, well – what could he say? The boy felt no responsibility for what his devilment had done to Jacob Thompson's boy. He thought of nothing but that cursed camera. It wasn't the first time he'd got himself caught up in something impractical. The panther. The fire at the camp meeting. He wouldn't be surprised if Alemeth had a hand in cutting the tail off Colonel Brown's horse. And then there was Reverend Vrooman. He'd never know how many crazy ides Vrooman had put in the boy's head. Once Vrooman's views on the slavery question were found out, the abolitionist had been sent packing, but by then, the man had had four years to steer the boy from his senses. This latest idea, to make money taking society pictures, was worse than his shenanigans with Leander McKinney. It had nearly gotten him killed, and Macon Thompson too. He was old enough now to know right from wrong. And he'd got told no, as clear as could be – yet he'd gone ahead anyway.

Then there was his disrespect for Eliza. The first few years, it had looked like he might grow out of it, but over the summer, it had gotten worse. He'd even turned his back on her once, while she was talking to him. It had nearly brought her to tears. She had her faults, sure, but there was no excuse for treating a lady that way — even if she wasn't your mother.

The simple fact was, Alemeth had his mind on all the wrong things.

The simple truth was, he didn't appreciate real value.

The simple conclusion was that until he started to turn himself around, he deserved no more responsibility.

Anyone with their eyes open could see how close they were to collapse in the natural order of things. It wouldn't be long before Bynum's Creek would have to be protected from free thinkers and abolitionists like Reverend Vrooman. How much use would Alemeth be then, when their very survival was on the line?

Amzi could only hope, and do what he could to bring the boy to his senses.

75

Semmy Lou and Medora left home for boarding school that fall. After they left, for Alemeth, there was no avoiding Eliza and Pa.

Avoiding Eliza would have been easy by staying outside with Pa. But staying outside with Pa was hard. He couldn't look at Pa without thinking of the camera. Absent outright defiance of his father, his only option was to keep quiet. All things considered, it was best to keep a distance between them.

Then one autumn afternoon, Amzi came up the road with a wooden crate in the back of the buckboard. He told Alemeth to get an iron wedge and a hammer and to meet him in the library.

The crate was on the table, next to Eliza. As Alemeth stepped closer, curious, Amzi began to claw it apart, prying out nails, twisting boards, banging them out with the hammer. The mystery of its contents did not remain a mystery long. Amzi lifted a wrapped package out of the straw in the crate, then tossed paper and straw aside.

"Well, would you look here. My new Model 1842."

He held the gun like he'd first held Walton, admiring it. He kept his eyes on the gun as he spoke.

"Alemeth, I'm giving you my old one."

The 1812. The flintlock.

"It's yours now, son."

"Thank you, Pa. To what do I owe – "

"We should be ready to defend the plantation."

"Oh, Amzi!" said Eliza. "Will you ever stop worrying about the negroes?"

"I'm not worried about *our* negroes, Eliza. But you never know about others. And there could be a Yankee invasion."

"Surely you don't think –"

"Eliza, I think it's time to be ready."

"Isn't it time for restraint, Amzi? Time for Faith that God will take care of things? We don't need to intervene in His plan."

"Don't worry, Eliza. I'm not planning to intervene in anything. I just want to be prepared, in case anything happens."

"But Amzi — "

The argument that followed was but one of many between Amzi and Eliza that fall, and it made life at home even less like it used to be. Alemeth talked to Uncle Johnson about living with him, but Johnson said no, he had to deal with his problems, not run from them.

76

Nearly nine hundred miles northeast of Bynum's Creek, at the confluence of the Potomac and Shenandoah, lay the U. S. Armory and Arsenal at Harper's Ferry. Amzi's 58 inch, .69 caliber Model 1812 musket – now Alemeth's – had been made there. The Armory was the largest source of weapons for the U. S. Army, producing ten thousand pieces a year. By 1859, it held a hundred thousand muskets and rifles.

Just days after Amzi's Model 1842 arrived, the telegraph brought news that the Armory had been hit. As soon as the operator finished scribbling the message, a boy carried it to Colonel Brown's house across the street. And from there the news spread to Howard Falconer at the Intelligencer, to Amzi Byers at Bynum's Creek, and to the rest of the community. It was that madman John Brown again. The abolitionists had seized the advantage. For a few hours, it seemed abolitionists had taken the nation's arms for themselves.

The following day, Reverend Vrooman was found in the Tallahatchie river – drowned. He'd been dead several days, maybe more, from the looks of him. Some said it looked like an accident; others, a suicide; others still, that someone else had done him in. No one wanted violence, certainly no one condoned murder (if that's what it had been); but regardless of the cause of Vrooman's death, it eased the tension some, on the roads around Oxford and Panola, to know there'd be one less abolitionist to deal with.

Federal troops retook control of the Harper's Ferry armory. The talk in the days that followed was about the trial of those taken alive. The trouble-makers didn't deny what they'd tried to do – they were proud of it, and glad for the notoriety. So people were asking, why bother with a trial?

"I say, just go ahead and hang them," said Amzi. "They're terrorists. If we don't send a clear message, there'll be no stopping others from trying the same thing."

"Surely, you don't think our —"

"If all the other negroes do, then why not?"

"But Amzi, most of them understand. how difficult it would be for them to survive on their own."

"Your granddaddy thought the same thing, I'll bet, before the uprising in Haiti. Eliza, how much of this John Brown talk has gotten to the negroes?"

"Oh, they've heard everything, from what Leety tells me."

"Alright then. What John Brown did in Virginia has nothing to do with them. They need to understand that. And another thing. I'm putting the guns on the mantel in our bedroom. Out of reach of Walton and Eddy. I'm going to keep them loaded."

77

A hundred and seventy miles of the Baltimore and Ohio Railroad connected the arsenal at Harper's Ferry to the Baldwin Locomotive Works in Philadelphia. As Harper's Ferry was to arms, Baldwin was to locomotives, putting out hundreds of engines for the new railroad industry. Like most of the engines Baldwin had built for the southern market, the *James Brown* had a five foot wheel span, and due to the narrower standard span in the north, the Colonel's new locomotive had to be shipped south on a flatbed car. Only when it reached southern soil could it be offloaded and placed on the proper size tracks.

Colonel Brown had paid for the engine and named it for himself. Though he planned to lease it to the M.C.R.R., he'd insisted its maiden run be to Oxford, where it now sat, on the right-of-way given it by the University.

Twenty-four tons of black iron, the 'iron maiden' sat heavy on the rails, the walls of her boiler thick enough to hold a hundred pounds of pressure per inch, her pistons tight enough to haul a hundred tons of cargo. A black chimney; a fine cab and a bell, all polished and new. Power. Class. A fitting statement of the Colonel's vision for Mississippi. And with the Colonel himself in the cab, the whole town turned out to see the eight-wheeler.

Alemeth, Gordon and Howard twisted their way through to be sure they could hear.

"How honored I am," the Colonel said, "to stand before you today, in the presence of this magnificent machine. When the M. C. R. R. starts using the *James Brown* to haul cotton to Grand Junction – when other lines take it on to Richmond, Baltimore, and Philadelphia – for me, as for a lot of you, it will be a dream come true. No longer will we have to face the perils of the sea. No longer pay the high cost of journeys under sail.

"But a locomotive is nothing without rails to run on. How grateful I am, therefore, to you, my friends, for your faith in the railroad. You who bought subscriptions will be rewarded with great dividends. And it isn't just you and me who'll profit. As we stand here at our University, it's good to reflect on the boon that the railroad will bring to town, with students, and parents, and visitors to academic conferences. With this locomotive engine, and these rails, we stand together, not simply at the cutting edge of learning and discovery, but along the best and newest link between our southern farms and northern factories. It's the modernization of America, my friends. In no small sense, we are building, for our sons and daughters, a promising, prosperous future, a new iron age that will benefit us all."

Alemeth's jaw had dropped at first sight of the massive machine. It was as if the steam-driven Calypso had been condensed, its wood turned into iron, and placed on iron wheels. He felt proud of his connection to the man in the cab, the man of the hour, the man who was bringing Oxford into the future, a future where the whole world would be united by railroad tracks, telegraph wires, and a shared understanding of how things really are. Alemeth could think of no finer future; how lucky he was to witness it's arrival!

When the Colonel had finished, Harvey Walter introduced Robert Shegogg. After Shegogg was through, Jacob Thompson said a few words. And when Thompson was done and Colonel Brown had thanked everyone for coming, he announced that Doctor Barnard had agreed to conduct a tour of improvements at the University for anyone interested. Alemeth wasn't the only one caught up in the magnificence of the hour; he and his friends decided to go along for the tour.

The President led them, first, along the track into the railroad cut. From inside the cut, embankments rose sharply on both sides. Stairways led up through nearly vertical banks.

"Imagine the weight of a wheelbarrow," said Barnard, "when it's half filled with rocks. It's no easy thing to push a wheelbarrow half filled with rocks. A lot of us couldn't push it more than a yard or two, if that. A locomotive like Colonel Brown's weighs more than two hundred such wheelbarrows. Now imagine pushing that locomotive up a hill. How many men, or horses, or mules, would that take? And finally, imagine the power required to push a locomotive up a hill along with tons of cars full of passengers, cargo, or both. And imagine the power required to get it to stop. To keep from having to climb up the hill, here at the University, only to descend again a few hundred yards to the south, over a *million* full wheelbarrows of rock and dirt have been removed from the cut where we're now standing."

As Dr. Barnard led the group to the new Magnetic Observatory, the boys reacted to what he'd said.

"It's easy to see why things flow through channels," said Gordon. "Everything follows the path of least resistance."

"A wagon on a pock-marked road," said Howard. "A driver naturally chooses the smoother side."

"It takes power to force a wagon wheel up and out of a rut," said Gordon. "And the more a path is followed, the deeper the rut becomes. The more we do something, the less we think about doing it. The more likely we'll do it without even realizing we're doing it."

"Well," replied Howard, "what's so bad about that?"

"Habit is dangerous. The more familiar it is, the more dangerous it is."

"Nonsense," said Howard. "It's the unknown we need to look out for. The unexpected."

"But it's the familiar we most take for granted, Howard. The familiar that we most accept without question."

"Interesting."

"Freedom, when you get down to it, is nothing more than the ability to get out of a rut. Out of *all* your ruts."

By now, the group had emerged from the cut and was approaching the new Magnetic Observatory.

"You have seen the way bar magnets behave," said President Barnard as if to a class of students. "Put two together and they snap into alignment, the positive pole always north, the negative always south. We've long known that some objects emit more powerful magnetic fields than others. We now understand that the earth itself, due to the energy of its rotation, has a magnetic field that works just like those two bar magnets. Practically everything on earth – ourselves included – has trace amounts of metal affected by magnets. Iron, nickel, cobalt, copper, silver, platinum, bismuth – they're all subject to the earth's magnetic field. Without our even being conscious of it, the earth is pulling us all toward alignment, north and south."

"Scary thought," said Gordon. "But fascinating."

Down the hill, the Colonel's new locomotive sat still at the Depot. Alemeth imagined the earth's magnetic field working to bring it into polarity. It didn't budge. It clearly took more than magnetism to align a locomotive.

"Variations in the magnetic field occur all over the globe," continued Barnard. "And the strengths of these fields are constantly in flux. Variations have an impact on the weather..."

Alemeth's ears perked up at mention of the weather.

"Our magnetometers can assess the strength of field here in Oxford. We can compare our data to that from magnetometers all over the world. Ladies and gentlemen, if I'm not badly mistaken, we will soon have a bird's eye view of the weather. Once we are able to track it with regularity, we'll be able to forecast it. Predict it. Before it's noticeable to our unassisted senses."

He'd have to tell Amzi about that.

"But everything depends on non-interference by any other force. Keep in mind that many substances carry their own magnetic fields, and that different electrical conditions create them. It's essential to the system that our readings be accurate. We need the most precise measurements we can attain. Which is why the magnetometers must be isolated from any sort of local energy. No vibrations. No loud noise. No radiant heat.

By this time, Barnard had led the group to the Magnetic Observatory itself. It was a small building, but as dense and stable as the "iron maiden," the *James Brown*.

"As you can see, the foundation is built into the rock. When it comes to our Magnetic Observatory, insulation is everything. We've done everything to isolate it. To keep it unaffected by motion, pressure, temperature, any source of extraneous magnetism, any external energy or influence at all. Even the presence of a person might affect the magnetic map of space around a magnetometer."

"Scary again," said Gordon.

"That's why we're calling it 'the Dead Room.'"

78

ART. 62. Any negro or mulatto, bond or free, shall be a good witness in pleas of the State for or against negroes or mulattoes, bond or free, or in civil cases when free negroes or mulattoes alone shall be parties, and in no other cases.

— Ch. XXXIII, Article 62,
Revised Code of the Statute Laws of Mississippi, 1857

"In no other cases," said Hugh Barr.

Dr. Barnard's servant girl, Jane, had been badly beaten and bruised. She had tearfully explained her condition by saying that Sam Humphrey had raped her. Sam had withdrawn from the University at Dr. Barnard's request. But after further consideration, Humphrey had reapplied. Adamant, Barnard had refused readmission. J. D. Stevenson of *The Oxford Mercury* and his friend Dr. Branham wouldn't let it go, complaining that, having taken the word of a negro girl over that of Sam Humphrey, Barnard was "unsound on the slavery question." When criticism of Barnard reached parlors and kitchens across the county, and much of the state, Barnard demanded a trial to clear his name. And when the Board convened on the first of March, affable, wispy-haired, hard-of-hearing Frederick Barnard finally got the trial he'd asked for.

From the very start, it was a comedy of errors. Since Dr. Barnard had demanded the trial, the Board naturally asked him to state the nature of the issue. But since there had been so much said around town about him, behind his back, which he had not heard, Dr. Barnard couldn't possibly know the scope of what had been said about him, or what people meant when they talked about him being "unsound on the slavery question." ("What does that even mean?" he had asked.) And having no idea what was being said about him, he saw no way to comply with the Board's request that he state the scope of the issue to be tried. So he demurred to the request for particulars, demanding that the trial cover "everything." After all, he wanted *complete* exoneration.

The Board was naturally reluctant to address a subject quite so broad as 'everything,' so to better understand the point they were agreeing to decide, the Board invited Dr. Branham to state the scope of his accusations. Dr. Branham insisted he had no desire to allege anything further than that Dr. Barnard had accepted the word of a negro over that of a white man. That alone was the only accusation, said Branham. That alone was enough to show that Dr. Barnard was unsound on the slavery question.

Why? "Because, through the law, the people have spoken. To willingly *break* that law, because of one's personal feelings about negroes generally, or one in particular, is to be unsound on the slavery question."

Barnard clearly *had* credited Jane (and her bruises) over Sam Humphrey's denial. He clearly *had* accepted the word of a negro over that of a white man. Did that mean Barnard was guilty? Branham and Stevenson thought so, and everyone knew they'd been doing everything they could to get others to agree.

After the Trustees had heard all the evidence, the Colonel suggested they take a recess. He and Barnard went to see Hugh Barr together.

Barr:	In no other cases.
Barnard:	Meaning?
Barr:	Meaning that a negro is simply not a proper witness, legally speaking, in *any* case against a white man.
Barnard:	So without a white witness, Sam Humphreys could never be convicted in a court of law?"
Barr:	That's right.
Barnard:	Amazing. As long as he does it without a white witness, a white man is free to do anything he wants to a black woman.
Barr:	Or a black man. But there's more.
Barnard:	More? That's not bad enough?
Barr:	In fact, it's even worse. If you say, publicly, that Sam raped the girl, that's slander *per se.* You'll be *deemed by the law* to have committed a slander against Sam, unless you can prove the truth of the accusation. And there again, with no white witness, you'd have no way to prove the truth of what you'd said. Sam could sue you, or anyone who says he's guilty, and win. You'd have to pay him money for the damage to his reputation.
Barnard:	My God, man. I can't believe what I'm hearing. The man can rape with impunity, and then collect money from us, in a court of law, if we say so?
Barr:	Exactly.
Barnard:	Heaven help us.
Brown:	My question, Hugh, is this: How can we ever explain ourselves to the community, if we can't say Humphrey did it?
Barnard:	Captain Boynton was there. He'll back me up.

Barr:	He didn't see the attack with his own eyes, gentlemen. He only heard about it from Mrs. Barnard and from Jane. Inadmissible hearsay.
Brown:	And Hugh is telling us Jane can't testify. That leaves only Margaret.
Barnard:	Well, I'll not put my wife through such an ordeal.
Barr:	It wouldn't matter. I can't imagine the lad did anything so brazen in front of Mrs. Barnard. I feel sure she only heard about it from Jane, too. And there again: anything Mrs. Barnard could say would be hearsay.
Barnard:	And so?
Barr:	And so in a court of law, there's no witness we'll be able to call, to testify about what happened.
Barnard:	And Jane?
Barr:	'In no other cases,' Doctor. Jane couldn't testify at all. Without witnesses, you'd be asking the members of the jury to accept as true something they'd heard no one say. Ultimately, since you're basing your conclusion on what Jane said, we'd be asking the jury itself to commit the crime – to credit the word of a negro over that of a white man.
Brown:	You can see how, being made to pay Sam Humphrey money for the damage to his reputation, you'd look guilty in the court of public opinion as well.

After Barnard was excused, Colonel Brown lingered with Barr a bit longer. During the private meeting, for the Board's ears only, Mr. Barr offered an additional opinion.

"By agreeing to conduct the trial in the first place," he said to the Colonel, "You've already conceded the public importance of the matter at hand. Finding Doctor Barnard guilty, as to such an important matter, you'd have no choice but to let him go, or look like fools throughout all of Mississippi."

The Colonel weighed everything he'd heard. On March 2, 1860, when the Board announced its decision, the words it used for the announcement were carefully chosen. There was *no* finding of guilt *or* innocence, for *either* Barnard or Humphrey. The Board simply found no reason to remove Dr. Barnard from his position. *That* was its decision.

Branham and his allies at *The Oxford Mercury* were furious.

The Colonel, and the rest of the Board, had escaped by the narrowest of margins.

79

Escape or not, Oxford's division over the Sam Humphrey affair had put the University itself on trial, and after the vote on Barnard, talk at the Board turned to whether the *Oxford Mercury* would always be hostile.

"How nice it would be to have a newspaper that could be relied upon."

"To be a friend."

"To the University. And to the state of Mississippi."

Colonel Brown volunteered to take on the problem, and to report back to the rest of the executive committee.

The Colonel knew Howard Falconer. One of the law students, he was the son of Thomas Falconer, publisher of the *Holly Springs Herald*, of Marshall County. The Colonel asked Howard if he thought his father might be interested in opening an office in Oxford.

"No, sir," replied Howard. "I can tell you for a fact he wouldn't. I've already asked him that very thing. He won't make the investment."

"That's too bad. I wonder – "

"But I'll tell you what, Colonel. I'm an able fellow. I know how to publish a paper. My brother and I grew up on a printer's apron strings. Besides, anyone who knows me can vouch for my loyalty."

"Your loyalty? To what?"

Howard gave the Colonel a confident stare.

"To Mississippi, of course. And to the University. All I lack is the money."

"If the University were willing to assist a young editor who held its interest high...?"

"Then I would be much obliged to it."

Colonel Brown didn't take long to reach a decision. The Trustees all knew Howard Falconer. After all, he'd been first in his class. The Colonel would tell the Trustees of his conversation with Howard; of how the young man had impressed him with his knowledge of the newspaper business, and of his considered opinion that buying a press and sufficient fonts to run a newspaper was surely worth a subsidy from the building fund.

80

One day soon thereafter, Howard Falconer came by Bynum's Creek.

"Good mornin', Alemeth," he said, getting down from his saddle horse.

"Good morning. What brings you out to Bynum's Creek?"

"Well, as it happens, I'd like to talk to you about a business matter. I'm starting a newspaper. You used to set type, as I recall."

"Yeah. I did, for *The Panola Star*. I'm pretty rusty, though."

"You could pick it up again. It's something you don't ever really forget. I thought you might like to join me. Gordon's going to help me out some, but fiction's his priority. I need somebody with an interest in the truth. And who can set type every day. Gordon suggested you'd fit the bill, and do a bang-up job."

Things had been pretty good at *The Star* – there was always something interesting going on. And Howard was likeable enough. But he couldn't be sure about Pa's approval. It would likely be just like the camera. In fact, he wondered if there was any point even asking.

Wouldn't it be something, to walk up to Pa and say, "I've already made my decision. I've already told Howard I'll go to work with him."

"I'm not sure. I'm interested, I really am. But I'm not sure."

"Alemeth, the north is getting behind Lincoln and Douglas. The abolitionists are intent on taking our negroes away. Great events are on their way. It's going to be a fantastic time to be in the newspaper business. You think it over, will you?"

"Yeah. I definitely will. How much will it pay?"

"That depends on how good you are. I'll pay you two and a half dollars a week, to start. If you're good, I'll pay you more."

"Alright. I'll let you know."

"The thing is, I have to go down to Jackson Friday and Saturday, for my father. But until Friday, you can reach me at Robinson's Hotel. You'll need to let me know before I leave for Jackson."

"Alright."

"Here."

Howard handed him a sheet of paper.

"You might want to read this while you think it over."

PROSPECTUS
OF THE
Oxford Intelligencer.

It is proposed to establish, at Oxford, Mississippi, a weekly journal, under the foregoing title, and to issue the first number on or about the 1ˢᵗ day of June, 1860.

THE INTELLIGENCER will not be the organ of any man, or of any clique or combination of individuals; but it will endeavor faithfully to represent the views and sentiments of the community of Oxford and Lafayette county, and to uphold and foster all the great interests – educational, agricultural, material, social, and moral – with which the highest welfare of our people is identified.

&etc.

Alemeth had always been interested in knowing the truth. Knowing how things really are, not just someone's half-baked opinion. Howard seemed intent on a newspaper that would restrict itself to what everybody agreed on. He could be happy as a part of such a paper, devoted to publishing what was obvious. He found Amzi in the tool shed.

"Pa, I thought you ought to know. Howard Falconer has offered me a job."

"Oh, yeah? Doing what?"

"Setting type for him. He's starting a newspaper."

Amzi didn't raise his gaze.

"I was hoping I'd get your blessing."

Then Amzi looked Alemeth in the eye. "You're telling me you're abandoning Bynum's Creek?"

"I'm not abandoning it, Pa."

"If you go to work for Howard Falconer, you are."

"Do I have your blessing?"

"You're wrong to be leaving your home, Alemeth. Your family."

"Pa, I won't be leaving."

Amzi's eyes were tired and sad. "Yes you will, son."

"What do you mean?"

"If you're going to spend all your time up in Oxford, working for Howard Falconer – rather than here on Bynum's Creek, where you belong – I can't support you in that. You'll have to move out of the house."

*   *   *

Robinson's
UNIVERSITY HOTEL

*   *   *

Thursday morning, Alemeth called on Howard at Robinson's. He'd be willing to accept the job – he *wanted* to accept the job – he'd long thought he might like to become a newspaper man – but he needed a place to stay, and he had no money for a room of his own.

"You can stay with me, if you like," said Howard. "I take my room by the week. You can have the bed when I'm gone, and can sleep on the floor when I'm here. Until you've earned enough to be on your own."

"Terrific."

"I've got a few minutes. Let's go over to the paper now. I'll show you what's what."

Howard and Alemeth walked to the Masonic Hall. On the first floor, a sign read "DOYLE'S," but instead of going into Doyle's shop, they took a stairway to the second floor.

"Welcome to the workplace," said Howard, leading the way up the steps. Upstairs, four men were at work on plastering rooms. One at the end of the hall had its own sign on the door: *"The Oxford Intelligencer."* Inside, basking in the chalky air of fresh plaster, were a press, and paper, and ink. On the wall, Howard had already hung a map of Mississippi and, next to it, a map of the entire country.

The letter cases were laid out on tables in several places around the room, but Howard had covered them with blankets to keep out the plaster dust. Alemeth removed several blankets and looked at the fonts.

"Thanks to Colonel Brown, we have plenty of sorts," said Howard. "We can have a good store of standby pieces."

Alemeth nodded. He understood the need for standby pieces.

In the adjoining room, Alemeth put his hand on a bearing bracket of the main steam press and gave it a tug. He put two fingers on the main roller and gave it a push. And then, when he'd satisfied himself that the roller seemed sound, Howard asked him to step into his office.

"Today is Thursday," he said. "We have five days to put together our first issue. We have to build up our standbys as soon as we can. We're going to have plenty to do for a while. But before we get to standbys, I have this." He handed a manuscript to Alemeth. "It's a Salutatory editorial I've written. It's going into the first issue. Why don't you see what you can do with it?"

Alemeth took the manuscript from Howard and carried it back to the letter cases. After studying what Howard had written, he found a font of large, ornamented Old English characters from which he picked out the sorts for the title. Then a more solid, block headline font for the second heading. And finally, some decorative dingbats to make the piece pop from the page.

𝕿𝖍𝖊 𝕺𝖝𝖋𝖔𝖗𝖉 𝕴𝖓𝖙𝖊𝖑𝖑𝖎𝖌𝖊𝖓𝖈𝖊𝖗.

HOWARD FALCONER, EDITOR.

WEDNESDAY, JUNE 6, - - - 1860.

We deem it not inappropriate, in the commencement of our enterprise, to mark out some of the principles and rules of conduct by which we purpose to be guided.

In politics, we belong to the Democratic party, and as far as we can, consistently with the interests of the country, and of the slaveholding States especially, we intend to strive for the unity and success of that party. But when our rights are jeopardized, and a domineering majority, refusing to recognize the great doctrine of equality of rights in the common territory, and making principles secondary to individuals, would exclude half the States from their birthright, and seal against them forever the blossoming fields won by their arms and consecrated by their blood, our allegiance to party will be thrown aside, and we shall gird on our armor to defend the right, and do battle for the sunny land which gave us birth, to stand with her or to fall with her.

Alemeth stopped reading. There was laughing in the hallway: the plasterers, sharing jokes. Better to read the rest of Howard's manuscript in the quiet. He closed the door.

Howard's manuscript called the "great" doctrine of states' rights the paper's "polar star." It called those opposed to slavery "devils," "champions of evil," and "ignorant fools." Every sentence had fighting words. They urged the readers to arms against the 'idiocy' of popular sovereignty. Urged people to be ready to protect their interests, "at all costs."

The Star had never been so passionate. Could these really be the feelings of the whole community? Manuscript in hand, Alemeth walked into Howard's office.

"Howard, would you like my opinion on your Salutatory?"

Howard seemed surprised, but said, "Of course, Alemeth. What is it?"

"I know a story needs a strong point of view. But I think you might want to consider toning it down some. You might lose your most important audience."

"Oh? And who might my most important audience be?"

"Readers sitting on the fence."

"What?"

"If you sound like an extremist, you might lose them. You want to grow your numbers, not shrink them. That's what Mr. Ward used to say."

"I'm well aware we want to grow our numbers, Alemeth. But the way things are going, a paper – well – alright. You make a good point. I'll tone it down some. Thanks."

Howard sat down and scribbled out a note, then handed it to Alemeth.

"Here. Make these changes. Scratch that last paragraph, and add this instead."

Alemeth read the note.

Good.

He felt a lot better setting the new paragraph.

Above all, it shall be our earnest effort to avoid dogmatism and strife. We are firmly convinced that a good cause loses nothing by extending courtesy to an opponent, and we are sure that a newspaper is not a fit arena for the settlement of disputes. We shall attack no one. We shall attempt to pull no one down. Such conduct does not, in our opinion, comport with the decency and dignity of the Press.

Alemeth breathed a sigh of relief. The changes and the addendum would add a less contentious flavor to the editorial; that could only be a good thing. And by fairness to the whole community, it was bound to get closer to the truth. Best of all, the new paragraph was (at least indirectly) his doing. He drew in a deep breath and exhaled long and slow. Satisfaction born of accomplishment was an unfamiliar feeling, and after the changes made at his suggestion, he saw himself in a new light. Not as just a worker in a lawyer's back office, like he'd been at *The Star*. Not as just a printer's devil. Not even as just a typesetter.

He had gotten Howard to commit the paper to decency. Who knows? Maybe his suggestion would influence the news for years to come. Maybe, he'd finally contributed something of value. Maybe, at *The Intelligencer*, he'd finally arrived at a place he really belonged. And maybe, if things went well, he'd have more chances for input into what the paper said.

That afternoon, Howard took the stage, off to Jackson to cover the states' rights convention for his father. Howard had left him instructions to set as many pieces as possible before his return. Alemeth found himself alone with the in-box.

He took a manuscript from the top, and composing stick in hand, began to set the next piece.

....

....

The Past and the Future.

No intelligent man can have given even a superficial attention to the history of American politics, for the period which has elapsed since the conclusion of peace with Great Britain in 1815, without perceiving that this history has derived its tone and color almost wholly from the operation of a single underlying cause – the hostility, secret or avowed, of one portion of the confederacy, to the industrial system provided by God and nature for the well-being of the other.

....

....

81

At the end of the day, Alemeth returned to Howard's room at the University Hotel. There was more to read than he'd ever seen. Nearly every surface had a book, magazine, or newspaper on it. Eyeing a space between the bed and the wall, he picked a place where Howard wouldn't step if he came in late, and lifted a newspaper from the spot, making a place to sit. It was a recent number of the *Memphis Daily Appeal*. Ben Dill, from the old Oxford *Organizer* was now one of its editors. The lead article described how the Methodist Church had condemned the use of violence to end slavery, stating, "We earnestly pray that the time may soon come when, through the blessed principles of the gospel of peace, slavery shall cease throughout the length and breadth of this fair land." Someone had marked the passage up, writing "Wrong!!" in big, bold letters, and "Wrong!!" a second time two other places further down.

The room wasn't like the one he'd had to himself at Bynum's Creek, but he could get to like it. Alone and free from the family, he no longer had Pa or Eliza to watch him. No one to express approval or disapproval. No one, even, to notice what he did. He was free to do whatever he wanted. But as if setting type all day had made him tired, he had hardly finished reading the piece when he fell soundly asleep.

The next day, back at the offices of *The Intelligencer*, he returned to the manuscripts in his inbox. One was a letter from Jacob Thompson proclaiming his loyalty to the people of Mississippi; another a reprint from *The Southern Herald* regarding the upcoming University Commencement Exercises; the third an article titled "Improvements in Oxford," describing new edifices in town "either contemplated or in the course of being erected." Ironically, not least among the improvements described was the very building in which he sat.

> The New Masonic Hall, in the second story
> of which the Intelligencer has its office, is
> so nearly completed that little more than half
> of the plastering remains to be done. One of
> the stores in the lower story is already occu-
> pied by Mr. Doyle; and the other will soon
> receive the stock of goods of Mssrs. Web-
> ber & Watkins, to whom it has been rented.

It was strange to be setting type inside the room the type described, as if he held the Masonic Hall in the palm of his own hand, as if he held the office around him between his thumb and his forefinger, looking in on himself from the outside. Smelling the plaster, listening to the trowels and jokes from the workmen, he pondered another irony: that he was informing the town of what was going on, but he was doing so by using Howard's thoughts and by reproducing Howard's words.

> A.L. Shotwell, Esq., it is understood, has
> contracted for putting up a residence, of an
> elegant description, at a cost of $15,000;

Andrew Shotwell and Julia Brown. The newlyweds – his cousins, if you bought how Eliza put things – would be neighbors of the bride's father. Very cozy.

And then another irony still: by setting the type, by composing the single sorts into words and sentences, he was a courier of sorts, carrying Howard's message to the rest of the world; but at the same time, he was a reader of that message. Composer, courier, reader, all at once – it was like looking into a mirror, seeing and being seen.

> Col. W. F. Avent has nearly completed a
> spacious and tasteful dwelling, near the Rail-
> road.

Col. W. F. Avent. Now there was an item of interest. He'd seen the construction. It was only a matter of time before the Avents – and Sally Fox – would be residents of Depot Street. The thought of it set his spine tingling. He had to rein in his thoughts of Sally, purposefully squelching them to concentrate on work again.

When the piece on *Improvements* was complete, Alemeth found an editorial manuscript in Howard's hand, and began to set it. The manuscript was titled, "Black Republican Disregard of Constitutional Obligation." It was tiresome work, but for the rest of the afternoon, Alemeth assembled Howard's legal argument that the refusal of the northern states to return runaway slaves was a violation of Article Four, Section Two, of the Constitution. And as best he could, reminding himself repeatedly of the task at hand, he tried not to think of Sally Fox.

He spent Saturday composing more pieces. That night, Howard returned with news of the convention from Jackson. Alemeth was busy all day Sunday and Monday immersing himself in the details of parliamentary maneuvering and Robert's Rules of Order as experienced by – or, at least, as related by – Howard. On Tuesday, two columns lay open in the galley, waiting for late-breaking news, but no such news came. Howard strutted around the office, walking back and forth to the courthouse, sending runners to the telegraph office, wanting *something* worth printing to happen. Alemeth couldn't help but share his anxiety, wishing that something – anything – would happen to let the paper demonstrate its immediacy – and to keep Howard from pacing. Finally, late in the day, Howard told Alemeth there wasn't time to wait any longer, to go ahead and use the standby pieces.

"Here," he said, his disappointment sharp enough to provoke sarcasm. "Late breaking news. Add it to the piece on the commencement exercises." The item simply noted that the commencement sermon would be delivered by the Rev. Robert B. White, D.D., of Tuscaloosa, on Sunday the 24th in the College Chapel, and that the orator of the two literary Societies would deliver his discourse in the chapel on Wednesday the 27th. Late breaking news? Alemeth had never seen Howard so out of sorts.

Tuesday evening the steam-driven press produced seven hundred copies, eight pages each. The press, an 'iron maiden' in its own right, ran like a locomotive, its steam doing the work of a hundred men, until well past midnight. First thing Wednesday morning, Howard took copies of the paper to Neilsons and the hotels. Alemeth loaded a hundred papers into Howard's buckboard and delivered them to paid subscribers. That afternoon, when Gordon came over to help Alemeth break down the galleys, they spoke of the satisfaction to be gained from publishing the written word. Then, late in the day, Gordon announced he had something he had to get down on paper before he lost the thought – some short story that had been in his head about good people doing bad things. He left Alemeth to finish composing Howard's words alone.

As Alemeth sat dropping the last sorts into the letter case, Eliza knocked at the door. He answered it hesitantly. She didn't wait to be invited in.

How was he?

Had he eaten?

The house seemed empty without him.

For a moment, she seemed caring and warm. But the peaceful mood did not last long.

No one had seen him on Sunday. Had he not gone to church?

Well, no. He hadn't been to church.

"Not to *any* church?"

"No, Eliza. Not to any church."

"Alemeth, in town you have First Presbyterian, the Cumberland, the Methodist, the Episcopal, and now even St. Peter's, all just a short walk from here. You're not that far from College Hill. You can go to any of them. Do you intend to treat the Lord's day so lightly?"

"I was planning to go."

"Really?"

"Yes."

"So why didn't you?"

"Howard needed me to work."

"I see. So you're working on the Sabbath now."

"He needed me, Eliza."

"God needs you in Heaven, Alemeth. Surely one day a week isn't asking too much."

"I did the right thing by helping Howard. Think of it as an act of kindness toward him. Didn't Jesus say something about doing for your neighbor what you'd have your neighbor do for you?"

"So you worked on the Sabbath to do something for your neighbor?"

"I did."

"And you were so occupied doing the right thing for Howard, you couldn't take two hours to do the right thing for God?"

"Eliza, I know you're my elder. And a woman. I mean no disrespect. But you're not my mother. The law no longer treats me as a child. Why do you?"

"I don't treat you like a child, I —"

"You don't think so? You should listen to yourself."

"I'll certainly pray about it. You know, Alemeth, as scripture says, 'To those who have faith — '"

"I know. Anything's possible."

"Alemeth, if a person has no faith, they'll be shut out of the kingdom of heaven. Hebrews three eighteen."

"*Why*, Eliza? *Why* do you have to quote scripture all the time?"

The words were already out by the time he realized what he'd said. Immediately, he regretted asking. He thought for a moment that she was about to cry, and he considered making a quick apology. But then her countenance hardened. She raised her chin slightly and glared at him.

"Alemeth, I have faith in the Word of God, even if you don't. You'll accept the Lord someday, as I have. Then you'll understand."

His neck tensed. What gave her the right to be so sure she knew something he didn't? It was clear she claimed some sort of 'special connection to God' that he lacked. Like salt in a wound, it outraged him. He had no more thought of forgiveness or apology. Jesus died for our sins – what more faith did a person need than that?

82

A few days later, after a brief item about the season's first cotton bloom and another about the arrival in Oxford of L.Q.C. Lamar, Alemeth's in-box contained a manuscript written in an unfamiliar hand.

Step-Mothers.

The opinion of the juvenile world, and indeed of the world generally, with regard to step-mothers, is not flattering to that class of matrons.

He could go along with that; it was an understatement, to say the least. What made stepmothers like Eliza and Mrs. Brown act as they did? He had no idea. Maybe they felt they had something to prove.

There is, however, a strong infusion of prejudice and injustice in many popular opinions, and this is one of them. Second wives are not necessarily, or indeed commonly, the unamiable creatures they are represented to be.

What? This ought to be good. A defense of step-mothers?

Who is there among us that has not known second wives whose tenderness to their step-children could not have been surpassed by the mother that bore them?

Others, maybe. He couldn't vouch for what he didn't know. Maybe Frances and Fredonia didn't mind Mary Ann Brown. But Eliza? She could never compare to his real mother.

The offspring of a first marriage are almost invariably disposed to look upon a step-mother as their foe. They regard her as an interloper, a task-mistress, an ogress, whose great end and aim in life is to monopolize their father's affection and his worldly goods, and between whom and themselves no feelings can exist save distrust and hatred. This predisposition, or rather predetermination, on the part of the

> children to consider their step-dame their
> foe, is likely enough to make her so. The
> temper and disposition must be of exceeding
> sweetness that can stand such an ordeal with-
> out souring; and there can be but little
> doubt that the origin of many family feuds
> growing out of second marriages might be
> traced to the aggressive acts of step-children.

Well. *He*'d done nothing aggressive. He could have happily left her alone altogether.

She, on the other hand: she insisted the family have daily Bible readings. Insisted he go to church. Insisted on Sunday School. Insisted on teaching Kep. If anyone had been aggressive, it was her. He felt no guilt. His hands were clean. Any difficulty she might be having, she'd brought it on herself.

Hackles up, accused, justifying himself, the next paragraph caught him off guard.

> But the law of kindness is a love-compelling
> ordinance, and its persevering observance
> will overcome the strongest antipathies. Let
> the second wife who desires to secure the
> affection of her husband's motherless chil
> dren, meet their hostility with the soft an
> swers that turn away wrath and the disinter
> estedness that disarms prejudice, and she is
> sure in the end to make a conquest of their
> hearts.

He hurried into Howard's office.

"Did you write this?"

"Does it sound like me? Does it look like my writing?"

"No. You're right. Who wrote it, then?"

"The lady asked me to keep her contribution anonymous. I gave her my word as a gentleman."

"I see. It wasn't – "

Howard looked impenetrable, and Alemeth was already too frustrated to take on any more of a challenge.

"Oh, never mind."

On Sunday, Alemeth went to church with Howard at First Presbyterian. Sally's absence made Alemeth glum, but Howard was as enthusiastic as ever.

"Micajah Wade is going to retitle his Commencement address," he said with a satisfied air. "The new title is 'The Anglo-Saxon Race.'"

Micajah Wade? Who cared anything about the Anglo-Saxon race? The writer of *Step-Mothers* had not taken her manuscript to *The Holly Springs Herald* or *The Mercury*, but to *The Intelligencer*. She had spoken to Howard. Pretty clearly, she was one of the University set. Could she be someone he knew? Could she be thinking of *him,* and his relationship with Eliza?

That afternoon, he went out on the square. A broadsheet on the door at Neilson's advertised the nominating convention in Baltimore. Buck Avent was there; he'd probably taken his whole family, including Sally. Alemeth walked down Depot Street anyway. When he got to the edge of town, there was no sign of movement at Colonel Brown's house. But in the Avents' yard, below the sweeping limb of a live oak, a bright white wooden bench swayed slightly at the end of two ropes. It could have been just a breeze he hadn't noticed. But another thought proved tantalizing. At some point, surely, *someone* had been sitting there. The idea – the image of someone sitting in the swing, someone lifting themselves out of it just moments before – refused to leave him alone.

Though work kept him downtown most of the time, he began to walk down Depot Street whenever he could. And one afternoon several days later, beneath the oak canopy, on the white swing, Sally Fox was there, sitting next to Julia Brown. Talking to them were Howard and Gordon. Upon seeing Sally, Alemeth's spirits soared.

They were talking about the Commencement Ball. Sally looked straight at him, her smile sad but enthralling. He hardly heard what Julia was saying: "Andrew and I are going. Mr. Falkner is going to escort Miss Sally. Who are you going with?" And he hardly heard Howard's answer: "I'm afraid I'll be attending on my own."

It took several seconds, picturing Gordon with Miss Sally, before Alemeth could say anything. "Me, too," was all he finally muttered. "I'll also be going on my own." But even that proved an embarrassment.

"The Ball's for students and alumni, Alemeth. You didn't get an invitation, did you?"

The night of the Commencement Ball, Alemeth sat alone in Howard's room at the University Hotel, imagining things he couldn't see, waiting endlessly for Gordon and Sally as the night dragged on. Virgil's *Georgics* – or more exactly, his lack of any experience with them – had come back to haunt him again.

83

Tuesday, July 17th, 1860, 9:31 a.m.
34.37° north; 89.52° west

Alemeth sat in the press room of The Oxford Intelligencer, scanning a proof he'd just set about an address by General George Bickley to The Knights of the Golden Circle. Bickley wanted to "southernize" slave-free Mexico, to take over the country and reinstate slavery there. People said Bickley was planning an invasion. Alemeth had no interest in an invasion of Mexico; he was staying right where he was.

Tuesday, July 17th, 1860, 9:31 p.m.
38.88° north, 77.03° west

Of ninety-six patents Philip Thomas signed that week, one had caught his attention: Patent No. 29,217, filed by Benjamin Garvey of New York, was for a steam generator with sheets of metal riveted so as to hold them together with a greater force than the steam to be generated between them could exert to force them apart. Thomas thought the invention comparable to the state of the nation, and hoped it would hold together.

Wednesday, July 18th, 1860, 9:31 a.m.
59.07° north; 64.02° west

Dr. Frederick Barnard, in Labrador to watch a total eclipse of the sun, observed the phenomenon known as "Bailey's Beads" – rays of light skirting the cratered surface of the moon, one becoming bright and diamond-shaped, the circle like an enormous wedding ring. The United States Coast Survey was there to assess the impact of the eclipse on the earth's magnetic fields. But the team was disappointed: clouds prevented a thorough observation.

Wednesday, July 18th, 1860, 9:31 p.m.
34.37° north; 89.52° west

Alemeth was walking toward the railroad depot when someone cried "Fire!!!" Great black furls of smoke were bellowing from a side window of Colonel Brown's house. Old folks and mothers were holding children out of the way. On the front lawn of Buck Avent's house, between Sarah Avent and Harriet Thompson, was Sally Fox, her eyes locked with his. But as Alemeth ran toward the fire, he lost her, as if she, too, had gone up in the smoke.

....

....

The Fire.

ON Wednesday night, July 18th, about 9 1-2
o'clock, our town was suddenly startled by the
alarm of Fire!   Fire!   It was soon ascertained
that the dwelling house of Col. JAS. BROWN, on
Depot Street, west of town, was on fire. A scene
of the utmost confusion ensued; but, thanks to
the great efforts of the citizens, no lives were
lost, and a large part of the furniture was saved.
The house was burned to the ground ; but the
frame double office in the yard, and a brick
kitchen in the rear of the dwelling, were saved.
The loss is estimated at $7000. The fire was
thought to have originated in the kitchen, connected with the dwelling, through some carelessness
on the part of the servants.

....

....

The fire at Colonel Brown's house would have changed things even if it had been the only arson in Oxford that summer. It would have changed things even if everyone really believed it had been caused by carelessness. But as it was, more fires followed, and the theory of carelessness became hard to accept. A fire at the new steam mill that very night prompted Howard to say the two fires were probably started by the same trouble-maker. When a fire razed Nathan Worley's house on Saturday morning, Howard slammed his fist on his desk so hard a pair of scissors fell to the floor.

After each fire, additional paragraphs appeared in Alemeth's inbox, with directions to add them to prior accounts. Saturday night, when Neilson's was the target, Howard decried the arsonist's nerve – to commit such a heinous act of terror in the courthouse square, right under the nose of *The Intelligencer!* Nothing in Alemeth's in-box named any suspect, but as the week passed, Howard voiced his suspicions of Captain Boynton, the chemistry professor, in a dozen different ways. As each fire broke out, his suspicion grew stronger.

One afternoon, Sheriff Bill McKee stopped by the offices, wanting to know if anyone recognized the red checkered shirt he'd found down at the steam mill. When Alemeth said he had a similar shirt, McKee asked where he'd been on the night of the eighteenth. When he pointed out that witnesses had seen him arrive at the Brown's house after the fire broke out there, McKee conceded that he wouldn't likely set fire to his own uncle's house. But then Howard started with questions of his own.

"Alemeth, that explosion you and Macon Thompson caused last year. You and Macon were making gun cotton, as I recall."

"We were trying to make collodion. For photographs."

"Yes. But the gun cotton you made – the material that exploded – there was nothing left of it afterward?"

"Well, maybe it escaped, as a gas, and left no trace among the ashes."

"And it was Captain Boynton who taught you how to make the gun cotton?"

"Well, yeah, I guess. He taught Macon, anyway."

That was Monday morning. Howard and Sheriff McKee went to see Captain Boynton Monday afternoon.

When Howard got back, he seemed bothered. He kept muttering about Captain Boynton. And on Tuesday night, after visiting Sheriff McKee to inquire of any last minute fires, he handed Alemeth one last piece to set.

....

....

Excitement among Oxonians.

FOR the last week, Oxford has been a scene of no little alarm and excitement. There has, evidently, been a determined effort, on the part of some depraved scoundrels, to burn down the houses of some of our citizens. Since last Wednesday night, up to this, Tuesday evening, only one night has passed without an alarm. In consequence, our people have been thoroughly aroused to the necessity of ridding themselves of the cause of all this trouble; and sentinels have been stationed about the town, every night, for the past week. Woe to the wretch who shall be caught at his fiendish work! We would not give a sixpence for his lease of life. The hempen cord and death by strangulation would be almost too good for the villain who could wantonly endanger the lives of whole families.

....

....

84

Captain Boynton was outraged, adamant he'd not had anything to do with the arsons. He had alibis for several, and unlike some, he'd never been seen in a red checkered shirt. So Mr. Chalmers told Sheriff McKee there was really no evidence against Boynton at all. McKee passed the lawyer's opinion on to Howard.

"It's plenty plausible he's our man," said McKee. "I have to admit. Especially as to the days he has no alibi. But Chalmers is right, Howard: there's just no hard evidence."

Howard complained. Captain Boynton's anti-slavery views were well known. And the man was a skilled chemist with access to cotton and ammonia. McKee pointed out that every doctor and druggist around had access to cotton and ammonia. Not only that, he said, there was no evidence that the fires had anything to do with cotton *or* ammonia. (This was the point which divided the two men most: Howard found the lack of cotton and ammonia proof of the arsonist's chemical expertise, which, he believed, was tantamount to proof of Boynton's guilt.) The next week, when an attempt was made to torch Judge Howry's house, Howard again urged his suspicions about Captain Boynton. But when the next fire was at Vince Johnson's in Caswell, Boynton could prove he had not been anywhere near Johnson's house.

"Alright," Howard conceded. "I'll grant you he's not the *only* arsonist. But innocence on one count doesn't disprove guilt on another. And if there is more than one arsonist, it makes catching them all the more important."

"Maybe…"

"In the meantime, Alemeth, remember this: we don't have to pretend to like the man."

Alemeth had taken a liking to Boynton at first. But Boynton's abolitionist sentiments could lead to agitation and worse. No one could approve of burning down houses of innocent people, putting innocent lives at risk. If Boynton had anything to do with such fiendish work, he deserved to be caught and dealt with severely. *Whoever* it was deserved whatever came to them. No one had cause to torch the home of another man, no matter what their differences.

The day might yet come when everyone could see things the same way, but it seemed no closer than it ever had, and Alemeth wondered, how many years would he have to live before he saw any chance of such clarity in the world?

From the New York Churchman.
The Slavery Problem.

———

*   *   *   *   *

WITHOUT taking an extreme theory, and afterwards putting down facts to fit, according to modern usage, we begin by saying that, from the inherent characteristics of the negro race, we deduce the fact that the black man is intended by God to be the servant of the white man, as much as children are intended by nature to be subject to and dependent on their natural guardians; that the natives of Africa are no more able by a spontaneous effort, to raise themselves from their debased social, moral, and religious condition, than a newly-born infant is capable of supplying itself with food and raiment without the care of its parents; that every Christian man must recognize the responsibility with which God's providence has laid upon the superior race, to provide for the wants, both temporal and eternal, of the inferior one; that, to accomplish this end, the white race must exercise a certain amount of control and authority over the black ; and that, as a natural sequence, negro slavery, in some form or other, is part of the harmonious system established by God, in His good pleasure, for man's governance.

    *   *   It is doubtless our duty as a Christian people to bring this degraded and brutalized race under the influence of Christianity and within the pale of the Church, *even in spite of themselves.*

85

As Alemeth set the reprint from the *New York Churchman*, he thought of the difference between Eliza's beliefs and those of Reverend Stewart. Eliza looked forward to the day God would bring an end to slavery. It was one thing he saw the way she did. The piece Howard chose to reprint from the *Churchman* mirrored Reverend Stewart's thinking that slavery, instituted by God, was a just institution that Christians had a duty to defend. Would God really have commanded his people to make slaves of heathens if to do so was immoral? If God planned to do away with it in the future? It didn't seem so.

A young negro boy six or eight years old, paddle fan in hand, shooed away flies from the dinner table.

"If they'll burn down my house," said the Colonel, "they'll do anything. People need to keep their ears open. There's no telling what the negroes could do. This isn't Connecticut, Mary Ann. There are a lot more of them here."

"More of them than us."

"And don't forget what the slaves did to your family's plantation in Haiti, Eliza. We can't afford to ignore the agitators. If we do, they'll convince our negroes Abe Lincoln is going to set them free."

"Some of them are calling it the promise of Abraham. Is that right, Harl?"

"Yes, ma'am."

"I'll have to go over that again in Sunday School this week. We need to be sure everyone understands Romans 13:7. 'Render therefore to all their dues.' What the gospel says about equality and redemption relates to spiritual affairs, not civil relations."

"So, Eliza, scripture never says slavery's a sin?"

"No, it does not; it explicitly condones it. Slavery is a part of God's plan, just as much as its elimination. The promise of Abraham may not be fulfilled in our lifetimes. It may be centuries before all souls are free."

"Ladies," interrupted the Colonel. "If I may address the reason I invited you here tonight..."

Alemeth looked up from his dinner plate.

"I've asked you all here because you are my family. And there is nothing more important than family."

"Papa used to talk about our bloodline," added Mrs. Brown to Eliza.

"Before anyone else, I wanted you – the members of my family – to know where I stand on our relations with the north. Wasn't it John Locke who asked, 'What is liberty, unless it is the freedom from any power except that established by consent?' If a man says, I don't have the right to secede from union with him, then as I see it, he's attempting to interfere with my freedom."

Heads nodded.

"And if, when he hears me talk of the possibility of separation, he tells me he'll resort to arms, if he has to, to preserve our union, when he has most of the power and uses it to my disadvantage, what should I call him then? My friend? And if at the same time he insists on having his way with me, then is he not trying to make me his slave?"

"You're right, dear," said Mrs. Brown.

"They would take what belongs to us. They've been burning our houses; mark my words, Amzi, they'll soon be burning our plantations. All a man has of any value is his land. If you take away a man's negroes, you take away the value of his land."

"Well said, Colonel."

"People say Abe Lincoln is an ape. I say he's a man who would like to be king, whether he realizes it or not. Tyranny is tyranny, whatever its source. What will we do if he and his allies are elected?"

Looks exchanged across the table.

"Anything less than our grandfathers did, when they faced the tyranny of King George?"

Silence. More looks exchanged.

"This is our chance to do what our grandfathers did."

"Revolution?"

"Nothing less. Andy Jackson got us through our second war for independence. I'd say it's time for our third."

Silence.

"We know that a sovereign state has a legal *right* to secede. And we know that in the face of tyranny, revolution is an obligation. All that's left to decide is how, and when, and under what circumstances, we should do so."

"People are saying we should secede if Lincoln is elected."

"Possibly so," said the Colonel. "But that brings me to the point. We don't know when, but we know the day will come. So we need to spend every day in the meantime, getting ourselves ready for the fight. We can't afford to give up the initiative. We need to get as ready as possible."

"Agreed," said Mr. Walter.

"Tell me, Colonel," said Mr. Shotwell. "What do you make of this Bickley fellow?"

"I think we need to hear what he has to say. I'm planning to go. Gentlemen, shall we retreat to the terrace, for cigars? Let the ladies be rid of us?"

K. G. C.

Gen. Bickley, father of the K. G. C., paid Oxford a visit on last Thursday. At night he addressed the public in the Town Hall, and, at the close of his address, organized a Castle of the celberated brotherhood. A number of our citizens enrolled their names among the faithful, and there is little doubt that a large number of our people will enlist under the banner of the K. G. C.

Colonel Brown had returned from Bickley's meeting saying he agreed with Bickley's theories, but in his opinion, Bickley's proposals were impractical. Brazil, he said, had no interest in forming a common state with any part of North America. Nor could the people of Mississippi afford to invade Mexico. There was a more important front to be concerned with: the need to combine against the threat to the north; to align according to *that* common interest.

Howard had agreed. There was no one with a better grasp on public affairs than the Colonel. So Alemeth had decided Bickley was not worth further thought. When he'd finished setting the type for the K.G.C. meeting, he turned to setting standby pieces and day dreaming of Sally Fox – the voice that sounded like the purr of a lioness. The red hair. The captivating smile.

He was about to marry Sally and start a family with her when there was a knock on the office door. He opened it to find Eliza on the other side.

"May I come in?"

"Of course. I'm sorry. I could have gone to church."

"Alemeth, that's not why I'm here."

"It isn't?"

"I came to talk to you about how your Pa. We all know he's upset about you. That's why he's been in such a mood. The rest of us can bear it, if we must, but we would prefer your Pa in better spirits. And we think it's because you've left us."

"I'm not going back to Bynum's Creek, Eliza. It's too far. I need to be close to the print shop, and to Howard."

Eliza looked down. "Alright. I understand."

Then she looked up, with hope in her eyes.

"But how about this: your Pa is going to the Knights' Castle meeting Wednesday. If you would go too, it would give you a chance to talk to each other."

His eyes met hers, but he said nothing.

"Your Pa has been reading *The Intelligencer*. He looks at the typesetting. He says he's found hardly any mistakes. Why do you think your Pa would mention something like that to me?"

"I don't know."

"I think he's proud of you."

"No – "

"He sees you doing well on your own, Alemeth. He wouldn't likely admit it, but I think he may regret how hard he was on you. He loves you, you know. Maybe, if you mend fences with him, he'd give you money for some better clothes. You need clothes more suitable for work in town, you know. If you'd just meet him half way, your Pa could be of help to you. Somehow."

"I don't know..."

"What harm could come from *talking* to him?"

It was true. Nothing Pa had ever done justified not talking to him.

*   *   *

Three dozen men attended the Castle meeting. Alemeth had never felt more out of place than he did at the gathering of men who wanted to invade Mexico.

"It makes good sense," said Lucius Lamar. "We should ally ourselves with all those who share a stake in the preservation of slavery: the states where cotton is grown. Tobacco. Sugar. Rice. The crops of the tropical climates, where labor must be suited to the heat. From Richmond and Memphis in the north, to Mexico, Cuba, and Brazil, the Americas are the land God gave us; He made us responsible for feeding and clothing the world. Will we not be stronger, if allied together?"

Amzi was on the other side of the room, not looking Alemeth's way. There was no way to tell what he was thinking.

"We should secede from the northern union. Re-center popular government toward the south."

Finally, Amzi looked up at him.

"Align in accordance with the climate, as Agassiz taught. Each species created by God to fit perfectly in its place. Each race as much so, all as sanctioned by Holy Writ."

It was not until Lamar stopped talking and started to mingle with the crowd that Amzi was close enough for conversation.

"Evenin', Alemeth. How have you been?"

"Alright."

"Are you ready to come home?"

"Pa, I mean no disrespect. But I'd rather not. I've got a job now, with Howard. And to tell the truth, I like living in town."

"I can't convince you to come home?"

"I don't think so, Pa. Remember, you're the one who said I couldn't stay at home."

"Alright, son. Have it your way. But if this Lincoln fellow is elected, he may invade. Like Cornwallis or Dessalines. What will you do then?"

"What do you mean?"

"What if abolitionists try to take the plantation? You will help us defend Bynum's Creek, won't you?"

"Of course, Pa. Bynum's Creek is my home. How could I not defend it?"

86

Ever since George Oliver's conviction for manslaughter, people had been wondering how the Mississippi Supreme Court would rule on Oliver's appeal.

Hugh Barr had pointed out a practical problem.

"If a slave absolutely refuses to perform labor, as directed by the master, what can a master do to assert his authority?" Barr had asked at oral argument. "Must he simply accept the refusal?"

"'Just punish him.' That's what Mr. Chalmers would suggest. But I ask you – what if the slave laughs at his punishment? What if he intentionally works so slowly as to amount to defiance, and won't give honest effort, regardless of his punishment? If no lesser form of punishment succeeds, if even the lash produces no work – is the master left with no remedy at all? The law requires him to feed and clothe his slave; must he continue to do so, while getting nothing but insolence in return? Surely the law has to be interpreted in light of the practicalities inherent in the master-slave relationship. If being a master is to mean anything, a man *has* to have the right to do whatever it takes to secure obedience – and, yes, in some extreme cases, that can include taking the life of his slave."

The argument, once made by Barr in the courtroom, had been repeated all over Mississippi.

Then one night the Colonel and Barr returned from Jackson with the news that the court had ruled in Oliver's favor. The killing of a slave by a master, when the slave is resisting his master, can be considered neither murder nor manslaughter. "The master may use just such force as may be requisite to reduce his slave to obedience, even to the death of the slave, if that becomes necessary to maintain his lawful authority."

Hugh Barr had won his case.

George Washington Oliver had won his freedom.

Mr. Barr, Mr. Oliver, Colonel Brown and other notables celebrated at Buck Avent's house that night with *coq au vin flambé*, snifters of Cognac, and toasts to the judges of the court, who had impressed all the planters in Mississippi with their insight and sagacity.

"They were simply fair-minded enough to listen to reason," it was agreed.

(There were fires in Oxford that night, too.)

87

One cloudy afternoon, when Howard had taken Alemeth to the cotton market with him, a wind picked up that rustled the branches of the cedar trees. Someone mentioned the risk of rain. An insurance man said that in his estimation, the greater risk was fire. Sheriff McKee got the insurance man to agree that his numbers were based on past claims, so didn't factor in the risk of sabotage, which in his judgment was considerable, considering current circumstances. Then Colonel Brown spoke up, in his commanding voice, and said, "There's a bigger risk than either rain or fire. If the abolitionists instigate a slave rebellion, we'll have no one to work the land. We'll all be wiped out."

Howard Falconer followed the Colonel's lead.

"God Himself has entrusted this land to our care," he said. "We can't allow it to go to waste. Good stewardship requires the defeat of abolitionism."

"Maybe we should sign up with General Bickley," said Mr. Smither.

"General Bickley has some strange ideas," replied Howard, stepping forward to impress Colonel Brown by parroting his own ideas. "But he's raised the right question: with what states *should* Mississippi align herself? To our East, we have Alabama, Georgia, the Carolinas, all strong sisters. Who doesn't have family there? To the west, Arkansas and Texas are also our close friends. Most of us have family there. We all know that the threat lies to the north, which is fast becoming a land of immigrants and foreigners. At the end of the day, we need to be focused on defending our northern border. We need to protect Mississippi at Corinth. We shouldn't give the yankees two inches of our soil." He threw a knife into the ground, its polished blade grating on entry. "And we need to do it to the last ounce of blood if need be."

Colonel Brown stepped forward.

"All said very well, Howard. I certainly agree about General Bickley; our concern *must* be with the enemy to the north. But I'll tell you what I would do. I would not draw the line on the Mississippi border."

He lifted the knife out of the ground.

"That would give up Memphis. And it would give up the Memphis and Charleston railroad. In my view, we draw the line over there."

He threw the knife. It stuck again, several feet further north.

"There. We have to have Tennessee with us. Otherwise, we abandon the railroad. Tennessee is Jackson country, at heart. Southerners have good friends there too."

....

....

A DEMOCRATIC BARBEQUE

at Col. Jas. Brown's Clear Creek Plantation, on
Saturday, October 20th.
HONS. L. Q. C. LAMAR and J. M. HOWRY,
...... and F. J. LOVEJOY, ESQ.,
will be present and make speeches. The people
generally, and the ladies especially, are invited
to attend.

....

....

Alemeth had never seen more pink, rose and lavender than among the sundresses and parasols that converged among Mrs. Brown's birds of paradise, as if the ladies were trying to match the flowers. But they were of no account to him. There was no point in conversation with Mary Jane, Sarah Frances or Julia Brown. He cared only for signs of Sally Fox.

She was nowhere on the patio.

Which had felt worse? Seeing Gordon with Sally on the swing? Watching her and Gordon at the Colonel's? Missing the Commencement Ball? Gordon and Sally saw something in each other; that was clear enough. But something didn't fit. She was the girl he'd danced with on Independence Day – the day he'd got drunk and scared her away – he was sure of it. Why had she denied it? Why, unless she felt *something* toward him? And hadn't he seen that same interest in the look she'd given him at other times – that radiant, enthralling smile that seemed reserved for him?

He turned to look elsewhere, but Amzi stopped him.

"Where are you going?"

"I was – "

"Stay here. You need to hear this."

For the next hour, Alemeth had to sit and listen, detained, as the lawyers gave speeches from Colonel Brown's terrace.

Howry spoke first: something about the right of free people to sever the ties that bind to an unjust ruler. Lovejoy followed, asserting that having joined in alliance with each other voluntarily in the first place, free states had the same freedom to withdraw from that alliance – "the very essence of freedom," he called it. Going last, Lamar got the crowd going with talk of Divine Providence, patriotism and the doctrine of Just War. Howard applauded. Gordon jotted notes.

When the speeches were done, Alemeth slipped off, ducking around the corner of the house – where, at last, he found Sally.

She was standing with Mary Ann Brown and several young women. A woman he didn't recognize was the obvious center of attention. Everyone – including Sally – was listening intently to what she was saying to Mrs. Brown.

"I'd just left Mr. Avent's house, later than expected, and I was alone. As I was passing the Depot in my buggy, I saw a colored boy – a very large colored boy – outside the warehouse. I couldn't imagine what he'd be doing there in the middle of the night, so I pulled up to get a better look. He was at a wagon parked outside the warehouse, opening a box in the back of it. So I called out to him. I asked him who he was, and what business he had there."

"You didn't! Weren't you afraid?"

"Yes. I was. But the men can't keep vigilant for all of us."

"So what happened?"

"Well, the way that boy answered me! I thought he would hide whatever he had, or make some sort of excuse. But he walked right up to me. And I realized then just how big a boy he was. He was nearly as high as I was, in my buggy."

"You didn't recognize him?"

"No. I asked him who he belonged to. The way he looked at me, like he was angry, like he was trying to decide whether to grab me and kill me or run away. He said he didn't belong to nobody, he was a free man. I asked him again what he was doing at the warehouse. He showed me a bag he'd taken out of the wagon. He pulled out a few pieces of cloth from it – high quality cloth, as best I could tell – and he asked me if I might be interested in buying some! Can you imagine?"

"No…"

"How strange."

"How terrible."

"I think he was lying. He'd stolen that cloth, I'm sure of it. Free or not, he was there for no good reason. I could feel it."

"My Lord! What did you do?"

"I said I was most *certainly* not interested in buying any of his cloth. He just turned his back to me. Got into his wagon and drove off. He never did tell me why he was there. But I'd had enough. I'd done enough, I should say, and in spite of the danger to my person. I wasn't about to follow him."

"You poor dear."

"A woman's not safe, at night, in a buggy by herself. Even in town."

"Something ought to be done."

"For all we know, Mary, if it weren't for you, we'd have had another fire."

"I'll speak to the Colonel," said Mrs. Brown.

The ladies huddled protectively around their distraught sister, forming a barrier that, whatever it did for her, cut Alemeth off from Sally Fox.

Resolutions of Our Agricultural Society

Resolved, That we recommend to the people of this county the rigorous observance of the policy set forth in the following regulations:

1. That no negro be allowed, under any circumstances, to leave home without the written permission of his owner, employer or overseer.

2. That no negro be allowed to buy or sell anything whatever, without a written permit, specifying what he is authorized to buy or sell.

3. That no negro, under any circumstances, be allowed, at night or on Sunday, to visit Oxford, or any other place where goods are kept for sale, for the purpose of trading.

4. That all negroes be required to be in their own houses from and after the hour of ten o'clock at night.

5. That the owner or manager on every plantation habitually visit each negro cabin, after ten o'clock at night, at least twice in every month, at irregular intervals, and oftener if necessary.

88

On Tuesday morning – election day – with the fat of the country hanging in the balance – Amzi, Uncle Johnson and Alemeth took saddle horses into Panola and cast three votes for John Breckenridge, the only pro-slavery candidate in the field. Alemeth was late for work, but everything had been set except space for the late breaking news. There was nothing in the office he needed to do. Eventually, Howard sent him to Clear Creek with a note for Colonel Brown.

Alemeth waited for the Colonel's reply in the garden. Harl was standing next to the parrots' cage, a pair of scissors in his hands.

"Hey there, Harl."

"Hallo, Master Byers."

"Where are the birds today?"

"Them birds won't stay put no more."

"Oh, yeah?"

"Mrs. Brown say, Make sure them birds get plenty o' time outside. So I leaves 'em on the terrace. Every day, they get up and fly around. Get their exercise. They always come back. Then, the other day, Calliope bit Miss Mary Porter. Mary Porter said she hadn't done nothing to rile her. But Mrs. Brown, she took her parasol to the bird. After that, both birds been away all day. Last couple days, they only come at feeding time. Now she told me I got to clip their wings."

Colonel Brown appeared at the doorway.

"Here's my reply," he said, holding it out for Alemeth. "And one other thing. Alemeth, tell your father, and tell Howard, too. Fire or no fire, I can't let the abolitionists drive me out of my own home. I'm going to rebuild the house at the Depot, without delay."

Before returning to the office, Alemeth swung by the Avent house. Workmen had finished clearing the rubble where the Colonel's house had been. There was no sign of Miss Sally. No voice, no hair, no smile.

*   *   *

That night, Alemeth joined Howard at the telegraph office. Howard had been on high alert most of the afternoon and evening. Most of the paper was set in the galley. All that remained was the news about the elections. Waiting. When the click-clacking began, everyone listened intently, but only Tom Barret, the Depot Agent, could understand the wire. The rest of them looked at Tom's face, trying to listen to whatever news they might read there.

When the message was finished, Tom read it aloud. Howard started scribbling on his note pad. Howard's shorthand looked like drivel, and Alemeth had long since given up trying to read it, so the story Howard was writing remained inscrutable. When he stopped, he said "Alright, let's get these results in print," and started for the office. As he walked out onto the street, he called over his shoulder, "You have any ideas for the headline?"

What Tom had read was no surprise, but it was still a disappointment. As predicted, the south had gone for Breckenridge and Democracy. The north had gone for Douglas or Lincoln. The result talked about by so many – no one with a majority – had finally come to pass. But Alemeth didn't know what sort of story Howard had written. And he learned that much from Martin Ward: without knowing the angle of Howard's story, how could he suggest a title?

Back at the office, Howard put his feet up on his desk, the butt end of a pen in his mouth. On a pad of writing paper held in his lap, he began turning his short hand into regular letters, speaking, half to himself, half to Alemeth, as he wrote. He'd hoped for an election night different from this. He'd hoped the Democratic Party would unite on the question of slavery. But not only was the news disappointing, it was hardly news at all.

"What do you think, Alemeth?"

"About what?"

"About the headline. What sort of headline is right, to announce news everyone's been predicting? Some angle, some point of view, that isn't expected."

"Well, since it seems he didn't even win a majority, what about something like 'Lincoln Elected By Minority'?"

"Oh, I don't know. I was thinking something more like, 'Victory to the Baboon.'"

89

At the Colonel's house, at the hotel, at Doyle's, and at Neilson's, secession from the Union was the topic of the day, and on that universal topic, everyone who could speak a language shared his opinion. Howard's opinion was evident in everything he printed. On November 14th, he bemoaned the win by the 'black Republicans' and called for loyal citizens to wear a blue cockade in support of a free Mississippi. The next week, he wrote of the Home Guard forming for defense against Yankee aggression. The next – a slow week – an opinion piece on the right of a sovereign state to secede. To continue willing submission to rule by northern government was unthinkable. To entertain any doubt about the wisdom of secession was treasonous.

Eliza's view was nothing like Howard's. She was upset by all the radical talk, consumed by worry that secession would lead to war, and looking to God for avoidance of bloodshed.

Howard tried to allay her fears. The Yankees, he said, were merchants, after all, and if reasonable minds prevailed, they'd realize the financial harm that war would bring. "They need our cotton as much as we do," he added. "As long as we put on a good show of strength, they'll back down."

Gordon's view was like neither Howard's nor Eliza's. Sporty and irreverent, Gordon said that if secession led to war, he'd have great and glorious deed to draw from for his fiction. *Arma virumque cano,* he said. *If the choice is between a bloody, painful war to write about, or nothing at all to test the character of men, I'll take the war.*

Amzi was mostly quiet, busying himself with preparations for the hostilities to come.

Alemeth was less interested in severing a relationship than in fostering one. When the Browns invited him to Clear Creek on Christmas day, he hoped Sally Fox would be there – but when the time came, she wasn't. When he received an invitation to the Agricultural Council's New Year's Eve Ball, he sent her a note, saying he wondered if he might be so bold as to ask for the honor of escorting her for the evening. But he ran into her unexpectedly at Clear Creek; he had to express his invitation orally; and he fumbled his words.

Still, Sally was kind.

"I'm ever so sorry, Mr. Byers. Just this morning I accepted Mr. Falkner's invitation. But I'm happy you'll be there. I'll so look forward to seeing you."

The thought of Gordon escorting her again drove Alemeth crazy. Every day, on his way back to the hotel, he passed Buck Avent's to look for her. But every day, the swing hung empty. A letter from Lou said she might be able to get him a copy of *A Sicilian Romance* at school, but Lou came home from

Huntsville for Christmas without one.

On the night of the New Year's Eve Ball, he watched Gordon talking to Sally, celebrating with her. Everyone was applauding, everyone making toasts to Rhett and Calhoun. Gordon was smoking a cigar, a crowd gathering around him and Miss Sally, attracted by the wit and charm. Alemeth was in no mood for celebration.

It was time to ask Miss Sally about Ann Radcliffe. If he couldn't say anything intelligent about her books, he could at least show Sally how interested he was. Maybe she'd enjoy telling him about Julia Mazzini. But late in the evening, as he was wondering how to come between Gordon and Sally, he was accosted by Howard Falkner and Colonel Brown. Colonel Brown announced it was nearly midnight. South Carolina had thumbed its noses at northern claims of unbreakable bonds. It had declared independence, as their grandfathers had done in 1776. The gauntlet had been thrown and everyone knew it.

'The northerners can read our newspapers," said the Colonel, "just as we can read theirs. Howard, Alemeth, don't print anything that suggests Mississippi's afraid to take up arms."

And so the hour had come. The following week, in Jackson, secession was the *only* order of business at the state house. Until now, the attention of the entire south had been on South Carolina. Now that she had declared her independence, the attention of Mississippians turned inward, knowing they were duty-bound to follow.

A MERRY CHRISTMAS

The good people of Oxford have been making merry as can be all the week. Pleasant parties have been given, we believe, every night, and the lovely ladies of our town have made happy the hearts of their chivalrous beaux, with gay laughter, and bright smiles. Long may the Christmas of 1860 be remembered by our readers for the store of pleasing memories it has bequeathed to them all. "Ring out the old, ring in the new."

AN ORDINANCE

to Dissolve the Union between the State of Mississippi and Other States United with Her under the Compact Entitled "The Constitution of the United States of America."

The people of the State of Mississippi, in convention assembled, do ordain and declare, and it is hereby ordained and declared, as follows, to wit:

Section 1. That all the laws and ordinances by which the said State of Mississippi became a member of the Federal Union of the United States of America be, and the same are hereby, repealed, and that all obligations on the part of the said State or the people thereof to observe the same be withdrawn, and that the said State doth hereby resume all the rights, functions, and powers which by any of said laws or ordinances were conveyed to the Government of the said United States, and is absolved from all the obligations, restraints, and duties incurred to the said Federal Union, and shall from henceforth be a free, sovereign, and independent State.

Thus ordained and declared in convention the 9th day of January, in the year of our Lord 1861.

To understand the world, some said, all you had to do was understand Mississippi. And Mississippi now understood itself – or at least understood its own desire to be a free and independent state. It was too late to put the news into that week's number. The issue had already been printed. Yet no one needed the paper. Everyone knew the news. The people of Mississippi had proclaimed their corporate will. They were no longer bondsmen of the north. No longer subject to domination by an uncaring, disrespectful, unjust neighbor.

Now that the act had been done, attention turned to consequences.

Would the Yankees invade? Attempt to force Mississippi back into the union? And if war came, would it mean loss of crops and profits? Would young men *die* in defense of the homeland? What would be the price of independence?

Gordon's words resounded in Alemeth's ear: gentlemen accept the responsibility of their actions. Free to choose the paths the courses they chart, they bear the burden of the consequences of that choice. Amzi's question, too, resounded in Alemeth's ear. What *would* he do, if there was an invasion from the north? Would he defend Bynum's Creek? Risk his own life, alongside his father? And for what? To protect *Eliza*?

Alemeth knew that the Bible condoned slavery. He knew that Providence was on the side of the southern cause, on the side of preserving the southern way of life. But he wasn't ready to decide whether the cost of preserving that way of life was worth it, to him, personally. It all depended on one thing, really.

A letter from Lou: "I have heard this past week from Miss Sally Fox. She mentioned that she enjoyed seeing you at the New Year's Ball."

There were other lines in the letter from Lou, before and after those twenty-two words, but he could see only them. He read them again and again, mulling them over as if Miss Sally herself lay waiting for him, her eyes and arms open, warm and welcoming, and he would see her in the ink on the page if only he looked hard enough, and where, once finding her there, he would be able to proclaim his love for her at last.

90

That spring, however, was never meant to be a time for love. March in particular was consumed by preparations for war. On Friday, the first of the month, Howard asked Alemeth to get the word to every shop and hotel in town. According to the Colonel, the role of the press in wartime wasn't just to print a paper, but to ensure support on the home front. *The Intelligencer* had to be devoted to that high purpose.

"We don't only need to report the news," said Howard. "We need to stir men to action. To transform belief in the cause into martial sentiment, and martial sentiment into martial action."

The message Alemeth was to deliver was simple. The great baboon scheduled for inauguration in just three days did not deserve to have his election preserved in newsprint. Therefore, everyone with a copy of *The Oxford Intelligencer* of election day past – or of any other paper reporting the aberration in democratic rule – was requested to bring it to the courthouse square on Saturday night, to serve as kindling for a bonfire. Everyone was welcome to behold the conflagration and to participate in the spirit of the hour.

On Saturday night, Alemeth put his head out the composing room window. Hundreds of people had gathered in the courthouse square. Those who'd brought papers announcing the election results laid them beneath a platform built like a gallows, where the effigy – a straw figure in vest and suspenders, sporting a beard of black tobacco and a stovepipe hat – was hung. After some pelting, Howard said that the great baboon deserved no further place in the public square. He struck a friction match and lit the effigy on fire. The flames rose skyward, enveloping the blackened character. At last, when the conflagration's full roar settled into something quieter, Howard introduced the first speaker, Lucius Lamar.

Lamar spoke in cadences of firebrand oratory. The great baboon was "not *my* President," he said. His Yankees would have no place in *my* Mississippi. The freedom that Jefferson said was every man's right, the freedom that was part of God's omniscient plan, was in danger of being taken away by European powers, industrial magnates, northern school teachers, and foreigners of every un-American ilk. Monarchy and papism could be next to invade our shores. Mississippi had to make her stand for freedom of the people. Men have a duty, to themselves, to their families, and to God, to stand up for what they believe in.

It was a stirring speech, even watched from the upstairs window of *The Intelligencer* by a man lost in concerns of his own.

91

The ceremony at the Cumberland Church was scheduled for eight p.m., but even before seven o'clock, the church was overflowing. The Oxford Mercury estimated the crowd at no fewer than twenty-five hundred people. "Every seat was taken, every spot occupied, while hundreds lingered around the door, unable to get in."

Howard and Alemeth stood in a narrow passage in front of a side door, off to the side of the pulpit. At eight o'clock, a group of young ladies were escorted to the front of the church in white dresses and blue sashes that bore the names of seven states in gold. Stepping onto the chancel on the arm of Captain Green, one of the ladies turned to face the center aisle of the nave, with Captain Green beside her. The rest of the group divided, on either side of her. Holding up a flag with white gloves that reached her elbows, "Miss Sally Wiley" (Howard whispered the name to Alemeth) addressed the officer beside her in a voice loud enough to be heard by all.

"To Captain Green, and the gentlemen of the Lamar Rifles: Allow me, as the organ of the ladies of Oxford and its vicinity, to present to you this flag, which I hold in my hand."

She lifted the flag slightly toward Captain Green, but without letting go of it, continued to face her listeners.

"But, before I do, I should say a few words in explanation of the feelings and motives of those on whose behalf I appear before you."

Capt. Green and the other soldiers stood at full attention.

"In the history of every people, there are times of security, and times of danger. In times of peace, the minds of men become engrossed by the pursuit of gain. Other ideas are excluded. Effeminacy sets in. The nation becomes weak."

Effeminacy? The words came from feminine lips, but sounded as if they'd come from the pen of Howard Falconer.

"The glory of a nation depends on the watchfulness and readiness of its citizens to defend their rights. Every encroachment must be resisted. Each denial of right must be resented."

She paused, examining the papers in front of her.

"Our country has now reached a crisis in its history. Our safety is endangered, and our honor is at stake. If we submit to those who seek to rule us, we shall not only be dishonored in the esteem of all true men. It will prove that the lofty spirit which inspired our Revolutionary heroes has passed away. That we, their descendants, are letting them down. Our State has nobly resolved that she will submit to no denial of her rights; and by volunteering to bear her flag, you have shown your determination to uphold her in that resolution.

"An attempt may be made, under the guidance of wild fanaticism, to constrain us, by force, to submit to degradation. Should that happen, it is to you that we look for protection. Mothers and maidens alike, we rely upon your arms to defend our rights and our honor. And we rely on your unfailing hearts."

When Miss Wiley turned toward Captain Green again, the flag still in her hands, Howard Falconer's words were gone. She talked without looking at notes.

"Therefore it is that we have prepared, and now desire to present to you, this memorial of our confidence."

She held the flag out to Captain Green and looked him in the eyes.

"Receive it and bear it with you in your marches and upon the field of danger, remembering when you gaze upon it, that our eyes are also upon you. We shall sympathize with you in all your labors and discomforts, and celebrate your triumphs. Whenever it shall be unfurled above your heads, we feel assured that your stout hearts will rally to its defense, and we shall be safe."

Captain Green put his hands on the flag, but Miss Wiley did not let it go. When she kept on talking, she sounded again as if she were reading Howard's words.

"There is one thought that gives us pain. Those whom you may soon meet as foes should be our friends. Instead of trespassing upon our rights, they should be among the stiffest in their defense. Ten thousand recollections of the past should impel them to throw their shields over our rights and wield their swords to protect our honor and our equality. But we fear that patriotism has abandoned their bosoms. Mad ambition spurs them on to our subjugation. If it must be so, let the trial come. Our brothers will prove sufficient for our protection."

She looked out over the whole audience, and spoke again without reading.

"As a man cannot love a woman, bereft of honor, so a woman cannot love a man, devoid of courage."

Then back to Captain Green. "Into your hands, we now commit this flag. It is an emblem of the independence and honor of our State. It must be maintained at any cost, and we rely on you to do it."

She finally let go of the flag and stepped back from the pulpit.

Captain Green returned thanks to Sally Wiley, and to all the ladies of Oxford, on behalf of his company. His thanks were followed by those of Captains Chalmers and Harris. Then, in a stiffly pressed gray wool jacket with red trim, brass buttons and a pair of yellow bars sewn on each shoulder, Fredonia's husband, Harvey Washington Walter, took the pulpit, giving thanks to the church and to those donors who had contributed to the ceremony in other ways. Then he thanked everyone for coming out to show their support.

Miss Wiley took the arm of Captain Green. Side by side, stepping down from the chancel, they started down the center aisle.   Only then, and for a brief moment, did Alemeth come face to face with Sally Fox. Unbeknownst to him, she'd been one of the ladies in white and blue on the other side of the pulpit, where he couldn't see her. Now, as she came forward on the arm of another officer, the gold lettering on her sash spelling out *South Carolina*, she smiled his way before following Sally Wiley out of the church.

Lieutenant Walter gave the order, "Forward, march!" The Jeff Davis Rifles obeyed, marching down the center aisle. The other units fell in behind them. The Buford boys from College Hill, Mary Orr's boys from Sand Springs, ranks of uniformed others, now all followed, now all positioned themselves between Sally Fox and him.

When the University Greys and Lamar Rifles received muskets and bayonets from Jackson, the Oxford *Mercury* reported, "We have now on hand, in old Lafayette, a pretty fair supply of war implements, and we have the men ready and willing to use them." Now well armed, the Rifles, Guards, and Grays drilled in Oxford daily, red trim on their collars and cuffs, eight red bars across their jackets, and with buttons at each end, preparing for the defense of Mississippi.

Miss Sally Fox

Requests the pleasure of your company

At a

Reception

To be held on Sunday, March 24th,

Eighteen Hundred Sixty One,

for the newlyweds,

Mr. and Mrs. David Hubbard

Time: Five o'clock in the afternoon

Place: The Avent Residence

R.S.V.P.

Alemeth hardly knew David and Sally Hubbard, so he knew he hadn't been invited at their request. And despite his connections to Colonel Brown, Howard, and Gordon, he was hardly at the core of the University set. His invitation to the reception for the newlyweds had to have been Miss Sally Fox's doing. She had wanted him there, he felt sure. For a week beforehand, he counted the hours until he could spend the evening with her.

But when the time came, he was anything but the object of Miss Sally's attentions. She was the host. She drew the new Mr. and Mrs. Hubbard from group to group, ensuring an even distribution of the newlyweds' time; she was in demand by everyone, servant and guest alike. So Alemeth was left to fend for himself. He tried to become a part of conversations with others, but with limited success. When the cake that Sally had made was brought in, people admired it. Deprived of the chance to spend the evening with Sally, he approached the cake as if her creation – made by her own hands, he heard – was the next best thing.

It was over two feet wide, four feet long, and iced all over the top. In one corner was a rectangular field of blueberries. Within the blueberries, arranged in a circle, were seven white stars, little pentacles of whipped cream. Three horizontal stripes, two of red (strawberries) and one of white (whipped cream), decorated the rest: it was a tribute to the Stars and Bars that had been raised over the confederate capital at Montgomery.

He was admiring the cake with something of the ardor he felt for Sally herself when Howard Falconer approached and asked what he was up to.

"Just admiring Miss Sally's cake," he replied.

Alemeth had been thinking about Sally's delicate hands making the cake – of a finger dipped in the batter, for a taste – but Howard was focused on the new confederate flag it represented. He repeated Lucius Lamar's line about a man's duty to stand up for his beliefs. He had joined the Ninth Mississippi regiment. His unit would leave in a matter of days. Colonel Brown had tried to persuade him to stay on in charge of the paper, but without success. Already in uniform, he criticized the design of the flag. "They made the new colors too much like the flag of the old Union. I'd rather have a flag that looks less like the Yankees'. But I'll stand by it, whatever it takes." His passion for his cause – the disdain in his voice when he said the word "Yankees" – set him on a path that challenged others to follow. Alemeth wondered why his own passions were so differently aroused.

He had promised the Colonel he'd work with the new man, Frank Duval, to see that the *Intelligencer* continued. Knowing of that promise, Howard mixed instructions for the operation of the paper into his predictions about deployment of the Ninth. With minimal interest in either, Alemeth looked at

Miss Sally from afar, engaging, exchanging, smiling, delighting the newlyweds with easy exposure to every guest in turn.

He had just put a big piece of cake into his mouth when she approached them. *The* Miss Sally: the focus of his dreams for the last several weeks, the focus of his thoughts for the last several hours.

"Good evening, Mr. Byers, Mr. Falconer. I believe you know Mrs. Sally Hubbard. May I introduce her husband, Mr. David Hubbard?"

Howard was gracious. Alemeth tried to squeeze his mouthful down. Both Sallys laughed.

"You have whipped cream on your cheek," said Sally Hubbard.

As David Hubbard reached out to take his hand, Sally Fox touched the tip of a finger to her lips to indicate the location of the cream. His hand could not shake Hubbard's and, at the same time, wipe cream from his cheek. He fumbled, wiped his cheek, and wiped his hand. By the time Alemeth had satisfied himself that his cheek was clean, napkin disposed of, hands shaken, apologies made, Miss Sally and the newlyweds were ready to take their leave. Alemeth was left to choose between listening to Howard's prognostications and fending for himself, while Sally went on with the constant duties of a diligent host.

He had hoped, at least, to have a chance to say something personal to Sally at the end of the evening. But when the time came, on his way out the door, Sally spoke first, her low, sultry purr catching him entirely off guard.

"Mr. Byers," she said, "If I didn't know better, I'd say you were making eyes at me all evening."

Howard laughed. Alemeth didn't know what to say.

"Oh, now, I didn't mean to make you blush!"

*   *   *

The next few days were long and tortured. The last day of March, 1861, was Easter Sunday, and Alemeth had dreamed of meeting her after the worship service at First Presbyterian, planning how to recover from his disastrous showing at the reception, imagining that if he finally handled himself with any self-assurance at all, he might even spend part of the afternoon with her. But when Easter Sunday came, Miss Sally had joined her Uncle Buck in Jackson. Once again, she was not at First Presbyterian. Alemeth spent the afternoon alone, wondering if he'd *ever* have a chance with her.

Call For More Troops from Mississippi

We stop the press this morning to announce that President Davis has just made a requisition upon Governor Pettus for 3,000 more volunteers from Mississippi. The dispatch was received here last night, and the news is reliable.

Lincoln had called for seventy-five thousand volunteers – enough to invade Mississippi and then some. The call for southern volunteers could prove insufficient. Even so, Alemeth arranged the sorts into the headline Howard had written even before he left, to be used when the time came. In old two-inch wood-block letters, the headline proclaimed "War! War!! War!!!"

92

People were taking stock of guns, provisions and horses. Howard and his Ninth Infantry Regiment had been ordered south to keep open the port at Mobile. The University Greys and Lamar Rifles had been ordered north to Corinth. Every young man in northern Mississippi was enlisting, or so it seemed, as every week brought the formation of new units. Those that didn't volunteer left town, or at least tried not to be noticed.

Mary Ann Loughborough wrote to Eliza and Mrs. Brown that her husband, James, had been assigned to the staff of Major General Price. That he'd warned her it wouldn't be safe in Carondelet; that she should visit relatives further south as soon as her new baby was born. Besides, she might like to visit her Mississippi aunts, if it would not put them out too much to receive her.

Mrs. Brown wrote back right away. Leave Carondelet at once. Come to Clear Creek, where it's safe, as soon as you can travel. Eliza wrote much the same thing. Both women wrote to their sister, Julia, repeating the invitation and suggesting she come along to help. In a few weeks' time, Julia Webster, Mary Ann Loughborough, and Mary Ann's two children came to Clear Creek for a visit.

The cousins brought alarming news from Missouri.

The federals had driven Governor Jackson and General Price into the countryside, accusing them of treason. The new German majority were nearly all for the old union. St. Louis had been overrun by Yankee troops and Yankee sympathizers. No loyal Southerner felt safe there.

Eliza predicted that General Price would find a way to rally. Julia said it would take friends in other states. Mary Ann said it would take volunteers, and as she said the word 'volunteer,' she looked directly at Alemeth.

She was no longer Mary Ann Webster; now, she was Mary Ann Loughborough – with two little girls of her own – devoted to another man. But marriage to James Loughborough hadn't changed one thing about Mary Ann: she was as direct as ever. She asked him, point blank, if he was going to enlist.

Howard. Charlie and Ira Orr. Peter Brown. Charlie Morgan. They'd all enlisted.

"I'm thinking it over."

"Well, how long do you think you'll have, Alemeth Byers? The war isn't going to wait for you to decide, you know. What's happening in Missouri today could be happening here in Mississippi tomorrow."

"I know. It's just that – "

"What is it? Has a young lady caught your eye?"

There was nothing he could say about Sally Fox, so he simply shook his head. But that was not enough to dispel the pressure of Mary Ann's persistent questioning. He could have been underwater, at the swimming hole, in need of coming up for air.

'I'll decide by tomorrow,' he said at last.

As soon as he could, he went out to the porch. Clio and Calliope stood on their perch, outside their cage, strutting and nervous. He was about to speak to the parrots when Amzi joined him.

"Alemeth," he said, putting his arm around Alemeth's shoulder. "About enlisting. I don't know if you care for my opinions any more, but as your Pa, I owe them to you."

"I understand."

"As I see it, Alemeth, it's about preserving our way of life. Mississippi isn't the land; it's the people. My grandfather, Colonel Brown's grandfather, they fought for a government that would guarantee them liberty. To do what they wanted on their own land. And every day for the last forty years I've worked toward preserving that freedom, for our family. If we can't do what we want on our own land, then what sort of freedom do we have? As far as I can see, it's a man's duty to protect his birthright. To defend his homeland."

"And?"

"It's every man's duty to stand up for his beliefs. Do the right thing, Alemeth. Make me proud and enlist. Defend your family's freedom."

"Thank you, Pa. Okay if I take some time to think about it?"

Amzi frowned. "I've said my peace, Alemeth. It's up to you now."

Eliza had been watching them. After Amzi walked away, in the midst of goodnights and goodbyes, she asked if she could offer her own advice.

"What's that?"

"Don't let other folks decide things for you. Ask God what *He* wants."

It would have been nice, if he could have done that. But he'd never been able to hear God's voice; for him, Eliza's solution was no solution at all.

Maybe he saw it as some sort of substitute for prayer. Maybe it was an effort to avoid the decision. Whatever the reason, back at the University Hotel, he stopped in the lobby and used some of his pay to buy a whiskey. Then another. After the second drink, he started thinking it *was* time to make a decision. He was half way through the third whiskey when Gordon sat down beside him.

"What's up?" asked Gordon.

"Nothing. I was thinking about volunteering. Are you?"

"Of course. Isn't a person always volunteering for something?"

"Well… Why? To preserve slavery?"

"Alemeth, I don't know about slavery. Sometimes I wonder if old Vrooman wasn't right about slavery. But a democratic government depends on the consent of the governed. A free people has the right to separate from an unjust government that won't respect that freedom. That's what the Declaration of Independence was all about, and that's what Mississippi's done by seceding. I'm enlisting to protect our freedom, Alemeth."

Alemeth mulled it over.

"Think of what the word 'volunteer' means, Alemeth. *Volo. Volere.* To exercise one's will. To go after whatever you want most. After all, if you're not exercising your own will, then whose are you?"

"Whoever you love?"

"Good answer, my man! A gentleman should always seek to please his lady. Say, Mrs. Robinson, please, could we have another whiskey here?"

"Be right with you."

"So, Gordon," Alemeth asked. "Do you think enlisting would please Sally Fox?"

Gordon's eyebrows shot up, then he settled into a friendly grin.

"Are you kidding, Alemeth? You heard what Sally Wiley said. "As a man can't love a woman bereft of honor, so a woman can't love a man devoid of courage."

"And you think Sally Fox wants –"

"You saw her in that South Carolina sash. I think it's obvious what Sally Fox thinks. I'm going to enlist, and you should too, if you fancy her."

"But I made a promise to Colonel Brown. I told him I'd stay on and help Frank Duval."

"Well then, do both, my friend. You can enlist and still have time, after drill, to set type."

"I don't know."

"I'll tell you what, Alemeth. Come with me, tomorrow morning. I hear George Foote is organizing a company. We can enlist together."

"George Foote? Howard's law school friend?"

"Yeah. So what do you say? Let's do it."

He'd promised Amzi he'd defend Bynum's Creek. Gordon was doing it. And a woman probably couldn't love a man who lacked courage. In the end, it seemed, *everyone* agreed. So on the 27th of April, Alemeth and Gordon stopped in at Hulihan's Hotel, where they signed up with George Foote. Foote's volunteers were calling themselves the "Vindicators."

93

According to the order of the military board, the uniform of Mississippi troops would be a grey wool frock coat and trousers with red trim. The Vindicators were supposed to receive a shipment of uniforms from Memphis, but Captain Foote said not to count on them. He asked that everyone furnish his own, or at least wear clothes as much as possible like that specified. Hopefully, all the boys had at least *some* gray clothes.

Alemeth already had a pair of gray wool trousers. He got another as a gift from Eliza. He got a new frock coat from Mary Ann Brown, and Eliza sewed red felt around the collar of a gray jacket. He got a black felt hat from Lou, and Aunt Leety gave him a wool blanket. The first time he put the uniform on, he looked at himself in Lou's tall mirror and thought he looked smart. If *he* thought so, it had to be true. Miss Sally would *have* to be impressed.

*   *   *

A – TENNNNNNNNNNN – SHN!

One pace – no more – behind the man in front. Heels on the line. Knees straight. Erect at the hips.

Shoulders square. Head erect. Square to the front. Chin in. Eyes fixed forward.

Face right. Pivoting on the left heel. *Face left.* Pivoting on the right heel. *About face.* Always right, left foot forward, twenty-four inches.

Squad: forward, march. March. March. Halt. Face right. Double quick step. One, two, one, two.

Over and over again.

After drill, Alemeth and Gordon crushed mint leaves and loosened their uniform shirts, rubbing the leaves on their shoulders. When the soreness eased a little, they traded muskets, inspecting each other's weapons. Gordon's was like most of the boys': an old smooth bore. Amzi had given Alemeth his new 1842, with its sight, its percussion lock, its rifling. When the time came, he'd be able to load and fire faster with it. He'd be accurate from further away. As Gordon pointed out, he wouldn't just be part of a volley; he'd be able to see the man he was about to kill.

The idea of it still made him tremble. A man was more than a deer or a rabbit. But in the morning, they returned to drill.

Support arms. Right hand on the stock. *Present arms.* Center of the body. Rammer to the front. *Shoulder arms. Order arms.* A dozen times. Another dozen. And *Rest.*

Captain Foote said men were out of line. That their weapons were at all sorts of odd angles. He went over, yet again, the proper grip and tilt of the musket.

Support arms. Right hand on the stock. *Present arms.* Center of the body. Rammer to the front. *Shoulder arms. Order arms.* A dozen more times. And *Rest.*

"Look at you, still struggling. Some of you look like you've never handled a musket before."

Support arms. Present arms. Shoulder arms. Order arms. And *Rest.*

His back was getting tired. Things would sure be nicer in the company of Sally Fox.

Load arms. Right foot forward. Heel against left foot. Muzzle down. *Handle Cartridge.* Cartridge box open. Remove cartridge, place in the teeth. *Tear cartridge.* Down to the powder. *Charge.* Raise the elbow. Shake the powder into the barrel. *Draw rammer. Ram cartridge. Return rammer.*

Cast about. Half turn right, on the left heel. Gun to the right shoulder. Into the left hand. Right thumb on the stock. Muzzle at the height of the eye.

Prime. Thumb on the hammer. Half cock. *Load arms.* Brush off the old cap. New cap from the pouch with the thumb and first two fingers of the right hand. Press the cap on the cone with the right thumb.

Shoulder arms.

Ready.

Aim.

Fire.

Load arms.

Fire.

Load arms.

Fire.

Mid-month, the people of Sand Springs celebrated: the Presbyterian Church had declared its "unabated loyalty" to the northern government, and the southern church had separated from its northern counterpart. Day in, day out, Alemeth went through the motions at drill, and every day, before and after, he heard the bragging of others. Indignation at the prospect of Yankee aggression. Resolutions to stand and fight for the land they loved. Vows to defend the honor of mothers and sisters, loved ones and wives. Talk of the courage that could, like nothing else, turn a boy into a man, and win him respect, and honor, and love.

94

On the evening of Monday, May 20th, still in his grays after drill, Alemeth rode down Depot Street. He was expected at the office, and Frank Duval knew how long the ride from Panola took. But Alemeth had started thinking about seeing Miss Sally again. By the time he'd reached Oxford, he'd determined to pass by the Depot before going down town. He could see the great oak. A hundred yards later, he could see the bough and the white swing. Twenty paces later, he could see her. She'd been watching him approach. She was alone.

"Good evening, Mr. Byers."

"Good evening, Miss Fox. May I call you Miss Sally?"

She smiled. "Heavens," she purred, "I can't think why not."

"May I visit for a moment, Miss Sally?"

"Why, of course."

He dismounted.

"Do you have to call me 'Mr. Byers'?"

"What would you prefer?"

"'Alemeth' would be fine – especially if I can call you Sally."

"Why of course, Alemeth. 'Sally' it is."

When he'd tied his saddle horse to one of the smaller trees, Sally asked if he'd like to sit down. Even as she asked the question, she moved to the side to make room for him. But the swing moved with her; when Alemeth went to sit, he nearly missed it. Gaining just enough coverage to keep from sliding off, he wiggled into a precarious position. And it wasn't just the struggle against gravity. An afternoon at drill in gray woolens had left him smelling like a field hand.

"I can only visit for a minute. I have to be at *The Intelligencer*."

The edge of her dress touched the leg of his pants. If he turned, his face would be just inches from hers. She was close enough to smell his odor

"What are you reading now?"

She glanced at the book in her lap. "Mary Shelley's novel, *Falkner*. Mr. – Gordon gave it to me. Said he hoped it would give me something to remember him by. Have you read it?"

"No. I haven't. Not yet."

"It's about a woman who works to bring her stepfather and her beloved together. I rather like the fact that she succeeds at the end. We can use a few stories of reconciliation these days. Don't you think?"

He stood up and turned to look at her. He had to get back to the office. He had to spare her from his body's odor. He had to understand what she meant by 'stories of reconciliation.'

But he'd caught her off guard. As the swing sprung away, she fell forward. He caught her arm, and for the briefest of moments, her body was pressed against his.

Lifting her forearm with one hand and her waist with another, he righted them both, with no great loss of dignity. But with her reddened face just inches from his, he could smell his own foul stench, and knew that she had to smell it too.

"I have to be going. Frank will be angry enough as it is. May I see you again?"

"I love the yard this time of day. Most days, you'll find me here before supper."

"Well then. I'll see you soon, I hope."

She gave him a nod and a smile.

Riding to the office, he held on to the touch of her arms, the memory of her waist, and lived them over and over again. Frank Duval *was* upset, of course. So that night, he worked late, and got everything caught up, even after Frank left for the evening. But when he got back to the hotel, taking a barrel shower, he could think of nothing but Sally.

By order of the Commander in Chief, the following companies... Panola Vindicators, Capt. George P. Foote... are hereby ordered into active service, and will proceed forthwith to Corinth, Miss., to the camp of instruction there established, and report to Maj. Gen. Charles Clark, commanding.

They will take with them all arms and military property in their possession. All deficiencies in arms will be supplied at Corinth. The companies will provide themselves with cooked rations sufficient to subsist them to Corinth. The several railroads will furnish transportation, and the companies will proceed by the nearest route.

> *- W. H. Brown*
> *Adjutant and Inspector General*

The orders to Corinth had the town of Panola stirred to an excitement never seen before. Everyone came out to watch as the Vindicators paraded to show off their training, marching in tight formation, vying to impress the admiring town, striving to shine in varying shades of gray. Afterward, when the parade was done, Bill Starr said that Al Cansler and some of the boys were going to get whiskey. Did any of the Vindicators want to go? To be honored? To be treated to a surprise no one was willing to divulge?

There'd been times Alemeth would have wanted to see whatever it was, but as soon as the day's drill was done, he had to be in Oxford for work. So he missed events in Panola. On horseback, he hurried to the Masonic Hall, where Frank Duval awaited him, the call of duty stronger than the call of adventure. Frank leaned forward from behind Howard's desk and handed him a pile of assignments.

"You've got a long night ahead of you," said Frank. "You'd better get started."

It was hot in the print room. Alemeth removed his jacket, then his shirt. Then he turned to the letter case. He would work in his undershirt.

> A GUN FOR THE TIMES.- A citizen of Charlotte has invented a gun which will fire 120 balls in a minute. We have seen it tried, but are not at liberty to particularize at present. Competent officers pronounce it a complete success. The inventor, an ingenious mechanic, has gone to Montgomery for the purpose of exhibiting it to the authorities of the Confederate States. - *Charlotte Democrat.*

He wondered. A hundred and twenty balls in just a minute? No gun could be made to fire so fast. Colonel Brown had said to print nothing that might suggest weakness. A gun that could fire a hundred and twenty balls a minute sounded like the *Charlotte Democrat* had a Howard Falconer of its own, ever tuned to the impact of the words he chose to print, ever mindful of the need to show strength as conflict loomed. Maybe it wasn't the same as facing enemy fire, but there was honor in what the paper was doing.

*   *   *

For the next week, drill filled his days, Frank Duval his nights. Some of the Vindicators had gone with Bill Starr, got drunk, and met some women they didn't care to describe except with laughter and the shaking of heads. At *The Intelligencer*, there was as much type to set as there had ever been – more, in fact, now that there was so much news. Only once did Alemeth manage to get down to Depot Street, but Sally was not at her swing. Then, on the night of the 29th, the very last before the Vindicators were to leave, with *The Intelligencer*'s run printed and out the door, there was a final opportunity.

The Colonel and Mrs. Brown were hosting a farewell party for the recruits. Busy at work, Alemeth had only had a piece of cornbread at noon, and he was hungry. He'd be late, but if he could see Sally for even a minute, it would be worth it.

When he arrived, the fried chicken was gone, but he had no trouble finding Sally. In fact, she'd been waiting for him, with a surprise. In a linen napkin, she had saved him a piece of peach pie. She invited him to the terrace and gave him a fork; he put a bite in his mouth. The pie was warm and flaky, the peaches fresh but not tart.

He ate it as best he could, with Sally watching him. The crust dissolved slowly in his throat.

"This is delicious."

"I left that piece in the oven for you."

"You made this yourself?"

"I did."

"You were kind to think of me. I wish I could show my appreciation."

If she'd suggested *anything* he'd have done it. But she only blushed, and for a moment, didn't look his way.

"Would you allow me – the honor of a walk?" he asked. "To get some fresh air?'

"Why, yes. That would be very nice."

"Where should we go?"

"Have you seen the new observatory? It's a perfect place."

His heart leapt, as if it wanted to join hers somewhere in the fragile, empty space between their bodies. From the observatory, they could look at the stars together. Was it possible? Would he finally have Sally Fox to himself? They walked side by side, his hand close to touching hers. As they walked from Colonel Brown's house past the cut and up the hill, he could hear her breathe. Out of the corner of his eye, he could see her chest rise and fall. He remembered the moment his hands had touched her arms and waist.

"It's not up there?" He nodded toward the top of the hill.

"Oh, no." Her hair was a lasting prism for the evening sun. "It's down there. We're going to the 'Dead Room'."

The magnetic observatory had been sunk deep into the ground, its parts anchored in rock, concrete and lead. Entering it was like entering a vault. But once inside, Sally began talking about the instruments. About magnetic substances. Forces that operate, invisibly, across thousands of miles. There'd been a day, not long before, he might have been at a loss for anything to say. But this time, when Sally said something about the relationship between magnetism and light, he told her what Dr. Boynton had said about the future of photography. She lit up in an unguarded, guileless smile.

He took a step toward her. She held her face inches from his, as if she wanted a kiss. He leaned forward. Her eyes were not leaving his. Her mouth was open.

"Alemeth –"

She looked as if a new thought had crossed her mind.

" — I have a question for you."

Momentum carried him still closer, but she had something else in mind.

"Did the explosion in the Chemistry laboratory leave you any scars?"

"Why, no." He stopped for what should have been only a moment. "I was lucky, I guess."

"Do you mind if I ask another question?"

"No. Why not?"

"Why were you and Macon in the chemistry lab in the first place?"

"We'd gone there to use the equipment. To make a plate, for a photograph –"

"What on earth were you going to make a photograph of?"

It had been a long time, but he would never forget, and she couldn't have asked a question he welcomed any more.

"Of you," he said with a smile.

Sally cast her eyes toward the ground. He wanted to kiss her, but her downward glance kept her out of reach.

"Miss Sally?"

She looked up. Alemeth reached out. He touched her on the forearm. He moved his lips toward hers.

She didn't back away, but she raised her hands and stopped him, denying him the kiss. Then she looked at him again, with a slight smile that made him wonder if his advance had flattered her.

He had to do *something*.

"I'd still like to have… I'd consider it a privilege … if you might have a photograph taken."

"For you?"

"Yes. For me to have with me, in the war."

"I'll tell you what, Alemeth Byers. I'll have a photograph made for you, if you have one of yourself made for me."

"Excellent! Thank you. I'll have one made for you, the first chance I get. I promise."

The sun was setting. If he was ever going to hold her, and kiss her, it would be here, in the magnetic observatory, or later, on the walk home in the dark. But in his moment of hesitation, she had already started to back away.

"We should probably be getting back."

Her words stabbed his heart. Could she mean it?

She took a step toward the door.

"Miss Sally – wait a minute. I have another question for you."

She stopped. He was leaving for Corinth in the morning. He couldn't let his last night at home end without *something* more.

"When I get back – from Corinth, I mean – do you suppose we'll have a chance to pick things up from here?"

"Of course, Alemeth. You mean a lot to me. Wouldn't it be wonderful if this evening could last forever? But first things first. You have things you have to do. And you have to keep yourself safe, or you'll never come back to me."

"Sally, I promise – "

"So we'll have to wait and see what happens. They say even the stars are moving. We'll never see anything *exactly* the way we see it tonight. Not the evening star. Not each other. Not the way the moon looks."

He wanted to take her in his arms, but she tilted her head, turned and walked out the door, leaving him alone in the casement of iron and lead. He'd been cut off – as much as scientifically possible – from the rest of the world, and looking not at the instrument dials, but at the door, he saw only dark night and shadow where Sally had just been.

It was all he saw of Sally on that, his last night at home.

*   *   *

It's easy to understand why the angels were named for men. Michael who would make war on Satan, for his Lord. At God's bidding, Gabriel gave Daniel seventy weeks to make an end of sin. Raphael was told by God to bury Azazel in the desert, under a pile of rocks, and leave him there until judgment day, and he obeyed.

Sally Fox was a messenger of a different sort. Her breath was as soft as fur. Her voice had the tone of wood nymphs, fauns, and other forest things. And hers was the voice that called out to him the night before he left for war, and would call to him for many nights to come.

95

The couplings jerked; there was screech and strain; but once the *James Brown* was underway, its cars settled into a steady northward carriage that seemed unstoppable. The order to Corinth had brought on bravado at first, but the sight of the Depot fading behind left a stark and deadening chill. Above the din of the tracks, there was little talk. Wondering how many weeks it would be before they were able to whip the Yankees and come home, Alemeth leaned on his bedroll and knapsack with his chest, forearms crossed to make a pillow of his own flesh, his gear a comfort against wooden edges that rocked and jarred from side to side.

North of the Tallahatchie, the *James Brown* climbing into vistas of turnips, beans and green cotton, its labored chug-chug drowned out most other sounds. Northern clouds seemed to move south, distances to disappear. Alemeth leaned his head out the window. For minutes, farmland; more farmland; then, through woods, a white-tailed deer bounded away. Above an open field, a hawk soared, scouring the earth for things that Alemeth, confined and grounded, couldn't hope to see. And all the while, behind the clackclackclackclack, the tracks behind them vanished at every bend.

When Alemeth's head came back in the window, Charley Morgan was asking how long it would be before they reached Grand Junction. Bill Elliot did a calculation. If the crossties were two feet apart, there were twenty-six hundred per mile of rail. Charley guessed they were passing twenty every second. If he was right, they were traveling at thirty miles per hour, and should arrive at Grand Junction in less than an hour. Whether Bill was right or wrong, he spoke with authority; everyone accepted what he said.

Travel to Memphis by stagecoach had taken nearly a day. Reaching Tennessee within hours meant the world was suddenly smaller, but the distance to Sally Fox grew greater by the minute. At Grand Junction, leaving the *James Brown,* Alemeth bid farewell to the locomotive as if it were the man himself. If not for Colonel Brown, Alemeth never would have met Gordon or Howard or Dr. Barnard, never worked at *The Intelligencer,* never met Sally Fox. Pulling the Curtis watch from his pocket, he mouthed thanks to the Colonel for all of them, resolving to protect them all. The cars of the Memphis and Charleston were painted black to match the locomotives, the letters on them fine and yellow rather than wide and white. Stepping aboard the eastbound train, he could see that the seats faced forward. The interior of the car was different. When the engine engaged, it sounded older. The jostling was smoother. For Alemeth, nothing was left of the familiar except his clothes, the Colonel's watch, and now, Pa's Model 1842.

96

The ancient city of Corinth sat on the southern side of a land bridge across a gulf that separated the south of Greece (the Peloponnesus) from the north (Attica). The isthmus was a strategic crossroads between worlds, a place where north met south and east met west.

Newspaperman W.E. Gibson suggested the name 'Corinth' for the city at the northern border of Mississippi because he knew his city also sat on the edge of a great gulf. Just as the Gulf of Corinth divided ancient Greece in the days of the first city states, Tennessee separated the states of the south and the states of the north. In the recent election, the people of Tennessee had voted to remain in the union; only the legislature had overridden their vote, at the behest of wealthy planters with different views about freedom and independence. Most common folk were for the Union. At best, Tennessee was a land of mixed sentiments on the question of southern confederacy.

Corinth sat not only on the Tennessee border, on the edge of that gulf, but also on the Memphis and Charleston railroad. One cannot appreciate the strategic importance of Corinth without understanding the significance of this railroad, and the aims of those who'd brought it into being. By connecting Charleston (home of the largest slave market in the east) to Memphis (home of the largest in the west), the Memphis and Charleston bound the slave states into a natural union. In fact, in laying out the railroad's path, the power brokers had made it meander into each of the states whose borders it skirted, like a suture stitching together two sides of a wound. In every state there were men who invested in the railroad, and as all those investors knew, a railroad is only valuable if it leads somewhere. So every state with access to even a small portion of the railroad had a stake in preserving the whole. Tennessee, on the north, was tied by the M&C to the cotton states of Mississippi, Alabama, Georgia, and South Carolina. The Memphis and Charleston, quite literally, held the South together.

Corinth was also significant for another reason. It was at Corinth that the Memphis and Charleston was joined by the Mobile and Ohio. For that reason, it was through Corinth that Ohio Yankees could descend upon Mississippi at railroad speed. By virtue of the natural importance of any crossroads, amplified by these factors, Corinth was a hub of extreme importance, vital both to the south and to the State of Mississippi. And like Spartans assembling to defend the Peloponnesus, the Vindicators joined up with the Confederate Rifles, the Magnolia Guards, and a score of other Mississippi companies outside Corinth, brothers come together to protect the border, and with it, the whole deep South.

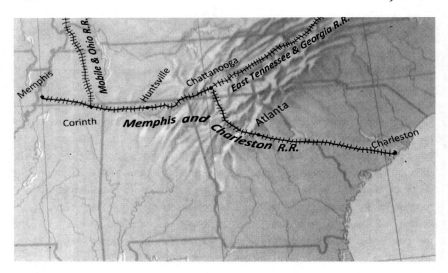

    As they settled into Camp Mott, outside Corinth, Gordon made notes about the soldier's life and mused about the debt modern warfare owed to the armies of Greece. He said camp life hadn't changed much since ancient times, but the army at Camp Mott was a hundred times larger than that of the Spartans at Thermopylae, and ten times as many tents than at a Sinner's Campground revival. But the order of the day at Camp Mott was not to save men's souls; it was to mold boys into soldiers, and there was more to being a soldier than having faith in the righteousness of a cause.

    Reveille at five.
Wash Dishes.
Roll Call.
Hope to God to pass inspection.
Squad drill from half past seven to half past eight.
Fix bayonets. Unfix bayonets.
Company drill from ten to half past eleven.
Quick step. Face right. Double step. Left right.
Squad drill again at half past one.
Fix bayonets. Unfix bayonets. Back getting stiff.
Company drill at four.
Quick step. Face right. Double step. Left right. Feet getting sore.
Dress parade at half past six.
Important to look fit and well disciplined. There was power to be had in large numbers of armed men trained to move on command.
    Then beans for supper, and sleep, and reveille again at five.

After a few days, Alemeth and Gordon suggested to Captain Foote that the boys could use some target practice. Captain Foote said he'd think about it. But the next day, the Vindicators became part of the 17th Mississippi Infantry Regiment, under Colonel Featherston; and that evening, it joined five other regiments on the field for review before Major General Clark and Governor John Pettus. By the time General Clark and Governor Pettus had thanked the men for their service to the great state of Mississippi, it was too late for target practice.

The next day, something unexpected happened. An announcement was made that changed every recruit's understanding of what they were about to do. The Seventeenth was not to remain at Corinth, to defend Mississippi, after all. With Virginia's decision to join the Confederacy, the capital was being moved to Richmond. The Seventeenth was shipping out, to assist in the defense of Virginia. Everything had to be made ready. After a morning of excited, confused scrambling, Alemeth, Gordon, and the rest of the Seventeenth boarded the Memphis and Charleston again, prepared to cross the gulf between them and the north. There'd be no time for target practice.

The Vindicators crammed into two cars. Through Mississippi and northern Alabama, six to a bench, clinging to bedrolls and muskets, they rode the jostling cars. In Chattanooga, when troops from Georgia joined the train, the Vindicators were crowded into a single car, shoulder to shoulder. (Gordon, with a pad of paper and pencil in hand to record what happened, said he said he felt like buck shot in a barrel.) Beneath the afternoon sun, the packed flesh of a hundred wool-clad boys sweated profusely. At Captain Foote's suggestion, the men got down to undershirts. But in very little time, the fine upholstery of the East Tennessee and Georgia Railroad, headed north, smelled as bad as they did.

Through old Cherokee country, the black loess gave way to corn country. Tennessee's oak and hickory were different. Railroad trestles over creeks added a high pitched racket to the rumble of tracks on solid ground. Towns had unfamiliar names. Up the valley to Knoxville, the long ridges of the Appalachians were covered by a vaporous blue haze that rose and spread above the canopy of spruce and fir. The locomotive's whistle was silenced at Colonel's orders as the 17th headed north through territory sympathetic to the Union. No whistles, no lights, nothing that would reveal them before the sounds of track and train.

*   *   *

They camped for the night at a church on the edge of Bristol, among tree stumps and bushes. On Sunday morning, the 16th, when orders arrived to move to Lynchburg, bravado returned for a time, with boasts of bringing Yankees to submission in spectacular ways. There was talk of defending Richmond, images of volleys fired from behind walls, Yankees charging up hills, southern boys picking them off. But the train sat empty on the tracks all day. Brave talk grew tiresome, seen for the empty boasting that it was.

Then, as soon as darkness fell, the train got underway again. When Bob Jolly and Charley Morgan said their ears were closing up, Bill Elliot said it meant they were climbing. The steep ascent into the Appalachians was building pressure. Alemeth felt it too – as if something was sucking his brain from his skull.

In Lynchburg, there was another halt, another day of waiting, new orders (for the 17th to join General Beauregard's army) and another night movement in the railway car. In the dark, the locomotive breathed easier: they were descending now, coming out of the mountains, into the Valley of the James, the homeland of George Washington and Thomas Jefferson, the birthplace of American history. Richmond was the last of the great American slave market cities: the apex of a triangle formed with Memphis and Charleston.

Standing in the aisle at the head of the car, Captain Foote made an announcement. A large force of federal soldiers had advanced into northern Virginia. The long-threatened Yankee invasion had begun. The presence of such foreigners in a sovereign state could not be tolerated – especially as they were poised for an assault on Richmond itself. Yet, only Beauregard stood between the Yankees and the new Confederate capital. The Seventeenth would join with Beauregard. There were no plans to attack. A few optimistic souls thought outright battle might yet be avoided. But if the federals were to engage in any further advances toward Richmond, they'd almost certainly seek control of the Orange and Alexandria. That railroad provided a speedy supply line north of the capital. Control of the telegraph lines meant instant communication across long distances. The federals' obvious target was the railroad junction at Manassas. And that was where their train was headed.

After the briefing, the boys talked over what Captain Foote had said. There was general unity of opinion: if all went right, they were going to be on the front lines within hours; and if there was going to be a fight, they'd be able to return home in glory, to the thanks of all Mississippi.

In time, the jostling of the train became as familiar as the gentle, rhythmic patting of a favorite nursemaid. Stories came to an end. The rocking back and forth lulled them to sleep. Battles paraded through their dreams, colors flying high.

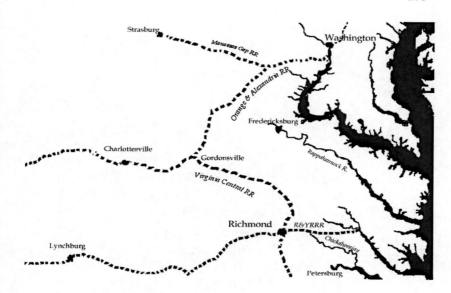

The following day the train made its way to Richmond, where there were another fourteen cars attached, and by mid-day, on to Manassas Junction, where the Orange & Alexandria line met the Manassas Gap Railroad to Strasburg. Camp Walker was an enormous mass of soldiers, far more even than at Corinth, tents sprawled across the fields in columns and rows as far as the eye could see, like endless columns of faces seen in opposing mirrors. Taking a spot of land between the Confederate Guards and the Pettus Rifles, the Vindicators spent the day digging in, cutting down trees for firewood and snake fences. After a meal of salt pork, bread and coffee, a couple of the boys were taken to the hospital with fevers; others brought out banjos and harmonicas. And that night, on stumped and rooted ground, they were surrounded by countless campfires.

"Why so many fires? We're like so many fireflies. Surely, we'll give away our numbers."

"I wonder if that's not the point," said Bill Elliott.

"What do you mean?"

"Come here. See those hills there, on the other side of the Creek?"

The creek ran through the wooded lowland that separated Camp Walker from the distant hills. On them, the glow of a thousand lights.

"Those are Yankee fires. If you ask me, Beauregard wants the yanks to see as many of our fires as possible. The more they see, the less likely they'll attack. With a little luck, they'll give up on the South. Head back north, to their sweatshops and factories, and be done with us."

BANDAGES – ARMY PATTERNS.— The following mode of preparing lint, bandages, etc., may not prove uninteresting at this time:

1 dozen 1 inch wide, 1 yard long.
2 dozen 2 inches wide, 3 yards long.
3 dozen 2 – 1-2 inches wide, 3 yards long.
3 dozen 3 inches wide, 4 yards long.
1 dozen 3 1-2 inches wide, 5 yards long
1 dozen 4 inches wide, 6 yards long

12 dozen, or one gross, in small packages.

The instruction heretofore has been, "wash the muslin;" but this is now said to be wrong, the unwashed being regarded best, as the surgeon prefers that it should shrink.

97

Bandages indeed. Bandages to shrink, of all things, —to help close wounds!

Eliza put down *The Intelligencer*. The issue of May 29th – the paper's last – was what life on Bynum's Creek had once promised to be. In the month that had passed since that final issue, most young men had left for war. The price of fabrics at Neilson's had gone up fifty per cent. People were asking twenty-five cents for a spool of silk thread, four dollars for flour and eight for salt. There was no money except some bank notes Amzi had got from Colonel Brown for some of his cotton. Amzi said he hadn't yet been paid by Buck Avent for the rest.

Nor was it just the absence of all the young men, or the lack of money, or the prices of things. The women at Sand Springs were concerned about their sons who had enlisted. Mary Ann was upset about Calliope biting her sixteen year old, Mary Porter. Sister Julia and her daughter, the younger Mary Ann – visiting from Carondelet with Mary Ann's two children – had brought more bad news. The federals had raided the Armory in St. Louis and made off with most of the weapons. Governor Jackson had fled westward with what was left of the militia. The streets were given over to thugs and vandals. Missouri was all but lost.

After her guests had gone to bed (for Jenty, the newborn, had tired both ladies out) Eliza prayed for peace in her heart, but for whatever reason, the Lord was not yet answering her. She got up from her chair on the porch. Using the north star as her guide as Alemeth had taught her, she determined the direction – just to the right – where the boys of the Seventeenth Mississippi had gone to fight for independence. She could hope there'd be no fighting. (There'd been none yet, as far as she knew.) She prayed that, whatever happened, the Lord would see fit to keep the boys safe.

Then Amzi came out, asking why she hadn't yet gone to bed. She confessed the cause of her worries. How terrible it would be if any harm came to Alemeth.

He put his hands on her shoulders. He assured her that everything would turn out for the best. He drew her body close, shielding her as if from enemy fire. To the tenderness of his attentions, she responded with attentions of her own. Before the night was through, Amzi and Eliza had lain together as they hadn't in a very long time.

98

The rain didn't let up. The creek rose. The soil turned to mud. For weeks, there was no way to dry clothes. Alemeth, Gordon and Bill Stevens – tent mates – passed their days at their campfire, taking shelter between drills, waiting, drinking stale coffee, trying their best to avoid constant saturation. Alemeth's crotch powder had run out. The itching wouldn't stop. His head and neck crawled with mosquito bites. One day, during a lull in the rains, trying to think of things to say in a letter to Dora, he felt a touch of dizziness. He shook his head, but the feeling would not go away. He put the letter down. Gordon went out of the tent, saying he felt sick. A few steps outside, he vomited. Alemeth could smell the stench, and his own dizziness worsened. Bill went out and covered Gordon's mess with dirt, but knowledge of what he was doing made Alemeth nauseous. He needed sleep. His back was sore. At supper, the bowl of beans didn't look like it belonged in his stomach, and he too vomited.

A visit from Lieutenant Fiser followed. Fiser said, "Look at me, private." He did. "Your eyes are red. And look at the rest of you! That's it."

Alemeth protested, but Fiser would hear nothing of it. The Lieutenant ordered Alemeth, Gordon and Bill to take the train to the army hospital in Charlottesville. After a few days there, Alemeth was released to rejoin the regiment at Centerville, but arriving in Centerville late at night, he found the regiment under orders to march north in the morning to Leesburg. He, like Andrew Dickens, wasn't yet fully recovered. It was decided they should remain behind, so as not to contaminate the others. They managed to eat some chicken and beans. His fever returned. Sore, uncomfortable, clammy and hot, Alemeth boarded the train again for Charlottesville. Perspiration soaked the mattress. The bed itself sweated, damp and cold. Alemeth woke from a delirium to hear Gordon Falkner nearby. "No battle is ever won," he said. And then, "the sooner we die, the longer we shall be immortal." His head ached. Nausea returned. He was lost in a tumultuous sea. There was no keeping track of time.

*   *   *

He didn't later remember the first ambulance, or the second, coming in from Manassas. By the time he could remember, the empty beds were occupied. On his stomach, arms and legs, the mosquito bites were gone, in their place even more measles. But it wasn't the measles that had gained his attention. It was the wounds of boys being brought in five and six to a wagon. Bandages and gauze were everywhere, moans rising from nearby cots, doctors with chloroform and ether attending, sawing bones at the point of injury, applying poultices, sewing patches of skin from severed limbs onto the stumps that remained. Disease was already familiar. Injury and fresh blood by the ragful were new and unfamiliar.

But talk in the hospital wasn't about the blood and scourged flesh. Having crossed Bull Run, McDowell's Yankees had been taught a good lesson. The South had whipped them pretty well. (Routed them, in fact, not just across the creek, but all the way back to Washington.) Amidst the groaning and moaning were tales of victory, honor, and pride. Even Gordon could only listen (too weak, he said, to take interest in his usual notes). Then, when Dr. Wise's daughter came in, passing out religious tracts, encouraging the bedridden men to read, Gordon took an immediate turn for the better. "I can't see," he said sending a wink Alemeth's way to signal that he was inventing again, for the sake of the doctor's daughter.

"What are the tracts about?"

"Holy war."

"Are they any good?"

"Yes. I like them very much."

"Tell me."

"They say war to preserve our southern way of life is a Holy War. They say there's no better way to show your love for God than giving your life for Him. Like the martyrs did."

"So, dying for the south is the same as dying for Jesus?"

"I don't know about that, Private. But it *is* service to His Will."

There was a shrill cry from a nearby cot.

"What was that?"

"A patient."

"Another amputation?"

"I'm afraid so."

"I'd have never imagined so many of them."

"A round musket ball slides off a bone; occasionally cracks one, at most. The lead of a Minnie ball is softer. It flattens out on impact, so it shatters the bone. When a bone's broken into little pieces like that, it blackens and dies."

"Delightful."

"These boys are the lucky ones. At least for them, amputation is possible. There's nothing we can do for those with wounds to the chest."

As hard as he could, Alemeth tried to imagine losing a leg to a surgeon's saw, or being hit in the head with a Minnie ball that flattened and shattered his skull.

Charlottesville, Va.

July 29th
Dear Sister,
I have not much news to tell, but as I believe a letter is due you, I will try to write you a few lines. There are at least fifteen hundred sick and wounded soldiers here. Four or five die every day. The hearse is continually on the go.
There are several Vindicators here. We are all improving slowly. I do not know how nor where to tell you to write to me at. I cannot say anything new about the battle, only we took from the Yankees thirty five thousand handcuffs, which they intended to iron our men with. (They expected to take Beauregard's whole army prisoners. But the joke was turned, we took about 1200 of them prisoners and sent them to Richmond with their own handcuffs on.)
A great many boys left today to return to their respective companies. I expect to stay here until I hear from Pa, then if I am stout enough to stand camp life I will return to my company. I wrote to sister from Manassas, if she has not written, she had better write to me here, to the care of Dr. E. S. H. Wise, as I do not know where I will have to go to when I leave here. When I leave I will write a few lines home to let you all know.
Charlottesville is a pretty place and one long to be remembered by the soldier on account of the kindness of the people. Mrs. Wise is just as kind a lady as ever walked on the Virginia soil.
Tell Pa I will write to him again soon.
Last Thursday six thousand soldiers passed through here. Every train is crowded with them. You may look out for the Capitol before many months, I can say no more.
Give my love to Pa, Ma, Sister, Walton, & Edy, and kiss Laura. Tell Aunt Leety and all the negroes howdy for me. Sister you will receive a brother's kindest love. I remain your affectionate brother.

J. A. Byers

Released from the hospital, Gordon and Alemeth got a ride to the front from none other than old Dr. Edgar. Edgar had appeared as if transported from an old dream into a new one. The old mentalist was driving the same wagon, but his sign had been painted over with green and a white flag hung out over the horses.

On the way to the front – Leesburg, this time – Gordon and the doctor traded stories. The doctor's began believably, credible tales about famous people like General Sherman and Abe Lincoln; Gordon's were about people less well known, people Alemeth recognized, people from Oxford and Panola, and Gordon's stories mixed things Alemeth knew to be true with tell-tale signs of invention, making Alemeth wonder if Edgar's were any more true than Gordon's.

Back in camp, they waited for over a month. John Jolly taught them to drop their hardtack into their coffee. (It softened the biscuit and let the weevil larvae loose, to float to the top, where they could skim them off.) Bill Elliot showed the boys how to mix hard tack with brown sugar, hot water, and whiskey, to make a sort of pudding. They became cooks, making bad food edible. Mostly, they played cards and dice, and waited.

Everyone had stories about the battle at Bull Run – but as Alemeth had only heard the stories of others, he kept his mouth shut, letting others boys talk about the parts they'd played. What could he say, in return? That he'd watched from a hundred miles away? That he'd had measles and had been taken from the field in advance of the action? The boys all knew he'd seen no danger. He'd committed no valorous acts. He'd not even witnessed the trial of other men's nerves. So the more he listened to the stories of others, the more he was left apart, alone, with nothing to do but dream of Sally Fox.

There was good news, at least, on that score: neither army was backing off. The Armory at Harper's Ferry was too important to be conceded by either side. *Sooner or later, he would have his chance to prove himself.*

He spent the rest of August tending fires, drinking coffee, wondering why one side, or the other, wasn't making a move.

Then, in September, he got sick again. Muscles ached. Fever and nausea again. When Lieutenant Fiser saw how dark his urine was, he looked into the whites of his eyes and said he had the yellow jaunders. The next thing Alemeth knew, he was on nursing detail at the field hospital at Carter's Mills, and Gordon was consoling him, telling him he was hardly the only sick soldier to miss the fight. That he should consider himself lucky he hadn't come down with the typhoid. Three Vindicators – Lorenzo Jones, George Capps, and Larkin Eastridge — had died of typhoid. That wasn't what Alemeth wanted for himself. Going home dead of disease was no way to win Sally's heart. But as far as Alemeth could see, staying in a hospital while others took to the battlefield was no way either.

By late September, the worst weakness passed, Alemeth convinced the surgeons to let him return to his company. For a while, it seemed he'd get his chance to prove his valor, after all. But on a Sunday morning at the beginning of October, when the Vindicators, roused at 3 a.m., were told to prepare for battle, Alemeth was already awake, a pain in his stomach so bad as to double him over. A tight knot twisted just below his ribs. When he stood up, he couldn't help but vomit again. Once Charley Morgan smelled it, everybody in surrounding tents knew of it. He could hide it no longer. Lieutenant Fiser assigned him to baggage duty in the rear, with others ruled unfit to fight.

And so, again, he missed the action.

When the fight was over, Gordon came back alive, uninjured, and full of fantastic stories, telling how Lieutenant Fiser and Captain Foote had proven themselves capable commanders, how the boys had showed all the courage a man could ask, how they'd run toward the front without a thought to courage or cowardice, only doing, in that moment, what they were doing, as if nothing else mattered.

Not being with the others at the hour of their trial sickened Alemeth's heart as much as the bug had sickened his gut. A sick solder can put his heart into the war, but until he faces battle, he can never go home a hero. It had been five months of army life in camps and hospitals, and he had nothing yet for Sally. Not even a photograph to send.

It was all he could do to wait for the next letter from home. The letters were welcome, when they came, but contained no good news. Jacob Thompson had lost his bid for Governor of Mississippi. It appeared that Mississippi was in a struggle for its very existence. And worst of all, it was all he could do to answer, yet again, questions from home about his own well-being, and complaints that in his last letters, he'd said nothing of the battle in which his fellow Mississippians had found either glory or death.

Camp at Carter's Mills... 6 miles from Leesburg

Oct. 26, 1861
Dear Father & Mother,

I received Pa's letter about a week ago, and Mother's today. When I wrote last, I was in good health, but about a week after I had a little of the jaundice or Yellow Jaunders. I am well now, with the exception of a bad cold, which I have had ever since I had the Measles.

About the battle. Sunday night and Monday morning 12 regiments of Yankees crossed the river. We had only four. They also had 17 pieces of artillery. Our regiments whipped the Yankees so bad they hardly knew themselves. About seven hundred prisoners were taken and about 1500 stand of arms. When the Yankees gave way they attempted to cross the river, but our little army followed them to the bank. A great many yanks stripped off their clothes, left them on the bank, plunged in to the river to swim over, and drowned in the attempt.

I am sorry I could not be there. Most of the boys got Yankee guns and overcoats & caps.

I have received the clothes you sent me some time ago. I will be glad to get the blankets and boots you said you sent me. I don't know that I need anything more, unless you send me something good to eat. Tell whoever knits gloves for me to knit fingers to them, the way in which we have to carry our guns, we cannot do it with gloves on our fingers.

I do not know when we will go to Leesburg again, or whether we go somewhere else. I can but send my love to you all.

Your affectionate son,

J. A. Byers

We also took four cannons.

99

Several months along in carrying another child, Eliza had been aching and tired. But Alemeth's letter bespoke a wonderful change in attitude. 'Mother,' he'd called her. 'Affectionate son,' he'd called himself. Could he be outgrowing his resentment? Had the kindness that disarms prejudice worked a change in him? It was the answer to prayer. She would offer it to the negroes at Sunday school, as testimony. She would ask them to pray with her that Alemeth's new attitude was a step toward his truly finding Jesus.

Strange, how the Lord uses suffering to bring out the good in people. Maybe something good would yet come from the war. Maybe, upon his return, Alemeth would become the sort of Christian that God-fearing people look up to. Maybe the whole war was just a part of God's Providential Plan and wondrous things would come of it, things no one could imagine.

She would knit Alemeth his gloves. She would get Dora to cook something good for him to eat. She would send it off in a package for him, as she had the clothes, the blankets and the boots.

Amzi's reaction to Alemeth's letter was something else entirely. When she finally got him to say what troubled him, it was evident his focus had been nothing like hers.

"He writes a lot about the battle."

"Yes, I thought so, too."

"But he says, 'I am sorry I could not be there.'" Amzi furrowed his brow. "I find that very strange."

"Oh?"

"I wonder if he did something he's not proud of."

"Amzi, why?"

"How can a boy be sick so often? What's wrong with him?"

Some days, she worried about Amzi even more than she worried about Alemeth. He was out of sorts about all sorts of things, not least that the price the State House had set for its new cotton notes was only five cents a pound for the crop to come. When Eliza asked him to take Alemeth's place as the other white person at Sunday School, he tried to get Johnson to do it, as if he didn't want to be there with her. His preoccupation with the war was a part of it, to be sure, but there was more. His disappointment in Alemeth was not how a father should feel about a son. Who knew why he couldn't feel better about his first-born son? And who knew what else he might be struggling with?

Able only to guess at the turbulent state of his troubles, she prayed for him every day.

She prayed, too, for Mary Ann Brown, who was in a terrible way over the demise of the University. With only four students registered, the University had closed for lack of a student body. Everything of high culture had been lost. Science. Philosophy. Literature. Education and culture would have to await the return of simpler times, but it seemed things would get worse before they got better. Captain Boynton had been dismissed for lack of attachment to the Confederacy. Professor Hilgard had packed up his soils. Dr. Barnard was leaving soon for Tuscaloosa.

So Eliza prayed, for Mary Ann's sake, that the University would be soon restored, that it would be allowed to thrive to His glory, and that her sister would someday be the confident, capable sister she was before the war.

Then, one Saturday afternoon, Mary Ann brought news that caused Eliza to pray for herself. Al Cansler was saying that her own stepson – yes, he meant John Alemeth – had called her an abolitionist. He was going all over two counties saying there'd be hell to pay if the Yankee schoolteacher (meaning Eliza herself) had been stirring up negroes at Bynum's Creek.

Could it be true? Had Alemeth accused her? Al Cansler was saying he'd heard it from Ben Spears. Why would Ben make up such a thing? And if Alemeth had said she was an abolitionist, what reason could *he* have had? She was no abolitionist. The idea was ludicrous. Alemeth had been a part of her classes with the negroes; he knew she'd never said anything to stir them up.

"You remember what happened to Captain Boynton," said Mary Ann, "not to mention Reverend Vrooman. You don't want to be the next one called to account for your sympathies. You'd better be careful what you say. People still talk about your school, you know. It's a lot for people to overlook. If you're going to keep on with it, you need other ways to demonstrate your southern sympathies."

"Alright, Mary Ann."

"Remember also, sister, that your voice is a constant reminder. Think of it as a challenge God has arranged, a burden you have to overcome. Tone down your Yankee accent; I can help you speak more like a Charleston lady."

So Eliza listened to Mary Ann speak, and tried to speak like she did, drawing her *tea* into *tay,* trying not to pronounce the *r* when she spoke of *war* or *fear.* Every chance she could, she mentioned her niece's husband, aide-de-camp to General Price, and her son who was with Beauregard's army in Virginia, and most of all, the doctrine that African slavery was a part of God's plan. She didn't like going to such lengths to protect her own reputation, but when it came to southern society, Mary Ann knew what was best, so Eliza deferred to her sister's judgment.

100

In late November, 1861, Mary Ann Loughborough and her children returned to Clear Creek. The teas and socials that followed were just what Mary Ann Brown said Eliza needed – an opportunity to affirm her southern sympathies to influential families. So Eliza repeated to the neighbors and invited guests just how much she supported the southern cause. How Mary Ann Loughborough's husband, James, was helping General Price regroup in Arkansas. How she'd just sent a package – along with her prayers – to John Alemeth, who was fighting for Beauregard at the front. She repeated such things whenever she could, her condemnations of abolitionists never forced, her loyalty to family never feigned. Her visits to Clear Creek to help entertain Mary Ann Loughborough did more good than any harm Al Cansler's letters could do.

At the same time, the Loughborough children brought a measure of pleasantness to the visits. Seven-month old Jenty made Eliza think of the child that she herself would soon bear. Three-year-old Julia Loughborough was perfect company for her own Laura. Little Julia seemed to love porcelain and lace, not to mention copying everything Laura did; the children made great entertainment for each other. When Mary Ann Brown invited Laura to stay at Clear Creek too, the children got to know each other well. Julia was especially fascinated by Clio and Calliope, and Laura proud to show them off. The first thing every morning, the girls ran down from their bedroom to greet them. They spent hours pretending the birds were their children. Harl told them not to be so loud and bossy around them, not to poke their fingers at them, but his warnings failed to end their fascination. After four days of unflagging attention, one of the birds gave a sharp nibble to Julia's outstretched finger.

Julia recovered – her pride hurt more than anything else – but after that, she kept her distance from the parrots.

When it was time for Laura to come home, she pleaded with Eliza to let Julia come home with her. The little girls were playing so well together, the adults couldn't refuse: Julia Loughborough came home with Laura; everyone readied for a joyful time of youth between the girls. But things did not go well at Bynum's Creek. On Monday evening, Julia refused to eat anything. While Aunt Leety put the little girls to bed, Eliza (whose back was aching, whose feet and knees were sore from another climb up the trail toward motherhood) went to bed early herself. Some time later she woke to hear crying. She put on a robe and entered the children's room. Leety was at Julia's bedside. An odor of excrement was in the air.

Julia was on her side, knees tucked into her chest; a flat of cotton flannel in Leety's hand was stained.

"That child's stool be awful sour, Miz Byers. She feels cold. Can't get her to eat a thing. We might want to get Annie in here, to see if she'll take some milk."

"Milk? Milk from – ?"

"Yes'm."

"I – I don't think that will be necessary, Leety. But have her send Gilbert to me. I'll want him to take a message to the child's mother."

The message said that Julia had come down with something and that, while she shouldn't be unduly alarmed, she should come as soon as she could. Gilbert left with it. Laura asked if Julia was going to be okay.

"Laura, honey, why don't you come with me. You may be able to sleep better in my room. Get your blanket."

"Why is cousin sick, mother?"

"Some bile must have crossed when she was bitten, Laura. But the parrots are fine, Mary Porter is fine, and no doubt Julia will be too, Lord willing. Be sure you say a prayer for her."

Across the hall, Walton and Eddy were sleeping.

When Laura was settled in and Bible study over, Eliza returned to the little girls' room. Leety had gotten things smelling passably clear, but the child herself was no better. As if to prove the fact, she vomited a clear fluid that looked like rice water.

"I's trying to keep her clean, Miz. Byers. And I's trying to get her to eat something. I don't know what else I can do. She ain't got no fever. You sure you don't want me to go fetch Annie?"

"No. The child's mother will be here soon. We'll leave that sort of decision to her."

Eliza went to the crib and took a close look. The child's hands were cold and almost wrinkled, her pulse quick, her breathing shallow.

"We'll summon Doctor Isom," she said. "He'll know what to do. Why don't you go fetch Gilbert."

"Gilbert's gone, Ma'am. Carried that note to Miz Loughborough."

"Then send Grote or Annie, for goodness' sake."

Leety left to find Grote, to fetch Dr. Isom. Eliza stayed with the child, helpless. When Leety returned, she went downstairs to wait for the doctor and pray that the Lord keep little Julia Loughborough safe.

*   *   *

By the time the child's mother arrived, Eliza was distraught, but had to hide it, best she could, for Mary Ann's sake. Julia had taken a grayish blue cast to the color of her skin; her eyes were sunken. Mary Ann took her from Aunt Leety and cradled her in her arms. For hours, the child moaned; the mother comforted. Over the course of the night, the moaning – which had started out strong and demanding – became gradually weaker. And then, at long last, the child fell asleep, and when her mother shook her, she did not come back to life.

By the time Dr. Isom arrived, there was nothing he could do. The child had already gone to her reward.

It's one thing to lose a baby on a birthing table. Eliza had known that anguish. But it was surely another to lose an infant you've come to know, a living human being who has sucked at your breast, learned to walk, tugged on your skirt, looked you in the eye and told you she loves you. Mary Ann Loughborough knew her daughter in the flesh. She had watched her die. Even *felt* her die. Eliza prayed for the child's soul to be taken straight to heaven, and for the mother's grief to be bearable.

Then she thought about the impact of the death on her sister.

"I hope Mary Ann doesn't take it too hard," she said to Amzi and Dr. Isom. "My sister, I mean."

The men looked at her curiously. "Explain?"

"I mean only that – what if Mary Ann – the child's mother – blames her?"

"Why would she blame Mrs. Brown?" asked Dr. Isom.

"Well, she shouldn't. I mean, she couldn't have known that the parrot would bite again, could she? And we can't *know* that the illness came from the parrot bite, can we?"

"My dear, I can assure you the child's illness did not come from a parrot bite. The child's runs had the distinctive odor of the cholera. Parrots don't get cholera."

"Oh! Well. Tell me then, Doctor – where did the cholera come from?"

"It's impossible to know, Mrs. Byers. Vapors, no doubt. We don't know causes. Only treatments."

"Poor Julia. There was no time for treatments."

"The child died of dehydration, Mrs. Byers. From diarrhea. The baby needed fluid."

"Oh. I didn't know."

"Eliza," Amzi said in disbelief, "she had the runs. You didn't even give her water?"

The idea that she might have done something to help the child was a knife through her heart. She didn't like the thought; she didn't like the taste of it.

She resented Amzi for suggesting it. It didn't belong in her thoughts at all; she was too upset as it was. There was no way she could have known.

That afternoon, the undertaker brought a child-sized coffin on his wagon. After he met with Amzi, he asked about 'disposition of the remains.' Mary Ann said the child would be laid to rest at the Loughborough family church in Carondelet. She kissed the coffin's lid. The undertaker put the coffin on the back of his wagon, and the wagon made its way from the house.

As it did so, Eliza's own child kicked inside her, making her heart flutter.

Christmas was right around the corner. Candied cakes, holly, readings from Luke – the Lord had given her many blessings. But the death of Julia Loughborough – at *her* house, from diarrhea and dehydration – weighed heavy on her heart. Amzi's unkind comment hadn't helped. And with Mary Ann Loughborough gone back to Saint Louis, there were no more socials to show her loyalties to the southern cause; only grieving, condolences, and a need to ward off nagging guilt.

As the holidays came and went, her feet and back sore, fatigued, Amzi muttering about money, the whole family in grief, and worrying about Alemeth and the war, the child inside her kept her up at night, fretting with the knowledge that the little he or she would soon face its own earthly trial.

101

It had been at least nine months. In a hundred ways, Eliza's body told her the baby was ready to come. Yet, poised against the Army of the Mississippi, less than a day's coach ride to the north, was the army of General U.S. Grant, his avowed purpose to invade, a battle expected at any time. Did God's instruction to bear children guarantee that bringing another baby into the world was the right thing to do? Was it fair, to bring a child into a world so beset by conflict?

Eliza worried about Amzi, and the family, and the church, and what the War might do to all of them. And with so much doubt, how could she *not* worry about the infant's future? All her perceptions signaled danger, all her instincts protection.

But worrying changed nothing. There was life inside her, and the child's future lay in God's hands. So when, on the 7th of March, a normal, healthy baby girl was born. Eliza reminded herself that the infant had as good a chance of making it as any child. She wrapped the newborn in a new cotton blanket Leety had made. Laura said the hair on the baby's head was like peach fuzz, and asked if they could name her "Peach." Amzi said that since the child was a girl, the name should be up to Eliza.

The birth had been a dim light in a very dark room. The passing of little Julia Loughborough had cast a shadow over everything, a shadow so deep it could not be ignored or forgotten.

"I've been thinking it would be an honor to Mary Ann if we named our little girl after hers. Don't you think?"

"Julia?"

"Yes, dear. Julia Loughborough Byers."

What the girl's future would be, no one could foresee. Whether war, or cholera, small pox or childbirth, would cut her life short, no one could know. How her father and she would get along remained to be seen. Whether she'd marry someday, and have children of her own, remained to be seen. But Amzi loved his daughters, and surely he'd love Julia too. And as long as she taught Julia to love the Lord, Julia stood as good a chance as the rest of them.

The Florence Gazette, of yesterday, says

We learned yesterday that the Federals had landed a large force at Savannah, Tennessee. We suppose they are making preparations to get possession of the Memphis & Charleston railroad. They must never be allowed to get this great thoroughfare in their possession, for then we would indeed be crippled. The labor and untiring industry of too many faithful and energetic men have been expended upon this road, to bring it up to its present state of usefulness, to let it fall into the hands of our enemy, to be used against us. It must be protected. We, as a people, are able to protect and save it. If unavoidable, let them have our river, but we hope it is the united sentiment of our people that we will have our railroad.

-- The Memphis Appeal, March 13, 1862

After Island Number 10 was lost, the Yankees swept down the Mississippi by steamship and barge. They captured Huntsville, cutting the Memphis & Charleston in half. They captured New Orleans. There was no sugar. No coffee. Nothing of northern manufacture – nothing, that is, save the hostile machinery of war. With no history as an independent state, Mississippi had to sustain itself with the resources on hand – whatever it could grow, or make, itself. And conditions for a cotton crop were hardly ideal when so much blood and sweat was being shed for the sake of the war.

Corinth protected not only the northern border, but with it, Mississippi's share of the M&C. Determined to maintain possession of Corinth, General Johnston attacked the Yankees at Shiloh, but along with seventeen hundred other confederate soldiers, he was killed. The effort failed to drive Grant from Mississippi. In addition to the dead, it left eight thousand Confederate wounded. The *James Brown* pulled carloads of them from the battlefield to Oxford. Townspeople brought mattresses, beds, cots, and bedding to the campus. Dr. Isom set up surgical tents and cutting tables, carts of chloroform, opiates and cotton gauze; young girls cut bandages, children scraped lint to be used in poultices. The University became a hospital, and the magnetic observatory, with its thick leaden walls, became a morgue.

On the sixth of June, Memphis was surrendered to the Yankee army. The western terminus of the M&C lost, Mary Ann Loughborough fled south to Oxford, joining Julia Shotwell as a volunteer at the campus hospital. Urged to volunteer with them, Eliza agreed, but she found the campus a horrid place of cotton gauze, white sheets, jaundice and gangrene; of typhoid fever, delirious soldiers, and bandages where limbs had been. She rolled up her sleeves, but among the many blood-stained wash rags in the barrel was one that smelled like the night Julia Loughborough had died. Corpses carried away for burial. Limbs harvested, for their skin, to be sewn onto stumps. Collodion shrank, helping to close wounds. Nausea threatened everywhere. No deadly disease would come to Dora or Laura, Walton or Eddy, if Eliza could do anything about it. She returned to Bynum's Creek, struggling to accept what a terrible place an army hospital could be.

North of town, as southern armies tore up the M. C. R. R. to slow Grant's advance into Mississippi, no one at Bynum's Creek noticed that Laura was pretending to be Julia's mother, telling her what to do with all the authority of an older child seeking to have her own way. It seemed such a natural thing – so inconsequential and ordinary – that no one took any notice.

102

The 17th Regiment of Mississippi Volunteers saw its first snow in camp that winter. Gordon found a sled in the barn of a farm house and some of the boys went sledding – a speeding, careening downhill ride – until Bob Patton sprained his foot and Lieutenant Fiser put a stop to their playfulness. In the days that followed, the thrill of that first snowfall gave way to the coldest winter in memory. Freezing rain made joints ache and left the boys wringing out cold, wet pants. The sun disappeared. The north wind brought sleet and a hailstorm. Feet stung as if iced, the wind so cold campfires couldn't keep them warm. Colonel Featherstone's negro, Joe, stole a wagon horse and rode off one night. To keep others from running off, the Colonel increased the watch and increased roll calls to four a day. A few soldiers deserted, but nearly all of Panola's Company H were re-upping. It was easy for Alemeth to go along with Gordon and the others, knowing he hadn't yet done what he'd come to do. And so he battled the cold his first winter in Virginia, waiting until spring for another chance to prove himself.

*   *   *

In March it was time for war again: the Vindicators hit the roads. Marching by day, bivouacking by night, they moved from the mountains of the Shenandoah to Middleburg, to the Rappahannock, and to the Rapidan. In April, further orders: travel by rail through Richmond, as far as West Point. From there, on foot again to Yorktown, to keep the Yankees off Virginia's Peninsula. Gordon said 'peninsula' meant an almost-island, that if the tides rose high enough, they all might find themselves adrift and headed out to sea. Alemeth was glad to have him along, as his gift for filling their heads made time pass far more quickly. Bill Elliott was different. Like Howard Falconer, he was a realist. He talked of how topography had to be used to advantage. How strategy and tactics had to change when one moved from the mountains to the piedmont, or from the piedmont to the tidewater. They were fighting on southern land. Their generals knew the topography. Knowing the land, they were bound to prevail. Different as he was from Gordon, Bill too was a pillar of strength. Bill, too, helped Alemeth fight off fear.

But as it turns out, the Yankees had two 200-pound Parrotts. They had twelve 100-pound Parrotts. They had four-and-a-half inch Rodman siege rifles. They had 10-ton mortars that fired 220-pound shells. And before too long, conceding the tidewater to the Yankees, the 17th and the rest of Magruder's division fell back to higher ground on the outskirts of Richmond.

103

On the twelfth of June, Gordon stayed in camp to work on a story he was writing while Alemeth, John Jolly and some of the other Vindicators made their way into the city, eleven dollars pay in their pockets. After a short search, they found the sign they'd been looking for.

Holmes, Booth, & Hodges
"Results in 15 Minutes."

Door bell ringing, they passed through the entrance to a large room and a voice from behind another door.

"Just a minute. I'll be right with you. Please, have a seat."

In the middle of the room, a large, tented camera on a tripod. Several lights on stands near the window. Arm chairs around the room – comfortable. Portraits everywhere advertising the proprietor's work. A sign on a wall read, "*All Confederate Notes Accepted.*" A door opened and a man emerged, a monocle gripped between an eyebrow and a cheek.

"Bob Hodges, gentlemen. What can I do for you?"

"We were wondering if you do any of those visitin' cards,' said Charley Morgan.

"No, I'm afraid we don't do *cartes de visite*. We do real portraits here."

"Daguerreotypes?" asked Alemeth.

"Ambrotypes."

"With collodion?"

"You know something of photography?"

"He knows everything there is to know about cotton," said John Jolly. "His Pa has a big plantation."

"Well then, gentlemen. Might I interest any of you in a group image, all of you at once? A remembrance of your days together?"

Hodges and the others all looked at Alemeth.

"No, thank you. We only talked about pictures of ourselves, for our sisters and our sweethearts."

"Come on, Byers. You've got enough money."

"You got your eleven dollars, same as me."

"But you got a whole plantation. A whole family that sends you things. You *know* I need money more than you do."

"Yeah," said Tom Carlock. "Me too."

In the end, Alemeth agreed to pay for the picture he didn't want. They all stood in a group, shoulder to shoulder, so they could remember their days together. Then, they posed individually.

When it was Alemeth's turn, Mr. Hodges pressed a finger against Alemeth's chin and moved it to one side. It wasn't a comfortable position, but after months of drills, he was used to holding uncomfortable positions. It was easy to hold still, despite the indignation. He'd soon have a picture for Sally Fox. She'd send him one of herself. Someday, he'd be with her again. He'd get a copy of that novel. Go home, eat another piece of her cake, and a piece of her pie. Exchange photographs. Have another chance with her in the Dead Room.

He could feel her lips close to his when Mr. Hodges handed him the finished photo.

It wasn't right.

"This picture isn't as sharp as the ambrotypes on the walls."

"You moved."

"I —"

"I told you not to."

Had he moved? Had his movement made the picture blurry?

"I didn't move."

"I'll tell you what," said Hodges. "I'll take another photograph for just a dollar."

The other boys were ready to go. Charley Morgan wanted to find a tavern. No one else cared about the blurry picture.

They paid for the photographs. At the bookseller, he couldn't remember the names of the books Sally had read.

Later that afternoon, after an hour at the tavern had left him tipsy, he was back in camp, looking at the ambrotype again.

It wasn't just the lack of sharpness to the image. He looked too young. The picture was of a boy, not a war hero.

A few days later at roll call, Colonel Holder offered his view that the stalemate outside Richmond would not go on forever. That if the Yankees didn't attack their positions soon, the 17th would be leaving their breastworks and attacking the Yankees. If ordered to do so, they'd attack the Yankees all by themselves – wasn't he right? (A cheer went up from the men.)

The presence of Yankees so close to the capital could not be tolerated. (Sober silence.) There'd be no more personal passes until further notice. (Hushed grumbling, audible only within the ranks.) He had, however, sent his negro boy into the city again. There was no guarantee of sweet cakes and bacon, like last time, but the boy was a capable boy, and when he returned, there was bound to be a good meal for everyone. (Smiles broke out on every face.) And one other thing: if any of the boys who had their own negroes wanted to send them into Richmond on errands, that would be permitted. Finally, he was pleased to say, there'd been a delivery of mail; the men should see their company commanders. *Dismissed.* (Smiling, anticipation, laughter.)

Lieutenant Wright read the names for Company H: Baker. Elmendorf. Lamb. Burleson. (A shame the picture in his coat didn't do him justice. The next time, he wouldn't move. He'd come out sharper, and more like a man. But when would there be another chance to get a photograph? And what action might there be, before then?) Pepper. Carlock. Perkins. Shuford. (The delicate photograph was all he had. It wasn't safe where it was. He could stuff it in his bedroll...)

"Byers."

(From Sally?)

No. The letter was from Lou, and it brought more bad news. Federal agents controlled the railroads down the line, preventing shipment of cotton north. You couldn't find things you'd grown to depend on. Walton had misfired a musket and nearly lost an eye. But Lou said there was goodness wherever she looked. Pa was distressed at the cotton market, but intent on finding a way to manage. Al Cansler was calling for an end to Eliza's negro Sunday school, but Eliza was standing up to him. Uncle Johnson had had more words with the man, and was seeing to it that Walton was fair to Eddie. And then, half way down the page,

I saw Sally Fox today. She asked about you.

He held the letter to his heart, then looked at the line again and again, trying to imagine the conversation, trying to hear exactly what Sally had said, and exactly how she'd said it, as if he could find the answers in the ink on the page.

But there was also, toward the end of the letter, a complaint.

I saw Sally Fox today. She asked about you.

"Oh, dear boy, what is a girl to do with a brother so ill-bred as you? Mary Fiser has received several letters from her brother. Sarah Jolly and Marjan Wright have heard from theirs. Do I have to write to your friends, and ask them to show my brother how a sister should be treated?

"We are so in the dark here. There is much news I want to hear. What has happened since Yorktown? Have you seen the enemy? Have you forgotten your sister? Please write, dear brother, or I can only conclude that you do not love me."

June 14th/62
Camp 5 miles east of Richmond

Dear Sister,

I received your letter yesterday, it gave me a great deal of pleasure, but you must quit complaining. You asked me if I had forgotten that I had a sister, and do you not love me, the reason you do not write. Such questions are simple and very foolish. Have you forgotten that your Brother lives entirely out of doors, and like the brute creation takes the weather as it comes, and has a very poor way to take care of paper? We have had no tents in nearly three months. My friends that you speak of are both officers, and have privileges I do not have.

We were on picket about two weeks. Our picket line ran through a field, where we could see the Yankees every day, in large numbers. Artillery, cavalry, and infantry. The Chickahominy, only, separated us. Their pickets were about four hundred yards from us. They frequently would shoot shell at our men when they could see them in squads. The Yanks kept at this till our men got tired of it and returned the fire. A general cannonading took place across the Chickahominy bottom which lasted about three hours.

On our march from Yorktown, we had a rough time of it. We lived two days on parched corn. Whenever we could get crackers & bacon, we thought we were doing well. I have not had as rough a time yet as I expected when I left home, but the worst is to come yet, and is fast coming on. There has been several fights around Richmond, but no general engagement, and I don't believe there will be one soon, though there are two large armies here close together.

The health of our company is tolerable good. Charley Morgan and Peter Brown are both well & look as well as any soldiers do. We have had a great deal of bad weather, but the last three days were clear.

The first chance Pa has, he must send me Gilbert. I need him. He will be safer here, and do me more good than at home. If there is any chance at all, I want him to send him.

I went to Richmond the other day. I had my ambrotype taken. It is not a good one, but I did not have time to have it taken over. I will have it taken again the first chance & have it put in a larger case. Please give my love to Miss Sally. I could enjoy a piece of that big cake now if I had it.

Give my love to Pa, Ma, Brothers, little sister, and accept a large portion for yourself, and tell the negroes howdy for me. This is enough. Put your letter away, for it is time to quit.

Your affectionate Brother,

J.A. Byers

Direct to Richmond, Va.
Care of H.W. Middleton
Company H, 17th Reg. Mifs Vol
Gen. Griffith's Brigade

104

In the beginning, gods created heaven and earth. And the earth was without form, and void; and darkness was upon the face of the deep.
--Genesis 1: 1-2

As if in memory of an earlier, Biblical time, the period of seven days between June 25 and July 1, 1862, has come down through history with the name, 'the Seven Days campaign.'

Before dawn on the first day, Robert E. Lee, the new supreme commander, faced a fundamental threat: General McClellan's Union Army, just miles outside the capital, would *have* to be repelled. And since the element of surprise is there for the side that dares to take it, Lee decided the attack would be the following day, as soon as Jackson arrived.

That following day would have been the first, if things had gone according to plan. But the opposing armies, close to each other and under considerable pressure, clashed before Lee had anticipated. With the first flash of gunfire at Oak Grove igniting a day early, historical accounts called *it* the first of the seven days.

Either way, as the day ended and succumbed to night, the new supreme commander couldn't sleep for going over his plans again, in every light he could.

*　　　　　*　　　　　*

On the second day, Lee examined his maps and organized his command. The enemy was both north and south of the Chickahominy. Heavy rainfall had made the river high and the ground wet, creating a swamp as much as a mile wide across the tidewater, divided into wetlands on either side of the river. The enemy line straddled the swamp. Communications between its right and left would be next to impossible. And so the plan took shape: Jackson and Hill would outnumber the Yankee right. And while they drove the enemy's flank into the muddy, shin-deep, cat-tailed river, Hager and Magruder, with smaller forces, would hold firm their positions to the south, on either side of the Richmond and York River Railroad.

Things went much as Lee had planned. As the day ended, A. P. Hill clashed with Porter on the Yankee right, but everything remained quiet in the center.

*　　　　　*　　　　　*

On the third day, General Magruder continued the plan for the outnumbered confederates to keep the enemy center occupied. While the real attack was underway on the left, he took the higher ground where he could be seen, marching his men back and forth along the nine mile road so that the enemy would mistake his movements for signs of imminent attack. In a scorching heat, Magruder's men marched east then west between the grassy fields, stirring up as much dust as they could and wondering, to a man, why their commander had set them to do what he had. Beneath the brutal sun, they thanked God for tobacco leaves and shady spots along the road, but as yet saw no real action.

*   *   *

On the fourth day, General Griffith's whole Brigade, including the 17th Mississippi, was held in the rear. Alemeth could hear cannon fire in the distance, and could see tiny clouds of smoke rising from the guns. He spent the day battle-ready, but with nothing to do, wondering if the Brigade would ever be sent to the front. Word had it that everything was going well to the left, but again, the center's orders were simply to stand its ground.

That night, during guard duty along the railroad tracks, neither the new moon nor the stars nor the lights of distant gunfire could fill the deep emptiness of space. While Bob and Gordon shared visions of what a cannonball could do to a Yankee observation balloon, Alemeth sat in the darkness, wondering what the world would look like from above, wondering if he'd ever get another chance to see the sky from Dr. Barnard's Observatories, wondering if his next evening with Sally Fox would bring him boldness and courage, whether he'd be able to prove to her that he was a man of valor.

*   *   *

The fifth day began with welcome news for those who'd already won their battle stripes: the Yankees were pulling back. They were abandoning their assault on the capital. For a moment, it appeared he might never get a chance. Then, when orders came in to pursue, his heart started pounding. If this was not to be his day, his day might never come.

A Confederate 32-pound siege gun, mounted on a flat car, moved east along the R.&Y.R.R.. The Vindicators were assigned to clear the path of Yankee rear guard on either side of the tracks. Peter Brown chose Alemeth and Bill Elliot to scout with him. They advanced through thicket and branch, under maple leaves with bright undersides, breezes opening the canopy to patches of sunlight, scouring the woods for signs of living creatures. They moved in short, quick advances, listening more than looking, Alemeth's own movements enough to give them away if he wasn't careful. Rabbits, squirrels and chipmunks all fled the woods before them as if aware a hunt was on. Then the ground became muddy, the woods humid. Sixty-five pounds of blankets and gear dragged him down. Pounding guns had driven all the animals away. There wasn't a bird in the sky.

With maybe ten minutes of daylight left, the crack of rifle fire just yards away, in the underbrush. John Jolly barked orders. Footsteps pounded. Fire hit the ground. Fence posts. Knapsacks. The heaving of lungs, the beating of the heart. Clouds of smoke. *Let death, if it comes, be sudden.*

Hitting the ground.

A nearby boy was lifeless, the mark of death on every feature of his face, on every awkward thing about the way he lay, as if the air and the ground had clamped him between them, unable to move from the instant he fell, frozen in time for ever, with Alemeth, just a few feet away, frozen too, the two of them feeling the same death. Inertia pulled his body forward, but his mind was locked onto the corpse on the ground behind him, and his thoughts stayed there, through time that had no measure.

Then, before Alemeth ever fired a shot, darkness fell. After dark, shooting blind just wasted ammunition, so there was only what was quiet, and what still.

*   *   *

The morning of the sixth day broke to reveal the Yankees gone. The Vindicators fanned out along both sides of the railroad grade, assessing damage to the countryside. Fields observed, farmers questioned, dead livestock noted. Human corpses on the ground, crumpled and misshapen. Heat. A stench in the air putrid enough to send his nose to his rib cage and his stomach to his throat. Captain Middleton said to search for guns and ammunition, and to take whatever else – food, razors, shoes or other personal items – they wanted to carry.

Wool. Brass. A pair of socks. A gold coin. A harmonica. Spruce gum.

At Savage Station, they came upon an abandoned field hospital. Under a large shade tree, Yankees sick and dying like so many broken animals. Men with severed limbs and tourniquets. Men with blood-soaked bandages around their heads. Rows of men, barely alive. The Yankees had been in such a hurry to retreat, they'd left wounded behind. One caught Alemeth's eye, lying on his back, his bandaged chest on display. Though his torso was still, he was raving like a lunatic.

"Me mother Mary, and me father, Austin, the whole lot of them. Damn Beaver Dam Creek. You say you saw a priest, now, did ye? Yes, I know. It started in Philadelphia. Such a lovely Cathedral. Think on it, do! Michael, th' Arch Angel, on his back for years, painting his ceiling. Tell Thomas I've died, would ye?"

Was the man talking to *him*?

"Tell him James is dying, will ye? Yeah. If ye could find it in your heart to be so kind. So Thomas could be free, you see. Would ye give a lucky medal and a message to me brother? ... Yeah. It's what I said. Thomas. 71st Pennsylvania. Company B."

The man was holding out a medal. He took it.

"Saint Christopher, do ye see? On his shoulder, that's Jesus. Jesus himself."

So it appeared.

"Now the message. Write it down."

"I'm out of paper."

"Alright then. When you get some. Tell him I said, 'May it give y' better luck than it ever did me.'"

The man started to laugh, and Alemeth started to laugh with him. Then the man's laugh turned to a tortured wheeze.

"You'll – you'll deliver the message. Tell me. (Wheeze.) Won't you?"

"If I can."

The man would be dead in a matter of hours. Remembering Captain's orders, Alemeth put the medal around his own neck.

*   *   *

On the seventh Day, the Vindicators spent the afternoon marching back and forth on a country road – the 'Quaker' Road, some said. Some wondered aloud if their march was another charade. But finally, late in the day, feet tired and shoes full of holes, they left the road altogether, crossing a wheat field to higher ground, the sound of pounding cannon and the crack of rifle fire.

The sunset was like none he'd ever seen. The air was thundering, the ground shaking, fire from federal twelve pounders engulfing them in screaming, whistling chaos. Wounded men urged them forward up what they said was Malvern Hill, but no order to charge ever came. If those in command ever gave such an order, it never reached Vindicator ears. Still, cannon blazed into the night as Alemeth loaded, rammed, aimed, fired, even after darkness and smoke made it impossible to see. It was not until the seventh day was nearly over that he was able to rest.

And with the Seven Days Campaign ended, what had transpired during those days – the pain, the suffering, the deaths that resulted – was left a mystery to remember for a very long time to come.

Executive Mansion
Washington
August 22, 1862

Hon. Horace Greeley:

DEAR SIR:

I have just read yours of the 19th, addressed to myself through the New York Tribune. If there be in it any statements or assumptions of fact which I may know to be erroneous, I do not now and here controvert them. If there be in it any inferences which I may believe to be falsely drawn, I do not now and here argue against them. If there be perceptible in it an impatient and dictatorial tone, I waive it in deference to an old friend, whose heart I have always supposed to be right.

As to the policy I "seem to be pursuing," as you say, I have not meant to leave anyone in doubt.

I would save the Union. I would save it the shortest way under the Constitution. The sooner the national authority can be restored the nearer the Union will be "the Union as it was." If there be those who would not save the Union unless they could at the same time save Slavery, I do not agree with them. If there be those who would not Save the Union unless they could at the same time destroy Slavery, I do not agree with them. My paramount object in this struggle is to save the Union, and is not either to save or destroy Slavery. If I could save the Union without freeing any slave, I would do it, and if I could save it by freeing all the slaves, I would do it, and if I could save it by freeing some and leaving others alone, I would also do that. What I do about Slavery and the colored race, I do because I believe it helps to save this Union, and what I forbear, I forbear because I do not believe it would help to save the Union. I shall do less whenever I shall believe what I am doing hurts the cause, and I shall do more whenever I shall believe doing more will help the cause. I shall try to correct errors when shown to be errors; and I shall adopt new views so fast as they shall appear to be true views. I have here stated my purpose according to my view of official duty, and I intend no modification of my oft-expressed personal wish that all men, everywhere, could be free.

Yours,
A. Lincoln.

105

When Lincoln's letter was read aloud from the pages of the New York Times, Charley Morgan asked if Mr. Lincoln wasn't trying to have his cake and eat it too. Charley wanted to know how Lincoln could wish for universal freedom while insisting on Union. Wasn't a permanent union, forced on the unwilling, exactly the opposite of freedom and independence? Peter Brown said that the independence of the people of Mississippi had to be preserved, "by *whatever* means it takes." By and large, Panola's soldiers, including Alemeth Byers, agreed. So for the next month, the Vindicators did what their leaders wanted. On the fifth of September, they crossed the Potomac into Maryland. The week after that, they stormed federal artillery positions on the heights above Harper's Ferry. After that, they were ordered to Brownsville. After that, to Sharpsburg. In every place, they did what their commanders told them. They made the best of pitching tents and digging trenches, and when an officer directed, they marched, or camped, or rested, or drilled, or took aim and fired – even shooting at clouds of smoke, if so commanded.

As the Vindicators followed orders, men fell around them. General Griffith. Captain Foote. Tom Foster, Sam McClure, Alex McIlhany, Clark Stevens, Will Canfield, Will Cantrell, Jimmy Wright. Command of the Brigade fell to William Barksdale. Command of the Seventeenth to John Fiser. And the more men died, the deeper grew anger among those still alive.

At the end of September, Alemeth, Calvin Morris, Dan Tharpe and Gordon Falkner sat around a campfire feeling the approach of winter. Gordon brought up the latest from Washington – yet another Proclamation, this one proclaiming that on the first of the year, the slaves of states sill in rebellion against the north would then and thereafter be free..

"How can a man so steeped in rhetoric about freedom talk about 'rebellion' against his tyranny?" asked Dan.

"The man doesn't know what freedom is," said Calvin.

Alemeth agreed. The only purpose in a threat to liberate slaves was to compel submission, and compelled submission was tyranny. What would the Yankees be willing to do, to carry out their threat? What would happen to men like Pa and Colonel Brown if the tyrant got his way? Alemeth looked at his pocket watch. Time seemed not to move. He waited for the minute hand, wondering aloud how long it would take for the South to be free.

"Just listen for a second," said Gordon. "Just listen to a single tick. Then imagine how long the rest of time has been, and how much has yet to come."

"Gordon, come down from the clouds. What on earth are you talking about?"

106

The visiting preacher at the Sand Springs pulpit cleared his throat, all eyes upon him. Eliza sat next to Medora and Laura on one side, Walton and Eddie on the other. Beaten by the terrible Christmas last and by Amzi's refusal to join her at church that morning, she needed her faith refreshed.

"Good morning," the preacher began.

"Good morning," answered the congregation.

"Let us begin this morning with the singing of *Lord in the Morning Thou Shalt Hear.*"

Eliza's efforts to speak like a South Carolinian had changed how she pronounced her words, but the New England apple remained. She sang as if in conversation with God.

> Lord, in the morning Thou shalt hear
> My voice ascending high;
> To Thee will I direct my prayer,
> To Thee lift up mine eye.
>
> Thou art a God before Whose sight
> The wicked shall not stand;
> Sinners shall ne'er be Thy delight,
> Nor dwell at Thy right hand.
>
> But to Thy house will I resort,
> To taste Thy mercies there;
> I will frequent Thine holy court,
> And worship in Thy fear.
>
> Lord, crush the serpent in the dust,
> And all his plots destroy;
> While those that in Thy mercy trust,
> Forever shout for joy.

The hymn's comfort was wasted on Eddie: he made shadows on the wall with his fingers until Eliza shot a look at him and mouthed *Pay attention!* Once Eddie had closed his eyes and bowed his head, Eliza was able to shut out other thoughts and turn her attention to the preacher.

"Brothers and Sisters in Christ. Given the current state of the world, and especially the abomination in Washington, your elders asked that I say a few words about *The Reward that Awaits the Obedient.* I will do my best.

"To begin with, I'd like to ask, who *are* the truly obedient? To answer that, we must consider the nature of the obedience that God demands of us. 'Thou shalt have no other gods before me. Thou shalt not bow down thyself to them, nor serve them: for I the Lord thy God am a jealous God, visiting the iniquity of the fathers upon the children unto the third and fourth generation of them that hate me; and shewing mercy unto thousands of them that love me, and keep my commandments.'

"'For this is the love of God, that we keep his commandments.' First John, Five Three. I say again: 'This is the love of God, that we keep his commandments.'   Love, says Holy Scripture, is obedience to the commandments of God. The tablets given to Moses spoke not of loving God, but of obeying him. Even John defined love as a demonstration of obedience.

"Now, this is no small thing, obedience – but what is it, really? To obey a command by doing what one would have done in any case, in the absence of the command: is that obedience, or is that self-indulgence, masquerading as obedience?

"How very different the obedience of Abraham, as he raised his hand to slay Isaac. How very different the obedience of Job, as he kept the commandments despite all his suffering. How very different the obedience of Christ to the will of the Father, despite the human suffering it required of him. Obedience to God expresses love for God only when we are willing to trust and obey Him, *despite* our desire to follow some contrary object, some preferable thing that pleads we follow it instead. The only time obedience can *truly* express our love for the Lord is when we do His will *in the face of our own*, when our own runs *counter* to his. *Submission.* That is the obedience that demonstrates our faith, our trust, and our love of God.

"Now, if the frame of mind required for true obedience is no small thing, then even greater are the consequences which flow from such obedience, or the lack thereof. 'Visiting the iniquity of the fathers upon the children unto the third and fourth generation.'

"What father can decline to obey the will of God, if he truly understands that he will bring the wrath of the Almighty onto his children, and grandchildren, and their children?

"In the Book of Leviticus, Chapter twenty-six, God tells us the consequences of our choice. 'If ye walk in my statutes, and keep my commandments, and do them; then I will give you rain in due season, and the land shall yield her increase, and the trees of the field shall yield their fruit... But if ye will not hearken unto me, and will not do all these commandments; I will even appoint over you terror, consumption, and the burning ague, that shall consume the eyes, and cause sorrow of heart: and ye shall sow your seed in vain, for your enemies shall eat it. And I will set my face against you, and ye shall be slain before your enemies: they that hate you shall reign over you.'

"What price is too high for our fields to bear fruit? What earthly desire could be worth having those that hate you rule over you?

"'He that keepeth the commandment keepeth his own soul; but he that despiseth His ways shall die.' Proverbs nineteen sixteen. If there be any here today who think obedience to the Lord's command is any less important than Scripture tells us, let him speak now."

Member looked at member; the congregation made no reply.

"Scripture tells us that servants should be obedient to their masters. Though he lived in the midst of widespread slavery, Jesus spoke not a word against it. He never encouraged rebellion against Roman rule, in an effort to stamp it out. Indeed, in Leviticus Twenty-Five, God *instructed* the Israelites to take heathen peoples as their slaves: 'Thy bondmen shall be of the heathen that are round about you; of them shall ye buy bondmen. And they shall be your possession. And ye shall take them as an inheritance for your children after you, to inherit them for a possession; they shall be your bondmen forever.'

"Brothers and sisters, Holy Writ does not lie. God *wants* his people to take slaves. He has *commanded* us to. But why? Some would ask, is slavery not an unfortunate necessity, to be discarded as soon as men find a way to dispense with it? The voices urging as much have grown. But it isn't so. Read Armstrong's *The Christian Doctrine of Slavery*: 'Some races have become so deteriorated by a continued action in opposition to the laws of God, that He has seen fit to care for them by placing them under the control of others; or by placing them, in mercy, under the guidance of a less deteriorated race.' God in his mercy has committed the Africans to our care. He has entrusted them to our households. It is our duty to honor that trust.

"Now, brothers and sisters, consider the civil law as well as the divine. The Supreme Court of the northern government, the supreme interpreter of the laws of *that* Union, has declared in no uncertain terms that negro slaves are the private property of their lawful masters. Yet, with his recent proclamation, the President of that same government has commanded that our slaves be set free. In what sense, I ask you, is this not a call for taking that which God himself has entrusted to another? Is this not stealing, on an *epic* scale?

"Yet, much as it troubles me to say, there are well meaning men who call for the making of peace with this enemy. Some of our friends and neighbors – perhaps even some of you sitting here today – have despaired of the war. Some can be heard whispering about laying down arms. About submitting to the northern aggressor on "honorable" terms. About keeping our lawful property by the only means the Tyrant would allow us – by disavowing the musket, complying with the dictates of tyranny, submitting once again to northern rule, out of what they call practical necessity. It is the only means offered us, by which to keep our negroes.

"It is tempting, no doubt, to some. But to such as these, I would suggest the reading of the Book of Numbers, Chapter Fourteen.

"Permit me to remind you. The Israelites have been wandering in the desert, northward from Egypt. They are camped outside the promised land. They receive the report of their scouts.

"'*The land, which we passed through to search it, is an exceeding good land. If the Lord delight in us, then he will bring us into this land, and give it us; a land which floweth with milk and honey.*'

"We all know the story. The journey had been arduous. Many had despaired, offering reasons not to trust in Moses and the promises God had made. The promised land was held by a powerful people, against whom there was scant chance of success – a tempting point, to be sure, for those whose faith was flagging.

"As our grandparents knew, America is the new Promised Land. Like the Israelites before us, we can't yet enjoy the peaceful occupation of our land because a foreign power has made claim to it. And we hear around us voices of despair. Voices that tell us our northern neighbors are too powerful to be driven from the land. That unless we lay down our arms and make peace with the powerful foe, they will take from us the dependent race which God Himself has entrusted to our care.

"Yes, brothers and sisters, Lincoln's armies are strong. But the Word of God does not lie. 'Neither fear ye the people of the land; for they are bread for us: their defense is departed from them, and the Lord is with *us*: fear them not.' Numbers Fourteen Nine.

"As it was for the Israelites, my friends, our choice is between easy and hard. We can do what seems practical and easy – avoid further conflict, avoid the further shedding of blood, and make peace – or we can trust in the Lord, obey His command, and fight to preserve the way of life He ordained for us.

"'I will smite them with the pestilence, and disinherit them, and will make of *thee* a greater nation – and *mightier than they*.' Numbers fourteen, ten through twelve.

"My good friends, the Yankee invaders are at our doorsteps, intent on enforcing a massive deprivation of our property. Intent on defying the commandments of the Lord on a colossal scale. And we can follow those who would submit to that army or, like Moses, Joshua and Caleb before us, we can maintain our trust in the Word of God.

"Our reward, if we obey? The land of milk and honey. The peace he promised to all who would trust and obey.

"I say to you, brothers and sisters, that He tells us what to do in no uncertain terms. When your hear a neighbor say it is time to make peace with the north – to lay down arms, to abandon the fight for freedom and independence, remember the lesson laid down in the Book of Numbers, Chapter Fourteen. Be not among the company of those who've lost faith. Trust and obey the Lord. Experience the most glorious reward!"

Silence hung over the room. For Eliza, the preacher's voice had been like morning rain, her strength and resolve refreshed and renewed. By the time the preacher led the congregation in the Lord's prayer and gave emphasis to one word above the others – *thy* will be done – his point about obedience was clear. The closing hymn turned her new resolve to the hardest steel.

> *Adore and tremble, for our God*
> *Is a consuming fire!*
> *His jealous eyes His wrath inflame,*
> *And raise His vengeance higher.*

None in the congregation sang the words with greater feeling than Eliza.

> *Yet, mighty God, Thy sovereign grace*
> *Sits regent on the throne;*
> *The refuge of Thy chosen race*
> *When wrath comes rushing down.*

> *Thy hand shall on rebellious kings*
> *A fiery tempest pour,*
> *While we beneath Thy sheltering wings*
> *Thy just revenge adore.*

For the first time, Eliza could feel, throughout her earthly form, the glory in Alemeth's path. How better emulate the Savior than to give one's life to protect what God has ordained! On that day, at that hour, in that place, Alemeth became her hero. He was, she realized, a soldier of the Lord as much as Henry Hitchcock or Lyman Beecher. As she led her children out of the church, she resolved to follow Alemeth's example of obedience; to make sure everyone at Bynum's Creek kept the first commandment as well as Alemeth was. Just moments later, when Gilbert's mother, Harriet, asked if she and Gilbert could stop attending Sunday School, Eliza didn't hesitate.

"Why, Harriet, you disappointment me. You have to keep the Sabbath holy. It's not an option, it's a command. 'If you turn away from the Lord, the Lord will not be with you.' We'll have no more wayward talk from anyone in my house."

107

The *James Brown* had been a workhorse hauling reinforcements and supplies from southern Mississippi up to the front at Corinth. But in the early morning hours of October 19th, 1862, pulling eleven cars behind it, it became an iron casualty of war. All twenty-four tons of it. Headed south on the M.C.R.R., just outside of Duck Hill, it ran headlong into a northbound train. Both locomotives, and the tender of the *James Brown*, were completely destroyed.

The damage to the oncoming train was even worse. The *James Brown* had sent two whole flat cars of it, filled with confederate soldiers, headlong into the collided engines, then buried them under another toppling car. Over thirty men were killed. Heard as far as three miles from the crash site, the wreck sent shock waves across Mississippi.

The north wind kept on blowing, and as it did, the trunks of trees began to shiver and snap. In October, Van Dorn abandoned Corinth to the Yankees. In November, Pemberton abandoned the depot at Holly Springs. In December, with Yankees pressing in even closer, Pemberton set fire to the railroad bridge across the Tallahatchie, pulling back again, heading south, abandoning Oxford to the Yankees.

Many Oxonians panicked. But though stung by the loss of his locomotive and now surrounded by an army likely to execute secessionist politicians for treason, Colonel James Brown remained decisive and as orderly as one of his watches. He wrote a letter to an insurance company he didn't expect to honor his claim, then rounded up his negroes and left town. The Colonel had no desire for martyrdom. To avoid capture, he took refuge in Meridian. Soldiers in blue swarmed through the streets of Oxford, setting up camps on lawns, helping themselves to the stores at Neilson's, Doyle's, and McGuire's. General Grant himself took the Colonel's mansion, next to the Depot and the telegraph office, for his residence. Yankees tended fires on the front lawn. Those not a part of the General's inner circle were not permitted inside, but in all probability, said the people of the town, "Unconditional Surrender" Grant slept in the Colonel's bed.

The indignity of enemy authority so close to home made the skins of loyal southerners crawl.

HEADQUARTERS
ARMY OF NORTHERN VIRGINIA
Camp near Culpeper Courthouse   November 18, 1862 2 p.m.
Lieutenant General THOMAS J. JACKSON

GENERAL:

The reports from our cavalry, individuals scouts, and citizens, represent that the enemy has abandoned Warrenton, fallen down to the Orange and Alexandria Railroad, and is moving in force to Fredericksburg. Their progress and direction is confirmed by their campfires at night, which are said to be plainly visible. ***

There are in Fredericksburg a regiment of cavalry, one of infantry, and two additional companies, and two light batteries. McLaws' division marched this morning for that place; also, Lee's brigade of cavalry, and Ransom's division from Madison. The rest of Longstreet's corps is prepared to move, and only awaits confirmation of intelligence. ***

I hope more shoes and blankets have arrived for your men, and that you will be enabled to keep them comfortable and in health.

I am, most respectfully, your obedient servant,
R.E. Lee
General

*   *   *

HEADQUARTERS
ARMY OF THE POTOMAC
December 9, 1862   11:30 p.m.

GENERAL: All the orders have been issued to the several commanders of grand divisions and heads of departments for an attempt to cross the river on Thursday morning. The plans of the movement are somewhat modified by the movements of the enemy, who have been concentrating in large force opposite the point at which we originally intended to cross. ***

The importance of the movement and the details of the plan seem to be well understood by the grand division commanders, and we hope to succeed.

A.E. BURNSIDE
Major-General, Commanding.
General G.W. CULLUM
Chief of Staff, Washington

108

Frank Middleton[1] informed the Vindicators of the orders for the defense of Fredericksburg. General McLaws had told General Barksdale to "hold the enemy in check until ordered to retire," and that's what they were going to do. The Yankees were threatening to cross the Rappahannock. The Buena Vista Rifles were guarding a dock at the end of Hawke Street, where a rope ferry reached the warehouse district at the north end of the city. Before the sun rose, the Vindicators had joined them.

From behind a shroud of fog that blocked the eastern shore and reflected the city's lights back into their eyes, Yankee guns started firing on the warehouses. From the thick night fog, a pontoon bridge emerged about half way across the river. They watched in silence as the Yankees busied themselves building it closer. About 5 a.m., the bridgehead about two hundred feet from shore and bustling with human life, Captain Middleton gave the order.

"Ready!"

Pull the paper cartridge. Bite and spit the end. Pour the powder into the muzzle. Drop the Minnie ball in. Ram.

Hammer back.

Percussion cap on the firing cone.

A large-framed engineer a good target.

"Aim!"

Alemeth lifted the barrel until the target was in sight: the man's chest.

"Fire at will!"

Triggers squeezed. The engineer fell into the water.

Pull the paper cartridge. Bite and spit the end. Pour the powder into the muzzle. Drop the ball in. Ram.

Hammer back. Cap on. Aim. Fire!

Yankees fell, Yankees jumped into the water, Yankees disappeared into the fog. Alemeth kept firing his Model 1842 as long as he could see Yankee bodies. But when the last of them had slipped below the water's surface and the last man alive had slipped into the misty night, when the last of the rifle fire had subsided, the waterfront gave way to exhaustion. Alemeth patted his chest, to be sure the metal case of the ambrotype was still there, and fell asleep in place, his finger still on the trigger.

As daylight began to show itself, Yankee guns began a barrage of cannon

---

[1] Frank Middleton had been given command of the Vindicators after Captain Holder was promoted to lead the 17th Infantry Regiment.

fire into the city. Between the shells, the morning fog burned away to reveal a crisp, clear day and a mass of blue on the east bank. Shots rang out. Burnt powder in the air; a cloud of smoke. Sheds, shrubs and evacuated houses gave cover from enemy sharpshooters. The Vindicators peppered the bridges whenever Yankees appeared. All morning, enemy cannon pounded, crumbling walls, toppling stairs, porches and chimneys.

In the mid-afternoon, sheer numbers proved their power. Blue troops poured from the end of one bridge, then another, into the waist-deep water, unstoppable. The Vindicators fell back, up the hill, to Caroline Street, begrudging inches, bayonets ready, firing at things they couldn't see, retreating in small steps backward, until standing their ground, in the end, at the Presbyterian church at Grace Street. Finally, then, the flashes of night fire subsided. Everything was in dark shadow, neither side inclined to move.

Across the church yard, a voice:

"Hey there, Johnny. You're there, ayn ye? Ay? Y' know y'are. Why don't ye come oot and let me take a better look?"

"I'm very sorry. I'd be right glad to oblige. But I'm not sure what you said, seein' as how I don't speak Irish. Why don't you come on out and show me what you mean?"

"You're smarter than the average country boy, y'are. Where you boys be from, eh? You rebels all talk alike, ye see."

"Panola County, Mississippi. You?"

"The City of Brotherly Love, my friend."

Philadelphia. The man who'd had the St. Christopher medal.

"What regiment you with? Not the 71st Pennsylvania, by any chance..."

"By Mary and Jesus," said the unseen man. "Who coulda known you boys had such intelligence? That's exactly who we are!"

"You know a Thomas in Company B? I might have something for him. It's a medal. A Yankee soldier gave it to me. Said this Tom was his brother."

"So?"

"Show me where you are, and I'll toss it your way."

"A right sly fellow, y' are. Why don't *you* show yourself?"

And so the evening passed on Grace Street, with taunts, dares, and a shared effort to deny the hot nearness of death. The city's defense passed until Frank Middleton put out word there were new orders: the 17th was to rejoin Barksdale at the base of Marye's Heights. The boys withdrew under cover of darkness, the medal still hanging from Alemeth's neck, the ambrotype still inside his jacket. Maybe he'd give the medal to Sally too.

109

The northern blockade had made supplies scarce. Grant's occupation of Oxford had eliminated the last vestige of southern authority. Yankee soldiers had descended like locusts, devouring scant provisions, tens of thousands of mouths, not a one of them producing food of his own. The price of beans was up, along with raisins, salt, sugar, soap. Corn and flour, confiscated. Hams and barley, devoured. Horses, mules, wagons taken from anyone suspected of rebellious activity.

When Yankee cavalry paid a visit to Bynum's Creek, it wasn't like a visit from Bill Starr. They came to satisfy themselves that Amzi posed no threat to them. He'd have felt justified blowing Captain Powell's head off with his old 1812, but that would have gotten him nowhere. As it was, every time Yankee cavalry came by, he did all he could do to convince them of his willingness to abide by Yankee law. So far, the Yankees had taken nothing from Bynum's Creek except what they could eat, and if that was the best he could do, he was determined to do it.

The only good news was the arrival of the Vindicators' Baxter Orr, injured and on furlough home. Baxter brought deeper news than any letter could convey. He told of how Alemeth and the boys had gotten used to the foul weather and hard conditions. They were heartier now, tougher, hardened men better able to handle their ills. He described in detail how the Yankees had pulled back from Fredericksburg, how the Seventeenth wintered there, camped on high ground and safe, as far as anyone could tell; how the Yankees had taken to launching balloons from which to observe their positions; how fortifications had dissuaded the Yankees from attempting another river crossing; how the weather was changeable; how some days, it was so cold they couldn't keep warm inside, even around their fires, even with big overcoats on, and how the river had frozen; and how, other days, there was fog and cold rain, but a little warmth; and how they were starved for mail from home; the chicken, beans, rice and porridge they had to eat; and the good days they'd had, when able to go into town and see regular people (though now, they all knew, they themselves would never be regular people again, as once they'd become soldiers, they'd always be soldiers).

Best of all, Baxter was able to answer their questions. Welcome as letters from Alemeth were, the time spent with Baxter was like being in camp with Alemeth for a day. It made them feel closer to him, as if they could see him the way Baxter saw him. Baxter answered Walton's questions about guns and ammunition, telling him glorious things, but always held back the unspeakable. And when Amzi asked him his view of the prospects, he hesitated. Some of the Yankees were good soldiers. If that were the only problem, the south would be sure to prevail. But to a man, the Yankees were better equipped. There were so many of them. Occasional captures proved how much better provisioned they were. The Confederate Army was depending on the homeland for food and was confident the planters and farmers of Mississippi would see them through.

Baxter was trying to avoid pessimism, but it leaked through the cracks of everything he said.

One day, Captain Powell offered Amzi fifteen cents a pound for all the cotton he had. Cotton was his one cash crop. Its sale supported everything else. And while cotton in New York was seventy cents a pound, it wasn't easy to get it out from under the eye of an occupying army, an army whose law prohibited trading with the enemy. There weren't a lot of other options to get any profit from the cotton. And to make the temptation stronger, Captain Powell said he'd pay in federal greenbacks.

The plantation was struggling. There wasn't money for supplies. There weren't supplies for growing a crop. There wasn't a crop to sell for money. But in mulling over the Captain's offer, Amzi hardened his resolve. The Seventeenth was suffering, and he would too. He would *not* submit to Union authority. He could let what cotton he had sit in the sheds a little longer. He could gather intelligence about Yankee troops and trains. He could look for a chance to haul his cotton south to Mobile, past the Yankee blockade, to the open sea. It was no less than his duty. He still had faith in the Confederacy. And Confederate law, same as Yankee law, forbade trading with the enemy.

Of course, Amzi could hardly tell Captain Powell he was hoping to run the blockade. Defiance could not be overt. Truth had no place in dealing with criminals like Yankee invaders. Biting his lip, Amzi told Captain Powell that he appreciated his offer, but he hoped the Captain would understand his hope to get a higher price elsewhere.

110

Gilbert was a hard worker who did what he was told, had a knack for flavors and loved to help out in the kitchen. He made an unlikely spy, but he had Grote's strong recommendation. Being so young, he also had room to move about unsuspected.

So Gilbert it was. Always given a legitimate task to explain his presence – a note for Mrs. Brown, or instructions to fetch mail from the post office – Gilbert's real task was to exchange information with Harl, who was still in service at the Brown's house on Depot Street, though now serving meals to Yankee generals. Gilbert would learn what he could about Yankee numbers and movements. Gilbert would report everything back to Amzi.

Each day for most of the month, Gilbert carried what news he could between Amzi, the Colonel, and their private correspondents. The Yankees were helping themselves to the Colonel's flour and pork. The General's staff had used Mrs. Brown's bone china. But they had caused no damage to the Colonel's mansion. The officers had also been discreet; Harl had overheard no military planning. The month was nearly over and Gilbert's weeks as a "spy" had uncovered nothing of importance. Then, two days before Christmas, when Gilbert returned from Oxford, he brought joyous news: the Yankees were packing to leave.

Amzi galloped into town, anxious to confirm the news. It was true. The Yankees were already gone. Oxford free again! Children paraded on Depot Street. "Hurrah for Van Dorn!" "The town is ours again!" Amzi wanted information. But Neilson's and McGuire's were closed. There was no sign of the sheriff. At the Butler Hotel, a boy behind the desk said Mrs. Butler had left right after the Yankees had moved out. Down Depot Street, Yankee litter was all over Colonel Brown's property; Harl had gone to Meridian to give the Colonel the news. Robert Shegogg was not at home, nor was anyone at Clear Creek. No one knew where General Forrest's rangers were. No one knew anything. No one had a plan.

Unable to learn anything, lacking a reason to do otherwise, Amzi headed back to Bynum's Creek. And there, at home, he ran headlong into the unfamiliar.

There were no cows in the pasture. The doors of the cotton barn were wide open. There were no goats. No pigs. A premonition of doom hung over the plantation. The house, the yard, the negro cabins, all were as a ghost town, silent and still. Then Grote appeared, as if from nowhere, Gilbert at his side, confirming that the Yankees had taken anything they might need, from carriages and wagons to flour, salt, and potatoes.

They'd also left a voucher. They'd taken forty-eight mules, it said, and fifteen horses, a hundred hogs, four hundred sheep, nineteen oxen, seventy-three cows, two hundred chickens, thirty turkeys, fifty geese, two thousand bushels of corn, seventy-five hundred pounds of cured meat, three hundred fifty dozen bundles of oats, a thousand dozen bundles of fodder, five hundred bushels of sweet potatoes, and a thousand bushels of Irish potatoes. Amzi would be compensated for all of it when the war was over – *if* he could prove his support of the Union.

"It says nothing about the cotton," he vented to Grote. "Durnit, boy, how could you let them leave off the cotton?"

Grote looked at Gilbert. "Tell Mast' Byers what you did, boy."

"I heard the Yankees was comin'; so I got Zack and Josh, and we put the cotton in the woods back behind Mas' Johnson's."

Amzi was taken aback. Gilbert had proven his worth. "I don't know what to say, boy. Good thinking."

Gilbert looked at his feet, concealing his smile.

According to Grote, while Amzi was in Oxford, Captain Powell had gathered the negroes in the yard. He'd told them that, as of the first of the year, they would be free to come and go as they pleased. Ike and some of the others had started talking about where they might go when they got up north. Abel had said it didn't matter, as long as they got out of the South.

But the Yankees were gone, and their authority over Bynum's Creek gone with them. Amzi met with every negro, assuring them the Yankees were lying, trying to disrupt the plantation; there was *nothing* that would change on the first of the year. The negroes seemed to understand.

When the first of the year came, Lincoln issued yet another proclamation. This one invited the slaves to join the Union in the war against southern planters. Word got out. Some negroes sang songs of Father Abraham's salvation. Ike and others ran off with plans to join the Yankees. Two days of heavy rain later, they came back; said the Yankees had no place for them. They'd been told to return to the Plantation, to see what terms Mr. Byers would give them, now that they were free. Rifle in hand, Amzi told them his terms: get back to work, or the sheriff and his dogs would be after them.

That done, Amzi told Gilbert to gather a bedroll and an extra shirt, and together they paid a visit to the Orr house. Baxter Orr was heading back to Virginia, to rejoin the Vindicators. At Amzi's request, Baxter agreed to take Gilbert with him, to the front, to be of use to Alemeth if he could.

111

Once Ike and the others came back, Amzi watched the field hands like a prison guard. He never went anywhere without his rifle. Nor was it just the negroes. He was short with the children; lost his temper at Eliza; bristled at the least distraction. He vowed to kill Captain Powell if he ever saw the man again, calling him vulgar names she'd never heard him use before. Sometimes there was nothing to do but walk away from him and come back later, when things were going better.

Worst of all, Amzi's poisoned spirits seemed to bring about a change inside *her* – as if his mood had somehow crossed into her, like some vapor, turning her own spirits dark. She found herself raising her voice. One afternoon she lost patience with Harriet for wandering off, and soon thereafter, lost it again on account of Dora's constant doleful humming. Amzi's spittoon had become a bother no matter how often Leety cleaned it. Little irritations festered like infected tick bites.

How different life might have been, had she remained in Connecticut or the finger lakes, or even in Columbus. What was the price she had paid for marriage? Would she ever finish paying it? Was it the war? Amzi? Would she leave Bynum's Creek, if she could? She worked herself up, then chided herself for asking such questions.

In May, when the Yankees took Jackson, Mississippi was left without a capital. When the Yankees got close to Meridian, the Colonel and Mrs. Brown returned to Oxford to their new house on Depot Street. Eliza hoped they'd have good news. But the parrots weren't with them.

"Where are Clio and Calliope, Mary Ann?"

"They're no longer with us, I'm afraid."

"Oh? Don't tell me…"

"Well, I couldn't leave them in Oxford. Tea, dear? Harl? When we got to Meridian, in the midst of everything else going on, the birds did the oddest thing. They started pecking at each other. Mutilated themselves. Bloody quills, bits and pieces of feathers all around the cage. Clio died right away. Calliope hung on for a while, but she was never the same again."

"Oh, dear. What got into them, do you suppose?"

"The house was chaos. They just couldn't handle the stress, I suppose."

"There's no telling what possessed the creatures, Mary Ann. We should pity them, I suppose. Ignorant animals, without souls, without any notion of God. Is it possible to account for anything they do, except to say they behave the way God made them?"

112

When Baxter Orr brought Gilbert into camp, Alemeth felt as if he'd brought a piece of home itself. The boy's familiar face was enough to remind him of the way things used to be, and a pair of gloves and new undershorts Gilbert brought, and a night of fresh news from home, and a chicken fricassee Gilbert cooked up, tempted Alemeth with the hopeful illusion that everything in Mississippi was like it had always been, that his service for the Army of Virginia and the service of all his comrades in arms, was protecting the south they'd all enlisted to save. But illusion it was, and even Gilbert's face – now two years older than the face Alemeth remembered – bore witness to the fact that things in Mississippi could hardly be the same as they'd been the day Alemeth had left. Alemeth arranged for Gilbert to work in the chow wagons. Gilbert had always been good with food and his kitchen service could put a little extra money in Alemeth's pockets. It so pleased Alemeth to have the boy nearby, and the sense of home he brought with him was so dear, Alemeth decided to let Gilbert keep half the wages he earned.

But while Gilbert's presence was pleasing at first, it increased Alemeth's longing for what he no longer had. For Aunt Leety's cooking, for conversation with Lou, for the fishing hole at Sand Springs. And mostly for Sally Fox. He wondered whether he'd be able to make it, if it were another month before he had a chance to hear that sultry voice again.

When Gilbert brought no news of her, Alemeth realized he'd never shared his feelings for Sally with the negro boy. As for Sally herself, for two months after his first letter to her he'd received no reply. When she'd finally answered him, she'd expressed concern for his safety and said (so sweetly!) that she thought of him often. But she'd failed to mention his suggestion that they begin a correspondence. Had she not had his letter in front of her? He'd written again, afraid to ask his question a second time, but saying he thought of her all the time, hoping for a like sentiment in return.

Again two months had passed without a reply. Thinking the army must have lost the letter, he'd written again, about how much he missed Mississippi, about how fondly he remembered every moment of their time together. During long marches, he'd remembered her in her white dress and blue sash. Over bitter coffee, he'd remembered the oak tree and the swing. While he crunched dry hard tack between his teeth, he'd tried to think of her Huckleberry pie.

Then, one day at mail call, Gordon's name had been called. Receiving his mail, Gordon cast a troubled, guilty, deceitful look Alemeth's way. Even before Gordon admitted it, even before he recognized the handwriting, Alemeth knew who the letter was from. When Alemeth asked him to read it aloud, he didn't, and when Gordon was through reading it silently to himself, Alemeth held out his hand.

"May I?"

The fact that Sally had written to Gordon was irksome enough by itself, but when Gordon wouldn't let him see the letter, the injury hurt all the more. Was it possible she felt something for Gordon, and nothing for him? For days, he tried to get Gordon to let him read the letter. He even offered to pay to see it, but Gordon refused.

He wrestled with the implications. To write a letter like those he'd written before would be humiliating. He could come right out and ask whether she preferred Gordon to him, but he didn't want to confront her. He wasn't even sure he wanted to hear the answer. He'd seen her in his arms. He'd felt her embrace. She had pulled him through two harsh winters, miles of marching and hours of enemy fire.

He'd been shot at and shelled for her. He had killed a man at a hundred yards for her. But had he done enough? He'd never been in an all-out charge at an enemy line, never picked up regimental colors, never taken a prisoner. Never done anything like Calvin Morris or Charley Morgan were writing their sweethearts about. The ambrotype he had for her was the picture of a mere boy. The medallion he'd taken was taken from a dying man. He could always make up some sort of story – about killing a Yankee Colonel, maybe, or risking his life to save another Vindicator – but he had nothing like Gordon's way with stories and words, and he didn't want to win Sally's heart with lies. Sally had to think well of him for something *real*. Something that would stand up to examination. And until he could give her *everything* he was prepared to give her, he didn't want to call her hand. He couldn't stand the thought of losing her, not before he'd even had a chance to win her.

So he'd decided he couldn't write to her at all. Rather than write again, he'd wait for a chance to prove himself completely. And he found it easier, in the end, to think of Bynum's Creek as little as he could, concentrating instead on the reality of what lay ahead.

The Yankees, after all, were just miles away. It was finally summer, when great battles were fought. One side or the other was certain to strike soon. This time, when the fighting began, he wouldn't flinch or hesitate. He'd do what it took to bring the big game home, regardless.

HEADQUARTERS ARMY OF THE POTOMAC
June 25, 1863 — 11.30 a. m.

Major-General *REYNOLDS, Edwards Ferry:*

Directions have been given for General Stahel to report to you with his command. Please send him in advance, in the direction of Frederick and Gettysburg, and drive from that country every rebel in it.

HOOKER,
Major-General.

*   *   *

HEADQUARTERS ARMY OF THE POTOMAC
June 30, 1863 — 12.45 p. m.

Commanding Officer Third Corps:

The major-general commanding directs that you move your Corps up to Emmitsburg. You will take three days' rations in haversacks, 60 rounds of ammunition, and your ambulances. Your trains will remain parked here until further orders. General Reynolds' First Corps, and General Howard's Eleventh Corps, are between Emmitsburg and Gettysburg. General Reynolds will command the left wing, consisting of the First, Eleventh, and Third Corps. The enemy are reported to be in force in Gettysburg. You will move without delay.

Very respectfully, &c.,

S. WILLIAMS,
Assistant Adjutant-General.

113

He couldn't remember what had happened. Time had been a stew of dreams, of Gordon, of Peter Brown, of Sally Fox, impossible to sort out, to fix, to see clearly. It had been endless night. Hearing a horse, and a shout, and drums. A chill in the air. Hard ground. Cannon fire. Rifle fire. A bugle. A headache. More dreams. Thirst, and rain coming down. Every sound the sound of darkness, and night that never passed, wondering if dawn would ever come, looking into the eyes of fish. Pa riding in from the darkness. Thirst again. Uncle Johnson pushing a plow. Parched lips. Walton shooting Uncle Johnson's gun at a jack rabbit. The night turning hot and feverish. A piece of Sally's Huckleberry pie. Getting sick. Red and orange leaves. A farm yard. A voice that said, *Keep moving; it's the only way to stay alive.* Thirst again. His stomach empty. Lapsing again into sleep. A door opening, letting in sunlight. Stark silhouettes. Voices of German girls. A stick in the ribs. Shoulder throbbing. Jaw sore. Rags around his neck. Around his jaw. Over his collarbone. On his back, on the ground. Breathing squeezing through the nose. Voices of Pennsylvanians. German men. Wentz. Spangler. Poerner. All unfamiliar. He'd been hit. But as far as he could tell, he wasn't dead.

"Doctor, this one just spit something up. It's very bloody."

Was she talking about him? He didn't think he had vomited. Then she bent over him, holding back her apron, looking into his eyes.

"Oh. You're awake. Can you hear me? Here. Take this."

"Wh– " Shots of pain in the jaw.

"Hurts, does it? You don't need to talk. Can you nod your head?"

He nodded.

"Good. Here. It's a musk pill. It'll help prevent gangrene." She put the pill between his lips, where it settled, unswallowed, unchewed. "Do you know where you are?"

Shaking his head caused pain; turning it slowly had to suffice.

"You're in my father's barn. When you were brought here, you were out cold. Your neck was – they took shell fragments from your jaw to your abdomen. I didn't think you were going to make it. But I've been praying for you."

He tried to connect the dots. Maybe it hadn't been the longest night ever. Maybe it had been days and nights. He remembered crossing into Maryland and Pennsylvania. He remembered Frank Middleton's description of the plan. He remembered Colonel Holder giving the command. The boys around him yelling like a bunch of demons and running forward. The peach orchard full of black smoke. A gap in the Yankee line. General Barksdale, on horseback, white hair streaming, the man falling from his horse. He remembered looking around, wondering what was going to happen next.

Nothing after that. Nothing of what happened right before he got hit. Not pain or bewilderment. No details. No photographs. The past had simply disappeared.

Now, on hard ground, a piece of litter, he swallowed the pill though it intensified the pain in his throat. A German girl changing his bandages. He was helpless. Hungry. Couldn't even get up to piss. Dependent on others for everything. He tried to call her, but his jaw burned in heightened pain. At last, unable to maintain his hold on the slope of an invisible bank, he fell beneath the surface again, back into the painless world of fishes.

After several days, perhaps, on his back, on straw, the German girl stood over him again, a writing tablet and pen in her hand, extending them to him. He was able to take them. She nodded her approval.

What's your name? he wrote.

"Sabina Spangler."

My things?

"You were brought in from the field over another man's shoulder. You and what was left of your uniform. But here." Miss Spangler reached into her apron. "They found this in your pocket." She handed him the ambrotype. "And this, they found in your neck." It was the medallion and chain given him by the Yankee at Savage Station.

His knapsack, his socks, his journal, Pa's 1842, all lost. But the ambrotype and medal had survived. The two things he had left, the two things he had carried for Sally Fox, had bother survived. It had to be a sign. He wrote another question on the tablet.

Will I be disfigured?

Miss Spangler took a close look.

"The wounds will leave scar tissue. But best not concern yourself with appearances. We're doing everything we can for you. We'll just have to wait and see."

My jaw hurts.

"I'll see if I can get you something for the pain."

Miss Spangler returned with a pill and a cup of water, which he took despite the hard pain of swallowing. Then a Yankee adjutant brought more news: The Confederate army had been driven out of Pennsylvania. Vicksburg had fallen. The whole of the Mississippi River, from Minnesota to New Orleans, was now under Yankee control. The adjutant said the Yankee wounded should be proud.

114

When he was fit enough to be moved, Alemeth was brought to the Confederate hospital at the College. The second week of August, he was moved to the General Hospital east of town, where all the remaining wounded from both sides were consolidated. After several weeks at the field Hospital, finally fit enough for travel by train, he boarded a flat car of the B. & O. that took him, under guard, to Baltimore's Jarvis Hospital.

Treatment of the wounded didn't change at Jarvis. "The stumps," as the doctors called the amputees, got soup, bread, and opium, the same as at Gettysburg. But other things were different. Jarvis was a quadrangle of buildings where men were lined up indoors, in cots, in neat rows. The diseased suffered a wider range of ills than the 'stumps,' and they received a wider range of treatments. Paregoric elixirs and tins of pills crowded the shelves. Camphor for putrescent sores. Alibert's pills and colocynth to promote bowel movement. Creosote pills for neuralgia. Strychnine for paralysis, Abernathy's mercury pills for headaches, and Dr. Turnbull's aconite pills for sedation. A pill for every purpose. A celebration of modern science.

As Alemeth considered the plethora of pills, the one which loomed the largest – the one he most dreaded taking – was the yellow one.

It was not the typical pill, a basis and corrective, powders rolled with bread or honey into a dough. Not like the blue mass, or Kendal's black drop. Nor was it a single dose of powder from a tin, measured and rolled into a paper wad with a suitable mixture for consumption. The yellow pill was a piece of paper – difficult to swallow not because it was paper, nor even because it was marked all over in ink, but because of the meaning to be drawn from the characters the ink spelled out.

"The yellow pill" was a nickname for the parole oath, and for the paper that had to be signed to record its making.

It was an oath to lay down arms.

The making of the oath was defensible, Captain Middleton had explained. It was in the training manual. It was a part of military tradition in the civilized world. Wounded prisoners are a drain on an army. Generals don't want to be burdened by them. A soldier could accomplish more from home, among family and friends, than from a far-off prison camp, ridden with disease and miasmic vapors. A wounded prisoner, asked to take the oath in return for release, was free to agree, by all the rules of war.

But despite everything Captain Middleton said, it was, still, the yellow pill. "A pill for cowards," said the Alabaman in the next bed. "The boys back in Maycomb County don't believe in giving parole. It's something weaker people do." The Alabaman wasn't alone. Of all the pills in the dispensary, it was most reviled by the men.

Lay down arms. Swear, under the all-seeing eye of God Himself, not to take them up again, in return for permission to leave the fight. To go home. Refrain from further opposition to the Union.

The war might end or go on – who knew how long – but swallowing the pill was personal surrender, submission to an alien will. The dream of coming home victorious and independent, gone. He couldn't bear the thought. So for a month, he languished at Jarvis, fearful of invisible infections, watching poultices changed, working through the pain in his jaw, taking only so much *pilae opii* as he needed.

Then one day, one of the volunteers from the Sanitary Commission asked him his name. To his delight, he found that he could answer her without the pain flaring at every movement of his jaw.

"Private John Alemeth Byers. Seventeenth Mississippi," he managed. His jaw was still sore. "Could you get me another pill?"

"How much do you hurt?"

"It's not unbearable."

"Well, then, I think it best if you not. They're not good for you."

"I've been taking them for three months. They've done nothing to hurt me."

"I'm sorry. No more for you."

The next day, the volunteer was back, this time accompanied by one of the Provost's men.

"This is Mr. Byers, corporal."

The Yankee looked Alemeth over, head to toe.

"You a private, soldier?"

"Yes."

"Seventeenth Mississippi Infantry?"

"Yes."

"I understand you've declined to sign the oath?"

"I see no honor in it."

"Soldier, do you understand what – "

"I understand." He looked the corporal in the eye to make his certainty clear.

"Alright, soldier; your choice." The man wrote something in his journal and left.

"Mr. Byers?" asked the volunteer.

"Yes?"

"Mr. Byers, may I ask you, why you don't take the oath?"

"Lay down arms against the Union?"

"Sure."

"No way."

"Do you really think Union is so terrible? We in the north are just plain people, same as you."

"You're not family."

"That depends on what you mean by family, doesn't it?"

"Call it what you want. I've sworn an oath to fight for Mississippi."

"Maybe you're wrong about Mississippi, private. Do you think it even *possible* that you're wrong?"

"With all respect, Miss. I have to keep faith with the people back home. Besides, there's a girl I couldn't face, if I went home a coward."

"I see. But maybe your faith is in the wrong things, private. Maybe the best faith is simply trust in the goodness of things."

"Excuse me?"

"Are you sure your sweetheart wants to see you be a hero?"

"Of course."

"What if she wants, more than anything else, to have you home, alive?"

Two years had passed since Sally had worn that South Carolina sash. A lot had changed since then. Alemeth was still mulling over the volunteer's question hours after she'd left the building. His sense of duty had been saying he should stick to his guns. But that night, lying awake, he wondered if it was the black loess of Mississippi he owed his duty to, or the people. And if the people, *which* people? Sally? And if it was her, did she really want him home, alive? Now, he'd come as close to death as a man could, and he'd done it for her. Maybe it would be enough. Her smile, summoned, spoke of that possibility, and nothing else. And as soon as he thought of eating a piece of her pie again, he could practically taste it.

JARVIS HOSPITAL
BALTIMORE, MARYLAND

There came before me, the undersigned, on <u>*15 Nov., 1863*</u> *,
one* <u>*Pvt. John Alemeth Byers*</u> *of* <u>*17th Regt. Miss. Infantry*</u>
*who having taken a solemn oath before me and in the presence
of God, vows to take up no arms against the authority of the
Government of the United States, or its armed forces, and to take
no action in opposition to that authority, or those forces, for the
duration of the present conflict, unless duly exchanged by the
belligerent powers.*

<u>*J. A. Byers*</u>

Signed before me at <u>*Baltimore, Md.,*</u> this <u>*15*</u> day of <u>*November,
1863*</u>.

Harrison Drew, Notary Public.

115

His solemn word, one hand on the Bible, his promise to cease all efforts against *The Union*, to give up fighting alongside Gordon and Peter and the others, to abandon the hope of coming home a hero: it was a distasteful choice, to be sure, especially when, cut off completely from Gilbert, he decided to take the train home without him.

But it was time to go home, even so. As soon as he signed the parole, he knew it had been the right thing to do. Released from Jarvis, free of the yoke of war, free to do anything he wanted, in fact, so long as he took no steps hostile to northern authority. And he'd be free, at least, to call on Sally, while Gordon wouldn't be anywhere near. Gordon hadn't heard from Sally again, as far as he knew. Maybe Sally would be more than glad to see him alive. Maybe she'd see how far he'd been willing to go for her. Receive him on a regular basis. Allow a courtship.

As the train approached Meridian, he patted his pocket, making sure the ambrotype was still there. From time to time, he took it out to see the image. It wasn't everything he wanted, but it was him, as he had been before Gettysburg. In Baltimore, he'd seen the jaw and neck wounds heal, the scars on his cheek congeal and harden, toughening to the touch. Once the scars had stabilized, he hadn't looked in the mirror much. He didn't need the reminder. He still saw himself as once he'd been – the man in the ambrotype. And if Sally Fox would never know how much he'd suffered for her, never know the stinging cold of a Leesburg tent in February, never know the terror of cannon fire, the horror of a bloody death, then at least, in that ambrotype, she'd have clear proof of what he'd given, for Mississippi, and for her. Looking at the image, he could feel good about himself; he could forget the scars; he could see himself the way she had seen him, that night in the observatory.

He nodded on and off, dreaming of calling at the Avent house, waking and dreaming again. In the last dream, he saw Sally get into a carriage dressed in white, ready to swear her fidelity, but he couldn't find his way to the church. And by the time the train pulled up to the Meridian station, he felt rested and refreshed, as if his dreams had shown him the way. He couldn't let her go again. Events would dictate his course no longer. Gordon had said he had to practice freedom; he finally understood. He would do what had to be done: he would take control.

A mile outside Oxford, he recognized turns of the road, fences, farms. But things were not what they'd once been. The fields had been ravaged. Hugh Pike's place had been burned to the ground. Other homes lay in the grasp of vines. There were no other wagons on North Street – just an solitary slave, an old man, with a pig on a tether. When the driver let him out in front of Neilson's, Alemeth ignored the people in the square, making his way straight down Depot Street. The weathered swing in the Avents' yard was empty.

Harl answered Colonel Brown's door. He was grayer than the last time Alemeth had seen him, and a little stooped over.

"Why, if it ain't Masta Alemeth. It's so good to see you is doin' alright, Mast' Alemeth. You *is* doin' alright, isn't you?"

Harl was talking to him, but staring at his jaw. (Everybody did, since Gettysburg.)

"I suppose I'm alright. How are you?"

"Good enough, I reckon."

"Is the Colonel at home?"

"Nosuh. He and the Missuz, they gone east, to Selma. Gone since last week. Only me here now. Just lookin' after the house."

Alemeth cast his eyes toward the Avent house.

"And Miss Fox?"

Harl cocked his head and furrowed his brow.

"Mast' Alemeth. You don't know?"

"Know what?"

Harl hesitated.

"Miss Sally – well – she be Missus Thompson now."

It hit like a sack of grain.

"Mrs. Thompson? *Macon* Thompson?"

"Yes, suh."

"When?"

"She be fixin' to have herself a child now, Mast' Alemeth."

"You mean – "

"Like to come this spring."

No sense asking where Sally was. It didn't matter. Was there any way to undo what had been done? No. (*No!*) The object of desire had been ripped away. Absent something dishonorable, never to be regained – never, even, to be thought about, in that way, again.

Maybe Macon's father had gotten to Buck Avent. Maybe the men had arranged the marriage. Maybe Sally had been pressured into it. Maybe…

He stopped.

False hope holds no promise. She hadn't called out for help. She hadn't sent him any sign of hesitation. She had agreed to wed Macon. She had *wanted* to wed Macon. And she hadn't even thought to send him a letter letting him know. (How little did he mean to her?) Face facts.

Anger at Sally. More anger at Macon. Nothing to be done. The outcome unbearable. The *longing* for Sally – now forbidden fruit – persisting. He didn't want to think about her, or Macon either. (How could she be happy with *him*?)

He paced in front of the house. If he could only get them both out of his mind, he could give thought to what else he could do. But as soon as he stopped thinking about one, the other was there to take over.

Macon and Sally were inseparable, bound by the bonds of marriage.

There was no one at the Depot except the telegraph clerk, slouched forward at his desk, his head on his arm, dozing next to the telegraph machine. *Sally Fox, married to Macon Thompson.*

There was no one at the University but Mr. Quinche, the professor-turned-caretaker, and a group of old men with muskets who said General Forrest was still out there, somewhere; he hadn't given up the fight for Mississippi, and neither had they.

She was carrying Macon's child.

He didn't want to be near her. He didn't want to think of her. So he went back toward town. Finding no one of interest, he had a whiskey at Butler's Hotel, listening to a conversation at another table. But all he could hear was Macon asking Sally to marry him, and Sally answering *Yes.*

He went from the hotel to the courthouse square in search of someone to talk to, but a man declaiming on a soap box kept looking his way. When he turned from the center of the square to escape him, there was only Sally and Macon.

And so on to the Masonic Hall. The shades were drawn at Doyle's. He climbed the stairs half expecting to find Frank Duval running *The Intelligencer,* but everything was quiet at the paper. The letter cases were empty. The dust on the table tops, and on Howard's old desk, was undisturbed. He ran a finger along the drum of the main press, leaving a dark line. Even there, beneath the press, in the shadowed corners, it always ended the same. What had happened? How had he been so wrong about what she was feeling? Had he known anything about who she was?

One thing seemed self-evident, though. And that was, that he had *let* it happen. The same way he'd let everything else in life happen. (He had failed, yet again, to see that things went his way.) He scrounged up a buggy at Butler's livery, and headed back to Bynum's Creek.

On the way home, he took a hard look around. The air was cold, the fields thin, the ground scarred by frost, old stalks falling over, limp and brown. (Sally and Macon had been together for more than a year. And there'd been letters from home.) At the old McKinney place, a stranger was driving a wagonload of split cedar logs. (Semmy Lou had written several letters and said nothing about Sally and Macon.)

As he pulled up to the house, Lou came rushing out and threw herself into his arms.

"Alemeth! Dear, dear Alemeth! I can hardly believe you're home!"

When Lou let go, there were hugs from others as well. Dora; Walton; Laura; Eddie. A warm embrace from Aunt Leety. A cheek-to-cheek with Eliza. Only the youngest – "Julia Loughborough Byers, meet your brother, John Alemeth" — turned away from him, too shy to show affection to a stranger. A great deal had changed. Dora was a young lady, Walton getting tall, Laura learning to play the piano. Aunt Leety's ham stew was better than anything he'd eaten in months. His old bed was inviting. But there was a contest played out in his heart: one side warming to the comforts of home; the other in no mood to find comfort in anything. For the comforts accused him of abandoning the Vindicators for stupid, selfish reasons, of abandoning them to another winter camp, and to the cold deprivations of war, and to fighting on without him. And when Harriet asked about Gilbert, he couldn't get her to understand that he had to leave Gilbert in Virginia with the confederate army. Her resentment was evident, and for reasons he didn't understand, it was directed at *him*, not at the damn Yankees.

Not long after supper, tired of celebrating angry, he announced he was ready for bed. He'd hardly gotten to his room when Amzi came in.

"Hey, son. I wanted you to hear it straight from me, one-on-one, man to man, while I looked you straight in the eye: I'm proud of you. And it's good to have you home."

"Thank you, Pa."

"Now I have a favor to ask. I'd like you to take your shirt off. I want to see it."

There was no doubt what Amzi was referring to. He removed his shirt.

"Jesus help us, Alemeth. It's a wonder you lived."

"I don't know why I did."

"Well. We'll see about that. What's that chain around your neck?"

"Oh. It's just a medal."

"It doesn't get caught in anything, hanging around your neck that way?"

"No. But it took a piece of shrapnel for me. Nurse said I might not have lived, if not for it."

"Well. It's a good thing for that. Good night, son. Get yourself a good night's sleep."

After Amzi left the room, Alemeth tried to sleep, but all he could think about was Sally and Macon.

*   *   *

When he finally awoke the next day, the sun was up. Amzi had already gone out. While he ate Leety's pancakes, Dora and Laura looked on with great curiosity, as if they'd never seen anything like him before. The children kept asking him questions – where he'd been, what he'd seen – always glancing at his neck and jaw. How little they understood what he'd been through. Laura asked if he had his own bed in the army. Dora asked if he'd seen Jeff Davis, and why he didn't write more often. Walton asked if he'd brought home any caps and powder, and Eddie asked if his jaw was always going to look the way it did.

He could have told them what war was really like, but he wasn't going to make anyone happy telling children about death from typhoid, or showing Eddie the rest of his scars. So when he finished eating, he said he'd like to be alone. He took the trail up the creek, toward Sand Springs, and by the water's edge, looking at his reflection, he saw the face of a man with nothing to desire beyond the utter destruction – the *obliteration* – of the Yankee army.

He looked up to see Lou. She'd followed him from the house.

"Alemeth – are you alright?"

He stood up straight, eyeing her.

"Alemeth, I – " She stopped, as if seeing a storm approach.

Then he let it out.

"Why didn't you write me about Sally, sis?"

"I would have if – "

"Wasn't it you who wrote, *Why do you not write to me?* And *Do you not love me,* and all that?"

"Alemeth, I – "

"Wasn't it you who complained about being starved for news? You knew Sally was on my mind. Why didn't you say anything?"

"Alemeth, I wanted to tell you. At least part of me did. But you were so far away. And already in danger. And – "

"So you thought it best to keep me in the dark? So I could make a fool of myself?"

Lou said nothing.

"Well. You're not worse than her. She didn't tell me either."

She cleared her throat. "Actually, Alemeth, she did. In a way. She wrote you a letter telling you everything. Marrying Macon. Starting a family. Everything."

"But I never – "

"She sent the letter to Gordon. He was in the best position to know if it made sense to tell you. She asked him to decide if he should give it to you or not. Well, Gordon wrote back. Said he agreed with Sally and me: it would be better if you didn't know anything."

He was angry at Gordon, angry at Lou. "You agreed with them?"

She tilted her head forward. "I was the one who suggested asking Gordon to decide."

"Well, you were wrong, Lou. You really messed up."

"I'm sorry, Alemeth. I really am. We all did what we thought was best."

Excuses only made him angrier. No one could deprive him of indignation. It was all he had left on which to base self-respect.

Back at the house, the younger ones made yet another fuss over him. Just when he didn't want anyone looking at him, everyone was. Eliza said again how glad she was to have him home. Lou said she'd worried every day about his getting killed. Eliza said she was right, and that no one needed anything more to worry about.

At dinner that afternoon, Uncle Johnson asked if anyone had seen Lincoln's newest proclamation – the one proclaiming a national day of thanksgiving. No one had. Johnson explained that among the things Lincoln was proclaiming thanks for were the recent advances of the northern army. The men gritted their teeth at the thought.

For the rest of the afternoon, Amzi and Uncle Johnson told Alemeth about the impact of the recent northern advances on Mississippi. The State's treasury had been moved from the capital to Mobile, judicial records to Selma, remaining armaments to Meridian. The Union had a stranglehold on the state. The capture of Vicksburg gave the Yankees control of the river. Their blockade of the Gulf ports had taken a huge bite out of trade, except with Yanks and Yank supporters. And their occupation of Memphis and Corinth, to the north, had taken the rest of it. The Union army had cut off communication with the rest of the world. Before leaving the capital, General Johnston had destroyed the city's stores of cotton and all the rolling stock of the M.C.R.R. that couldn't be saved. A Yankee flag had been raised over the capitol and the government was on the run. The legislature was meeting in Columbus. Governor Pettus had urged the legislature to mandate the removal of all slaves to safer parts of the state and to compensate planters for the loss of their labor, but the legislature had declined the mandate. Trade was all but impossible. The cotton market had been split in two – those willing to trade with the Yankees, at a profit, and those who risked their lives by holding out for trade with others.

Dealing with one side all but guaranteed retribution by the other. "I just floated two bales on a raft down the Tallahatchie to the Yazoo," said Johnson.

"Got a dollar a pound from a man hoping to get $2.50 in Memphis."

"But the point is, he had to risk his life to do it," added Amzi.

Bynum's Creek had not been spared. First General Van Dorn's army, then General Price's, had fed themselves off the plantation. They had taken everything that was left – every hog, horse, and mule, and near every laying hen. It cost two dollars a pound for sugar, a dollar for a half dozen eggs. They'd been eating root vegetables from nearby farms. Bartering beans for corn, scrap for scrap. "The Yanks figured out they couldn't whip our soldiers," said Johnson, "so they been making war on our farms and plantations."

Swept up in the current of a thousand resentments, Alemeth's resentment at Sally, Lou, Gordon and Macon began to fade. The next morning, Amzi sent what negroes were left to the fields, where they collected what they could, picking the cotton clean like Amzi told them, notwithstanding the cuts to their fingers. Amzi told Alemeth to go to the gin house, to check the cotton as it came in. Accustomed now to unquestioning obedience, he did. Twisting and squeezing it for signs of moisture, he watched Annie and Harriet mote seed husks from its fibers, making sure they *all* did what Amzi expected.

116

The war had made everything hard; once sweet Bynum's Creek was in ruins. Alemeth had failed to defend the Plantation. He didn't bear sole responsibility, but he was part of an effort that had floundered and now was facing collapse. He didn't have to look in the mirror, for the scars on his face were evident in the land outside the window that stripped him of everything he'd ever been, as Sally's betrayal had stripped him of his heart. Inside and out was a great void, a vast emptiness of feeling, an utter lack of meaning to life.

Deep within, beneath all that was hard, there remained tightening, uneasy hunger. Not a hunger for food, but for something – anything – that was good. There *had* to be something good, something on which to build, if there was ever to be meaning to life. As he cast about for hope, he found there was, in fact, one thing that made him smile.

Alemeth's newest half-sister was innocent. Unscathed by the sharp edges of war. Oblivious to the sense of the loss felt by everyone else. Unable to pronounce *Julie,* Laura had called her *Dudie*, and the name had stuck. Stand-offish the first few days he was stuck, Dudie had gotten used to him quickly. After church on Sunday, she dared to join him in the parlor, alone by herself, and stood in front of him, sizing him up. And when she saw him smile, knowing she'd captured his attention, she twirled about and began to perform. Able to walk, excited at making decisions of her own, she sought out off-limits places, provoking Eliza by moving in the direction of the bone china or the sweet potato pie Aunt Leety had left to cool on the table. Alemeth arched his hand into the form of a spider, fingers crawling along the arm of his chair, arousing a giggle. She came at him with two spiders of her own; he pretended to be afraid of her; she giggled again. And when her laughter seemed about to wane, he placed a finger of each hand on her sides, beneath the rib cage, and tickled. Producing screams of delight. From the other room, Eliza called out, "Miss Julia Loughborough Byers? What *are* you doing? You'd better not be doing anything you shouldn't." Dudie looked over her shoulder at Eliza, then back at Alemeth, as if for his assurance that everything was alright.

The object around his neck caught her eye. She clearly wanted it. She held out her hand, as if to touch it. Sally certainly didn't want it. He could have given it to Dudie. But his own hand stopped before it reached the chain, and he drew away from her. Lucky or not, the medal was an emblem of the war. Dudie was free from any trace of hostility, from any thought or care about it whatsoever. To give her the icon, damaged by shrapnel meant to maim, would have been to sully her innocence. That he couldn't bear to do. Anguish and pain were his burdens to shoulder, and Amzi's, and Johnson's – not hers.

In late December, a deep freeze took all the vegetables. The day before Christmas, Eliza came down with a fever, and the holiday passed with little celebration. A few weeks later, Colonel Brown brought news that Howard Falconer had come home. With the Colonel's help, he'd been elected to the Mississippi state house, and thereby exempted from further military service.

Was it possible that Howard would start up the *Intelligencer* again? That the old world would, somehow reconstruct itself, along old lines?

No. Howard was not coming back to Oxford. Until the legislature next met, he was going to stay in Holly Springs with his own family. There was hardship there, too. His family needed him. It seemed hardship was everywhere. No one had good news. No one felt joy.

No one, that is, except Dudie. Alemeth resolved that would do what he could to keep it that way. If he couldn't protect Bynum's Creek, maybe he could protect her.

117

One cold morning in February, Alemeth and Eliza were in Oxford on errands when they came upon a disheartening scene. Coming down Pontotoc Street was some sort of parade: teams of horses pulling wagons, interspersed with Confederate soldiers, some mounted, some on foot. Civilians looking on from both sides of the street. But this was no parade. In the wagons were gray-clad soldiers under guard, their hands bound, sitting on what had to be coffins. And they were blindfolded. Nineteen soldiers under guard; nineteen coffins.

Word spread through the crowd: these were the soldiers who'd defied General Forrest's orders to stay in winter camp during the recent freeze. They'd gone home to find warmth, against orders. They'd been convicted of insubordination and desertion; they'd been sentenced to execution

The procession came to a stop. The nineteen convicts were taken down from the wagons and formed into a line, side by side, some of them shivering. A master sergeant barked an order and a squad of soldiers, wheeling around from the column's tail, took up position about twenty yards from the sentenced men.

The officer in charge – a colonel, by the looks of him – read out the name of each, one by one, rank first, then cleared his throat and eyed the audience with authority. "We are assembled here at the order of General Nathan Forrest, who orders me to make clear, first, to all assembled, that he continues to maintain military control over northern Mississippi. Do not overrate the importance of occasional Yankee incursions. As long as we can cut off Yankee supply lines, they'll never be able to maintain a presence here.

"Second, he orders me to make clear *why we are here in Oxford this morning*. As to this point, I direct my remarks to you condemned men. As you know well, ordered by your commanding officers to remain in camp, rather than follow those orders, you chose to defy them. You deserted your posts. For your desertion, in the face of direct orders, you have been tried by a duly constituted Court Martial. And you have been sentenced to death by a twelve-rifle volley."

Alemeth looked at Eliza, searching for assurances; she offered none.

Discipline demanded it, no? What was about to happen was necessary, no?

"A soldier's duty is to obey his superior officers. The chain of command on which an army depends cannot survive insubordination. General Forrest's orders shall now be carried out. Ready!"

In unison, the squad pulled the hammers of its rifles back.

Hadn't the condemned brought it on themselves?

"I don't know if I can watch," said Eliza, covering her eyes.

"Aim!"

The squad raised its rifles, pointing them directly at the blindfolded line.

"Ladies. Gentlemen. Prisoners." The officer's words were deliberate and slow. "By order of General Forrest, I hereby inform you that the General has issued an order of reprieve. The sentences of execution, previously ordered, have been commuted. Rifle squad, stand down."

A moment of silence was followed by hurrahs from the street. Eliza cried out, "Thank you, Lord!" and others followed. Blindfolds were doffed and there was smiling and weeping. Then, without more, the soldiers were put back on the wagons, re-seated on their coffins, and carried off to the stockade.

Once she'd recovered her senses, Eliza's joy gave way to a frustrated anger. For the rest of the morning, she fretted.

"What have we come to, Alemeth?" she asked, shivering in her shawl.

"I don't know, Mother. That was tough to watch, wasn't it."

"How a man can make sport of killing his own soldiers! Like it was a game!"

"No less so than when the angel put Abraham to the test, no?"

Eliza looked him in the eye, mulling over what he'd said.

"Anyway, that's the way it has to be, Mother. The General was just letting his men know the truth."

"The truth?"

"When it comes to military discipline, a man's disobedience deserves whatever his commander sees fit to do. Anything short of death is an act of mercy."

His words did nothing to steady her nerves. But on the ride home, she steadied herself through a rough turn by putting her hand on his arm. She left it there even when the road turned smooth. And when they got back to Bynum's Creek, Eliza went straight inside: with Alemeth looking on, she took Dudie in her arms and told her how much she loved her.

Within a week after General Forrest's demonstration, his Confederate cavalry disappeared into the woods. Within days, Yankee cavalry were in Holly Springs again, tearing up the railroads, destroying crops, picking up slaves by the hundreds. Two columns of Yankees were cutting east across Mississippi, and Bynum's Creek lay directly between the two. No one was sure whether the Yankees were headed for the port at Mobile, the railroad depot at Meridian, or somewhere else. No one was sure how expensive next month's sugar and salt were going to be. No one was sure what the negroes might be talking about. With uncertainty prevalent, it was hard to tell the difference between opinion and fact. But when Union forces passed Abbeville, word of Yankee promises must have got out, one way or the other: Ike and Abel disappeared, along with most of Al Cansler's hands. They'd run off together, people said, to join the Yankees. With Bynum's Creek all but under direct attack, Amzi and Eliza argued.

"Now take a look at what all your teaching of negroes has done. How'll we grow a livable crop without field hands?"

"Amzi, you can't go blaming this on me."

"I can, and I do, Eliza. I've come to a decision you're not going to like. You'll have to stop your colored Sunday school."

"Amzi, you can't really mean that. You've been there. You know I teach them nothing but good."

"Eliza, I don't have time to listen to your Bible stories. Not when there's a war going on. Not in hopes of turning Africans into civilized Christians."

"Alemeth." She turned to him. "*You* can come back. *You* can sit in on negro Sunday school, like you used to. Will you?"

"It doesn't matter," said Amzi. "It's time to stop anyway, Eliza. That's all there is to be said on the subject. I mean it."

There were more words that night, both bitter and ugly, but Amzi held his ground, repeating his edict. *No further consideration.*

Over the days that followed, it became clear that his decision had struck a blow to Eliza's mood. She took to saying the twenty-third psalm, praying for the Lord's will to be done. She fretted over the children. She got impatient with Aunt Leety. And the more disagreeable Eliza became, the less Amzi seemed inclined to trouble himself about her. When Alemeth asked him about it, all Amzi said was, "She'll get over it."

Happy as Alemeth was not to have to go to Eliza's negro Sunday school, he felt sympathy for Eliza. Her negro school was what she cared about most, and Amzi had taken it away from her. Ike and Abel's running away had nothing to do with anything Eliza taught them, not as far as he could see.

118

The Yankees ended up taking Meridian, with its railroad crossing, munitions, and stockade of Yankee prisoners. For a few days, it seemed they had all Mississippi in their hands. But then General Forrest appeared (as if out of nowhere) and handed the Yankees the defeat Mississippi had been waiting for. The northern half of the enemy army was driven all the way from Okolona to Tennessee. The southern half returned to Vicksburg. For the first time in months, Mississippi was essentially free of Yankee soldiers. As March began, the wind grew warm, the ground grew soft. By the middle of the month, the future looked like it might bring good news after all.

One warm March day, one of Colonel Brown's negroes brought a message to Bynum's Creek. The state legislature had been called to meet. Howard Falconer would be stopping at the Colonel's on his way to the session, to consult with ex-legislator. The Colonel thought Alemeth might want to join them.

Alemeth missed the feeling of purpose that life as a newspaperman had brought him. Howard had seen the war up close. Howard had been injured. Howard had left the army. He and Howard had a good deal in common. He couldn't have explained it if he'd had to, but reconnection to Howard and the Colonel might mean reconnection to himself, reconnection to a purpose beyond Bynum's Creek. So Alemeth didn't hesitate.

The Colonel's columned mansion at Clear Creek needed a fresh paint, and the shrubbery was overgrown, but when Harl let Alemeth into the ante-room, the staircase was still imposing. Harl was grayer, and the parrots were gone, but the portraits of the Colonel's father and grandfather still faced each other on the wall. Howard and the Colonel sat beneath them, deep in discussion about the future of Mississippi.

When they rose to greet him, the Colonel did not seem as large as he'd once seemed – his shoulders, his spine, something about him not as imposing. When Alemeth shook his hand, the Colonel's grip seemed, for the first time, no stronger than his own. He'd seen so many imposing men in the two years he'd been gone; maybe the Colonel only seemed more human by comparison. Howard, on the other hand, had grown even stronger. There was no sign of the injury he had suffered, no loss of energy about him. He sported a pointed goatee.

"Well, now, good to see you, old friend!" said Howard, glancing at Alemeth's neck. "I see you pulled through! Good for you, old boy! We've done what we could on the battlefield. Now it's time to do our part behind the lines."

At Howard's insistence, Alemeth told him of Fredericksburg, the Seven Days Campaign, and Gettysburg, Howard told Alemeth of leaving the Ninth Infantry after a year; along with his brother and father, he'd enlisted in the 37th Infantry, marching into Yankee-held Kentucky to stir up support for the southern cause. He'd been wounded and taken prisoner at Perryville, spent three months in a Yankee prison, and exchanged. Once back with his unit, he'd fought at Chickamauga and Chattanooga.

Howard and the Colonel had been strategizing for some time. Their discussions had focused on the role of the partisan ranger. While organized armies fought traditional battles in open fields, partisan rangers had been proving the value of smaller units, men on horseback who penetrated enemy lines, stealing enemy horses and guns, destroying enemy stores. Howard and the Colonel had been trying to get the government to back them in such an enterprise.

The bonds issued by the legislature in its last session were all but worthless. The state had collected no taxes in years. Since the capital was too close to federal troops near Vicksburg, the legislature was meeting on the Alabama border. With no money, no capital, no way to enforce its laws, there were many who felt the government was lost. But Howard and the Colonel were agreed: with local resistance, the war in Mississippi could yet be won; even if the armies couldn't prevail, even if the government couldn't survive, resistance of the people could succeed. They could operate under cover indefinitely. A northern army could never maintain control if, farm by farm, the people held firm to their convictions and refused to submit to northern authority.

Howard left, that afternoon for the legislative session in Macon, where the Governor gave a rousing speech about the "brighter day" dawning on the South, proof that "the Almighty favors our cause."

With her husband still on the front, Mary Ann Loughborough brought her children to Clear Creek, along with her own high spirits and predictions of good things to come. There was a sympathetic publisher in New York that was going to publish the book she had written about her time in Vicksburg. Surely, Sherman had learnt his lesson about trying to invade Mississippi, she said. Surely the railroad would be repaired by the end of the month. Like Howard, she seemed incapable of giving up. Her energy was hard to resist. She was shaping her own life the way Alemeth had always wanted to do with his own: managing a house by herself, raising two children, publishing a book. She told Amzi not to give up hope, and she blushed at compliments from everyone else, saying she didn't deserve them. Then she turned to Alemeth.

"Tell me, Alemeth. Have you followed up on your interest in the newspaper business?"

"Well, no, not really. I've been —"

"Didn't you want to run your own newspaper or something? I'm sure the Colonel would let you start up Howard's old press. You could print war news."

"Well, now – if only I weren't needed at Bynum's Creek."

He looked at Amzi for confirmation, but Amzi offered an even more convincing reason: the Colonel had taken all the type and had melted it down for bullets.

However briefly, Mary Ann's enthusiasm had become his, too. He realized how much he still longed for a life beyond Bynum's Creek. He found himself sharing Mary Ann's disappointment. For the rest of the afternoon, he watched Dudie play with Jenty Loughborough. The younger girl followed the older everywhere she went. She hung on every word she spoke, copied how she sat, and how she walked her doll along the arm of her chair, how she cradled it in her arms. Dudie took delight in doing whatever Jenty could do. She seemed excited just to be alive. And as the sun descended that evening, when the two girls faced each other, silhouettes centered before a sky of mottled pinks and blues, hands and two tiny dolls between them, the beauty of the image was unquestionable. Alemeth wanted to make it last forever.

Then it dawned on him. Not only could a camera capture such things, but several months' pay – Confederate notes – had caught up with him. If he could somehow find one, he could afford a camera and equipment after all. He wouldn't need Amzi's permission. If he could find a camera, he could take pictures, not only of unusual sunsets, but of cedar trees and spider mites, the growth of seedlings, the breaking open of bolls. It would be the world as it really was, and he could focus on any part of it he liked. He told Mary Ann that if he could find one, he was going to buy a camera.

Mary Ann needed to hear no more. Before the week was out, she had contacted her publisher in New York, and within days, Alemeth had ordered a camera: a new Kinnar type camera with a tapered leather bellows that used thin iron sheets rather than glass.

As he contemplated all there was to photograph, he started seeing pictures in everything, as if he'd grown a new pair of eyes. In April, when it was warm enough to prepare the seedbeds, he saw pictures of loose soil run over with the harrow, furrows filled with puddles of glistening rain. Watching a field hand work, he saw the contrast between the glistening sweat and the dusty grime on an ebony arm, and he wanted to capture it. Watching the seedlings shoulder their way through the topsoil, he wished his camera would come so he could take pictures of the twin leaves unfurling. As the seedlings sprawled across the acres in neat rows, field hands and hoes chopping out the weed grass and turning the soil into beds, he imagined photographs of how the good life really was. A camera could record it all. Plants. Pests. Livestock. Children. There was no end to the images he wanted to have.

That was the problem, of course. Every image would require its own metal plate. In order to capture how things were, he'd need an endless supply of them. He knew he'd have to scale down his ambitions. To make good use of his camera, he'd need to prioritize, to decide what he thought most important. He would have to decide where to focus his lenses.

*   *   *

When the new camera and plates finally arrived, he rushed to open the crate. It was a beautiful thing: the Harrison lens from Scovill in New York, the wood of dark walnut, with brass knobs and polished lenses, the leather billows tapered so as to collapse upon itself. He couldn't wait to try it, the only question being what he'd choose as his first subject. And considering all the thoughts he'd had about photographs of nearly everything, he surprised himself, when the answer finally came to him, how obvious the answer was.

He asked Dudie if she'd like to be first. She was, after all, the least engrained in the habits of her elders, the simplest and purest life he knew. And as it turns out, there was little that could have pleased her more than being asked. She was the perfect subject to catch in a moment of discovery, and a moment of discovery was the ideal thing to preserve. He set everything up in the natural light of the front hall. As Dora, Laura and Walton gathered to watch, Dudie went into the kitchen, got the stool, and picking up her new birthday ragdoll, climbed up, balancing proudly on top. After checking all faces around her to confirm she was the center of attention, she took the doll by the neck and rocked it side to side as if it were walking, the way Jenty had done.

"Hello," she said, "My name is Dudie." Then, raising the pitch of her voice, "My name is Sarah," she answered for the doll. "Pleased to meet you." She used both hands and the higher voice every time it was the doll's turn to speak. "Now, Sarah, you sure are pretty. Are you hungry?"

"I'm so *very* hungry. The Yankees took all our food."

"Would you like Aunt Leety to go down to the smokehouse and bring you back some bacon for dinner?"

"Oh, yes, Mamma!"

"Okay. Leety? Sarah's hungry…"

Dudie was deciding what the doll would do and say – only two years old, acting like a mother already, and proud of everything her child did that she directed.

When Alemeth returned from his darkened tent with his metal plate still wet, he had little time in which to make the exposure before the collodion dried.

"Okay now, Dudie," said Alemeth. "Can you be still for just a minute?"

Dudie didn't stop. Giggles persisted.

Eliza called out from the other room, "It's time to stop playing around. Be still, now. *Julia Loughborough?*"

Dudie looked to Alemeth for a smile or nod that it was okay to keep playing, regardless of what Eliza said. Alemeth put his first plate into the camera.

"It's time to make the exposure, Dudie. You *will* have to be still."

She pouted.

"Dudie, the plate is drying. You'll have to stop that if you want your picture taken."

The struggle lasted several minutes. In the end, Alemeth was only partially successful. For his first portrait – a likeness of Dudie sitting on the stool in her dress, doll under her arm, glum-faced, resentment stiffening every limb – sister Laura had to stand beside her. Retreating to the darkness of his space, beneath a black blanket, Alemeth fixed the exposure into the plate and emerged with his first negative.

He'd have loved a likeness of laughter, or play, or anything that would sustain the joy of the little girl's life. Instead, he had to settle for the frozen, still portrait the exposure required. But that was alright. He had his camera and equipment now. There'd be time enough to see how he could capture more. For now, he started a list of everything – horses, trees, rivers, trains – he wanted to preserve on metal plates.

GENERAL ORDERS, WAR DEPT.
ADJT. GENERAL'S OFFICE
Washington, D..C.
No. 191   May 7, 1864

DECLARATION OF EXCHANGE OF PRISONERS OF WAR.

It having been officially reported that Mr. Ould, rebel commissioner of exchange, has declared, without consulting with the authorities of the United States, that all rebel prisoners delivered at City Point up to the 20th of April were exchanged, it is
Ordered
that all Federal prisoners of war and all civilians on parole prior to May 7, 1864, be declared exchanged, and they are thus declared exchanged accordingly.
By order of the Secretary of War:

E. D. TOWNSEND, Assistant Adjutant-General.

*   *   *

CONFEDERATE STATES OF AMERICA
WAR DEPARTMENT
Richmond, Va.
Exchange Notice No 10
June 6, 1864

The following notice is based upon a recent declaration of exchange made by the Federal authorities, bearing date May 7, 1864, and is supported by valid Federal Paroles on file in my office:
SECTION 1. All Confederate officers and men who have been delivered at City Point, Va., previous to the 1st of June, 1864, are hereby declared to be *exchanged*.
SECTION 2. All Confederate officers and men and all civilians who have been captured at any place and released on parole prior to May 7, 1864, are hereby declared to be *exchanged*.

ROBT. OULD, Agent of Exchange

By order:

S. COOPER, Adjutant and Inspector General

119

Alemeth learned of the exchange when Uncle Johnson came back from Oxford with a message from the provost marshal. It took time to digest it, terse as it was, but as Uncle Johnson explained, he hadn't been *actually* exchanged, man for man, under a flag of truce. He had been *declared* exchanged. Meaning that as far as the Confederate authorities were concerned, his legal status was the same as if he *had* been exchanged.

"What's all that mean?" asked Lou.

"It means your brother's relieved from his parole. A prisoner who's been exchanged is allowed to return to the fight, to take up arms again."

"Alemeth, please don't do that. You've done your time. We need you here at home."

"There's time enough to think about that, Lou."

But that evening, at the supper table, there was further discussion of the order of exchange. Laura asked what it meant to be exchanged. Eddie suggested that Lord Jesus gave his life in exchange for ours, to which Lou said, "This is about Alemeth's exchange, Eddie; not Jesus's," and then, turning to Alemeth, "You need to promise you won't re-enlist."

Before Alemeth could respond, Uncle Johnson cut in. "Alemeth, maybe you should ask yourself what you'd be willing to give your life for."

"That's just it," said Lou. "He doesn't know."

"For my family, I suppose."

"You *suppose*?" asked Amzi, leaning back in his chair.

"I think he should stay home, Pa. Alemeth, your family is more important than anything. Mother, what do *you* think he should do?"

"I think you should pray about it, Alemeth. Ask it in *His* name, and you'll get your answer. If you follow that answer, you can be sure of yourself."

"Sometimes, mother, that makes very little sense to me."

"Whatever do you mean?"

"Sometimes, I feel like I've been standing on sand in a creek bottom. As the water moves under my feet, I sink deeper. Some things seem real enough at first, but then fade away and disappear."

"Well, God is not going to disappear."

"I thought he was invisible already," said Walton.

"Your immortal *soul* is not going to disappear, either. Believe in that, Alemeth. And in the promise of the Lord. The devil lurks in doubt."

Eliza set her jaw and nodded deliberately, as if she'd said it all. Into the silence, Amzi leaned forward.

"Alemeth, son. I must tell you how *I* see it. If you care about my opinion."

"Of course. I want your opinion."

"You enlisted. Gave your first oath to the South. To Mississippi."

"That's right."

"As I recall, you did it for the duration of the conflict."

"When I re-upped, I guess I did."

"Well, then. Nothing about your injury or imprisonment changed that. Your parole was cancelled out by the exchange. Nothing has relieved you from your first oath. Eliza, isn't there something in the Book of Numbers about keeping one's oaths?"

"Very good, dear. Numbers chapter thirty tells us: 'If a man vow a vow unto the Lord, or swear an oath to bind his soul with a bond; he shall not break his word.'"

"There you have it, Alemeth. You've sworn an oath to Mississippi. You've bound yourself. A man's word should be as good as his bond."

Bound himself?

After dinner, he retreated to his room, wondering what it meant to say he'd bound himself. It meant, he supposed, that he'd offered himself up to punishment, should he fail to make good on his vow. But an oath taken two years ago? Before Gettysburg? When he was doing everything he did for Sally Fox? How would it make sense to follow *that* oath, now that Sally had abandoned him?

Eliza came to the doorway. Standing in her nightgown, Lou behind her, she said, "Alemeth, I didn't get a chance to finish earlier. The old law mandated keeping oaths. But here's what the Lord said. Matthew chapter five:

But I say unto you, swear not at all. Neither by heaven, for it is God's throne, nor by the earth, for it is his footstool... Neither shalt thou swear by thy head, because thou canst not make one hair white or black.

Out in the hallway, Lou's voice:

"Alemeth, if the Lord tells us not to swear any oath at all, then how can you be bound to keep an oath you made two years ago?"

Reverend Vrooman had given a lecture on oaths at Mount Sylvan. To make an oath was to be a witness, to swear to something's veracity. It was the same whether the witness was swearing to something in the past – some crime observed, some statement overheard – or swearing to something in the future – making a promise, perhaps, or a warranty. To take an oath was to put your honor on the line, for the truth of something. What did Jesus really mean, then, when he said to never swear an oath? To never vouch for the truth of anything?

With scripture sending mixed messages, Alemeth turned to logic.

If not bound by prior oath, he was free to re-enlist or not, as he alone saw fit. Left to his own authority. So. What did he want? What was worth volunteering for? He certainly hated everything the Yankees stood for. But to rejoin the Vindicators – he'd have to pledge obedience, again, to the command of military men with military commissions. He'd have to make yet another oath. Numbers said that an oath, once made, should be kept, and if anything was clear, it was that subjecting yourself to an oath could put heavy constraints on your freedom.

Into the middle of his quandary came Lou asking, "There's nothing so important as your family, is there? Stay home. You've done your duty. You know you want to be a photographer. I've never seen you so happy as when you're taking photographs." Putting the family first was easy; for a moment, it answered all his questions. Family was what he knew best. Whatever the conflicts, whatever the disappointment, family was what would always be there, in the end. Family should come first.

But what did it mean, to put family first? Did it mean making Lou happy, by staying home and making photographs, or Amzi, by going back to the front? Or even Eliza, by asking the Lord what to do? Or did it mean doing what *he* thought was right? Standing up for what *he* believed in? He asked himself what his heart said. The Bible made clear that slavery was God's will. The southern cause was just. The Yankees were tyrants to impose their own values on southerners by force of arms, in a union the south didn't want. And Howard had been convincing: while military victory might be in doubt, ultimate victory, through sheer force of will, through sheer refusal to submit to the oppressor in a perpetual war fought underground, couldn't possibly fail. It boiled down to willpower.

The Yankees had invaded the South. The Yankees had killed his friends. He'd been wrong to think in terms of obedience to Pa. It was more important to obey his convictions, and all he had to do was decide on those convictions.

Then it dawned on him: Maybe he didn't have to choose between his passions. Maybe he could use his camera to show the world the terror and misery that the Yankees had brought on the country. He could never carry all his equipment, but if he only shot in daylight, outdoors, he wouldn't need lights. Just a camera tent. Plates. Chemicals. A dark place to work. It could be difficult, but not necessarily impossible, especially with Gilbert's help.

The more he thought it over, the more certain he became.

The next morning he gave Amzi his decision. He would return to fight again, for the cause of the South. Lou asked if he'd leave the ambrotype with her, so she'd have something to remember him by, and he was happy to oblige.

120

This time, with the Yankees in control of Grand Junction, the train route went through Alabama, Georgia and the Carolinas, up the Atlantic coast. He'd have liked to be take pictures of the passengers, packed in tight rows, their faces sullen and worn with the weariness of war. But his chemicals were dangerous, especially when a man sitting next to them lit a cigar. There was little space. No way to get enough light. Subjects rocking back and forth. Photography was out of the question.

When the train arrived in Richmond, he had little trouble finding the Vindicators. Gilbert was still attached to the regiment, but it was a torn and tired remnant of the unit he remembered. The men were ill-clothed, mostly unshaven. They'd been living on little more than hardtack, tobacco, and coffee. They'd all lost weight, many had no shoes, knees of trousers were patched or threadbare, arms bandaged. But the seeming hopelessness of the cause, and their doubts, only made him more determined.

When Alemeth told his comrades of Baltimore and parole, of finding Sally married to Macon Thompson, Bill Elliot said he was luckier than some. Sixty-five of the regiment had been killed at Gettysburg; seven more at Chickamauga, and five more at Knoxville. Frank Middleton had been killed, Captain Govan had lost a leg, and Colonel Fiser had lost his right arm. That winter in East Tennessee, they'd lost more men to disease.

There were things in the faces Alemeth had never seen before, looks of weariness and grimness, resolve hanging on by a thread. More than bones had been broken by the war. The spirit of the men had changed. They now talked of survival; whether peace might yet be won; how badly they were needed at home. Only Gordon seemed to have kept high spirits. "Welcome back," he said, eyeing Alemeth's camera. "You were right to come back. You and I aren't needed at home. We're different. Our place is right here."

When Alemeth found Gilbert among the chow wagons, it was a sweet reunion. Gilbert asked about the medal that still hung around Alemeth's neck; Alemeth told him how it had stopped a piece of shrapnel at his throat. Gilbert gave him a pouch of cherry seeds he'd rescued. But there was a new order regarding negro servants. They'd been impressed into a company of laborers subject to the Colonel's orders, available for their masters only when relieved from military duties. They had to be kept under close watch. Owners had to ensure their servants were back at the negro camp no later than nine o'clock. Gilbert's time now belonged to the Colonel, and Alemeth's plans to make him a photographic assistant had to be postponed.

After a few days, Alemeth found time to write home.

At Gains' house near Richmond

June 6th/64

Dear Father

 I will write you a few lines, as I can't tell when I can write again. There was some skirmishing last night, There has been no general engagement yet, but I think there will be before many days. Our boys have to lie close in the ditches day & night, & whenever one sticks his head above the works he is shot at.

 I have not been to the regiment yet, but will to day. Our line & the yanks are about 250 yds apart. The yanks are said to be moving from in front of Ewell, on our left, toward our right.

 The company numbers 11. Tom Carlock was shot in the mouth. Wright was wounded & has gone home, Elliott commands the squad. Jim Brown & all the boys that are here are well. The brigade is about 2 miles from here.

 Tell Harriet I saw Gilbert yesterday, he is well and is as fat as a little beef, & looks better than I ever saw him. He is staying at the wagon yard & helps to cook for the regiment, as the boys can't do their own cooking while in line of battle. He draws his rations just the same as the soldiers do. The boys say they get plenty to eat, but they get corn bread instead of flour. They draw tobacco, sugar & coffee.

 Tell Miss Ella David McEwen was killed. Give my love to Sister & all the rest. Write soon & direct to Richmond.

   Your affectionate son,

   J. A. Byers

 Here is some fine cherry seed, plant them in some good place & see what they will come to.

As time allowed, Alemeth explained his photographic equipment to Gilbert, that Gilbert might yet be of use to him. How to keep the plates secure and protected, how to keep the chemicals dry. Gilbert found an old wagon and a tarp Alemeth might use for preparing his plates, but the wagon needed repairs. All things considered, there was too much to be done to allow for photography. There was no place to set everything up. In the evenings, there was no light. During the days, they were busy. There was no way to take pictures, for now.

For nearly three weeks outside Richmond, Alemeth spent his days building chevaux-de-frise and watching negroes dig ditches, finding no chance to set up his equipment. Then, in the early morning hours of June 18, the men were told to pack their personal gear: General Kershaw's brigade had been assigned to the defense of Petersburg, and they were to be aboard the train in thirty minutes. When Bill Elliot saw Alemeth packing his camera equipment in the wagon, he told him there'd be no place for such nonsense in the trenches. So Alemeth had to leave it all behind. He and his equipment went their separate ways, photography now impossible until he got his equipment back, whenever that might be.

*   *   *

Just as Richmond sat at the fall line of the James, Petersburg lay on the fall line of the Appomattox, the twin sisters overlooking the Tidewater together, arm in arm, as it were. Petersburg was connected by rail not only to Richmond but west to Farmville and Lynchburg, east to Norfolk and the ocean, south to Weldon, North Carolina. Its tracks provided a supply line from the whole south to the capital, like a spine supporting a brain. If the enemy couldn't take Richmond or Petersburg outright, they were intent on disrupting the line between them. Twenty-five miles of trenches had been dug to protect that line.

For seven days, the Seventeenth lay bellies in the trench dirt, waiting to be attacked. Early in the day, the sun weak; shadows. At mid-day, no walls, no shadows. All but motionless, most of the time. The sun bearing down, the mud turning to dust, counting minutes till time for another swig from canteens. It was no place for a camera. No place for explosive chemicals. Dust and dirt would have gotten into the lens the way it got into writing papers and pen points.

Outflanking the trench line, Yankee cavalry had destroyed parts of the railroad to Weldon, cutting the rebel army off from all points south. As long as the Weldon road was out of service, there'd be no supplies going out or coming in, no packages, no letters. Without Gilbert, without the camera, without letters from home, without a working pen to write with, there was little to do but look at the men on either side of him, wishing he could capture their images in the face of their mortal enemies.

They weren't allowed to get up and move around without permission (Captain Wright's orders). Every day, they changed alignment, so they wouldn't have to be next to the same two soldiers all the time. So one day was passed between Charley Morgan and Calvin Morris, another between Peter Brown and Bob Patton, a third between Charley and Gordon Falkner. Looking into faces, feeling the sun, breathing the dust, they waited for an increase in cannon fire, a battle cry, some sign it was time for bayonets. But the attack didn't come. The Yankee army dug in too. So they dug in more themselves, with lumber reinforcement. Boards swinging into place sent dirt like little shells among the larger ones around them.

Face to face with his fellows for hours on end, in the face of death, Alemeth had a chance to know them as he never had before. Charley Morgan, the heir to his father's plantation, was most like Alemeth on the surface, but shallow and immature: he made light of everything, he pretended he cared about nothing, he proclaimed his intention to bed as many girls as he could before he died. Calvin Morris started speaking of salvation, describing his visions of the afterlife, one after another, each more vivid than the last, proclaiming his Faith in the Lord. Peter Brown spoke of the failings of Jeff Davis, and the reasons the situation could have been better had Judah Benjamin been able to win support from the English or French. Peter thought everyone ignorant, from the generals and politicians down to Colonel Fiser and Captain Wright. Bob Patton held the opposite point of view. As far as Bob was concerned, General Lee and Jeff Davis could do no wrong; their decisions were bound to prove brilliant in hindsight. They deserved complete loyalty and total obedience.

And then there was Gordon. Gordon liked to hear himself talk and his imagination knew no bounds. The others had limited interests, returning to the same points like pendulums, unable to escape the pattern of their own observations; but Gordon was like a firefly: you never knew where he'd come from next. Sometimes, he was all but impossible to follow. One day, he said the past had never existed, and challenged Alemeth to prove that it had. In the discussion that ensured, he said that facts and the truth had nothing to do with each other. That people had invented God for their own reasons. And that one never knew, maybe Reverend Vrooman had been right, maybe slavery was an abomination.

"What?" blurted Alemeth. "Slavery evil? Gordon, what's gotten into you? I hope you're not going daft on us."

"Daft? No. I don't think so."

How can you deny the past? And God? How can you be unsure about slavery?"

"Alemeth, I've never felt sure about anything – certainly not about slavery."

"Gordon, it was you that got me to volunteer. You've spent more than three years putting your life on the line. And you're telling me you're not sure you believe?"

"Oh, I believe, Alemeth; I believe, alright. I'm just not sure."

Alemeth protested, challenged, tested, complained, but Gordon wouldn't budge. Gordon agreed that northern aggression was an evil attempt to subjugate the people of the south by force; he agreed in the righteousness of the south's fight for freedom; he remained willing to die for the south. Yet he refused to commit himself to anything. He seemed to believe in nothing beyond his own imagination.

After a week, the Vindicators were relieved from the ditches and returned to their camp in the rear, closer to Richmond. The old camp was a welcome sight. The servants were right next to them again, so Gilbert was nearby in the evenings. But there was bad news, news that, piled on top of everything else, grated on all Alemeth's earlier frustrations. His camera, his chemicals and his plates had all disappeared. No one in the quartermaster's tent knew anything about his 'imaginary' wagon. Their journals made no mention of such things.

He had held out hope that he could capture the world as it really was. Now, with the disappearance, with the lack of any evidence that it had ever existed, with its own reality called into question, Alemeth felt violated. Anger rose up in his gut as never before.

It didn't help that there was so little freedom in the life that was left for them: day after day, the Vindicators cleaned weapons, drilled, kept camp, and waited for orders.

On Independence Day, amidst the sutler's fireworks, there was talk about the importance of independence. Gordon asked the others what they thought that meant.

Calvin: Independence is what our ancestors fought for: the right of a free people to decide their own affairs.

Charley: For me, independence means freedom to do what you want.

Alemeth: Independence is more important than anything. It has to be defended, whatever the cost.

Bill Elliot: That's why there'll always be a need for armies. My uncle George says being a soldier is the best career a man can have.

Charley: But inside an army, independence is the last thing you want. What an army needs is obedience, not freedom.

Bill: An army needs discipline, of course. Where would we be, without discipline?

Gordon: For me, real independence is about telling stories.

Charley: What?

Gordon: Really. Telling stories is a great way to be free. You get to invent a world of your own choosing, to see the world from your characters' eyes. It helps a lot, to get outside yourself.

Alemeth: Leave it to you to get outside yourself, Gordon. But seriously: we're putting our lives on the line for something here and, I mean no offense, but I don't think it's your *s*tories.

That evening, back in the tent, Alemeth asked Gordon if he'd been serious. When Gordon said he had, Alemeth asked if he didn't think there were more important things to be fighting for. Southern rights, for example. Independence from northern authority.

"And slavery?" asked Gordon.

"Sure. Of course."

"Isn't it dangerous to be so sure of anything?"

"I have the strength of my convictions. Don't you?"

"If you ask me, Alemeth, certainty is the greatest sin. Once we feel certain of anything, once we build that wall, that's when we really give up freedom. As for submitting to authority, the best thing to do is to be the author of myself."

Petersburg, Va.
July 7ᵗʰ, '64

Dear Sister,

   I am getting anxious to hear from home, and hope you will write to me soon. We have been relieved from the ditches about two weeks, and may have to return again soon to relieve some other troops, unless something occurs to require us elsewhere. There is nothing unusual going on. Everything is quiet, except sharp shooting and some cannonading. It is hard to tell what Grant is going to do. He is still digging away in our front. If he continues at this he will die with old age in some of the holes he has caused to be dug, which will serve him a resting place, and never get to Richmond. A few shells go into Petersburg every day, but do but little damage. They knock a few holes in some of the buildings, and scare the women and children.

   It takes 15 dollars to get a meal of vituals in Petersburg. Flour is 400 dollars a barrel, Bacon 7 & 8 dols a pound, Sugar 12 dols, Onions 1 dollar a piece, Corn field peas 60 dollars a bushel, Milk 23 dollars a quart, Butter 14 dollars a pound. The Weldon road is not yet fixed, but I hope it soon will be.

   The weather is very hot, dry, and dusty. Everything in the way of vegetation is parched up for the want of rain. There has been no rain here to do any good in two months. But the boys are all in fine spirits and are ready for the Yanks whenever they come. We are all confident of success. You must have plenty of good things for me if I ever get home again, and send some to me if you have a chance. Send me some pickles, onions and pepper sauce. If you can get sugar, make me some blackberry cordial & brandy peaches.

   Tell Dora to write to me, I would like to hear from her. Tell Walton I will send him some caps & powder the first chance I have. If he was here, he could get as much as he wanted, and shoot at Yankees from morning till night, if he wanted to. I have no war news. I sent several papers home. Have they been received? I will send more when the way is open. Give my love to all at home & all my friends,

   Your affectionate brother,

   J. A. Byers

If I ever get home again.

He'd wanted to explain to Lou the danger he was in, with Death everywhere, but he couldn't write home about his fears. He wouldn't even admit them to himself. That's how you got the jitters. There was a lot of talk about who would get them next. Everyone knew that it could be anyone, but if you started thinking about it – if you started to doubt yourself – that could be the beginning of the end. He wanted nothing more than courage, to be a man of valor, to have the strength of his convictions – but the reality around him required resignation to one certain reality: that if God had death in store for him, or worse, so be it, death or worse it would be.

So it was all he'd been able to write, *If I ever get home again.*

That night, he dreamed of Aunt Leety making corn pudding, of putting a line in the water at Sand Springs, of a blue sky that filled with cannon fire, and more exploding shells. Then he dreamed of Dr. Edgar in his ambulance. The ambulance was full of severed limbs that spilled onto the ground at his feet.

Petersburg, Va

July 10th/64

Dear Father,

We are still lying quiet, but there is a prospect for a march, I have not the remotest idea where to. Three days rations are ordered. Everything is quiet on the lines. There was a great deal of picket sharpshooting last night. On the 8th the enemy made an assault on our lines, but were easily repulsed. The cannonading & musketry was quite heavy, but it did not last long. Our brigade was ordered into line and kept under arms ¾ of an hour, but was not called on, when we all went back to quarters.

There are a great many conjectures, as to where we will go if we have to march. Some think we will go down on the Weldon road to guard it, or go back towards Richmond, and some think we will go to reinforce Early in Maryland, but no one knows when we will go. We may not go at all. It is evident that Grant's Army occupies a bad position for water. The refugees from that region say there is no water except wells & they go dry in time of a drought. We have had no rain here in two months.

I sent a notice to you in sister's letter taken from a newspaper telling how you might send things to me, if you have anything to send. I would like for you to get Ragan to make I & Gilbert another pair of shoes, 5 & 8, on a plain last, like the one he made before. They are the best shoes to march in I ever wore. And be sure to put in very stiff counters. Send me about 10 pounds of well dried beef, if you kill any, and coffee, pickles, brandy peaches, & such nice things as a soldier would like to get from home.

I have sent you some papers. Have you received them? If you get them, I will send you some more. Please write to me soon. I want to hear from home. I hope the time will soon come when we will see each other again, and enjoy the comforts of the family circle at home. I may be spared this war throng or I may find a soldiers grave, but I am happy to say that I am reconciled to whatsoever is my fate. God will deal with me, as is consistent with his own good will, which is just and right.

Give my love to all at home. Write soon & often to your affectionate son,

J. A. Byers

PS. This move may be to go into a fight close at hand, What Beauregard & Lee intend to do is not for us to know every time.

When the Weldon Road was repaired, Alemeth received a letter from Eliza: she said she hoped she'd earned his acceptance as one of his family. That she looked forward to him coming home, to him going up to Sand Springs and bringing back some catfish for Sunday dinner. He wanted to say yes, he had accepted her, and yes, it would surely be nice if he could get away from all the dust, and come home again, to her and to all the rest of them. He even thought of saying he'd enjoy going to church with her. But he wasn't sure if it were true anymore. He wasn't sure he really *wanted* to go home. He'd had a growing sense that his unit was where he belonged. That camp would always be his home. That the Vindicators would always be his family.

Besides, he'd run out of paper, so he had to keep his silence until he could get some.

The next Sunday, when they both had some free time, Alemeth spent some time with Gilbert. Watching him count the money Alemeth had given him Alemeth wondered what would become of him, if he were to be killed in battle. He shared with Gilbert what was on his mind.

"I imagine you miss being home some, Gilbert."

"Yes, suh. I s'pose I do."

"I've been thinking about the promise I made to your mother. To treat you like I would Walton."

Gilbert furrowed his brow.

"And I was thinking. If I'd brought Walton up here to Virginia with me, and he wanted to go home, I'd let him."

Gilbert said nothing. But as Alemeth saw it, a dead man needs no servant.

"Gilbert, if you want to go home, you can."

"Don't you go worryin' yourself about that, Mast' Byers. I don't want to go back to Mississippi. I'm very well satisfied right here where I am, for the moment. Fact is, I expect this here's about the best place I've ever been."

Gilbert grinned. In the midst of war, he had somehow found satisfaction. And a short while later, he appeared with several sheets of writing paper, which he handed to Alemeth.

"Tell them – tell my mama – tell 'em I'm doin' fine. Alright?"

Alemeth agreed, but as he found a spot to sit and write, the wagon train came up. The Seventeenth had been ordered to a new position.

North of the James, near Malvern Hill, below Richmond

July 28th/64

Dear Mother,
I received your kind letter a few days ago at Petersburg. We have been moving around considerably since then. Circumstances would not permit me to write before this, & only a short letter now. We are all in line of battle, throwing up breastworks. I think we will have some hot work here soon.

Our brigade has been in no engagement since I have been back. Bob Patton and Tom Carlock were wounded at Cold Harbor. Carlock has been sent home. Tell Harriett Gilbert is in good health, and is very well satisfied.

I wish I was there to enjoy the fruit this year. You must have something fixed up for me & send to me, or keep for me if I ever get home.

The weather is very hot & sultry. There has been some skirmishing on our right and left today. I have nothing of importance to write. Tell Uncle to write to me. Out of so many at home to write, I might get two letters a month. I have received but one since I left. All of you please write soon & often, Mother. Give my love to all.

Your affectionate son,

J. A. Byers

121

Sunday down time together. Gilbert is dealt a hand of his own.

Gordon: So let me ask you, Alemeth. How did it feel to take the yellow pill?

Alemeth: I'll tell you. I felt like a fool.

Charley: Go on.

Alemeth: I'm just sick, thinking about it. Imagining things with Sally Fox, the way I did. Then I fell hook, line and sinker for that nurse's nonsense. Blind as a bat.

Charley: Which nurse? (He has so many.)

Peter: The only good thing about a hospital.

Alemeth: The nurse that told me Sally might want me home. I was so taken by Sally, it was all I needed to hear.

Gordon: So the oath was easy, then?

Peter: I bet half a dollar.

Charley: I fold.

Peter: Byers, the bet's to you.

Alemeth: (*Glancing at his cards*) Yeah. Not at first. But it got to where it was easy. (*Again*) I fold. I just got swept up in it.

Gordon: Happens to the best of us, Byers.

Peter: Gilbert. It's to you, my friend.

Gilbert: I check.

Peter: Gilbert, you can't check. You have to bet or fold. Byers, I thought you said your boy knew the rules?

Alemeth: Sorry, I thought he did. Gilbert, if you have nothing, just fold. I guess I was thinking so much about her and me. Just imagining things, at first. Then I started to think it was real.

Gilbert: I call.

Gordon: Ideas are like Sirens, I suppose. The voices of some are hardly audible, but they all vie for attention.

Peter: Are you calling, Gordon?

Gordon: No, really. Have you read *Moby Dick*? People get set in their ideas. Especially ideas they've had for a long time. Make it two dollars.

Peter: I think you're full of it. I call.

Gordon: Think of the latin. *Convinced* comes from *convictum*. *Vinco, vincere, victus*. It means you've been conquered.

Peter: It's your bet, Gilbert. A dollar and a half to you.

Gilbert: I call.

Gilbert places another dollar and a half into the pot and looks up as if to ask, *what next?* Gordon fans out his hand for all to see: three jacks. Peter throws a pair of kings onto the table. Gilbert spreads out his cards, naming each of them. He has nothing.

Calvin:	Why did you call, Gilbert?
Gilbert:	I thought I had it.
Alemeth:	Gilbert, have you forgotten so soon?
Gordon:	*(Raking in the pot)* I'll tell you something. A good poker player knows the power of an idea. We're either drawn to one, or not. The closer we get, the more familiar it becomes. If you want to play poker, you've got to take advantage of that.
Calvin:	Whose deal is it?
Alemeth:	Like Gilbert thinking he had a winning hand there?
Gordon:	Sure, if you like. Make your opponent believe in something. When he accepts it as fact, he's all yours.
Charley:	It's my deal.
Alemeth:	Like being in a rut?
Gordon:	Exactly.
Charley:	I wish you'd stop all this talk and hand me those cards so I could deal.
Peter:	Give them to me, Charley.
Charley:	But it's my deal.
Peter:	No, private, it's mine.

Gilbert is staring into space, his mind elsewhere. Alemeth, wondering if he should hold on to Gilbert's money, lest he lose it all, is distracted; he loses his medallion to Gordon on the next hand. A few hands later, a showdown begins when Gilbert calls Gordon's bet of a dollar. Gilbert's position being lousy, Alemeth winces. Behind Gilbert, Charley raises two dollars more. When the bet comes back to Gilbert, though he's trapped between two strong hands, he calls yet again. After the draw, when Charley opens for three dollars and Gordon raises to ten, it's past time for Gilbert to fold.

But when it's his turn, he doesn't.

Gilbert:	My turn to bet?
Gordon:	Yes, Gilbert.
Alemeth:	Gilbert, pay attention to the hand.
Gilbert:	I'll raise it this last five dollars I got. If I can.
Peter:	You can, Gilbert.

Alemeth wants to say *No, Gilbert, you don't know what you're doing,* but Gilbert puts five more dollars into the pot, and Gordon calls, and when they lay down their hands, Gordon's tens and eights loses to Gilbert's full house.

Alemeth: Of all the luck. Congratulations, Gilbert. You've either got the best poker face around, or you had no idea what you were doing.

Gilbert: Gordon, how 'bout, 'stead of the pot, you give me that medallion?

Alemeth: Gilbert, don't be a fool. That was a very big pot.

Gordon: Don't underestimate the boy, Alemeth. I think we've been underestimating him. I think he knows exactly what he's doing.

Gilbert looks down to the ground, concealing a smile, and Gordon gives him the medallion.

122

The preacher had set up an empty rifle crate in a peach orchard next to Company C, to serve as his pulpit. Once black arm bands had been passed out and rolled onto arms, the service began.

"We mourn for the dead," he said, "as a way of relieving emotion. Of giving form to lamentations. Of voicing respect for the departed. Our sadness comes from the value we see in life. The denial of the potential that life brings is a tragic loss to those who remain, to remember. (For today, for the time being, not yet among those who've passed on, it is we who are left behind; and it's all we can do to remember.)

"And so, this evening, we deal with these fallen men as memories. Not to judge whether they were good, but to pay our respects to them. For every man is a sinner: we can be assured, not everything they did was good. Rather, let us remember that few men, if any, have *never* done *anything* good. And much good might yet have come of each of them, had Death not cut them down prematurely, like plants in early spring.

"So let us mourn for the good they might have done. And let us remember. As I read each name, remember what you can of them. For no matter how short, their lives meant something to us, in some way, large or small. They each became a part of us."

Beginning with Company A, the preacher began reading the names of the dead. James M. Moore. Patrick Moore. William W. Ormand. John L. Parker. William J. Parker. James A. Pickett. After Alemeth remembered one man, he tried to remember others. William H. Pittman. T. B. Robinson. John E. Smith. William Perry Taylor. James E. Whitworth. Hamilton H. Wood. James L. Worsham. G. B. Addison. James M. Blackard. Albert Bronhors. William Gast. Andrew Robison Govan. John M. James. George W. Julian. Horace F. Keeble. James F. Laws. Samuel F. McClure. Alexander H. McIlhaney. William T. McRaven. David G. McWilliam. Frank S. Ross. Andrew V. Spillers. James L. Tucker. John Watson. Solon L. Whittington. James W. Birge. Thomas H. Bodinhammer. William A. Cates. William N. Cox. John J. Crippin. Mitchell S. Davis. Joseph E. Douglas. Archibald Y. Duke. Rufus C. Eaves. Washington P. Eaves. Daniel R. Edington. Thomas J. Foster. Rollin C. Grisworld. William Hodges. F. M. Hogan. Gabriel T. Holmes. Dr. M. Mayfield. William B. McGee. Jefferson R. McNutt. David W. McWilliams. Woodson B. Mears. George W. Morris. George W. Owen. Andrew P. Parks. Rufus A. Robbins. Dixon H. Roberts. John G. Stapp. John Samuel Stokes. William H. Stokes. James Barrett. George W. Casey. Joseph D. Cochran. James G. Cook. George

H. Cox. Joseph A. Culver. William J. Grier. Joseph B. Holland. John H. Howell. John V. Jones. M. N. Lockard. Randal McDonald. John H. Morgan. James P. Owen. B. F. Peck. Nelson L. Strong. Newton J. Tedder. Wright H. Tedder. John L. Watson. Thomas B. Watson.

The names meant nothing. Somewhere in Company E, Alemeth's mind began to wander. But it was brought back when the preacher came to Company H. The Vindicators were from Panola. He'd known each of them well.

Tom Bradford, the first person he saw kissing a girl. George Capps, Bob Jolly's neighbor, who liked to hunt for raccoons. Jimmy Eastridge, first to die of typhoid fever. George Foote, who'd got the Vindicators together. And Richard Jones, Georgia boy, fingers all yellowed from tobacco. Frank Middleton, who cared how his mustache was waxed. (He'd been a good captain, though.) Johnny Morise, jokester with a laugh to match. Jimmy Parker. Dick Perry. The Rhodes boys. George Shuford, who never tired of saying he was from Coahoma County. Jimmy Wright, who'd signed up the same day Alemeth did, and bragged how many Yankees he'd killed.

When the reading of the names was finished, the preacher paused, then cleared his throat and continued.

"Lord, let us remember these men, who gave their lives for the South. And let us remember the families who gave up their sons to preserve our freedom – we'll be forever in their debt. I commend to you, soldiers, Mississippians: contemplate your fallen brothers.

"We have all felt the grief of Lamentations. 'I am the man that hath seen affliction by the rod of his wrath. He hath led me, and brought me into darkness, but not into light. Surely against me is he turned; he turneth his hand against me all the day. My flesh and my skin hath he made old; he hath broken my bones. He hath set me in dark places, as they that be dead of old. He hath hedged me about, that I cannot get out: he hath made my chain heavy. And when I cry and shout, he shutteth out my prayer.'

"But the prophet also tells us, 'The LORD is good unto them that wait for him, to the soul that seeketh him.... For the Lord will not cast off for ever: but though he cause grief, yet will he have compassion according to the multitude of his mercies.'

"Through faith in our Lord, we've come to understand there is reason for hope. Death needn't be that terrible darkness we all have feared. It can be the gateway to heaven. A reward for Faith, and for obedience to the Lord. Martyrs, my brothers, live forever.

"And so I'd ask you to join me in prayer for the souls of those already taken. Lord, we pray that each of them was saved before he was called to judgment. For those who have, in these terrible times, not yet found their way to you, Lord, we ask for mercy, and for respite from the pain of eternal damnation."

The preacher closed his eyes and bowed his head, his palms facing the sky. After a moment of silence, he lifted his head again.

"And now, a question for the rest of you. Are *you* ready to declare yourself among those faithful to the Lord? Let us search our souls. Let us lift up our hearts unto God. Death can come without warning. A stray shell can cut us down without notice, leaving no time to confess our faith."

A man rose and stepped forward. Three more followed. Then Charley Graves and Jimmy Lamb. Alemeth stood up. As he watched the preacher baptize those who went forward, he thanked the Lord for his own baptism, and his own Faith. The years he'd spent resisting Eliza came back, painful reminders of his disobedient past. He wanted to cut them out of his heart, the shame almost too much to bear. How could he have doubted? How could he ever have waivered? Was he not in service to the cause of Christian honor, justice, and right? Could there be anything to fear, but doubt itself?

He asked the Lord for forgiveness that he'd ever tried to resist, and he vowed he'd be obedient to the will of the Lord, come what may.

Dear Pa,

I know not what will have taken place, or where we will be when you hear from me again. We are not surprised at any time to get marching orders. Our wagon train has just come up.

Jim Brown starts for home tomorrow. I was going to send Gilbert with him, but he has declined the idea of going home for the present, which suits me very well. I & Gilbert both are blessed with good health. He is a little slow but an honest good boy. I will send him home when the campaign is over.

We have preaching in our camp every night when things are quiet. A goodly number of mourners go up every night. Six were baptized the other day.

Tell sister to make me two good shirts tolerable heavy, & two pair of thick wool socks. If you can get any drilling, get enough for two pair of drawers. I don't like to wear rough cloth for drawers. Make them some larger than those little things at home.

Don't forget to send my gloves.

On the 7th, we took the train, and came to within 6 miles of Culpepper, where we now are, near Slaughter Mountain. About 2 miles from the railroad in a nice piece of woods. Nothing of interest has occurred since we have been here. I received Mother's kind letter & answered it. Somebody write to me. I have received but one letter from home. I have nothing more to write. Give my love to all at home.

Your affectionate Son,

J. A. Byers.

123

Amzi surveyed the embers of the house on Depot Street. This time, it wasn't just the Colonel's house that lay in ashes. The Yankees had burned down much of Oxford, including every building around the Square. They'd even burned down the courthouse. *The courthouse,* for God's sake.

There was no military advantage to what they did. No practical purpose. Even when the Yankees had taken livestock and stores, they'd done it to supply their army. There'd been a sort of perverse logic to it. The present destruction was different. It was entirely, completely, absolutely, senseless.

The courthouse, for God's sake.

Like all acts of terror, it was meant to intimidate people into submission. It was just plain *evil*, that one man could do that to another.

The legislature had authorized the sale of more state bonds, but who in his right mind would buy state bonds? The Yankees had taken Memphis, Vicksburg, New Orleans – indeed, the entire Mississippi River. They'd taken Corinth, and they'd taken Mobile Bay. Sherman's army was bearing down on Atlanta, and General Forrest's efforts to disrupt his rail supplies had been repulsed. Its railroads torn up, its treasury empty, its plantations ravaged,

Mississippi was on the verge of collapse. Men of fighting age were taking jobs as constables and sheriff's deputies, exempting themselves from military service.

In the face of such setbacks, it was hard to see a path that led to success. There'd long been talk of making peace. There'd even been talk of surrender. The only real hope was that Lincoln would lose the election. A less tyrannical man, like George McClellan, might yet agree to the preservation of slavery. Jeff Davis had vowed to fight to the death for a free South. Al Cansler and Jim Murdock were lining up behind Howard Falconer to form an underground, continuing the fight regardless of what happened in November, regardless of what the army did, regardless of the fate of the government. You could see it in the granite eyes of the figures milling about among the ruins: the eyes of men who'd committed themselves, men whose identities lay in being resolute. Eventually, they said, the Yankees would have to give up; Mississippi would have to be free. God himself had given the land to this people. The war could only be truly lost if they gave up their faith, gave up their conviction that theirs was the cause of righteousness.

Amzi looked up from the ashes. His gaze settled northward, toward Virginia, where the Vindicators were carrying on the fight. Though scarred for life from jaw to chest, Alemeth was still offering his life against evil. His courage was something a man couldn't help but admire. Maybe he'd done a good job with the boy after all. If nothing else, Alemeth understood there was something more important than himself. Understood his call to duty. Understood what it meant to stand up for what was good, and just, and right.

Abraham had been willing to sacrifice his son. Would it be right for him, Amzi Walton Byers, to do any less, if God so willed it?

124

On the 15th of September, the 17th left Winchester on the Valley Pike. At Middletown, they crossed the Blue Ridge into the Luray Valley. As the regiment made camp, Alemeth left in search of something to eat. Reaching the banks of the Shenandoah, he found a small farm where a stranger let him fill his canteen with milk and the bottom of his mess kit with preserves. Two more miles upriver he was given all the pie and butter he could carry. A mile farther, he was given peaches. The food and sympathy warmed his heart.

Lou was right. There wasn't anything as important as family. He'd do anything to protect them from Yankees. Medora. Laura. Walton. Eddie. Little Dudie. Pa. He wished he had photographs of all of them. As he passed through the woods on his way back to camp, he saw them on the roadside, on the porch, in the doorway of Sand Springs Church. He tried clinging to the images, but couldn't maintain stable pictures of faces, their images dissolving into a resurgent fog. The disappearances made him want them all the more. But he was beginning to understand the nature of obedience. It required self-denial. It didn't matter what he wanted. He was prepared for the future, whatever it might bring.

That night in camp, Alemeth told Gordon he was ready to die for his family, if need be.

"For *any* family?" Gordon asked.

Despite his resistance, Eliza had taught him about Faith. "Yeah. I think so."

"Well, what about Gilbert, then?"

"Well. Gilbert isn't *really* family."

"Are you so sure? Don't you recall the Latin word *familia?*"

"Sure. The Latin word for *family.*"

"Yes, but remember Reverend Vrooman's point about it? The *familia*, originally, were the household *slaves*. A *famulus* was a slave. "

"You're saying the 'family' got named after *them?*"

"Exactly. They've been 'family' even longer than we have. So if you're going to say your family's all important, you need to be able to say who is, and who isn't, family. And that includes your slaves, Byers. Be careful about getting into a rut. It's not enough to claim freedom; you have to practice it."

Easy enough for Gordon to say. Gilbert didn't belong to *him*. But that's the way Gordon was, he thought: always a dreamer, always refusing to accept things as they really were.

"I hope you're not getting soft on the cause," Alemeth said.

"No. I've always believed. I just know that we could all be wrong."

Leaving the camp in Luray, the 17th marched back and forth through the mountains, to Thornton's Gap, to Woodville, to Culpepper, to the Rapidan, to Gordonsville, to Stanardsville, to Brown's Gap, to Port Republic, to Waynesborough. Then came word that Phil Sheridan's Yankees had been burning the Shenandoah Valley. The Confederate Army had been dancing with the enemy for weeks, their presence veiled by the mountains, matching the Yankees move by move, waiting for the right chance for an advantage – and all the while, Sheridan had been leaving crops blackened and charred.

When the Yankees withdrew northward, the Confederates entered the wasteland they left behind. In the morning, with the red and gold of the trees hidden in a world full of smoke, scorched fields were all they could see. And as the men moved north down the macadamized Pike, past razed barns and crop stalks bent and black, Alemeth dreamed of striking back for the south and for God. In his mind's eye, he saw acres of white cotton, and Bynum's Creek warm and familiar, where there'd always been a crop at harvest time. He saw Mary Jane, and Pa, and Lou. But in the midst of memory was fire and smoke. Bynum's Creek had been ravaged as well. The burning had charred his heart, and the Yankees deserved no mercy.   He would do what he could to hold them accountable – give his life, if need be, toward that end.

On the 6th, the Seventeenth marched to New Market. The day was clear and warm, the road dry and dusty. Aching ankles, calloused feet, blisters, worn out shoes: weeks of marching had taken their toll. But at last, at New Market, they made camp. The next day brought a crisp, warm beauty. There were no orders for more marching. Alemeth began a letter home.

Oct 7th/'64

Dear Sister,

I will try and give you an account of our tramps and marches. The 15th, we left Winchester and marched out on the Staunton pike. On the 16th we crossed two branches of the river, and passed through a narrow gap in the mountains which brought us into what is called Luray Valley, a kind of basin in the Blue Ridge. We camped at the foot of a mountain near a little creek.

I left the regiment before it got to camp & took a ramble in the mountain for something to eat. After rambling for some time from place to place, without any success, I turned to right and went across the mountain and soon found myself again on the bank of the Shenandoah. Here I found some little farms. The first place I went to I got a canteen full of milk, and the bottom part of my mess can filled with preserves, but could get nothing more there. I went about two miles up the river to a house where there was a butter boiling going on, and preparations were being made for a frolic that night. I think there were seven girls at this place. Two or three of them were dressed up as fine as hard times and a back woods life would admit of, and entertaining some straggling soldiers that had got there ahead of me. One was weaving, and one was baking pies, and one was stirring apple butter, and another was feeding a sugar mill, while the old man was driving the horse around. The old lady of all was sitting in a corner, knitting. Here I got pies and milk as much as I could eat and the top part of my mess can full of apple butter. I went a mile farther up the river, and got my haversack full of peaches. The sun by this time was getting low. I started across the mountain, again for camp, and got there, a little after dark.

The 17 we marched to Thornton's gap. On the 18 we crossed the mountain and camped at Woodville. The 19 we went to Culpepper and from there to Gordonsville, Stanardsville, Port Republic and Waynesborough. On the 5th of October, marched to Harrisonburg. The yanks retreated before us and burned wheat stacks, barns and houses on the way. It seemed as if the whole world was full of smoke…

Alemeth put down his pen, wondering if he could write what he was thinking. Bill Elliot was standing over him, saying the slaves in Gilbert's unit had been released from duty. He put the letter, unfinished, into his haversack, and got up to fetch his servant.

On the way back from the negro camp, Alemeth told Gilbert he was a good boy: he wanted only the best for him. "You'll always be important to me, Gilbert. You're a part of my family, I suppose."

"That bein' the case, Mas' Alemeth, then could I buy my freedom?"

Alemeth had no answer.

"Here." Gilbert held out the medallion he'd won back from Gordon. "Your lucky medal. I'll give it back to you – for my freedom."

He'd imagined he might give Gilbert freedom when he died, or when he was a grown man. It was a custom among some to reward a slave for faithful service, through one's last will. But he'd never thought of doing it *soon*. Even he had waited until he was twenty-one for emancipation. Gilbert was just a boy. Alemeth wasn't sure how much he understood the responsibility that freedom involved. What would Gilbert do with his freedom, if he got it? Leave camp in the middle of a campaign?

Besides, Gilbert had earned less than a hundred dollars, and he was worth more than that.

"Gilbert, you're worth a lot more than that silly Catholic icon."

"You could lend me the money. I would pay you back."

Thinking of Gilbert's poker play, Alemeth wondered if he'd be able to.

"Forget it, Gilbert. You need to learn to be patient. Your day will come. I promise you that."

"Much obliged," Gilbert said, with a little bow. His thanks seemed genuine. He was a good boy. Alemeth liked him a lot.

"Say, Gilbert. How about seeing if you could find us something to eat?"

"Yes, suh."

*   *   *

On the 6th of October, the Seventeenth marched to New Market. On the 12th, to Mount Jackson, and on the 13th to Strasburg. Not until there did Alemeth find time to complete the letter home. When he finished it and handed it to Gilbert to mail, Gilbert held out the Saint Christopher medal in return.

"Here," he said. "You need this more'n I do."

"No, you keep it. It'll be a token of my promise to you. To do right by you. For all your help to me."

"No, Mas' Alemeth. I need you to have it. For me."

You could never be sure what a medal might do. It had saved his life once. He held out his hand, and Gilbert let the medal fall into it.

"Thanks. Now, it'll be nine soon. It's time we get you back to camp."

*   *   *

Alemeth lay awake for what felt like hours, watching flickers of light dance across the tent, imagining what Gilbert would make of himself when he was finally given his freedom. What Gordon had said kept coming back to him. Gilbert was his *famulus*. And he wondered, what if he were to die on the battlefield tomorrow? Who, then, would the boy belong to? He couldn't see leaving him to Pa, or Walton, or Lou. If he were to die, Gilbert ought to be free. In the morning, he'd make that clear. When he got home, he'd make a will, and make it his bequest. Or maybe he should give Gilbert his freedom now, when Gilbert was still young. But then, what would he do if he lived, and needed the boy?

He was still mulling it over in the wee hours, when he finally fell asleep.

He woke up. Bill Elliot was shaking him, and shaking Gordon next to him. Elliot word from Captain Wright: they were moving out.

"Be ready to move in half an hour. Wear black buttons. No tin cups. No shiny objects that could give us away."

As he sat up and began to dress, he considered the medal. The Saint Christopher was shiny. How could it bring him any luck, hidden away in his haversack?

The silver watch Colonel Brown had given him was shiny too. Aside from his camera equipment, the watch was the most valuable thing he owned. He wondered if, leaving these objects behind, they too would disappear, as the camera had. He rolled the watch and the medal in a handkerchief together, put them deep in the bottom of a sack, and left the whole package in his bedroll. Gordon was waiting for him. They walked out of their tent, into the fog together.

There were all sorts of reasons the Yankees would be surprised. The northerners had beaten them at Winchester, at Fisher's Hill, at Tom's Brook. They'd seen the effect of the burning on the Valley farms. They had to know the rebels were tired, weak, and ill-nourished. They would be confident. And as Captain Wright said, that very confidence would make them vulnerable.

Through the foggy night, the Vindicators could see the lights of campfires on the crest of the hill. Wading across Cedar Creek, the cold water up to their hips, trousers and boots wet, they climbed up the hill, Gordon on one side, Peter on the other, moving the way they'd trained for movement at night. As Alemeth lost sight of Gordon in the thick pre-dawn, as he caught glimpses of Calvin and Peter, he imagined ending up in the Yankee camp alone.

A couple hundred yards out, Captain Wright gave the signal to attack. With a shrill yell, they charged into the night, falling on the Yankee camp as if leaping from the limbs of trees, using the embers to guide their descent, firing into tents of terror-stricken Yankees, grabbing abandoned rifles, seeing Yankees hop and stumble in bedrolls like one-legged men, most not taking the time to grab their guns before they were gone in the darkness and the fog, and Alemeth shooting at every one, every squeeze of his trigger sending thrills through his veins.

There was an order to pursue. For the next two hours, the Vindicators did so, advancing over the ridge, through woodlands, fenced farms and the Valley beyond, firing at backs they hoped were not their comrades. The surprise had worked. With the Yankees in full rout, their panic spreading across the Valley Pike, Gordon and Alemeth let out shrieks of rebel yell designed to impart terror, but the shrieks were helplessly mixed with cries of joy. And as the day emerged from the pre-dawn fog, the Yankees' disarray evident, Alemeth and Gordon were euphoric. By mid-morning, the enemy had abandoned their headquarters farmhouse and fled still farther down the valley.

The boys had been up most of the night. They were cold and still wet. They'd been in combat for ten straight hours, and some of them needed a rest. When Captain Wright announced orders to hold their position, they warmed themselves over the Yankee fires. Some got out of their wet clothes. There was bacon and salt pork, already cooked for a Yankee breakfast, just sitting there, waiting for rebel mouths. Abandoned equipment and personal belongings were everywhere.

Alemeth and Gordon had survived. It didn't matter anymore what was shiny and what was not. They moved from bacon to copper, brass and silver. Alemeth pocketed a two dollar gold piece. Then Peter Brown said, "Private Byers, Private Falkner: come with me."

They stood, of course, but Alemeth also had a question.

"Where're we going?"

Peter tossed his jaw, motioning over his shoulder in the direction the yankees had run. "I thought we'd go do a little reconnoitering. That's all."

Orders were to stay put. Whatever Peter had in mind, it was his own doing. But Gordon said, "Let's go." Peter had already started off in the direction of the Yankee line. Excited by their success, flush with the conviction their cause was righteous, Alemeth saw little reason not to follow.

"Where are we going, Sergeant?"

"We're going to get ourselves some Yankees for breakfast, Byers. You okay with that?"

"Damn straight I am."

125

Eliza sat on the porch, looking out toward the cotton house. She'd written hard letters before – to Aunt Harriet; to Henry Hitchcock; to Julia, after William died. But this time, after writing *Dear Alemeth*, her pen lay idle on the paper.

She'd decided to write because Alemeth needed encouragement: news from home to keep him from feeling alone. But how could she encourage him when she was so discouraged herself? Even Scripture seemed silent this particular afternoon.

Amzi was at the cotton house; he was *always* at the cotton house; he said he had to be, at harvest time. But she knew it wasn't so. The words didn't ring true. It was as if he didn't want to be with her, as if he wanted to be alone with his spittoon and his flask of whiskey (— oh, yes, she knew he still used them; she knew his promise to give them up meant nothing.) How could she be a source of comfort to Alemeth when she felt no warmth from Amzi, for herself? Amzi was angry at Grote for abandoning Bynum's Creek, angry at Uncle Johnson for paying his negroes even if they were only confederate notes no one else would take. He was angry at anyone who disagreed with him, angry when she tried to make helpful suggestions. Sometimes, when his anger wasn't raging, he stared blankly at the emptiness before answering the simplest questions.

I'm worried about your Pa, she wrote.

She stared at the words. She could see Alemeth in a trench somewhere, thirsty for water. She scratched them out. She crumpled the paper and dropped it onto the porch beside her. She wrote *Dear Alemeth* on another sheet. Alemeth had his own concerns; she'd be wrong to add Pa to his worries.

But what news?

Grote took off, she wrote. *And several others too.*

She paused and tried again to think of something positive before continuing.

Aunt Leety might soon be the only one left. The other day, Pa said I shouldn't feel too sure about her, but I think he's wrong. Leety will still be here when you come home, I'm sure. But your Pa is determined to make things work without any of them, if he has to. If anyone can, he can, I know, but please pray for him.

Alemeth's prayers could help.

But was it good for the boy to worry about Amzi? Did it help take his mind off his own troubles, to think of his father's? Or did it simply add weight to his burden? She took a corner of the page, as if to start crumpling again, then stopped.

I can scarcely express myself these days.

She could write about Dora, and Walton, and Eddy, but the truth was, they were little better off than Amzi. Their father's mood had gotten to them all. How many times had she told them not to complain? That they were lucky to have a roof over their heads? She could write that she'd been busy keeping house. That they scarcely had anything to eat, and no meat for a week.

About the photograph you took of Laura and Dudie: I've put it in Dudie's baby things. Laura thinks she looks awful in it.

But what did Alemeth care about that? If she was going to be honest, she had to share her own troubles.

Despite trial after trial, we are all healthy here. I ought not dwell upon our difficulties, when you have your own, I know – but if I ought to share news, as you want, I'm obliged to say there's right little of importance that isn't a difficulty of some sort or other. Do you still have the Bible I gave you? I read mine right often. I hope you're reading yours.

She stopped there. Alemeth got annoyed when she mentioned Scripture. The last thing she wanted was to annoy him. But what could she write that would bring joy to the young man? Reflecting, she remembered a sermon Uncle William had given on Habakkuk. In the darkest hour, God was more important than ever. She knew she needed the hope that faith could bring. She knew Amzi needed it. She knew Alemeth needed it too, whether he liked it or not. So she found the verses she remembered, and copied them into her letter.

Although the fig tree shall not blossom,
Neither shall fruit be in the vines;
The labor of the olive shall fail,
And the fields shall yield no meat;
The flock shall be cut off from the fold,
And there shall be no herd in the stalls.

Yet will I rejoice in the Lord.
I will joy in the God of my salvation.
The Lord God is my strength,
And he will make my feet like hinds' feet,
And he will make me to walk upon mine high places.

When she had finished, she gave the letter to Amzi to mail.

Amzi rode into town with it, and once there, he inquired whether there was any incoming mail.

October 24th, 1864

A. J. Byers, Esq
Water Valley P.O.
Mississippi Central Railroad

Colonel Byers:
    I have chosen this hour for the purpose of informing you of the death of your son, A. J. Byers, who was killed in the battle on the 19th inst, near Strasburg, Virginia. He was shot through the heart and died instantly. I don't suppose he ever spoke after he was shot. There was no one of the company near him at the time but found him a short time afterwards.

    We got his pocket book and what money he had besides other articles of clothing and will send everything with Gilbert as soon as the opportunity presents itself.

    His loss is very much felt by every member of his company. He was a friend that I highly prized. He had never gave me any trouble, always being at his post of duty, and I humbly trust he has found a home in Heaven. He had been quite a moral man. I don't think he ever swore any at all and think he had become very much devoted to Christ. I trust God will comfort the hearts of you and your bereaved family and friends. Almuth has always acted very gallantly on every field and has shown to the world that his whole soul was in the cause.

    When we first attacked the enemy they were completely surprised and routed. We drove them six miles, captured their encampment with everything they had, eighteen pieces of artillery among the rest, but late in the afternoon the federals attacked our lines and the Divisions on our right and left gave way and fell back in confusion, and of course our Division followed, but my Brigade rallied behind a rock fence and checked the whole army, and I did hope that we would retrieve the fortunes of the day, but soon the enemy flanked us and we left the whole ground in the hands of the enemy with the loss of 12 pieces of artillery, a few wagons and some prisoners. Our loss was very light. We captured twelve thousand prisoners and brought them off safe.

    There is something due Almuth by the Government which I will collect if you will forward me the power of Attorney. My kind regards to your family. If I can do anything for you I will be happy to serve you.

                        Very respectfully,
                        Jesse. C. Wright, Captain, Co. H
                        Camp 17th Mississippi Regiment
                        New Market, Virginia

Outside the post office, Amzi let the letter drop to his side, overcome with memories of Alemeth, memories of things he'd imagined, things that, now, would never come to pass. Alemeth's pride at catching his first fish, his encounters with poison ivy, his troubles with Leander McKinney. Alemeth was supposed to inherit the land. He'd been everything the future promised, everything for which it existed. Now, none of it would ever come to be. Amzi stood on the corner, motionless, blind to the leaves that fell from the trees around him.

When he came to, he went to the cotton house. He couldn't be with Eliza now. Couldn't say anything to her, not yet. What could he say to her? What could he say to Semmy Lou? To Walton? He had to be alone. To shut out everything trying to rain down on him, everything that shed light on what the letter had said, on the unspeakable future it foretold. He had to crawl into a private place.

Inside the cotton house, Harriet and Mary sat on separate benches, picking out motes. He said nothing to them. He spit a plug into his spittoon. He bit off another.

I insisted he return to the front, he thought. *I am responsible.*

He stood up, as if in a hurry to be somewhere else. He turned around. He sat back down again.

Alemeth, can you ever forgive me?

He looked down at the floor, summoning strength, holding back tears. He had given Alemeth his rifle. He had encouraged him to enlist. Back at home with scars from his jaw to his chest, he'd sent him back to the front again, hundreds of miles away, into the jaws of death.

But what was he blaming *himself* for? Had it not been God who'd taken him? It was God who'd let it happen. It was God who – no. He stopped himself. God was not to blame. Responsibility lay on Yankee shoulders. *They* had taken down Alemeth, same as they'd taken his plantation, same as they'd taken his cotton, same as they'd taken his negroes. It was the Yankees who'd destroyed the life he'd been trying to build. It was Captain Powell who tried to steal his livelihood, and now had stolen his son. Tyrants. *Murderers.* He might live another twenty, thirty years, but if he lived for another five hundred, he would *never* forgive them.

Alemeth's service had been so right. God must have had his reasons. But it was plain that he was no Abraham. There was no angel explaining he'd been misled, as a test of his devotion. He'd gone the whole way. He'd done exactly what God wanted. And yet, now, despite everything he'd done, and everything he'd tried to do, everything he'd given, everything he'd sacrificed for what was good and right, Alemeth was dead.

"Devoted to Christ," the letter had said. It didn't matter if it was true. Captain Wright had done the right thing by saying it; it would make it easier to break the news to Eliza and Lou.

*   *   *

Eliza's tears began as soon as she started reading. She had to stop. She started anew, but quickly had to stop again. She leaned forward. She put her hand on the table, trying in vain to support the weight of her grief. "No!" she cried out. "No! Lord help us. God – say it isn't so!"

She cried, and lifted the letter again, and read a few words more between a flood of tears, wiping her eyes. Then she put the letter in her lap, and closed her eyes, and prayed.

It was several minutes before she raised her head again. Holding back her tears, she was able to finish the letter.

"He says he thinks Alemeth was devoted to Christ," she said when she'd stopped. "I wonder, Amzi. Do you think he was saved?"

"I don't know, Eliza. He sure wasn't saved for use here."

"Well. Of course. But we have to accept that the Lord had a reason for taking him. Don't we? Accept that the Lord's will has been done? "

Amzi didn't answer.

"What is hope, Amzi, if not trust in the goodness of God?"

Still, he didn't answer.

"Amzi, the only thing that really matters is whether Alemeth is in heaven, no? Gilbert will be back soon; we can ask *him* if Alemeth finally found Faith."

After the service at Sand Springs, Eliza gathered the family for prayer. Lou, Medora, Laura, Walton, Eddy, even Dudie sat around, all contributing to the tears as Eliza spoke of the divine reward for Faith in the one true Lord.

Eddie asked when Gilbert would be back. Eliza hesitated. At length, as if to convince herself it was true, she said, "I'm sure he's already on his way home."

126

Phil Sheridan's defeat of Jubal Early at Cedar Creek was the final action the 17th Mississippi Regiment would see in the war. Within the next six months, Lee had surrendered at Appomattox. Lincoln had been shot. Mississippi's declaration of independence had proven illusory. A state was *not* free, *could* not be free of its union with other states. By force of arms, Lincoln had demonstrated northern authority. The south saw no alternative to submission. As a condition of re-entry into the Union, the citizens of rebellious states were required to take loyalty oaths. They had to adopt new constitutions that outlawed slavery forever. Never again could a state doubt the supremacy of the Union. Every citizen owed a duty of obedience to it. It wasn't pretty, but Lincoln had preserved The Union. All that remained was the elimination of slavery, in all the states, and in all of its forms.

Amzi Byers, sixty-three years old when the war came to an end, was left to put the pieces of his plantation back together again. But he had to do so without most of his negroes (who had gone north) and, more importantly, without the cash he'd need to pay those who remained. He imagined spring plantings to come: would he have to yoke the plow to himself, in complete subjugation? In search of a way out, he wondered if Irishmen might meet his labor needs He wrote to the war veteran, James Loughborough – Mary Ann Webster's husband – seeking his advice about whether Irish labor could be found in St. Louis.

Having ended the war with his honor and health intact, Loughborough was working as a railroad agent and buying cheap real estate. His reply informed Byers that "the Irish generally are gregarious in their natures, and require to be looked after by someone to whom they are accustomed." It was a trait that would necessitate employment of an overseer, and even then, the Irish couldn't be counted on. All things considered, it just wasn't feasible.

"All the elections have gone Radical," Loughborough wrote, "and we are drifting with the current, to what God alone knows… There are many texts of scripture we can apply, and from them gain comfort: unless we are much deceived in the signs of the times, we will have exceeding great need of comfort in the future."

As Amzi was distressed about the loss of his field hands, Eliza was distressed about the loss of her household servants. As the war wound down, Mary Ann Loughborough had loaned her negro, Cinth, to Eliza, but even Cinth had not stayed on. On the twenty-third of January, 1867, Eliza wrote to her daughter Dora, complaining that she was working harder than ever before:

My dear, *very* dear *Child,*
    ... I have no news of much interest to write. My time from morning until night is taken up in keeping house. I feel as if I was fairly into the business, for the first time in my life. I had such a good honest cook last year, and Cinth in the house, that I scarcely missed my old house servants, but now I have no one but Jane and Puss and a very dishonest *and indolent cook, neither has she any management at all to get through with her work, so I am obliged to follow after her getting out* everything *for each meal and do all the planning besides, and of course I have all this to see after in the house, besides, to get it kept in any order at all.*
    I am so wearied when night comes, and still these short days I can find scarcely any time to even fix work, and cut out for Gracy, who is sewing a while for me until crop time, when Dick wants her to help him. It seems to me that I haven't a half hour to sit down without neglecting something, & I have to go right after Jane and Puss to see that their sweeping etc. is half done.
    But I will not worry you with any more of my trials. I ought not to think so much of my own annoyances, when your Pa has so much weightier trials to contend with, which is breaking him down very fast. His disposition you know is so different from mine. If he could cast off care sometimes as I do and feel cheerful and happy. But his spirits want that elasticity with which I am blessed, although mine flag right often these days, and I feel sadly *in need of my dear dear daughter's sympathy and love.*
    I must close. I shall be uneasy if you do not write soon. I want to hear how you enjoyed Christmas week. Good bye.
        Your loving mother. E. S. Byers.

Eliza saw no need to burden Dora with concerns about Alemeth's soul. Captain Wright had said he thought Alemeth was devoted to Christ, but some said sharing such thoughts with grieving families was sympathetic protocol, and no more. Eliza wanted to resolve her doubts, to know for sure whether Alemeth had been saved. She knew, from the thief on the cross, that salvation could come in one's last minutes on earth.   She tried to imagine what Alemeth's last hours.

But when Gilbert returned to Mississippi, he told her he'd been assigned to the supply train; he hadn't seen much of Alemeth at the end; Alemeth never spoke to him about God, and he knew nothing of Alemeth's last hours at Cedar Creek.

Amzi told her to let it rest, that Captain Wright could be trusted, that she had nothing to gain by trying to dig deeper.   But the seed of doubt, once planted, had started to grow. She wrote to Captain Wright, but no sooner had her letter been posted than the war was over, the army disbanded, and her letter lost in a sea of uncertainty.   She tried to locate other Vindicators. George Foote, Tom Bradford and Kale Bryant were all dead. Others had been dismissed from service, returning to Panola before Cedar Creek. Baxter Orr had served in a different regiment. The few Vindicators Eliza was able to reach offered general assurances of the sort she didn't trust, or said they didn't recall Alemeth saying anything about Christ. None knew of Alemeth's last hours.

Gilbert and others suggested she talk to Gordon Falkner, as Gordon had been Alemeth's tent-mate. All she had to do was find Gordon, and all her doubts would be resolved, one way or the other. So Eliza's search for Alemeth's final hours became a search for Gordon Falkner.

But her search for Gordon Falkner went no better. No matter what she did, she couldn't find Gordon. Mount Sylvan had closed, Reverend Vrooman was dead. Lou recalled that Gordon had come from Ripley, but none of the Falkners of that place knew anything about him. Eliza asked Colonel Brown for whatever information the University's records might have, but to Eliza's amazement, the Colonel said he didn't remember him, and the University had no record of his attendance. It was as if Gordon had been swallowed up by the past he so loved.

Gordon had worked for Howard Falconer at *The Intelligencer*, so Eliza contacted Howard, who was starting a law career and publishing a paper in Marshall County. Howard was a tireless investigator; if anyone could find Gordon, it would be Howard. But Howard fared no better. After Gordon went off with Alemeth in October of 1864, neither had been heard from again.

Howard's advice to Eliza was like Amzi's: she should simply accept what

Captain Wright had said. As for Alemeth's last hours, Captain Wright had said it all: no one had been with him when he was killed, but he'd been shot through the heart. He'd died instantly, without uttering a word. There was nothing more to be said. There was nothing more to know.

So life went on, Eliza trapped inside the confines of doubt as to Alemeth's salvation.

As for the former slaves of Bynum's Creek, most of them took the last name of Byers (a.k.a. Byars, or Barrs) as was the custom – and all of them quickly discovered what it meant for them to be free. On October 8, 1867, a former slave named Louis Barrs complained to the Freedman's Bureau that two white men had come to his house in the middle of the night pretending to have orders from civil authorities to search his house. They took his pistol (a revolver) and ammo. One of the men threatened to shoot Barrs's wife.

A year later, agent James Pierce of the Freedman's Bureau office in Panola wrote to his superior in Vicksburg:

"I find many well-disposed citizens who express a desire to see the freed population prosper, and who, by good advice, assist them in getting along," he wrote. "But there are others, and they are the source of numerous complaints, who desire to see them remain in a state of extreme poverty or dependence, who, by their superiority of attainment, seize every opportunity to cheat and defraud them of their scanty earnings.... In the southeast part of this county, in the last two months, five murders have been committed on freedmen and several instances have occurred where freedmen, through fear (whether well grounded, or not, I cannot say), have left their crops and came away from that part of the county."

Pierce wrote again on the ninth, describing a murder on land that belonged to one A. P. Cansler of Long Creek. The murdered man, a sharecropper named Godfrey, had left the field in which his hands had been picking cotton, taking with him a single barrel shotgun, saying he was going to hunt turkeys. Soon after Godfrey left, and again some thirty minutes later, his shot was heard. It seemed he had found his game on Cansler's land. But then, after another half an hour, three more shots were heard, these in quick succession, and the following day, Godfrey's body was found, fourteen buckshot in his right side and some more in his head, above the left eye. The murdered man's gun was lying at his feet, still loaded with shot.

Pierce reported that "no person was seen on that day passing through the neighborhood; and I could get no clue to the perpetrator of the foul deed."

Two months later, Pierce wrote again, this time of an organization known as the Ku Klux Klan.

"About one night in every week, the Ku Klux assemble, in numbers varying from ten to fifty, and go through the country, whipping, robbing, and sometimes killing freedmen."

Pierce described how three white men had entered the home of a former slave named Allen, fired their pistols in his house, and robbed him. After Allen complained to the Freedman's Bureau, a white man named Murdock – who'd been identified by Allen as one of the three who'd robbed him – went back to Allen's house, and in the presence of a justice of the peace, "drew his revolver and stated that if he (Allen) went before the jury and swore to anything against him, he would kill him on sight....

"The evidence that this man Murdock is a member if not the leader of the Klan is indisputable. Nearly a dozen witnesses – persons whipped and robbed by him – can be brought to prove the fact."

But the records of the Freedman's Bureau reflect no further action in the case of the man named Murdock.

As the Klan brought terror to the freedmen, Amzi found himself chained to a failing plantation. In 1868, after three years of struggle, he began to break it into smaller parcels, selling some to Lou and her husband, some to strangers, until the plantation was a fraction of what it once had been. Meanwhile, many of those loyal to the south were prohibited from running for office. On November 3, 1874, the Republicans won a major victory in the elections, effectively taking over the government of Mississippi. Two days later, a letter from Dudie Byers to her mother Eliza referred to "Poor Papa." The following year, a group of whites known as Red Shirts threatened any blacks who dared to vote; their campaign of terror helped the Democrats take back the government again.

Walton Byers – next in age to Alemeth, next in line to take over what was left of Bynum's Creek – had been eleven years old when the war began. He'd never dreamed of running a vast plantation with scores of field hands working the land. He'd never dreamed of a prosperous future. He'd only felt grief at the loss of a brother he'd always looked up to, seen despair at the loss of Bynum's Creek, the anguish of his mother and father. The letter from Captain Wright, informing the family of Alemeth's death, had arrived just days after Walton's fifteenth birthday. Voices of vengeance against the north had filled his world; he'd have been a giant of a man to resist them. If those voices ever ceased their pleas, they could have left nothing but resentment in their wake. In any case, it's easy to imagine that the suffering of Bynum's Creek's freedmen was not his greatest concern.

How and when Walton met his wife is not known. Jennie Harper had been born and raised thirty miles north, in Marshall County, where Howard Falconer was practicing law and running another paper. Whether it was Howard who introduced Walton to Jenny, or Walton's courtship of Jenny that brought the men together, has been lost on the passage of time, but Walton did spend time with Howard during his courtship, and in May of 1877, when Walton and Jenny were married in Holly Springs, Howard Falconer was there.

During their times together, the two men talked of Alemeth's days at the Intelligencer, and of his last days in Virginia. They talked of Gordon as well, Alemeth's tent-mate and the last man, by all accounts, to see Alemeth alive. Howard said he missed his old nemesis in debate about fiction and fact, but that he'd met a fitting end, lost in a foggy end that could never be known.

For their parts, the newlyweds thought nearly as much of Howard – champion of history, defender of fact, passionate advocate for the southern cause – as they did of each other. How else to explain the fact that when their first child was born in July of 1878, Walton and Jenny named him Howard Falconer Byers? Howard was a survivor. It made sense to name the child for the injured war veteran, the lawyer, the member of the Mississippi House, who stood up for what he believed.

Once the child had been christened, the new parents must have looked forward to their next visit to Holly Springs, when they'd be able to share the honor done with Howard.

But even as the child had been growing in Jennie's womb, a different form of life had come to Mississippi. When the steamer *Emily B. Souder* pulled into New Orleans on the 23rd of May and moored at the foot of Calliope Street, the ship's purser, a man named Clarke, was ill. He boasted that he'd "beaten" the quarantine doctor by being allowed to disembark despite a slight neuralgia. Over the next two days, in the capital of decadence and depravity, Clarke's headache turned feverish; he had a severe pain in his loins; he urinated green, then suffered convulsions and delirium; within two days, he was dead.

Meanwhile, an engineer on the same ship, one Thomas Elliot, died on the 29th, a few blocks away. An autopsy performed on the 30th included examination of body tissue. The microscope used wasn't powerful enough to discover the cause of the disease, but successfully confirmed its manifestations. The mucous surface of the stomach was reddened and softened, with appearances of dark, grumous fluid contents. The kidneys had the appearance of severe congestion, and the liver was of a light yellowish hue.

The public health authorities determined that the disease was caused by germs brought to life in hot weather, not moving through the atmosphere above the ground, but "capable both of spontaneous locomotion along the ground and other surfaces, and of transportation in the clothing of persons..." The authorities' conclusion was that the death had been caused by "wingless *animalcula.*" They took immediate precautions as best they knew how: sprinkling the streets with carbolic acid and spreading sulphur fumes indoors.

But despite the efforts of the experts, the *animalcula* continued their deadly crawl through city streets, ship's quarters and sailors' clothes, heading northward, up the Mississippi River. Within weeks, the *animalcula* were causing sickness in Vicksburg and Memphis, delirious death the all too frequent end. In August, a hundred cases of the epidemic were reported in Grenada, Mississippi, and by the first of September, the disease had reached Holly Springs.

Walton wanted to speak of the honor he'd done Howard, by naming his son after him. But when Walton visited Howard in early September of 1878, he was taken aback by Howard's reaction.

Howard thanked him for the honor, but quickly changed the subject. He' had finally found Gordon, he said. In fact, Gordon had come to Holly Springs, to visit him.

"You may remember how Gordon was," said the newspaper man. "Fascinated by the impossible. Told me of Scylla's six heads. Polyphemus and his one eye. Birds with faces like women. He was making no sense. I told him he was crazy. You know what he told me?"

"What?" asked Walton.

"'I can imagine they're real' he said. 'If not today, in the past, or in the future. And if I write about them, I make them real.'"

"I see," said Walton.

Howard wiped his brown with a wet cloth. "Excuse me," he said. "I've not been feeling well. But it was all nonsense. History, science – there's hard evidence for some things. Don't let Gordon fill your head with nonsense."

"I don't imagine he will. I haven't seen Gordon in years."

"Good. You're a good man, Alemeth."

"Alemeth?"

"Yes, Alemeth. You agree with me, don't you?"

"What?"

"You told me, when you came with Gordon. You know I'm right."

"What are you talking about, Howard?"

"Last week. You know."

"Howard, Alemeth died – a long time ago. In the war."

Howard cocked his head, giving looking befuddled. Then, grimacing, he put his hands to his loins.

"I'm really not feeling well," he said. "I think you'd better go."

By all accounts, the *animalcula* took Howard three days later. Gordon and Alemeth were never heard from again.

אלמת

Postscript

It's easy to recognize the names ancestors pass down to us. (My great grandmother, Julia ("Dudie") Byers, named my grandfather William Loughborough, after James Loughborough; his daughters – my Aunt Ellie and Aunt Mary Anna – were sisters to my mother, Julia.) It's harder to see the other things our ancestors pass down to us – strands of culture and belief so familiar, so taken for granted, that we can't recognize how much they shape who we are.

As a young northern white boy, I was taught that slavery was a thing of the past; that I could condemn it, safely and righteously, as the cruelty of other generations, regions and cultures. I eventually learned about my distant ancestors who'd once owned African slaves, but the evil, having been discovered and condemned, did not point a finger at *me*. The sins of my people offended me, but they were *their* sins, not mine.

Or so I once thought. As time passed, I came to question that belief. Verging on old age, I've begun to understand how similar I am to those who came before, as if time has been cleaning a lens and I can finally see my people, my family, in myself. Among other things, I've discovered vestiges of racism in my own unconscious habits. And I keep stumbling into evidence of that most distasteful personal trait – the ease with which I can condemn the sins of others while unable to see the wrong in myself.

Many of the people depicted in *Alemeth* are my maternal ancestors. In writing this work of fiction, I have tried not so much to create a story as to discover whatever story my ancestral research revealed. That has required portraying not only the characters' wrongs, but their justifications, rationalizations and lack of self-awareness. I have also tried to write about the larger family to which I belong – and it hasn't always been pretty.

The fact is, while not given at Sand Springs on Christmas eve of 1856, the sermon in Chapter 59 was given at the First Presbyterian Church in New Orleans four years later, and Howard Falconer printed it in the *Oxford Intelligencer* on December 12, 1860. The fact is, Howard wrote the strident words ascribed to him on pages 232 and 236. The fact is, while many Christian churches opposed slavery, there were many that argued for its perpetuation as well. Though the trial testimony presented here is imagined, the manslaughter conviction of George Washington Oliver for the killing of his slave, John, was in fact overturned by the Supreme Court of Mississippi, as described in Chapter 86. The fact is, our national heroes, Thomas Jefferson and George Washington, wrote the offensive, racist words ascribed to them on page 94. The fact is, John Alemeth Byers, like nearly all the characters in this work, were real people, and Alemeth (along with tens of thousands of other Americans) gave his life in the effort to preserve slavery. The fact is, though we now understand the horrific injustice of that institution, hundreds of thousands of Americans believed that God had created it, their beloved Holy Scripture endorsed it, and their duty as "civilized Christians" was to defend and preserve it. Incredibly, they did all this in the name of freedom.

Such discoveries have led me to ask two questions: First, how could *so* many people be *so* wrong? And second, how can even a large group of people be so certain of their beliefs as to seek to impose those beliefs – by various degrees of influence, pressure, and in some cases, force – on others?

As hard as those questions are to answer, I'm also loathe to succumb to an opposite reaction: that of condemning all those who fell prey to the attitudes which supported the horrific institution – as if all of them (unlike you and me) were somehow purely contemptible people, and nothing more. Alemeth Byers asked his sister to "tell Aunt Leety and all the negroes howdy for me." He was concerned enough to ask Amzi to "tell Harriet Gilbert is in good health." In Alemeth's heart and mind, as he perceived it, he *cared for* the people of color around him. And if this was rank self-deception, as I believe it to be, it was the same type of self-deception to which I believe we all fall prey when we rationalize and justify things that serve self-interest.

My mother's family were southern Presbyterians; my father's northern Roman Catholics. I grew up knowing my maternal grandparents to be extremely kind, generous, loving people, one was a church elder, the other a Sunday school teacher. And I knew them to be tolerant people, who went out of their way to see that my brother and I got to our church on Sundays though ours wasn't the same church as theirs. Later in life, as the remnants of my family's racist past became increasingly evident, I found myself asking how such good people could have been blind to such obvious evils as slavery and racism. And the more I researched, the more apparent it became that the defenders of American slavery grounded their views in the Bible.

Five years ago – the year before she died – my mother expressed regret about the religious conflicts that had marked much of her life. She urged me to remember that there are no Catholics or Presbyterians, as far as Jesus is concerned. His was a message of love, she said, pure and simple. And this isn't just about Catholics and Presbyterians, she said. It applies to *everyone*. Baptists, Methodists, Greek Orthodox, *all* people of faith. We're all the same, she said. Religious differences have to be put aside; we *all* need to be more tolerant – and now, more than ever, *so we can defeat the Muslims.*

And so I ask who, among Christians, would acknowledge the role that Scripture has played, and may yet again play, in blinding people to their own wrongs? And who, among all the world's religions, would concede that passionate, self-righteous *faith* – by which I mean *conviction* that one correctly understands the will of God – can lead one to the use of force and, sometimes, inhumane wickedness? And who, among agnostics and atheists, can see that this blindness isn't some special affliction of the world's religious alone, or present only in examples from the past? Doesn't *anyone* who has absolute convictions feel superior to those who see things differently? When people cease to admit the possibility of being wrong, don't they run the risk of losing compassion? Of being no better than those they most despise and condemn?

In his book The Gulag Archipelago, Alexander Solzhenitsyn expressed a wish for an easier world:

> If only there were evil people somewhere insidiously committing evil deeds and it were necessary only to separate them from the rest of us and destroy them. But the line between good and evil cuts through the heart of every human being. And who's willing to destroy a piece of his own heart?

In short, I think of Alemeth as a testament to the one thing I believe all of us share, regardless of our religion or lack of it, regardless of our politics or philosophies, regardless of our different shades of racism: namely, an intrinsic, inescapable, nearly infinite capacity for being wrong. Indeed, it sometimes seems that the more familiar we are with a belief, the more we take it for granted, the more we refuse to question it, and the more likely it is we'll be blind to the error it contains.

I offer up *Alemeth*, then, as a reminder that, no matter how passionately we hold our beliefs, they (and we) may be wrong.

8 November, 2016.

Acknowledgments

I am indebted to my grandmother, Corinne Logan, and to my aunt, Mary Anna Rogers, for preserving so much family history, and most especially the letters of John Strong and John Alemeth Byers. I am indebted to my grandfather's niece, Frances Maginnis, and her daughter, Carol Lehr, for additional letters by Alemeth, for Eliza Strong's autograph book, and for the 1862 ambrotype of John Alemeth Byers.

For my understanding of the history of Oxford Mississippi and Colonel James Brown, I am indebted to many sources, but most especially to the University of Mississippi, for its records of the University's early days and for its extensive newspaper collections on microfiche, including the *Star,* the *Signal,* the *Mercury,* the *Organizer* and the *Intelligencer.* I am indebted to my great grandmother Eliza Byers's niece, Mary Ann Webster Loughborough, for *My Cave Life in Vicksburg*, the book that first introduced me to Oxford, Mississippi, to James Loughborough, and to the Gayoso Hotel. To Barbara and Tommy Ward, I give thanks for their hospitality, understanding and insights into the early Sand Springs Presbyterian church. I'm indebted to Don Doyle, who, through his published work, provided valuable insight into the people of Lafayette County, Mississippi at the time of the civil war.

I also thank my teachers, and especially Paul Czaja, David Coffin, Alan Vrooman, and Fred Tremallo, for their encouragement, decades ago, and I thank my brother David, and James and Lisa, and my wife Karen, and my friend Clint Burr, for their review and suggestions for improvement. I thank Jim Horton, for teaching me about typesetting. Finally, for a thousand subjects of miscellaneous research, my heartfelt thanks go to Wikipedia, Google Books, Ancestry.com, and the U.S. Census Bureau.

The following also provided valuable information:

For various aspects of Mississippi history:

Barnard, F. A. P., *Autobiographical Sketch, 1888,* Publications of the Mississippi Historical Society, Vol. 12, 1912, p. 107.

Board of Trustee Reports and Minutes (MUM00524), The Department of Archives and Special Collections, J.D. Williams Library, The University of Mississippi

Catalogue of the Officers, Alumni & Students of the University of Mississippi, 1860-61, http://www.kemper.msgen.info/schools/catalogue_of_the_officer s.htm)

Chamberg, James, *Premium Essay on the Treatment and Cultivation of Corn* [sic: should be *Cotton*], *The Working Farmer,* Vol. V, p. 151, Frederick McCready, New York, 1853.

Choppin, Samuel, *History of the Importation of Yellow Fever Into the United States, from 1693 to 1878,* Public Health Reports and Papers of the American Public Health Association, Riverside Press, Cambridge, 1880.

Claiborne, John, *Mississippi as a Province, Territory and State, With Biographical Notices of Eminent Citizens,* Power and Barksdale, Jackson, 1880

Commons, John, et al., *A Documentary History of American Industrial Economy: Vol 1, Plantation and Frontier,* Arthur H. Clark Co., Cleveland, 1910.

Conrad, Alfred, and Meyer, John, *The Economics of Slavery in the Ante Bellum South.* The Journal of Political Economy, Vol. 66, No. 2 (1958).

Deed Books in the Courthouses of Panola and Oxford, Mississippi

Doyle, Don, *Faulkner's County, The Historical Roots of Yoknapatawpha,* University of North Carolina Press, 2001

Ezell, Norman L., P.O.Box 186, Duck Hill, MS, *Tragedy at Duck Hill Station: Collision of the James Brown and the A. M. West,* 1990, reproduced by Reba Alsup at http://www.tngenweb.org/benton/tragedyatduckhill.html

Faculty Reports and Minutes, The Department of Archives and Special Collections, J.D. Williams Library, The University of Mississippi

Goodell, William, *The American Slave Code, in Theory and Practice,* American and Foreign Anti-Slavery Society, New York, 1853

Hartshorne, Henry, ed., *How to Make Gun Cotton, The Household Encyclopedia of General Information,* Thomas Kelly, New York, 1881.

Helpful Hints for Steamboat Passengers, 1855, reprint, Explorations in Iowa History Project, University of Northern Iowa, 2003

Hill & Swayze, *Confederate States Rail-Road & Steam-Boat Guide,* Hill & Swayze, Griffin, GA, 1862, Call number 2672.05conf (Rare Book Collection, University of North Carolina at Chapel Hill), Electronic Edition, U. of N. Carolina, 2001, accessed at http://docsouth.unc.edu/imls/swayze/swayze.html

Historical Catalogue of the University of Mississippi, 1849-1909, Marshall & Bruce, Nashville, 1910

King, Calvin and Dorothy, *The Byers*, in *History of Panola County, Mississippi,* Vol 1, Panola County Genealogical and Historical Society, 1987.

Jernegan, Marcus, *Slavery and Conversion in the American Colonies*, The American Historical Review, 1916

Johnson, John W., *Sketches of Judge A. B. Longstreet and Dr. F. A. P. Barnard,* Publications of the Mississippi Historical Society, Vol. 12, 1912, p. 122

Lowry, Robert, and McCardle, William H., *A History of Mississippi,* R. H. Henry & Co, Jackson, MS, 1891.

Lafayette County Heritage, Vol I, Skipwith Historical and Genealogical Society (1986)

Lloyd, James T., *Lloyd's Steamboat Directory and Disasters of the Western Waters*, Cincinnati, Ohio, 1856 accessed at https://play.google.com/books/reader?id=67hEjmDIo4MC&print sec=frontcover&output=reader&authuser=0&hl=en

Mayes, Edward, *History of Education in Mississippi*, Govt. Printing Office, Washington, 1899

Mayfield, Jack Lamar, *Oxford and Ole Miss,* Arcadia Publishing, 2009

Mayfield, Jack Lamar, *University Trustee Col. James Brown and Student Malicious Mischief,* The Oxford Eagle, Nov 12, 2010, page 2B.

Pearson, Charles E. and Birchett, Thomas C., *The History and Archaeology of Two Civil War Steamboats*, Coastal Environments, 2001

Prescott, George B., *History, Theory and Practice of the Electric Telegraph*, Ticknor and Fields, Boston, 1860.

Raboteau, Albert J., *Slave Religion: The 'Invisible Institution' in the Ante-Bellum South*, Updated Edition, Oxford University Press, Oxford, 2004.

Records of the Field Offices of the State of Mississippi, Bureau of Refugees, Freedman and Abandoned Lands, 1865-1872, NARA Microfilm Pub. M1907, National Archives

Report of the Commissioner of Patents for the Year 1860, George W. Bowman, Washington, 1861.

Rowland, Dunbar, ed., *An Encyclopedia of Mississippi History*, Southern Historical Publishing Assoc., Atlanta, 1907.

Ruffin, Edmund, *Slavery and Free Labor, Described and Compared, 1859,* reprinted in *From Slavery to Freedom: The African-American Pamphlet Collection, 1822-1909,* Rare Book and Special Collections Division, Library of Congress.

Sansing, David G., *The University of Mississippi: A Sesquicentennial History, University Press of Mississippi,* Jackson, 1999

Slate, Frederick, *Biographical Memoir of Eugene Woldemar Hilgard, 1833-1916,* National Academy Of Sciences, Washington, 1919.

The Astronomical Expedition: Observations of the Total Eclipse of the Sun on the Coast of Labrador, New York Times, August 10, 1860.

Thomson, Dave, *Samuel L. Clemens' Mississippi Steamboat Career,* accessed at http://www.twainquotes.com/Steamboats/CubPilot.html

Vernon, ed., *The American Railroad Manual,* The American Railroad Manual Company, 1873

Waddell, John N., *Memorials of Academic Life,* Presbyterian Committee of Publication, Richmond, 1891

William and Marjorie Lewis Collection (MUM 00266), Department of Archives and Special Collections, J.D. Williams Library, University of Mississippi

Williamson, Joel, *William Faulkner and Southern History,* Oxford University Press, 1993

***

For information on nineteenth century Christian churches:

Armstrong, George D., *The Christian Doctrine of Slavery,* Charles Scribner, New York, 1857

Bell, Nyleen Barnett, *College Hill Presbyterian Church, College Hill,* Skipwith Historical and Genealogical Society, Oxford, Mississippi

Jones, Charles C., *A Catechism of Scripture, Doctrine and Practice for Families and Sabbath Schools, Designed Also for the Oral Instruction of Colored Persons,* John M. Cooper, Savannah, 1837

Moore, William E., *History of the Second Presbyterian Church of Columbus, Ohio: An Address Delivered March 3, 1889, on the Fiftieth Anniversary of Its Founding,* Hann and Adair, Columbus, Ohio, 1889

For information on the Webster, Blow and Loughborough families, and Carondelet:

Beecher, Lyman, *A Plea for the West*, Truman and Smith, Cincinnati, 1835, available at http://books.google.com/books?id=MMdM9vX32jYC&dq=Lyman+Beecher+%22A+Plea+for+the+West%22&printsec=frontcover&source=bn&hl=en&ei=kbVfS9LuB5GtlAffm4TmCw&sa=X&oi=book_result&ct=result&resnum=4&ved=0CBQQ6AEwAw#v=onepage&q=&f=false

Fehrenbacher, Don. E., *The Dred Scott Case: Its Significance in American Law and Politics*, Oxford University Press, 1978

Harris, Nini, *A History of Carondelet*, Patrice Press, St. Louis, 1991

Hyde, William and Conard, Howard, eds., *Presbyterianism in St. Louis: The Carondelet Presbyterian Church*, Encyclopedia of the History of St. Louis, Vol. III, Part Two, The Southern History Co., New York, 1901, p 1806.

Loughborough, Mary Ann, *My Cave Life in Vicksburg*, The Reprint Co., Spartanburg, South Carolina, 1988

For the Civil War, including troop movements, companies, routines and battles of the 17th Mississippi Infantry:

Ainsworth, Fred, Kirkley, Joseph, and Scott, Robert N., eds., *War of the Rebellion; A Compilation of the Official Records of the Union and Confederate Armies*, Government Printing Office, Washington, published in seventy volumes between 1881 and 1901.

Davis, George B., et al., *Atlas to Accompany the Official Records of the Union and Confederate Armies*, Government Printing Office, 1895

Bowman, John S., ed., *The Civil War*, World Publications, 2006

Byers, Alemeth, *Manuscript Letters 1861-1864*, private collection. (Also available at the Mississippi Department of Archives.)

Combined Military Service Record for Private John Alemeth Byers, Company H, 17th Mississippi Infantry, National Archives, Washington, D.C.

Cox, Walter F., and McCoy-Bell, Melissa, *Muster Roll of the 17th Mississippi Infantry*, 1997-2006, at http://www.rootsweb.ancestry.com/~mscivilw/17thms.html

Davis, William C., *The Battlefields of the Civil War*, University of Oklahoma Press, 2006

Enzweiler, Stephen, *Oxford in the Civil War: Battle for a Vanquished Land,* The History Press, Charleston, S.C., 2010

Esposito, Vincent J., ed., *The West Point Atlas of War: The Civil War,* U.S. Military Academy, 1995

Felton, Silas, and Mott, Wayne E, *In Their Words: Recollections of Visitations at Gettysburg After the Great Battle in July 1863,* The Gettysburg Foundation, accessed at http://www.gettysburgfoundation.org/media/assets/Felton-Motts.pdf

Flannery, Michael, *Civil War Pharmacy: A History of Drugs, Drug Supply and Provision, and Therapeutics for the Union and Confederacy,* CRC Press, 2004

Ford, Jennifer W., *The Civil War Letters of Lt. William Cowper Nelson of Mississippi,* University of Tennessee Press, Knoxville, 2007

Gallagher, Gary W., ed., *The Shenandoah Valley Campaign of 1864,* University of North Carolina Press, Chapel Hill, 2006

Gilham, William, *Manual for Instruction for the Volunteers and Militia of the Confederate States,* West & Johnson, Richmond, VA, 1861

Hasegawa, Guy, *Preparing and Dispensing Prescriptions During the Civil War Era,* Apothecary's Cabinet, No. 10, American Institute for the History of Pharmacy, 2006.

Holzer, Harold & Symonds, Craig L., eds., *The New York Times Complete Civil War,* Black Dog and Levanthal Publishers, Inc., 2010, for Lincoln's letter to Horace Greely

Johnson, Curt, and McLaughlin, Mark, *Civil War Battles,* Fairfax Press, NY, 1981

Johnson, Jemmy Grant, *The University War Hospital,* Publications of the Mississippi Historical Society, Vol. 12, 1912, p. 94

Lewis, Thomas A., *The Guns of Cedar Creek, 2d Ed.,* Heritage Associates, Strasburg, VA.

Massey, Mary Elizabeth, *Ersatz in the Confederacy: Shortages and Substitutes on the Southern Homefront,* 1952 facsimile edition, University of South Carolina Press: Columbia, 1993 (p. 168)

Mayfield, Jack, *Grant Arrives,* The Oxford Eagle, Dec. 10, 2010.

Mayfield, Jack, *Oxford Town,* The Oxford Eagle, Aug. 26, 2004

Moore, Robert Augustus, *A Life for the Confederacy: as Recorded in the Pocket Diaries of Private Robert A. Moore, Co. G., 17th MS Regiment, Confederate Guards,* Holly Springs, MS, 1959.

O'Reilly, Francis Augustin, *The Fredericksburg Campaign: Winter War on the Rappahannock,* Louisiana State University Press, Baton Rouge, La., 2006

Rowland, Dunbar, *Mississippi: Comprising Sketches of Counties, Towns, Events, Institutions,* etc.; Article on the Army of Northern Virginia at pg 111.

Salmon, John S., *The Official Virginia Civil War Battlefield Guide,* Stackpole Books, 2001.

Sears, Stephen W., *To the Gates of Richmond: The Peninsula Campaign,* Mariner Books, Boston, 2001

Seventeenth Mississippi Infantry, Regimental History, at http://www.firstbullrun.co.uk/Potomac/Third%20Brigade/17th-mississippi-infantry.html

Smith, Andrew F., *Starving the South: How the North Won the Civil War*, St. Martin's Press: New York, 2011 (p. 32-33)

Smith, Timothy B., *Mississippi in the Civil War: The Home Front,* University Press of Mississippi, 2010

Standard Supply Table of The Indigenous Remedies for Field Service and the Sick in General Hospitals, CSA, Surgeon General's Office, Richmond, 1863

Swinton, William, *Decisive Battles of the Civil War*, Promontory Press, NY, 1986

Tucker, Philip Thomas, *Barksdale's Charge: The True High Tide of the Confederacy at Gettysburg,* Casemate Publishers, Havertown, PA, 2013.

Whitehorn, Joseph W. A., *The Battle of Cedar Creek,* 3d Ed, 2006